The Deed

A NOVEL

KEITH BLANCHARD

To Sean—
You have an awesome
sister—she said she's getting
full price for this one
out of you!

Keith
Blanchard

SIMON & SCHUSTER
NEW YORK LONDON TORONTO SYDNEY SINGAPORE

SIMON & SCHUSTER
Rockefeller Center
1230 Avenue of the Americas
New York, NY 10020

For information about special discounts for bulk purchases,
please contact Simon & Schuster Special Sales: 1-800-456-6798 or
business@simonandschuster.com

Designed by Lauren Simonetti

Manufactured in the United States of America

1   3   5   7   9   10   8   6   4   2

Library of Congress Cataloging-in-Publication Data

Blanchard, Keith
The deed / Keith Blanchard.
p.   cm.
1. Manhattan (New York, N.Y.)—Fiction. 2. Deeds—Fiction. I. Title.
PS3602.L36 D4 2003
813'.6—dc21
2002029435

ISBN 0-7432-2387-X

To my best friend, Leslie, the love of a thousand lifetimes

Three things are necessary for the salvation of man:
To know what he ought to believe,
to know what he ought to desire,
and to know what he ought to do.

—ST. THOMAS AQUINAS

The Deed

Prologue

The burgher fell in love with the rotten log the instant he spied it, by the side of the forest path, sprawling wantonly across a tangle of ferns. Hours of slogging through the brackish wilderness behind his joyless companion, on half rations and no meat, had left the oversize administrator drained and weary; the log's horizontal surface, framed to idyllic perfection by a green little clearing dotted with toadstools, exerted an almost magnetic influence on his heaving frame.

He gazed lewdly along the length of the fallen trunk as he approached, small eyes expertly locating a section where some internal erosion had gently collapsed the bark and formed a mossy natural saddle. *Merciful heaven,* he said to himself. *Sixty guilders for a pot of beer and an hour to sleep it off.* Measuring off the last few yards with heroic strides, he sat down heavily and pinned the precious satchel to his knees. The dying wood creaked in protest at his bulk.

Glancing up, he saw his subordinate stop without turning, contemptuously, at the far edge of the clearing, and the burgher discreetly tried to merge his wheezing with the whistling sea breeze that somehow penetrated to this spot deep in the island's interior. An early frost hung heavy in the air, though October was still loosening summer leaves from gnarled branches, and even as the burgher wiped cold sweat from his brow with the back of a pudgy hand, he felt the onset of a too-familiar chill laying claim to the flesh of idle toes and fingers. Another merciless winter seemed imminent; it was as if the Creator himself could not abide this wretched hinterland without an annual furlough.

A few paces farther along the path, where the clearing dissolved seamlessly into forest, a young soldier stood impatiently, staring into the trees, having missed instantly the leaden crunch of his superior's footfalls. He ran his slender fingers along the smooth breech of the gun slung over one shoulder, and cursed silently as he measured the shadows ahead. *The third rest in as many miles*, he mused. *It beggars description*. At this rate, he estimated, they would be lucky indeed to complete their mission in time to beat sunset back to the fort—and braving these northern reaches of the island alone at night was a fool's gamble.

At the rickety Dutch barracks on the southern tip of the island, grandly called Fort Amsterdam, a rough consensus had formed among the grumbling soldiery as to the nature of this secretive mission. Though the soldier's orders were straightforward enough—to see this politician safely to and from the Haansvoort house in the north—he thought he knew exactly what was sealed in the burgher's mysterious leather bag, and the knowledge disturbed him to the edge of violence. Towing this bloated cow through the forest was vexing enough, but for such a cowardly purpose . . .

Turning at last, the soldier stared coldly back across the clearing, into the worried little pig eyes of the loathed politician. The burgher made a fat and easy target for his hostility, and though the soldier knew his audacity bordered on treason, he cared little whether his disgust could be read. An incautious bravado had slowly begun to take possession of him, out here in the wild, and he could feel his heart in his chest, pounding invincibly. The jungle was a pitiless equalizer, and they were far from the fort.

"'Tis no great hurry, Jacob," the burgher suggested, shielding his eyes from an imaginary glare with one pink hand, and giving the log next to him a sensuous pat with the other. "Rest thou a bit."

"I prefer to stand ready," replied the soldier.

The burgher smiled nervously. "Certainly, certainly, always the warrior. But Jacob, the Manahata are peaceable. We *have* a treaty," he encouraged, hoping to spin out a few precious minutes of respite with any sort of conversation.

The soldier unshouldered his musket and began to make a great display of checking the dryness of the powder. "I don't share your trust of the savages," he replied without looking up. "They are irrational, as like to turn on you as not, and treaties be damned. Also, these woods are full of bear, and panther, and all manner of unnameable beasts with which we have no treaties." He glanced over with this, eager to see his words take their calculated effect, but the other's face remained smoothly impassive.

"Tut-tut, Jacob," said the burgher with professional breeziness. When the soldier returned to the powder horn, though, the administrator cast a wary eye into the woods that ringed the clearing. They were completely and irredeemably surrounded, he suddenly felt sure, and in the dark and shifting shadows he caught brief, inconclusive glimpses of slitted eyes and twitching whiskers, of velvet muscle hunched beneath dripping fangs.

A mild breeze swept across the path, combing the light grass gently westward and rustling up little whirlwinds of fallen leaves, as if setting the forest floor ablaze with its passing.

"Van Cleef," said the soldier bluntly, "I have a right to know our purpose."

The burgher kept his composure through no small effort of will. For not the first time, he wondered whether he ought to fear this man— whether the bonds of civility, strained by the Indian wars and the myriad other troubles at Fort Amsterdam, were yet strong enough to hold violent nature in check.

"Jacob," he purred tentatively, controlling his emotion and quickly cobbling together a strategy, "do you have any food left in your bags there? A bit of that bread from this morning, perhaps? Anything?"

The soldier only stared.

"Well," said Van Cleef, smiling. "*That's* why we're here. We have to secure provisions enough to see New Amsterdam through the winter and beyond. We *have* to. There's no choice in it."

The rumors at the fort thus half confirmed, the soldier met his superior's eyes squarely. "At what cost?"

But Van Cleef shook his head. "That we may not discuss, I'm afraid, you and I."

"Bah," Jacob sneered. "The terms are well-enough known. This is madness."

"You've seen the storehouses, Jacob," said the burgher patiently. "Shall we eat the powder?"

"The savages have food to spare."

"Which is why we are here."

"But damn it—not to parley, and trade, and beg," hissed the soldier, his increasing agitation animating his angular features.

This is really too much, worried the burgher, struggling to steady his voice. "What would you have us do, Jacob—massacre them for their grain? We have scarce enough men to hold the walls as it is. We dare not risk another war."

He watched as Jacob grunted and looked away again, into the shivering gray branches. A squirrel crabbed sideways into view around the trunk of an enormous maple, then started at something and scampered up into the canopy. The burgher realized his pulse was racing, and squeezed his hands together.

"But . . . *him,*" said the soldier, squinting in disgust.

The burgher feigned nonchalance with a shrug. "Who else can entreat with the savages?" he asked rhetorically. "They practically revere him." He considered this for a moment. "He holds the keys to Pharoah's larders."

"God gave man dominion over the earth and everything in it," Jacob countered as his passion, defeated, began to cool into sullen resentment. "This is unnatural. If the savages will not give us what we require, then we will take it by force."

"Perhaps," allowed the burgher with a condescending smile. "But not today." He moved as if to rise, but at the shifting of his weight, the log cracked ominously, then caved in all at once. With an involuntary little cry and a loud crash, the burgher landed hard on his back in a cloud of dust and pulp.

"Spawn of Satan!" he sputtered, enraged, heaving himself to his feet with surprising agility and furiously plucking the satchel from the crumbled wreckage.

The soldier prudently turned to check the dryness of the powder again, his sides shaking. *Oh, praise God I didn't miss that,* he thought merrily. Later that evening, among his fellows in the barracks, it would be the soldier himself tumbling backward off a bench with a womanly screech, stuffed pillows bursting out of his shirt, to the unrestrained mirth of drunken cohorts. For now, though, he bit his tongue as Van Cleef slapped dust from his voluminous breeches and grimly resumed the silent march. The soldier's spirits were quite renewed, though a dark foreboding kept his eye sharp.

For the burgher, red-faced and seething, bruised dignity scarcely scratched the surface of what ailed him. A terror had begun to clutch at his heart in recent months. Never in his life had he felt so helpless, at the mercy of every New World beast and savage hungry with the onset of winter, his only protection a handful of such ragged men as this. The very island itself seemed carnivorous; for not the first time since coming to this wretched colony, the old Walloon conjured up a pleasant image of himself curled by the little fire in his study back at Hoorn, sipping Madeira and contentedly burping up the ghost of a succulent feast. Then something small and restless rustled in the brush, and the burgher, suddenly afraid his man would outdistance him and leave him to the wilderness, clutched the satchel to his heaving breast and forced his aching legs to hurry.

And all around them, the primeval forest pounded with life. Fox scared up pheasant; rabbit and whitetail bounded along on invisible errands; insects buzzed and seagulls cried into the wind that swept the island and rained gold and ruby leaves upon the ferns and wild blackberry and meshed pine needles of the underbrush. The air seethed with the earthy smells of moss and mushroom, of violets and cattails and rough animal musk. Above it all, immeasurably ancient stands of elm, beech, and birch, raised interlaced fingers in a sheltering canopy the midday sun could penetrate only in patches. It was breathtakingly beautiful and subtly terrifying, an untamed and chaotic land bristling with treacherous landfalls and dark predators, a place of raw wonders and terrors that had never known the stabilizing force of civilization.

✧ ✧ ✧

Nahoti heard the cloddish white men crashing through the woods long before they appeared in the little window over her cooking table; she watched with unblinking eyes as they parted the forest wall at the edge of her clearing and made their way toward the house. The skinny one, the one with the gun, she did not think she had seen before, but she recognized the other only too well. Dropping the curtain, she stepped away from the window and closed her eyes.

He smelled like meat, she remembered. He had come with two others, and they had met with her husband for hours, talking and smoking while the sun blazed across the sky, while she milled around outside, idly pulling weeds and drawing little circles in the dirt. Pieter later tried to assure her that the strangers' visit was actually a great blessing, but Nahoti's heart would not give her peace, because she knew an awful truth her husband refused to believe: These men wanted him dead. Her husband's refusal to entertain her fears, and his continued dealings with these men over all her protestations, filled her with an emptiness that shook her faith in their marriage to its core.

Ever since she had left her people to live with this white man in his square little house, Nahoti had felt isolated. She was the daughter of the chief of the Manahata, and a woman of standing by birth. But Pieter was considered a virtual god by her people, for his healing potions and his quick fluency with their language, and from the moment her father had offered her to Pieter in marriage, she found to her dismay that the women of her village would no longer meet her eye. Their adulation left her so uncomfortable that she could no longer bear their company; for almost a year now, Nahoti had washed her and her husband's clothes at a distant bend in the river, at odd hours when she could be assured of solitude.

Pieter, though, was a refugee as well. He'd long ago forsaken his own people to live among the Manahata, and though the gulf between himself and Nahoti was vast, the couple quickly found themselves bound by exile and mutual curiosity. From the outset, their investigations into each other's culture became inextricably twined with discovering one another as individuals, and as man and woman, and they explored each other's minds and hearts insatiably. With Pieter, Nahoti had found a love beyond imagining.

6

Three quick raps on the door resounded hollowly through the little one-room house, each one a sharp reminder that Pieter was out in the woods somewhere, hunting, and not expected back. A wave of supernatural dread washed over her. She quickly wiped her hands on her apron and draped the cheesecloth back over two little seedcakes she'd been preparing for supper. As she crossed toward the door, it creaked open of its own accord, spilling a sheaf of sunlight onto the packed-earth floor.

"Good day, madam," said the fat one, peering around the corner, ruddy and out of breath. "Is your husband at home?" A quick look around the one-room house answered his own question, and without awaiting an invitation, he threw the door open wide and entered, leaving a trail of wet leaves as he clomped over to the rough-hewn wooden table by the fireplace. The strange thin one followed, casting a disinterested glance her way as he first leaned the black gun against the wall by the door, then thought better of it and carried it with him to the table.

Quietly thankful they'd left the door open, Nahoti watched as the two men settled onto the benches by the table, where the noon sun slanted steeply through the unshuttered window, illuminating dancing motes of dust and deepening the crags and pits of the white men's faces.

"Pieter's not here," she said with measured calmness, standing stonily by the door as the thin man laid the gun on the table before him and began rubbing part of it with a cloth drawn from his pocket.

Having already set the bag on the table, just within the swing of his meaty paw, the burgher plucked the hat off his head and dropped it on top, before casting his eyes around the cabin again.

"I suspected as much," he confided, and the man with the gun snickered. "Perhaps you'll be good enough to entertain us yourself until he returns?" he continued, licking his lips lasciviously.

Nahoti froze, and the burgher rolled his eyes. "Something to *eat*, my dear. And beer, if you have it."

"We . . . we have only water," she replied in a near whisper, eyes dropping to the floor.

The gunman, with his back to her, turned halfway around and sniffed the air, a grin spreading across his face. A moment later he had risen and muscled past her to the cooking table, where he scooped up the cakes with a laugh, shaking off her halfhearted attempt to clutch at his sleeve and carrying them triumphantly back to the table.

"Here's goodly water, Van Cleef," he offered with a grin as he reseated himself and distributed the booty. "Drink your fill."

"Oh, be civilized, Jacob," the burgher demurred, even as his wet tongue ranged over his lower lip like a blind, pink animal.

The gunman broke one of the cakes with his hand, and without looking up, addressed Nahoti: "We'll have that drink now, woman. And be quick about it."

"Get out of my house," came a voice from the doorway.

◇ ◇ ◇

The burgher started visibly, and his expression further paled on seeing Pieter, his rangy but muscular frame outlined in the light, a pair of game-birds in one hand and a musket, held at the trigger, in the other.

The soldier was not impressed. He knew Pieter Haansvoort to be a bookish weakling and despicable traitor to Holland. Rising from the table to his full height, Jacob skidded the rough wooden bench away behind him, where it caught on the floor and tipped over with a crash.

"Well, Haansvoort," he said with an oily smirk, bowing mockingly, one hand on the table. "My humblest apologies to you *and* your brute," he added with a sidelong glance at Nahoti, who had retreated safely to the corner by her window.

"Enough, Jacob, enough," directed the burgher nervously. "Pieter, I'm afraid my companion lacks the—"

But Pieter silenced him with a cold shake of his head. His eyes stayed with the soldier as he stepped farther into the room, and though his gun remained pointing at the floor, his finger curled sensually around the trigger. "Either he leaves or you both do, Van Cleef—it's all one to me."

The soldier met Pieter's glare with his own unblinking gaze for a moment or two before looking to the burgher for support. But Van Cleef only turned away, glancing at the satchel on the table as if to make sure it had not crawled away in the confusion. Scowling, the soldier snatched up his blunderbuss with one hand, spat on the floor, and lurched past Pieter to the outside, slamming the door shut behind him.

✧ ✧ ✧

"Well, what a bit of unpleasantness," said the burgher. "I deeply apologize."

"No, no; I'm exceedingly glad to see you, Van Cleef," said Pieter, smiling grimly and dropping the gamebirds on the table as he righted the fallen bench and seated himself, propping his own gun against the table.

"I can well imagine," said the burgher soberly.

Pieter grinned. "I expected you sooner, if truth be told."

"Securing an escort proved . . . problematic," replied the burgher. "The savage hovers about the fort like a flock of hellish crows. There are few enough able soldiers to man the walls, and none to spare for hiking half the length of the island." His eye drifted toward Nahoti, who picked at the hem of her dress from the relative safety of the cooking-bench.

"Well," said Pieter knowingly, "that is your governor's fault."

Van Cleef sighed wearily. "You intend to start that again, then."

Pieter shrugged. "If you continue to throw your soldiers' lives away attacking peaceable Indians, you cannot also have them available for defense." He smiled affably. "Mathematics is quite invincible on the point."

Van Cleef's eyes narrowed. The disastrous event to which Pieter alluded had occurred some weeks earlier, when a few hundred Algonquin Indians had massed outside Fort Amsterdam, seeking shelter from a pursuing band of warring Iroquois. The Dutch colony's famously paranoid Governor Kieft, crying conspiracy, denied the refugees entry into the fort, and his army seized on this prohibition as a license to open fire. The terrified Algonquins fled, and gleeful soldiers pursued them across the river to Pavonia, largely obliterating them in a weeklong massacre of men, women, and children. Though technically a "victory," a frightful number of Dutch had been killed in the campaign, further thinning the troop strength of the fort to a disheartened two hundred or so, including conscripts.

"I only tolerate your insolence because of our great need," Van Cleef chastised diplomatically. "Rest assured, we still have army enough to protect ourselves. The fort will stand, Pieter, trust to it. Though I'm sure it little contents you."

"On the contrary, my dear Van Cleef," replied Pieter, folding his hands on the table before him. "I sleep better knowing I'm under the protection of the Royal Dutch soldiery." His eyes twinkled. "They are a vanishing breed."

A hint of real anger began to crystallize at the edge of Van Cleef's voice. "It is not my business to question the affairs of our governor, nor yours either," he replied tersely. "I remind you, you are still a Dutch citizen."

Pieter held out his palms in conciliation. "My apologies, Van Cleef," he relented. "I mean no disrespect." He glanced over at the satchel by the portly man's elbow. "Come, that *is* the document, I presume?"

Still officially slighted and muttering, the burgher retrieved and unbuckled the leather bag. From its depths he withdrew a snowy piece of vellum, a foot square and curling slightly at top and bottom. Thirty or forty lines of text snaked their way across the page, revealing the ad hoc nature of their contents in hurried, spidery penmanship, anchored by a brown wax gubernatorial seal at the bottom. Laying the document on the table, the burgher scanned it briefly, then reversed it and slid it across the table.

Pieter lifted the page gingerly, by one edge, trying not to betray his excitement. Van Cleef, normally a keen observer of men, missed the sudden brightness in Pieter's eyes, as he was otherwise engaged in the act of producing a quill pen and a sealed inkstand from a deep interior pocket of his greatcoat.

"A witness is . . . customary," Van Cleef began, drawing ink into the pen. He glanced back toward the door.

Ignoring him, Pieter slowly examined the document. He found no fault in its construction—no great surprise, as he'd dictated its terms himself—and was amused to note peripherally the burgher shifting in increasing discomfort. Satisfied at last, Pieter took up the pen and signed his name before passing the quill on to Van Cleef, who signed beneath him.

Retrieving the page, Pieter turned toward the far side of the room. "Nahoti?"

Van Cleef's mouth opened in automatic protest, but he held his tongue as Pieter summoned his wife to the table and handed her the quill with a nod of encouragement. Nahoti expertly signed the Dutch translation of her name, while the burgher produced a few other, smaller papers, which Pieter also looked over, making a change here and there before signing. These Van Cleef replaced in the satchel; the vellum scroll remained on the table.

"You've taught her Dutch," said Van Cleef.

"She taught herself. There, it is done," said Pieter, satisfied, with something like wonder in his voice.

The burgher smiled warily. "You have performed a noble service to the Dutch West India Company . . . and to your people."

"Hurrah for me," Pieter said dismissively. "A detail of Manahata Indians will bring the first provisions to the fort within three days. Please try to remember not to kill them."

"And . . . the beer?"

This brought an indulgent smile. "All in good time, Falstaff; all in good time. Rest easy: The terms of the contract will be fulfilled."

Satisfied, the burgher redeposited the pen in an interior pocket and gathered up his bag. "Then that is all. Thank you for your hospitality, madam," he said to Nahoti, tipping his hat with disingenuous grace before putting it back on.

"Van Cleef, I'm curious," said Pieter, waving his hand over the page. "What do *you* think of this little bargain of mine? It will not make the Company's ledgers sparkle, precisely."

"Very true," Van Cleef allowed quietly, resuming his seat and taking a deep breath. "But we are in an . . . unprecedented position, as you well know. A governor's first duty is to the people of the colony; the good captain does not let the passengers die to salvage the ship."

"Well put," Pieter said, nodding. "And yet, New Amsterdam is a business venture, not a colony. Governer Kieft serves the Dutch West India Company before Holland."

"Oh, not before Holland," protested the burgher.

"The masters in Amsterdam will be furious," Pieter continued. "Van Cleef, speak plainly with me. We are both men."

The burgher focused his eyes on the table before him for a few long moments; finally he shrugged.

"What else can we do?" he said quietly. "You know the strength of your position. The outlook for the settlement—colony, trading post, what you will—is black. The farms are ravaged, and already the first frost—"

"The farms are ravaged," Pieter interrupted eagerly, "because your soldiers raid the Indians and then retreat behind the walls of the fort, leaving the farmers to fend for themselves."

"Pieter, if we are to speak plainly, I must say that your sanctimoniousness is really quite unbearable," said Van Cleef.

"It's Governor Kieft, there's the problem," said Pieter. "I've said so from the beginning. And now you all know it, too."

Van Cleef was nodding slowly, with a sneering expression underlined by a tight-lipped smile. "Yes, yes, you've always said so. Even back when you still deigned to live among your fellows, you barked incessantly about"—here his voice grew suddenly, acutely sarcastic—"our catastrophic disruption of these aboriginals. If I may say so, it's the most outrageous hypocrisy yet visited on this New World."

Pieter's eyes widened in real surprise at the vehemence, but Van Cleef was not yet finished.

"*You're* the one teaching them our language, Pieter," he continued, with a sidelong glance at Nahoti. "Training them in Dutch cultivation, Dutch architecture, giving them our clothes, our tools, our guns. Who's the colonist, here—you or me?"

"I do *not* give them guns."

"No? And yet they get them somehow. Perhaps they have invented them simultaneously," suggested the burgher, drawing up his dignity; he was in his element now. "And now let me ask *you* something, Pieter." He tapped a bejeweled middle finger on the document between them. "Had the company refused your demand, would you have truly let your countrymen starve? Knowing it was in your power to save them?"

"Don't be facetious," said Pieter. "It's Kieft's outrageous policies that threaten you with starvation—whatever power I have to intervene hardly bloodies my hand with his crime."

"That does not answer the question," noted the burgher.

But Pieter only smiled. "All I have ever intended, Van Cleef, is to do what I can to arm these aboriginals against the abuse of Europe."

"You know they will only sell it again, the moment your back is turned."

"That is why it's in my name, and not theirs."

"Yes," said Van Cleef, "but one day you will be gone, and they will lose it, or bury it with some esteemed chief, or warm their hands over its ashes in winter."

"Perhaps." Pieter shrugged as together they rose and headed for the door. "We must all of us follow the dictates of conscience, and trust Providence to reward us in kind." He smiled broadly. "Keep one hand on your scalp, Van Cleef."

✧ ✧ ✧

Moments later, as Nahoti cleaned the pheasants at the cooking-table, Pieter was in the throes of a euphoria that was half uncontainable excitement, half dreamlike haze. He returned to the table and sat on the bench by the window, the better to catch the sunlight, and as he settled in to revel in the intricacies of the document, a triumphant smile spread across his face. He had forbidden himself to anticipate this moment. And yet here it was, in the flesh, and the possibilities swirled in his mind like dandelion seeds before the wind. Time itself seemed to have ground to a halt, stranding the sun high in the sky as if unsure of which way to fall.

"'Go now, write it on a tablet for them,'" Pieter said aloud, quoting Scripture from memory. "'Inscribe it on a scroll, that for all the days to come it may be an everlasting witness.'"

Any shift in power invites retribution, he knew. But of the danger to himself he took little note: If the peril was not insignificant, neither was it immediate. He'd set in motion a course of events he hoped would outlive his mortal husk, and what Pieter *did* fear, intensely, was for the life of the document itself. Van Cleef's derision pointed up a real concern—the deed was the Word, legal and binding, but it was parchment as well as document, a fragile paper thing subject to the ravages of fire and water, earth and air, human accident or—deadliest of all—sabotage.

Though Pieter's disputes with the Dutch were mainly of a philosophical nature, his fear for his adopted people was real. He knew that the Company, and the Dutch government generally, intended to loot the New World of all extractable riches, and the unreal stories that filtered back from other colonial outposts bore testament to the extremes of cruelty men could muster toward this end. While Pieter had an almost supernatural faith in the power of the written word, he was forced to concede that the Manahata, with no written history and no real sense of property, could only dimly, at best, comprehend the importance of this deed. If they were ever to benefit from it, they would somehow have to be convinced to protect the page itself, to keep it safe and dry and out of the hands of the grasping Dutch, perhaps for long years.

Such was the conundrum that faced Pieter now, but for this, at least, he'd had months to prepare. He turned to find Nahoti, a bone knife clenched in one blood-spattered fist, butchering the luckless pheasants with a rare exuberance. Smiling, he called her over.

As his wife approached, with those sad, impenetrable eyes that never held laughter long, Pieter marveled, not for the first time, at the natural transparency of her emotion. Fear, excitement, anger, love—all coursed violently through her body like a river pent underground, seeping conspicuously from every pore, unhindered by disguise or artifice. Sometimes she seemed more animal than human, utterly in thrall to the basest excitements of the flesh, wary and untameable. At other moments, though, the thrilling simplicity of her naked honesty inspired him to wonder whether civilized society, in the end, was anything more than artful camouflage.

"This paper is a great mystery, which I want to explain to you," he began, smiling in an ill-fated effort to ease her distress as she approached the table and sat beside him. "Nahoti, a few months ago a dream came to me . . ."

"Well, he signed it," said Van Cleef, as he met the soldier and together they began trudging back toward the forest.

"Was there doubt?" retorted the other. "The devil himself couldn't have drawn terms more favorable."

"That's as may be," the burgher replied with a shrug and walked on, a few steps ahead of his subordinate. Before they left the clearing, however, at the wide and grassy mouth of the path that threaded back through the trees, Jacob placed a bold hand on his superior's arm and turned him around.

"Just know this, Van Cleef," said the soldier firmly under his breath. "I'll happily come back and finish this business, on a word from you."

"Peace, good Jacob, peace," urged the burgher. "It's Pieter's food that will be feeding you, his ale you'll be drinking this winter."

"One word," reiterated the soldier, maintaining his iron focus. "On your authority—official or not."

All the humor drained from Van Cleef's face. "Now listen to me carefully, Jacob," he replied, boldly poking a fat finger into the soldier's chest. "Whatever slights you believe you've suffered, however inequitable you think the agreement between this man and the Dutch West India Company, it is *not* your business. You *may not* lift your hand in anger against him. Is that clear?"

The gunman's brow darkened, and Van Cleef slid past him, striding purposefully into the woods, muttering, as he passed, "Not until spring, anyway."

Jacob, caught wholly unawares, nearly laughed out loud.

✧ ✧ ✧

Back inside the cabin, Nahoti listened quietly as her husband relayed a terrible vision of the future. He was speaking of a time when the god of her people would desert them, when her tribe would be driven from their land and made to walk among strangers.

Nahoti tried to pay attention, though the images disturbed her deeply;

prophecy was not to be taken lightly. But her thoughts kept scampering away like children. She was remembering a warm winter's night when she and Pieter had slipped through the forest down to the shore to walk in the white foam at the edge of the sea, beneath the stars. There, as the dark wind whipped her unbraided hair about her head, he had pointed out over the sea and told her of his own land beyond the water, where the people crowded together in impossible cities, and he foretold that more men would be coming, ship after ship after ship, like the icy waves lapping at their feet. It was here that he'd first promised he would never leave her, no matter what happened.

At the table now, again holding her hands, Pieter was saying that the paper the men had brought contained a great magic that must be kept safe until Manahata's return, for it would one day restore their land and bring her people home again.

Nahoti argued with him then, though she knew it was futile, protesting, as she always did, any further involvement with these horrible men. Pieter reasoned with her, tried to calm her, and finally resumed his narrative, accepting her sullen silence as acquiescence. But he was wrong. She was brooding, quietly fixating on the terrifying image she'd seen through her little window just moments earlier, when the man with the gun had turned back and stared coldly at the house, as if memorizing the scene for some future horror.

The page and the land are one, her husband was telling her; the page and the land are one.

Unsure whether the devil had seen her, Nahoti had pulled herself back violently from the window, heart pounding. But the spell had been cast; the thin man's last icy glare would never entirely leave her thoughts and dreams, for all the rest of her days.

Chapter One

MANHATTAN, 1999

THURSDAY, 9:05 A.M.

COLUMBUS CIRCLE

As Jason Hansvoort stepped off the curb and into the path of the oncoming taxi, his eyes never wavered. From a park bench on the far side of the street dangled a pair of female legs, sweetly agape, their northern reaches discreetly sheathed in a slack blue-jean wrap skirt. It was this steadily improving celestial view that had blotted out all earthly considerations; a last, curious image absurdly poised to fizzle with his soul into universal static at the crush of metal and bone.

Had Jason peripherally glimpsed the yellow behemoth bearing down on him, or heard the anguished squeal of badly abused brakes, or otherwise sensed the rusty creak of the scissors yawning open to snip short the thread of his life, there might have been just enough time to pointlessly brace for the impact. But he remained oblivious, right to the end. His perception of the event did not collapse into a series of staccato images, like photographs flipping through his consciousness; he did not suddenly see all the colors of the world framed in unusual clarity. His life in no way flashed before his eyes, even as a deadly metallic juggernaut the color of sunshine desperately ground to a halt a few feet from his knees.

"*Asshole!*" shouted the irate Indian cabdriver, leaning out the window.

"Doo you tink dot you are Shuperman?" he wondered angrily. In the center of his turban, a purple stone glowed dully.

Suddenly the world was filled with sound and light, and Jason's brain scrambled to untangle the knot of input that assaulted his senses: the braying of horns, the pungent incense of burnt rubber and roasted peanuts, the sudden, undeniable presence of a steaming vehicle practically in his lap.

"My bad," Jason mumbled reflexively, heart belatedly thudding as he rewound, stepping backward onto the curb.

The morning crowd took little notice, but here and there pockets of diverted bystanders watched expectantly, hoping for further drama from the scene. A single white male, twenty-three and reasonably good-looking in dirty blond hair and a clean gray suit, Jason saw himself reflected in their eyes as the perfect urban straight man for a bit of cosmic slapstick. Any minute now, his briefcase would unlatch comically and scatter white papers like doves all across Columbus Circle, to roars of canned laughter.

"Asshole!" the cabbie repeated apoplectically, punctuating his rage with a cryptic two-handed gesture that was probably quite obscene in his country of origin. Without waiting for a response, he floored the pedal with another screech and exited, stage right.

"That's *Mr.* Asshole to you, buddy," said Jason bravely into the cabbie's exhaust, but his audience had already dispersed.

Jason's near-death experiences were the stuff of legend among his friends. He had fallen in front of a city bus; he had toppled, arms windmilling in the expected way, from the edge of a subway platform, clambering to safety just in time. He had witnessed a stabbing outside the Port Authority bus terminal late one night, scarcely ten feet from him, a noisy act of public violence that had sent adrenaline shooting around his bloodstream like fireworks trapped in an air-conditioning duct. In Washington Square, two summers ago, he'd been part of a crowd that had scattered like spilled marbles when a limousine hopped the curb and careened into the park, killing two Ohio tourists paralyzed by the sheer *interestingness* of what was unfolding. The limo had also critically injured a street mime performing at the time; the poor bastard's animated back spasms were misinterpreted by many as a sick attempt at black humor.

Jason reached behind the knot of his tie to undo the "choke" button, as onlookers lost their cohesion and devolved into the usual pedestrian chaos, and the traffic stream reassuringly resumed its course. From a rational standpoint, he had long suspected these recurrent near misses could not be attributed to mere chance. But warning himself to be more careful was an empty ritual; it always felt disturbingly as if he were trying to be his own parents.

Jason switched back to his left hand a burgundy hand-tooled leather briefcase, the gift of his mother and father on the occasion of his landing his first real job, at Young & Rubicam advertising. The case's elegance belied Jason's moderate income—it was pretentious and overstated, relentlessly *adult,* and it had always felt somehow wrong in his hand, though of course he would never part with it now. He stretched the knuckles of his free hand, wiped the palm on the convenient leg of his trousers. *Once more unto the breach, my friend,* he rallied himself, looking uptown and downtown like a five-year-old. When the light changed, he stepped into the crosswalk and successfully forded New York's only traffic circle.

One bystander waited a moment, then stealthily crossed the street after Jason, following him to the far corner and watching him head east on 59th Street, holding safely to the sidewalk along the southern edge of Central Park. She peered after his retreating figure for a moment before leaning lightly against a utility pole, dizzy with relief. Glancing down, the stranger saw that her hands were actually shaking, and she thrust them into the pockets of her raincoat as she glanced around, inscrutable behind cheap sunglasses.

If she'd been looking for a sign that the iron was hot, this surely had been it. The screech of the taxi's brakes had chilled her heart; twenty yards or so behind, she'd found herself literally unable to scream or even speak, incapable indeed of any action beyond groping spastically toward him as if trying to propel him to safety through the sheer force of her panic. Now she closed her eyes, relaxed, and breathed deeply, seeking out a familiar inner pool of strength, not yet to tap it, but simply to reassure herself that it was intact and primed.

Jason had turned out to be as expected: somewhere around twenty-five or so, she guessed, roughly her own age. A nice coincidence. In closeup he had genial, good-guy looks: tall, with green eyes and blond hair. No wedding ring, which presumably meant no children—the important thing, of course. He *seemed* approachable, anyway . . . but perhaps that was hope speaking. The thrill of the prospect of fulfilling a destiny more than three hundred years in the making was tempered by visceral worries: apprehension at the sheer weight of the task ahead, and a dread of ramifications unknown.

When her eyes opened, the girl was pleased to find that her clever hands had drawn two cigarettes from the pack in her coat pocket. She lit one and inhaled deeply, snapping the other cigarette in half and grinding its broken body into the sidewalk with the toe of her cowboy boot. Stepping lightly over the legs of a sprawled homeless person clad in a mink coat mottled with red spray paint, she hopped the four-foot crumbling brownstone wall that girdles Central Park and disappeared into its abruptly green interior.

✧ ✧ ✧

Jason hit the light switch of his office and laid his suit jacket over the back of the extra chair, where it promptly doubled over in a half gainer and collapsed onto the seat. *Seven point five from the Russian judge,* he mused. *That's gotta be a disappointment.* The voice-mail indicator on his phone console blinked sleepily in the sudden light.

After grimly zipping through the familiar sequence of buttons that would play back his messages on speakerphone, Jason took up a position by the window, clasping his hands behind his back and flaring his nostrils like an executive. The view was dominated by the imposing glass-and-steel forest of Midtown's skyscrapers. But twenty-six flights below, Madison Avenue snaked along the base of his building in multicolored scales of morning traffic, and at the extreme right of the view, up beyond the East 60s, a small but treasured corner of grassy park could be glimpsed—slightly more, if he pressed his cheek against the glass.

There were two messages. Nick, his best friend from Princeton, called to relate "a tale of disgusting, unspeakable debauchery that I hope you'll find inspiring," and to remind him about their lunch today. Jason smiled at this, anticipating a welcome break from his usual solo routine.

The other message was less benign. Pete Halloran, his project manager, wanted him to come around to his office as soon he got the chance, and could he please bring the Hair Peace file. Jason's lip curled into an involuntary sneer as his easy morning dipped sharply toward earth, flames streaming from both engines.

Jason's sudden gloom didn't spring from the fear of reprisal. Halloran was a notorious soft touch, relaxed and genial to an absolute fault, the textbook hands-off manager. But Hair Peace—the nightmare of the moment, an ill-conceived combination hair gel and scalp treatment—had stubbornly thwarted Jason's every attempt at a coherent positioning strategy. After two weeks of gale-force brainstorming, the requested file remained a pitifully thin manila sandwich. And while he *thought* Halloran genuinely understood the problems endemic to the new account, Jason's continuing failure to come up with a creative breakthrough appeared, to himself if not yet to his boss, more and more of a personal statement.

"Knock, knock," said a voice at his half-open door, to a harmonizing chorus of knuckles, and *they* swept in.

It was Nivens and Walters, an inseparable pair of dorks from personnel who periodically swooped down on Jason's office like wacky sitcom neighbors. Nivens was the more loathsome of the two, small and froggy, with a shockingly pale freckled face framed by thinning orange clown hair. Walters, bald and pear shaped, wore ridiculous Buddy Holly glasses on a face billowing with flabby jowls and permanently transfixed by a snarky, murderous smile.

By virtue of their positions, perhaps, the two had an inside line on company gossip, and for some arcane reason usually invited Jason to feast on the first fruits of their inside knowledge. For all his disdain, though, he could never quite bring himself to throw them out. They were legendary office fixtures, and their intermittent presence suggested some mythic, eternal quality that he had no right to challenge; therefore, he endured them patiently.

"Howdy," he said.

"Nice tie," said Walters, with an oddly brazen sincerity that stopped just short of sarcasm.

"Thanks." Jason had no idea what tie he was wearing and resisted the temptation to investigate. "Made it myself."

"Yeah . . . *right*," Nivens replied nerdily. Walters—who did little of the talking, although he gave most of the knowing glances—slapped his hands on his formidable paunch and looked slowly around the office, nodding his head in a way Jason found deeply disconcerting.

"So what's up, guys?" said Jason, feeling itchy and unproductive. "I'm kind of in a rush this morning."

"Nothing much," said Walters. "How was your weekend?"

"Fine," Jason replied woodenly. "And yours?"

"Oh, you know," said Nivens. "The usual."

Jason tried to will some dramatic event into being to break up the tedious scene that loomed—the long and terrible endgame of extracting from these two the information they were so desperately eager to unload. A terrified executive bursts through the door, gurgling blood and clawing at a knife in his back, and does a face plant into the fica; a muscular reptilian arm crashes up through the floor, splitting the carpet and dragging somebody screaming down to hell.

"Someone get fired, or something?" Jason prodded, opening his briefcase and removing an orange from an infinitely wrinkled brown paper bag inside. As Nivens and Walters looked sideways at each other, he began denuding the fruit, tossing the little orange scabs with practiced ease over the edge of his desk, where they dropped through the miniature hoop that hung above his wastebasket, just out of sight.

Suddenly he paused, thumb buried in orange rind, and looked up slowly, scanning both of their idiotic faces. "Wait a minute. It's not me, is it?"

Nivens smiled slightly. "No, it's not you, you paranoid asshole."

Jason nodded suspiciously. "But it's *somebody*."

The pair again exchanged schoolgirl glances. "Okay," Nivens gave in. "Let's just say somebody's *leaving*. But it's not official yet, so don't spread it around. We're only telling you this because it concerns you directly." He

paused as if expecting still more encouragement, but Jason abstained by popping an orange segment into his mouth.

"It's your boss," said Walters in a melodramatic whisper.

"My boss?" mumbled Jason semicoherently through the citrus, keeping up a show of disinterest. "Who, which boss? Halloran?" Since the merger with Grey, his company had become the biggest of the Big Five ad firms, and "boss" now had all kinds of orders of magnitude.

But Nivens grinned impishly and touched his finger to his nose. "Bingo," he confirmed, and Jason resisted the impulse to smash the fruit into that pasty little face.

"That's a stupid rumor," declared Jason. "A month ago, you told me we were supposedly getting bought by Disney/ABC. Where the hell do you guys hear this crap?"

"Don't get your panties in a bunch," Nivens assured him. "You're not scheduled to go down with the ship. Even if you don't get along with the new guy, you'll probably just get shifted to another account group."

"Or the new *gal*," chimed in Walters.

"Or the new gal," Nivens agreed.

But Jason was shaking his head. "I don't think so," he declared, out of equal parts loyalty and conviction. "Halloran's the golden boy." He looked down at his hands, then the orange, a suddenly pointless prop, and set it down, trying to maintain a credible nonchalance.

"Suit yourself," shrugged Nivens. "But I get his file cabinet."

"You can have it," said Walters. "*I* get his office."

"You can't call offices," said Nivens. "They're assigned, you moron."

"Guys, thanks for the scoop," said Jason, holding up his hands as if preparing to applaud, "but I've really gotta get some work done."

"Beware, O unbeliever," said Nivens. "Seriously, though, you didn't hear anything from us."

"I certainly didn't," said Jason. "Mark my words, gentlemen: Halloran will still be here when we're all wearing mahogany overcoats."

After they finally left, Jason sat in quiet contemplation for a few moments. He'd never bothered to track the always-dire forecasts of the Brothers Grim over his three years of employment, but they seemed to be

right at least half of the time, making them difficult to dismiss out of hand. It *was* preposterous . . . and yet, there the notion remained, a grinning barnacle securely attached to his forebrain.

His still-tentative grasp of office politics encouraged him to keep the information under his hat, although he had no idea what private use he could possibly make of it. In the end, he based his decision to say nothing to his boss on purely practical concerns. Even if Halloran *did* have his walking boots on, what could calling attention to the situation prematurely accomplish beyond embarrassing them both?

The buzz of the phone called Jason back to reality, and he decided to make haste and let the machine answer. Picking up the Hair Peace file and grabbing a notebook to pad his insubstantial load, he stepped out and headed for that big, quiet corner office at the end of the hall.

✧ ✧ ✧

Pathologically tidy, furnished in a colorless, antiseptic institutional style, Pete Halloran's office had all the plastic charm of a suburban model home. On the far wall, behind a smooth, gray art-deco desk subdeveloped with pristine little stacks of neatly clipped papers, a three-paneled picture window anchored the room's preternatural symmetry. Identical file cabinets graced the end walls; a pair of chairs on the left balanced a small couch on the right; twin ferns buttressed the window, arching in gently opposing angles toward the sunlight. As usual, Jason felt oddly compelled to run a comb through his hair before entering.

As the room's sterility made clear, Halloran no longer engaged in any messy acts of creation, and Jason could not avoid reading the evidence here of some desperate, alien thirty-something crisis of the soul.

The opening door revealed his boss in the act of chain-smoking, a fresh cigarette caught in the corner of a Popeye sneer, the still-smoldering cherry of another held tenderly to its naked tip. "Howdily-doodily, neighbor," said Jason from beyond the threshold.

"Morning," Halloran replied between puffs, drawing in the fire. His haircut was a well-manicured auburn lawn, his suit crisp and unruffled.

"There's a lung surgeon out in the lobby to see you," said Jason.

Halloran managed a wan smile as he inhaled deeply to establish the flame, dropping the old butt in a smokeless ashtray and closing a teeny garage door to pinch off the smoke. "Tell him to come back tomorrow," he replied. "I'm having a drink with my liver specialist."

Jason pulled up a chair and watched in mute fascination as his boss wet his little finger and picked up single ashes from his desktop.

"You're not interested in half a ten-K share at the Jersey shore this summer, are you?" said Halloran. "It's all the weekends."

"Not unless you called me in here to give me a fat raise."

Halloran smiled. "So . . . not in this lifetime. Well, I had to ask. It's been a complete nightmare. Yesterday, I interviewed a woman who wanted to bring her entire group-therapy group down for the month of July. She's already called twice to let me know she's not taking my rejection personally."

Jason smiled. "I think I'll just skip the traffic again this year," he replied. "I see enough New Yorkers in New York."

"Fair enough," said Halloran.

Though Halloran had assumed the paternal duty of guiding Jason through his fledgling corporate ascendancy, the two enjoyed an almost peer-level friendship, limited only by their age difference and the asymmetric power axis. Halloran had once even tried to set Jason up with his younger cousin, a dismal experiment that was never, ever spoken of, even in jest.

"That's the Hair Peace project, I take it?" Halloran wondered, indicating the folder. "Looks rather . . . svelte."

Jason tried not to wince visibly. The casual humor only underscored his unshakable concern that his inability to come through for Pete amounted to some sort of personal betrayal. "I've got some ideas cooking," he replied.

Halloran nodded. "But nothing you're ready to share just yet."

"That's pretty much it, yeah."

"I warned you that this was going to be a tough one," said his boss. "Talk to me."

Jason laid the file on the desk and took a deep breath. "I don't even know where to start. It's problematic pretty much across the board."

"Well, let's see," said Halloran, checking his ceiling for inspiration. "For one thing, it's an idiotic product."

Jason smiled, relieved already. "Yeah," he agreed enthusiastically. "That's it in a nutshell. It's supposed to soothe itchy scalps and provide an appetizing 'wet' look. But it doesn't actually, medically, address dandruff or any of the *causes* of itchy scalps; it just sort of *greases* the itch. Which is soothing, I guess, if you're in deep denial. And the 'wet' look hasn't been appetizing since Fonzie."

"True," said Halloran. "This is one of those miracle products conceived by some sixty-year-old would-be Ron Popeil while he's sitting on the john. So start by fine-tuning your demographics: What kind of consumer *is* likely to think this sort of thing is cool?"

Jason was shaking his head. "But it's more than that," he complained. "I mean, Hair Peace, for Christ's sake. It's a lame pun on toupees, which aren't that funny to start with. And the whole thing's a blatant attempt to latch on to enviro-chic. Borderline-toxic, animal-tested ingredients, in a conscience-soothing forest-green package. I mean, look at the damned *bottle*," he protested, opening the folder and pulling out a product shot, a photograph of a green Hair Peace bottle illustrated by several lines of glowing text. "These guys actually had the temerity to press a damn *peace sign* right into the petroleum-based, landfill-gagging plastic of the bottle. It's the most baldly cynical thing I've ever come across."

" 'Hair Peace' also sounds like 'herpes,' " Halloran noted, looking up from the photo. "If you say it with sort of a French accent."

Jason grinned. "Right. So you agree."

Halloran took a healthy drag from the cigarette, and guided a precarious ash cone to the tray. "Well, what does *that* mean? That it's impossible? It's a tough sell, granted," he continued, forestalling Jason's interruption with an upraised hand. "But so what? If it were easy, they'd do it in-house."

"I know, I know," said Jason, signaling his perfect understanding with an exaggerated nodding of his entire upper body. "I guess . . . I guess it's just hard to get fired up extolling the virtues of a product you don't stand behind."

"Well, let's not get all starry-eyed," said Halloran dismissively. "The reason it's hard to extol its virtues is because it hasn't *got* any, that's all. But that's the *challenge*, Jason. Don't be so concrete." After a perfunctory puff of his cigarette, he began waving it around as an abstract pointer. "I mean, really, a potbellied pig with a number-two pencil can sell Coke and Pepsi. If you can peddle *this* piece of shit"—here he tapped the product shot with his free hand—"it will mark you as a player. This is a made-to-order opportunity to prove yourself."

In the unbearable floodlight of Halloran's scrutiny, Jason's thoughts kept twisting themselves into maddening phone-cord tangles. "Maybe . . . it's just hard for me to get away from the idea that it's already taken a lot longer than it should have."

"Listen, this is not worth choking over," said Halloran. "Hair Peace is just an ill-conceived product that needs a lot of help—that's all." Jason started to speak, but was again silenced by an upraised finger as Halloran exhaled a smooth stream of smoke out of one side of his mouth. "I understand how paralyzing this kind of pressure can be, believe me. Just try and think more abstractly; don't tie yourself to the product. Think lifestyle. Think joy, happiness, dancing supermodels. Think sex."

"Yeah," Jason agreed, smiling. "Okay, that sounds good."

"Don't be so concrete," Halloran reiterated, sliding the Hair Peace photo back into the folder, which he then closed and held out before him. "And don't abuse my leniency. I still very much expect you to produce."

"I understand," Jason replied with a sober nod, accepting the folder and rising to his feet. "Listen, thanks, Pete. I appreciate the vote of confidence."

"Give me something in a week," said Halloran.

✧ ✧ ✧

Running his fingers through his own shaggy blond mop, Jason closed his eyes and pictured great disembodied tufts, cute dangling braids and ringlets, embarrassingly spare comb-overs. He focused in further, on slender individual fibers, long tendrils of dead cells excreting themselves backward out of the head and into the waiting jaws of eager clippers, tumbling end over end to the barbershop floor. He was running through a forest of hair on the head of a giant, sidestepping sweat-oozing sinkhole pores, hacking his way through gently curling thickets with a nano-machete. Suddenly the heavens darkened: Looking skyward, he yelped as an immense plop of noxious Hair Peace, impelled by a monstrous hand, blotted out the sky.

The buzz of the phone broke up his reverie; hungry for the interruption, he scrambled forward to pick it up on the first ring and barked his knee on the desk. "Y and G," he said wearily.

After a long moment of silence, a female voice tentatively began. "Jason Hansvoort?"

"That's me," he replied cautiously. "Can I help you?"

Another long pause. "I think so," the voice continued at last. "Yes, I definitely think so. I'm sorry, it's just . . . amazing to hear your voice."

Jason frowned. "Who *is* this?"

"My name's . . . Amanda," the caller said haltingly, as if constructing a pseudonym on the fly. "You don't know me."

True enough. Her voice was wildly unfamiliar . . . unprecedented, really, with a gently modulated, almost musical quality he couldn't quite identify. The effect was quite hypnotic, and Jason had to remind himself of the danger of first impressions made over a phone. He shuddered at the mental image of a nude four-hundred-pound woman on the other end of the line, swatting a cockroach on her naked belly with a wet slap.

"Amanda," he affirmed, glad for the handle. "What can I do for you, Amanda?"

Again the caller remained silent, and Jason frowned. "I'm not really sure where to begin," she said at last. "I've been watching you for a while now." A pause, then an audible breath. "Well, that isn't it. I'm not a stalker, or anything. I'm calling you because . . . our lives are connected, in a strange way."

Curiouser and curiouser, thought Jason, as a faint aroma of prank reached his nostrils. The handful of Princeton friends he hung out with in the city were not above enlisting a stranger's help to pull off a practical joke, and a woman with a sexy voice was a famous Achilles' heel of Jason's.

Ever since high school, he hadn't had—or desired, for that matter—

any real long-term relationships, confining himself instead to balmy summer romances and a string of one-night to one-week stands. He had become a sort of catch-and-release fisher of women, and flirting had become
a virtual end in itself—not just a carefully honed skill, but a raison d'être.
He was strictly a vegetarian when it came to relationships, but by God, he
loved the hunt.

"You're that woman who breaks into Letterman's house, aren't you?"
he wondered idly, in no particular hurry to get back to smacking his head
against the wall.

"No," she replied, with a devastating little laugh—an easy mark. "Let
me explain . . . I'm sorry, but I need to make absolutely sure I'm talking to
the right person. Are you from Westchester?"

"I grew up there," he confirmed warily, eyebrows narrowing. "What's
this about, Amanda?"

"I'm sorry; I must be making you terribly nervous."

"No, no, I'm intrigued," he said. "Just promise me you're not pregnant
with my baby."

Another laugh; she had a dangerously fetching little chuckle, this one.

"Okay. Last question," she promised. "Has your family ever changed
the spelling of its surname?"

The bizarreness of the question caught Jason off guard; unable to
scramble a witty riposte, he had no choice but to deliver. "Yes, I believe
we did. It used to be spelled with a double *a*, or so I've been told, anyway.
Haansvoort," he pronounced, elegantly spreading the dipthong.

"Bingo," said Amanda in quiet triumph. "Oh, my God, I *found* you, you
elusive son of a bitch."

"Excuse me?" said Jason, as the amorous daydream coughed up a spray
of dust.

"Nothing, I'm sorry—that's not about you. Listen, Jason, I . . . I have
to see you," said Amanda. "Can you meet me for lunch? I'll explain everything, I promise."

Jason pulled the handset away from his face and regarded it strangely,
the bewildered bushman wondering how they got that tiny person into
the phone. "Of course not," he said, returning the phone to his ear. "No."

"No?" she said in real surprise. "Why not?"

"Why *not?*" he repeated. "Are you serious? Because I can't just go around having lunch with escaped mental patients—this is New York City."

He was only toying with her now, but her voice took an agitated turn. "I *swear* I'm not crazy," she protested. "Jason, I—I just need to talk to you face-to-face. It could mean a lot to you . . . a *lot*. Oh, my God, more than you could possibly imagine. I know this probably isn't making much sense, but just hear me out. A *lunch*—that's all I ask."

"Listen, you sound like a nice person," Jason replied, "but you've got to give me something to go on."

Having apparently sensed his crumbling resistance, the stranger brightened. "Lunch today. I'll meet you in any well-lit public place," she urged. "If you're not overjoyed that I tracked you down, I'll buy."

"No," said Jason.

"Why *not*, damn it?" she demanded.

He grinned involuntarily. Whoever she was, the girl had attitude. "Because I already have a lunch," he said.

"Oh. Okay, okay," she said hopefully. "Well, how about after work, then?"

"You're relentless, aren't you?"

"You have *no* idea," she replied smoothly. "How's seven o'clock?"

"Fine," said Jason, crossing himself. "Where do you want to meet?"

◇ ◇ ◇

Jason watched, entranced, as his pal Nick shook clotty Parmesan cheese onto a slice of pizza already swimming in tangerine grease. The two occupied one of five tiny tables in the frenetic shoe box of a Midtown pizza joint, the smell of bread thick in the air, faux-Venetian mosaics on the wall, plastic bottles of pizza spices loitering in intimate trios on every horizontal surface. A line of lunchers straggled along the length of the counter, sizing up the pies to the tinny call and response of the swarthy doughboys on the other side.

Nick, the lady-killer, looked tanned and dashing in tailored ocean-blue pinstripes, with an authoritative, almost swashbuckling jade tie and a patterned, yet somehow coordinated, shirt. He was preparing two slices of some meat-lover monstrosity; shake-shake-shake went his little off-white blizzard, clogging and coagulating the sprawling system of greasy rivers and lakes that spread over the raw, red meat–strewn landscape.

"That may be the most disgusting sight I've ever seen," Jason observed, grabbing a sheaf of napkins from the dispenser. "I can hear your arteries gasping from over here." He began laboriously blotting the grease from the top of his own plain slice.

"Actually," Nick replied, putting down the nearly exhausted shaker, "did you know that sausage has, ironically, been shown to reduce the risk of some types of coronaries?"

"That's a filthy lie," said Jason. "Even *you* ought to be ashamed."

Nick shrugged. "It may be a slight exaggeration," he allowed, dark eyes flashing as he leaned his body into the edge of the table, protecting his Brooks Brothered lap. "Ah, the glorious first bite," he said, addressing his slice, which was now poised, curled and aimed, just outside his mouth. "The heart meat, sliced from the pizza's soft belly." He closed his eyes in anticipation and sensuously sank his teeth in with a low murmur. "From here on in," he proclaimed, still chewing, "it just gets colder and stiffer as you inch your way toward the dry and dusty hills of the baked crust-bubbles."

"Uh-huh," Jason nodded, still blotting.

"When I win the Lotto, I'm never eating two bites out of the same slice again."

"When *I* win the Lotto," Jason countered, "I'm never eating anything in the shape of a triangle again."

"Snob," sniffed Nick.

The two munched in silence for a few moments, watching through the blocked-open front door as jacketed passersby braved the light rain that had begun to fall. The sky was bright but overcast; it would probably shower on and off all day. A bicycle messenger rocketed by, scattering terrified citizens in his wake.

"What do you think *their* life span is?" Jason wondered, still focused outside.

"Four years," Nick asserted distractedly. Jason didn't bother to spare his friend a glance; he'd almost certainly made up the number on the spot.

A young mother soldiered by, squinting, trying to keep her oversize umbrella from buckling in the wind as she pushed a stroller sealed in plastic like a miniature oxygen tent.

"I've been thinking I might want to start looking into possibly getting a new job," said Jason.

Nick paused in midbite, intrigued, then continued chewing. "You sound awfully sure," he laughed. "New position? New company? New career?"

"I'm not sure. That's actually the first time I've put that thought into a sentence."

"And what a sentence it was," said Nick. "Does this have to do with that Afro-Sheen stuff?"

"Hair Peace," Jason reminded him, for the dozenth time. "That's part of it. It's turning out to be a really phenomenally hard sell. I just don't know if I can do it. I don't even know if I *want* to do it."

"You know what your problem is?" said Nick.

"Tell me," Jason encouraged, with all the sarcastic patience he could muster. "What's my problem?"

"Well, you've mastered perspiration," said Nick. "But you don't have any feel for inspiration. You stack bricks as fast as you can, but you never design the building." He folded the slice deftly with one hand and waved it before him. "Instead of throwing more and more hours at the problem, you need to work smarter. Step away from the engine and look around and let your cerebral cortex make wild, magical connections for you."

"What a delicious blend of metaphors," Jason replied. "Unfortunately, the reality isn't that romantic. A positioning strategy doesn't just come to you while you're eating a Pop-Tart. There's actual work involved."

"How long have you been beating your head against the wall on this thing?" Nick wondered.

"I'm not beating my—"

"A month?"

"I'm not beating my head against the wall," Jason insisted.

"This falls right in line with your usual M.O.," said Nick. "You put all this pressure on yourself because you can't be satisfied unless you change the course of Western civilization with your trailblazing approach to this particular fish sauce or whatever. And then, surprise! You can't focus because there's too much at stake."

"Thank you for your adorable, childlike insights into the creative process, you fucking banker," said Jason with all the disdain he could muster.

Nick laughed at this. "You *can't* be implying that you don't think I'm creative."

Jason grinned. "You're right; I can't say that."

"You may not remember this," Nick continued, "but right out of college I was offered a job in Saatchi and Saatchi's creative department."

Jason's eyes opened wide. "Really?"

"I've never told you this story?"

"Nick, I'm *kidding.* It's the biggest whopper you've told in . . . well, in minutes."

"Jesus," said Nick. "What a jaded old skeptic you've become. I was having a Sapphire martini with this account executive at the Temple Bar, and—"

"Don't," said Jason, shaking his head, a ghost of a smile still on his lips. "Don't waste a goody on little old me."

Nick shook his head sadly and took another bite. "I frankly don't know why you stayed in advertising *this* long. What do you get out of it that makes it worth all this busy work?" He paused, shrugged. "Do you get *any* kind of orgasm at the end?"

Nick's predilection for asking the big questions was at once his most and least endearing quality. On the positive side, going for the conversational throat turned dialogue into a rich, layered experience; the pale conversations that sufficed for most people seemed, in comparison, like so much insipid banter. At the same time, though, friendship with Nick meant subjecting your soul to constant, often harrowing scrutiny; his conversational excesses were at their most charming when their object was anybody else.

"Let me put it this way," said Nick, filling the pause. "You're either doing what you want to do for the rest of your life, or you're paying the rent while you figure it out. So which is it? You ought to at least know *that* much about yourself."

Jason gave him a quizzical look. "Well, come on—there's a big middle ground there. Who knows for sure what they want to do for the rest of their life? That's like saying, 'Promise me you'll love me forever.'"

Nick was smiling. "Ah, but you see, lots of people *do* promise they'll love each other forever. There's a whole diamond industry predicated on the concept. It doesn't mean they're necessarily right; couples break up all the time. It just means they *know* they're right."

"Say again?" said Jason.

Nick shrugged. "They're not paralyzed by inaction."

"But they may be acting wrongly. Or foolishly."

"Yep."

"Okay . . . ," Jason began slowly. "So can you look me in the eye and tell me you're sure you want to be a currency trader for the rest of your life?"

Nick leaned calmly into the table and said methodically, "I'm sure I want to be a currency trader for the rest of my life."

A moment of silence followed. "Jesus," said Jason, running one hand through his hair. "Look at me. I'm playing Truth or Dare with a pathological liar."

"I'm sure it's what I want to do for the rest of my life *right now*," Nick clarified. "And the instant I'm no longer sure, I'll make the necessary changes, or I'll move on."

Jason marveled, not for the first time, at his friend's uncanny sense of conviction. Nick had been cocky when they were roommates in college, but in the years since their graduation, his brazen swagger had blossomed into an absolute certitude, an *authority*. It no doubt served him well in poker-faced trading; clearly, Wall Street had been good to Nick, and Jason didn't doubt for a minute that his friend really *did* intend to make the Street his permanent home. He envied Nick's confidence and resented it, too, as it stood in such embarrassingly stark counterpoint to his own wheel-spinning postcollegiate limbo.

"Well, maybe that's where I am," Jason said.

"Which . . . ready to move on?"

"Maybe," Jason replied. "I'm not sure." He looked out the open doorway again, where the rain was coming down harder now, graying the afternoon sky and sweeping the street in thin, misty sheets. "Maybe I just need a vacation. A nice little three-day bender."

"You just need to get laid, my friend," prescribed Nick, the eternal sybarite.

"Hey, that reminds me," said Jason. "This morning I got a phone call from this girl who says she's been following me."

"Interesting," said Nick, clearly amused. "Old squeeze?"

"I don't think so," replied Jason. "Not that I recall, anyway."

"They're the most vindictive," Nick observed. "The ones you can't recall, I mean. Almost by definition. Did I ever tell you about the time an old girlfriend chased me through Tijuana with a machete?"

Jason ignored him. "Anyway, she doesn't sound dangerous."

"Okay," sighed Nick, rolling his eyes. "Look, if you need to do the witness protection thing, I know a good plastic surgeon."

"I'm surprised you *aren't* a plastic surgeon."

"So what does she want?"

Jason recounted the mysterious morning call, ignoring Nick's ineffable grin and self-consciously leaving out his own odd attraction to the mystery girl.

"I'd roll with it," Nick advised, semi-surreptitiously checking his watch. "Go have some drinks. Don't look a gift babe in the mouth."

"Oh, I'm definitely intrigued," Jason assured him. "I'd just feel more comfortable if I knew what she wanted."

"Assume she wants a ride on your banana boat," he advised. "If you're wrong, she'll let you know." He stood up and grabbed his plate.

Jason shook his head. "I don't think she wants my banana boat."

✧ ✧ ✧

Outside, they joined a bedraggled handful of pedestrians huddled under the awning as the rain pounded the street. Jason, noticing that Nick was unarmed against the elements, tapped his own umbrella on the ground with a jaunty little Gene Kelly lilt.

"So when are you meeting her?" Nick asked, ignoring him.

"Tonight, after work."

"Nice," Nick observed. "Go for the kill."

"Her idea." Suddenly, Jason brightened. "Hey, maybe she *does* want a ride on my banana boat."

"Aye aye, cap'n."

Jason grinned. "I'll keep you posted."

They shook hands, an absurd piece of formality Jason always wished could be accomplished with a bit more irony. "Good luck tonight," said Nick. "If you have any equipment trouble, tell her she can give me a call."

Nick stepped into the rain with one arm upraised, and managed to haul in a taxi on the first cast. The choreography was incredible—the cab swooped in to the curb just as he arrived, and a single giant step over the swollen rain gutter took him into the warm, dry interior of the car. As the door slammed, Jason shook his head in amazement, trying to lock open the stupid, capricious umbrella as Nick's window rolled down.

"Make sure she pays!" shouted Nick over the rain. "This ain't 1960." His friend's hair, Jason couldn't help noticing, had acquired an appetizing wet look.

✧ ✧ ✧

Ye Olde North Taverne, two and a half stories of peaked wood gables, shuttered eight-pane windows, and a faded swinging sign lettered in bony Old English script, crouched like a decrepit old rummy among the strapping young glass-and-steel titans of Midtown.

It was a calculated deception. In truth, there was nothing olde about ye taverne at all, not the calibrated sag in the roofe, not the artificially lumpy bricke floore, not the broade, fake beams spanning the quaintly lowe ceilinge. The building itself dated only to the mid-seventies, when the marketable cachet of Old World architecture was at a relative high. Naturally, Ye Olde North proved much more popular than the authentically ancient bars that dotted New York, with their déclassé locations, their messily crumbling facades, and their inconsistent multigenerational decoration.

Jason smirked contemptuously; even a naturalized New Yorker is entitled to some sneering rights. Now a journeyman of the urban scene, he reveled in his disdain for places like this, which were useful only insofar as they tended to centrifuge out the most obvious and clueless tourists.

Checking his watch as he entered, Jason found he had plenty of time for a preliminary cocktail before his appointment. An early buzz conferred a certain positional advantage on a first date . . . if that's what this was. An afternoon of expenses and busywork had forged in him a powerful thirst, the type o' thirst that can only be slaked by an ale served in an authentic replica pewter tankard.

Finding an empty booth beyond the end of the bar, Jason leaned his briefcase against the seat back and carefully folded himself into the narrow seat, taking pains not to foul his suit on the unwiped vinyl tablecloth. Bouncing once on the too-cushiony Naugahyde perch, he cast an eye around for waitress service, watched a few mute moments of ye olde basketballe on the little TV behind the bar, and gradually let himself be absorbed by the quaint local fauna. A trio of women in identical blue dresses—flight attendants?—erupted in laughter over some petty scandal; a pair of nerdy double-breasted vultures (mustaches, furtive eyes darting down blouse tops) made a lazy infinite loop around the bar.

As always, Jason paid particular attention to the female denizens, unabashedly poring over their forms and faces with voyeuristic intensity from the shelter of his booth. None of those immediately visible warmed his gravy in particular, but girls would come and go over the course of the evening, naturally, and all available plays would eventually make themselves known. Of course, he wasn't here alone, he reminded himself, resisting his mind's impulse to continue pointlessly speculating about the morning's enigmatic phone call.

With authentic replica waitresses apparently in scant supply, Jason hauled himself up with a sigh and strolled to the bar, leaving his briefcase to guard his seat. There, he watched with mounting annoyance as the unconcerned barkeep squeaked glasses with a hand towel, oblivious to all entreaties and crumpled offerings, shifting his weight in a casual way that made it clear he hustled for nobody, bub. It was minutes before Jason could lure him over with a twenty so crisp it felt counterfeit to the touch.

A woman in red glanced over from a nearby stool, and Jason smiled conspiratorially but noncommittally—*Jeez, can you believe how slow this joker is?*—waiting until she turned back to her friends to check her out. Nice face, okay smile, sort of a jumbo can. He fiddled with a pressed-paper St. Pauli Girl coaster and relented; nothing deforms the human posterior like a bar stool.

Sauntering back toward his seat with beer in hand, Jason was jostled hard, perhaps intentionally, by a harried, scowling waitress in period dress, an impact that cost him most of the beer.

He looked up angrily from the disaster, but the protest died on his lips because there *she* was, sitting in his very booth as if it had actually been hers all along.

It had to be Amanda; she stood out from the undifferentiated bar-scene background like a Cadillac in a swimming pool. She was attractive, to be sure, but in a strange, exotic sort of way that seemed somehow incidental to her . . . *presence.* Or maybe it was the hat, a flat, straw-colored number, almost a boater, bound with a black ribbon and set jauntily askew, that seemed so out of place in the dry-cleaned conformity of the crowd she was beckoning him through with one cupped hand: *Come on, come on.*

He tried to stare as casually as possible while threading his way toward her. She wore a tan suede vest over a black button-down shirt, a simple outfit that just managed to clamber over the threshold of his natural reluctance to notice such things. Her long, black hair was drawn back in a couple of waves; a smoothly tanned face and a pair of dark, smiling almond eyes became gradually distinguishable as he approached and sidled smoothly into the seat across from her, Naugahyde squeaking unhelpfully.

"Hi," she said brightly.

Jason smiled and shook her proffered hand in a presumptuous, finger-contact-intensive way. "Hi. Jason Hansvoort," he replied, adding, "as if you didn't know."

An almost goofy grin spread across her face. "Yes, I know. It's nice to finally meet you."

"So—am I your prisoner?" he said with a smile, firing up the flirting engines as she sat back and adjusted the rolled-up sleeves of her shirt. Overall, he decided, quite a package.

"It's a long story," she laughed. "You—"

"Wait one sec," Jason interrupted, freezing her with an upraised finger and smoothly catching the lacy sleeve of a different, but equally sullen, waitress quite intent on swooping past.

"Could we get a couple of—" Jason paused, turned to Amanda. "What would you like?"

"Oh—um, yeah," she replied, glancing at his beer before looking up at the waitress. "I'll have, um . . . uh . . . planter's punch."

"We don't have that," replied the waitress, late for something and straining at the leash.

"I know, I know," Amanda confessed. "I panicked. I'll just have what he's having."

"Two Basses," said Jason. "Bass. Whatever."

The waitress nodded her dull comprehension and sped away, and Jason hooked a thumb at her retreating form as he turned back to Amanda. "Take a good look," he advised, "because you will never, ever see her again."

Amanda made a face. "I should have gotten a rum and Coke."

"You want that? I can get it from the bar," he said, half-rising. The chivalry card was an easy one; he'd already planned to make every effort to buy all the drinks.

She shook her head. "No, no; this'll be fine. I can wait."

"I'm warning you—the last time she came by she was only this tall," said Jason, holding his hand at chest level.

Amanda smiled wanly. "You're kind of a class clown, huh?"

Wounded slightly, he shrugged. "I thought you knew aaaaall about me."

She shook her head. "I know almost nothing about you."

"Well, in that case . . . why *are* we here, exactly? If you don't mind my being blunt. But you did say it was a long story."

Amanda leaned toward him, taking a deep breath as she gathered her weight on her elbows and pressed her palms together, interlacing long musician's fingers as she flashed him a conspiratorial grin. "I'm here to unravel an ancient mystery," she said at last, not quite under her breath. Her eyes sparkled with electric excitement.

"You sound like Leonard Nimoy," he said, to break the spell. He turned to check on the waitress, simultaneously reaching for his wallet. "I'm thinking we should run a tab, right?" he queried, seeing the waitress returning.

"Oh, yeah," Amanda confirmed with a nod. "You're going nowhere, buddy."

✧ ✧ ✧

"I hardly know where to begin," Amanda confessed after a preliminary sip. "You'd think that after all this time I'd have it written out on three-by-five cards."

"Who the hell *are* you?" he asked gently, with a shrug. "That seems like a good place to start."

But she continued to trace her own path. "I think I'll begin with the story," she replied, "and then tell you where you fit in, and why I've been trying to find you. And then everything will become clear, I promise." She gave him a reassuring smile.

I'm thinking flake, said Jason to himself. *I turned her down at an eighth-grade dance, and she's been tracking me ever since. In her studio apartment is a shrine to me: candles, yearbook pictures, a lock of my hair. And all over the walls is scribbled, over and over again, a thousand times: "'Sorry, I don't dance to Foreigner. Sorry, I don't dance to Foreigner.'"*

Amanda stared at him blankly, maybe confused by the sudden wary look in his eyes, maybe running her fingers over a ten-inch steak knife strapped to her thigh. Her question, when it surfaced at last, took Jason completely unawares.

"How much do you know about the European settlement of this country?" she asked simply.

Jason blinked. "Excuse me?"

"You know, when the—"

"Yeah, yeah, I know," he interjected, then shrugged. "All right, it's your game. Let's see," he began. "'In fourteen hundred and ninety-two, Columbus sailed the ocean blue.' Except the Vikings were here first, I seem to recall."

"That's right."

"And this is all going to make sense?"

She nodded sincerely. "Yes, yes. I promise."

"There was Columbus," Jason continued, "who I believe actually went to the Caribbean first, and then Florida, and then later there were the Pilgrims, fleeing England, I guess . . . for religious reasons, who came over on the *Mayflower* and landed at Plymouth Rock."

He looked up, trying to gauge her intentions, but as Amanda only nodded expectantly, there seemed nothing to do but continue. "The Pilgrims set up colonies in New England, where a lot of them died of beriberi and syphillis and tomahawks. If the revisionist historians haven't decided that that was all bullshit."

"Very good," she said. "There were a lot of settlers, though, who weren't English. French, Swedish . . . Dutch."

"That sounds familiar." Jason nodded. "I think I vaguely remember my grandmother trying to drill that into my young skull." He added, "Her husband was Dutch. That whole side of my family is Dutch."

Amanda nodded and continued. "The Spanish had St. Augustine, in Florida, and the English set up a colony in Virginia, at Jamestown, which you may have heard in your history class was wiped out. Cholera. The Pilgrims up in Rhode Island made a better go of it. But it was the Dutch who were the first to really grasp the . . . *earning* potential of the new land. They were traders—they didn't care so much about establishing colonies. What *they* saw in the New World was a bottomless supply of goods, with no one to keep them from it but essentially unarmed indigenous people. In 1621, the Dutch West India Company was chartered, with the express purpose of looting the New World of furs, gold, and whatever else of value could be carted back to Europe."

"Whatever they could keep the pirates from getting," Jason suggested.

"Well . . . that really became more of a problem later on," said Amanda. "Anyway, England's star was only just beginning to ascend, and at this point, Holland's power on the sea was still more or less uncontested. They were able to thwart French efforts to establish colonies in Maine and Maryland, and eventually laid claim to the entire North American coast from Newfoundland to the Chesapeake Bay."

"*Jeopardy* scout," said Jason.

"Excuse me?"

"You're a *Jeopardy* scout," said Jason. "Or a grad student."

Amanda raised an eyebrow. "NYU law," she acknowledged.

Jason raised an eyebrow at this. "They teach you this in law school?"

"No, no," she replied, shocked, shaking her head. "*God*, no. Law school is dull—deathly, deathly dull. This is all independent research." She staved off his next question with a wave of her hand. "Wait—let me do this in order, or I'll never get through it all. You just nod and drink your beer."

He nodded, and took a sip. *The wench grows bold.* Confidence held an almost narcotic attraction for Jason, and though he still burned with curiosity as to where this could possibly be heading, he was more than content to drink deeply as she boldly held forth on whatever she damn well pleased.

And for the next twenty minutes or so, he let her guide him back through the earliest days of New York history. How Henry Hudson, an Englishman working for the Dutch government, had been charting the Delaware Bay in 1610, heading north along the coast, looking for the Northwest Passage to India, apparently a sort of Holy Grail for navigators at the time.

"When Hudson reached the northeast corner of what we now call New Jersey," said Amanda, "he came upon this enormous bay. To the left there was a mighty river cascading out of the woods, jumping with fish. And to the right—or, more precisely, sort of dead ahead—there lay a beautiful, pristine little island, covered with deep forest. Manhattan. It was in the fall, so all the colors would have been out. Must have been an unbelievable sight. So guess which one he chose to explore?"

"The Hudson River. I mean, the river."

"Exactly," she said. "You *are* paying attention. Hudson was a sailor, after all, and who can blame him? But he always remembered the island fondly; in his diaries, he actually describes it as being an ideal spot for a trading post. He was right, of course. Unfortunately, two years later, he was dead."

"Natural causes?"

"Not exactly," said Amanda with a wry smile. "He was set adrift by his own men—in Hudson Bay, between Canada and Greenland. But his dream was eventually realized. The Dutch established settlements all over the mouth of his river, and in 1626, the Dutch West India Company, through their colonial governor Peter Minuit, bought the island of Manhattan from its native inhabitants."

"Now, that I remember," said Jason. "For thirty pieces of silver, or something."

"Well, that's Judas Iscariot." Amanda smiled.

"Right," said Jason, nodding. "How ugly American of me." *Here I am*, he thought, *just sitting in a bar, getting a history lesson from a hot chick*. Concentration was proving more difficult than he'd hoped; this felt tantalizingly like a dating scenario, yet the one-sided conversation yielded little opportunity for him to dazzle her with his wit and charm.

Amanda kept up the brisk pace. "They also didn't buy Manhattan with a trunkful of junk jewelry, as a lot of history books have it," she asserted. "It was quality Dutch merchandise—tools, clothing, knives—worth about sixty guilders at the time. It's historically translated as about twenty-four dollars, though with inflation it should be up to a couple of hundred bucks by now."

"Still, the deal of the century."

She nodded. "No question. The deal of four centuries."

"Crazy Injun Joe: His prices are in-*sane!*" said Jason in an extravagant TV voice, hands outstretched to suggest the extent of Injun Joe's insanity.

She smiled thinly. "Yes, now pay attention, please. So *anyway*, the Dutch bought the island from the natives, a tribe called the Manahatas— that's where the island gets its name—and they set up a fort and a major trading post at the south end of the island. What's now the Wall Street area."

"That's kind of funny," Jason interjected.

Amanda glanced quickly both ways as if to see if anyone else was laughing. "Why is that funny?"

"Just the idea that Wall Street used to be a trading post," he replied. "It's what it is today, too, if you think about it."

Amanda shrugged. "Sure, but there's nothing ironic about that—it never stopped being a trading post."

While Jason mulled this over, she stole the opportunity to sip her beer. "Anyway," she continued, "the Manahatas, like many other Native Americans, were a primitive, migratory people with no real idea of 'property.' They've sold the island to the Dutch, but they aren't even sure what that means. So they take all their new stuff back to their huts and continue to inhabit the island, which is technically no longer their own. Essentially, they just move north, off the beach."

"Makes sense," said Jason. "The housing's better north of Fourteenth Street anyway."

"But the point is, they don't really know what they've done; they aren't culturally capable of figuring out what's happened to them." She paused, as if to let this take effect, and Jason realized with a start that Amanda was Indian. Or part Indian, he amended, as her hazy, exotic looks began at last to resolve in his mind into distinct features: high-swept cheekbones, a generous mouth with an upper lip that curled smileward with every few dozen words, as if endlessly amused by some running in-joke playing hide-and-seek beneath the surface of her commentary. Her skin tone was on the olive side, and her hair had a defining wave that didn't fit the native stereotype, but the context made the conclusion inescapable. Still, it seemed the wrong time to bring it up, and Jason tried quickly to recall the conversation.

"So the natives were taken advantage of," Jason summarized.

Amanda nodded. "They were a Stone Age culture dragged to the bargaining table of colonial Europe. It was much, much easier than taking candy from a baby."

He concentrated on drinking as she went on; he was clearly going to have to focus on buzz management this evening. For her part, Amanda slid her thumb up around and around the rim of her beer mug as if trying to coax out a resonant hum, as she described New York's subsequent history. By the 1650s, the Dutch were hopelessly overextended, and starting to lose it. The Portuguese had driven them out of Brazil; the French had retaken Quebec; and in 1664, the English had counterclaimed the territory from Delaware to Connecticut, including Dutch New Amsterdam, a.k.a. Manhattan. Ultimately the island was surrendered by its one-legged governor, Peter Stuyvesant, much against his wishes. He'd declared his willingness to fight the entire English army himself if he had to, until all his men called his bluff by defecting.

Tempting though it was to construe the girl's excited energy state as an unquenchable jones for his man flesh, there was no point in deluding himself. It was becoming disturbingly clear to Jason that Amanda had no carnal interest in him whatsoever. Oh, he amused her in a general sort of way; they seemed to get along well conversationally. But he'd seen all kinds of romantic prospects melt away over the years . . . it was the curse of the comic, and he knew the signs too well. And while the raw fact of her platonic disinterest didn't dissuade him from persevering, it was more than a little disheartening.

"And now," said Amanda, leaning back dramatically, "we're at the turning point. Everything I've told you so far is history; you could find it in a hundred textbooks. I did," she added parenthetically. "But *now* we dive into uncharted waters. Some of what I'm about to tell you is only conjecture; some of it is surely not quite right. But taken all together, there is truth to it."

"Sounds like a good time to break for more drinks," Jason decided, flashing a peace sign to a nearby waitress. "Oh, wait—" he said, turning back to the table. "You wanted a rum and Coke, or something."

"Oh, please, I don't care," replied Amanda, opening her purse and withdrawing a pack of cigarettes and a lighter. "What's your time frame like?"

"I'm definitely a night owl," he assured her. It wasn't precisely true, but he *had* optimistically blocked out the entire evening, as was his habit on those rare occasions when he had actual formal dates. "What about you— you live in the city?"

"Upper East Side," she replied. "I can just catch a cab back whenever." She pulled two cigarettes from the pack, and before he could decline, broke one of them in two and dropped it into the ashtray, then nonchalantly placed the other between her lips. Following his intrigued gaze, she lifted the pack: *Want one?*

"I'm on the Upper West," said Jason, refusing the cigarette with a shake of his head, wondering what sort of ritual he'd just witnessed. "Eighty-first and Amsterdam. We're ten minutes from my apartment."

"Good," she said, lighting the spared cigarette, "because we're only about halfway done."

Holy shit. "Listen, Amanda," Jason began, wincing slightly. "Don't take this the wrong way, I'm having a good time. But where's this all going?"

Amanda frowned in real surprise. "I'm not boring you, am I?" she asked, as if fascinated by the notion.

Jason shook his head. "No, no, that's not it. It's just that . . . well, none of this seems to have anything to do with *me*."

"I'm sorry," she said. "I know, I get carried away. You've been very patient with me; I appreciate it. But I really do find this story fascinating, personally, so it's hard for me to—"

"I do, too," said Jason. "Really. I mean, I'm not a history guy, but I'm definitely intrigued. I just need . . . a context. The 'Why me?'"

"It's coming," Amanda promised. "Or rather, that *was* the context. The *story*, the reason I asked you here, is coming right up."

"Okay," he said warily.

"I promise," she said sincerely, crossing her heart with one index finger, giving him an excuse to steal a glance at her grapefruit breasts. The waitress clunked the drinks on the table with one hand and scribbled a few digits on their bill.

Amanda watched her leave as if waiting for her to drop out of range. "Okay, you ready?" she said.

"Let's do it."

Amanda took a deep drag, then sneered at the cigarette and abandoned it on the edge of the ashtray, where it began slowly cremating itself, thin soul departing in a long gray wisp. Turning her head, she exhaled away from him. "Here's where the story takes . . . sort of a mythic turn," she asserted. "Most schoolkids learn about Peter Minuit and the Manhattan sale from that famous painting by, um, someone or other. It shows the Dutch traders shaking hands with the about-to-be-defrauded savages, as they were known."

"The natives," Jason suggested.

"Yes, the Manahatas. As I said, that was in 1626. And by the 1660s, Stuyvesant had surrendered the town to the British, and the Dutch occupation was done. New Amsterdam became New York, the city we all know and love today."

Jason tried to come up with a quick caustic remark, but couldn't formulate it in time.

"Now, Jason," Amanda continued quickly, as if to forestall any further interruption, "what would you say if I told you that I believe that storied sale never in fact took place? Or that, if it did, it was rescinded not long after our little painting?"

Now we're getting somewhere, thought Jason as he considered this. "I could believe that," he decided. "It wouldn't be the first time history's lied to us; Randy Johnson couldn't throw a silver dollar across the Potomac, for example."

"I have reason to believe that there was a mysterious benefactor," Amanda said. "A Dutch settler who was very, very close to the Manahatas, probably lived among them. He may even have been married to one. Somehow, this man came into legal possession of the island, and agreed to hold it in perpetuity for the Manahata people, who clearly had no business transacting for themselves."

She had paused again, expectantly, but Jason only shrugged in confusion. "Okay . . . ," he said simply.

"There was a document," she went on, "or a deed—some sort of bill of sale—that established this guy's ownership of the island, and all it entails, devolving it on his heirs in perpetuity. Essentially, giving him and his descendants clear title to the land forever," she paraphrased. "But, again, he was to hold it for the Manahata people. This may be explicit in the document, or it may not."

"I'm guessing we're deep in conjectureland now, right?" said Jason.

But Amanda was shaking her head slowly. "No. Jason, the document *exists*. Now. Today."

This genuinely surprised him. "You've seen it?"

"Well, no," she conceded. "Not yet."

"Well, if you're right, that's amazing," he acknowledged, taking a slug of beer. "That's got Discovery Channel written all over it."

"No, no; you're missing the point," she complained, putting her hands to both temples as if preparing to communicate the point telepathically. "I'm not talking about a historical curiosity; I'm talking about a valid deed to property."

"What, to Manhattan?" he said incredulously. "This guy's been dead for how long?"

"I told you, the deed confers the land on all his heirs, in perpetuity."

A perceptible shift in Amanda's tone brought his attention into sudden sharp focus: She was quietly assertive now, her eyes ablaze with passion, and suddenly he had it.

"And I'm the heir," he said. "The great-great-great et cetera grandkid."

Amanda smiled and sat back in a sort of ecstasy of relief. "Bingo," she confirmed.

"You seem awfully sure," he said suspiciously, eyes narrowing.

"Yes," she replied, nodding soberly. "I am. I can't prove it yet, but yes, I'm quite sure."

"But come on, Amanda," he said. "You're a law student. You have to know a document like that would never be enforceable. Not after four hundred years, or whatever. There must be half a million landowners in this city."

"You're *wrong*, you're wrong," she insisted, shaking her head violently. "Why do you think they run title searches every time anyone transacts property anywhere? Why do you think they have title insurance in the first place? The courts at every level, including the Supreme Court, have *always* upheld prior titled ownership. *Always.* And there's no statute of limitation, either. Old wills, old deeds, et cetera are sufficient evidence to oust long-established residents. If someone can firmly establish prior title, they own the land, free and clear. It really is just that simple."

Jason suddenly remembered his beer and took a long, hard swallow. He needed time, needed to drag himself out of the conversation and steady his whirling thoughts. But Amanda had no patience for him.

"In 1972," she continued breathlessly, "the Supreme Court overturned an 1892 act that had opened up the Klamath River reservation to white settlement, and restored it to the aboriginal Indians. In 1991, in Connecticut, local tribes successfully sued the state and won a significant plot of land, including part of downtown freaking Hartford, that had been unlawfully settled." She paused, waiting for input that wasn't coming. "I go on like this for days when nobody stops me."

They stared at each other across the table for what seemed like minutes, not speaking. Her dark eyes kept him riveted; the rest of the bar had long ago faded into peripheral darkness. Apparently, fate had fiendishly decided to present Amanda to him as some vague agent of mystery: not the Lady, but the tiger. He clasped his hands together as part of a monumental effort to focus, but Amanda grabbed his hands between hers and pulled him forward, into the table. Their faces were now inches apart, and Jason felt a physical rush. The din of the crowd swelled hotly around his ears, closed his throat.

"This is *real*, Jason," she said quietly, without blinking. "*You're* the descendant . . . it's your deed."

She released his hands and clasped her own together as she sat back in the seat, touching her forefingers to her lips as if in prayer.

"Your island."

Chapter Two

Casually spreading the blinds with two fingers, Ronnie Dovatelli peered out his conference-room window and watched a golden retriever relieve itself on a fire hydrant across the street, two stories below. *There truly is nothing new under the sun,* he mused, thoughtfully swirling the surface of his hot chocolate, where slowly deliquescing puffs of foam, tattered remnants of a once-formidable armada of mini-marshmallows, dispersed their essence in coiled white streaks. No coffee since the goddamned ulcer, of course, not without a Maalox chaser; this humiliating child's drink was the most caustic thing his jittery stomach walls could handle. Not that anyone in the organization dared to meet his eye and make that particular observation.

The pooch wagged his tail as he delivered his pungent critique, the inverted triangle of a red bandanna swinging loosely from his fat neck. Ronnie let the slats of the blinds spring back into place and reluctantly allowed the animated voice of his excitable son-in-law to drift back into his awareness.

Vince Furnio, dapper in off-the-rack Armani, stood with hands on hips, sandwiched comfortably between a project easel (currently featuring a pie chart under the heading "Kids Today") and a projector painting a

PowerPoint presentation on the far wall. Around the overlarge table, backed up nearly to the walls on all sides, lounged a dozen or so business-men and one woman, all casual in attire and attitude, none paying partic-ularly close attention to the demonstration that was, as anybody could have guessed, entirely too good for the room.

"So I'm seventeen," Vince was saying. "I want to participate in mobsta culture, but I don't wanna actually get arrested, or shot, or otherwise screw up my happy little suburban life." He punctuated his speech with smoothly interpolated hand motions, wrists locked as if in handcuffs, a pair of thumb-cocked finger pistols. "I wanna be a Soprano, not a Gam-bino."

Again with the frickin' Sopranos, thought Dovatelli, and the bile churned merrily up the back of his throat. *Bane of my existence*. Kids com-ing up now didn't want to hear word one about spreadsheets or manage-ment; you could practically hear them turning the music up in their heads. All they wanted was to whack somebody. It was a full-time job just keeping them off each other's throats. No one coming up through the ranks understood that this was a business; if you didn't let 'em carry a gun, they'd drift away, and if you did, you had to watch 'em slip their hands into their pants to finger it constantly, rubbing it like a goddamn rabbit's foot. When his generation handed over the wheel . . . and it wouldn't be long . . . the violence unleashed in the East was going to be a thing to be-hold.

He cast his eye over to Gina, his poor only child, Vince's bride of al-most a year. Dovatelli watched his daughter trying vainly to spin a pencil on her finger, staring in cross-eyed frustration at the stick through lashes gummy with mascara, her awkwardly masculine features framed with a dated Jackie O. bob. Gina had come up snake eyes in the genetic crap-shoot, winning Dovatelli's looks and his wife's simpleton brain (God rest her soul). It wasn't hard to see what Vince, the clumsy little machinator, saw in her; his cockiness since marrying Gina made it clear he believed he'd now simply inherit the business from the old man, like an heirloom watch or a blood disorder. What she saw in him, who knew? Maybe just an option. *Sorry, kid.*

A glance around his circle of listless pencil pushers reminded Dovatelli that he wasn't exactly flush with options himself. Maybe he *would* hand the reins to Vince; the only other candidate, obviously, was Freddie Marone. A hulking giant with dark eyes and a bodybuilder's tight-lipped smile, Freddie was Dovatelli's second-in-command, and privy to virtually all the company secrets. Nobody would question his succession . . . still, his thirst for the dark side of the business scared Dovatelli not a little. He'd watched Freddie position a crying businessman in his office doorway and slam a steel door on an exposed leg hard enough to break it, then shift the man, quivering and screaming and pleading, and break the same leg in another spot. That terrible cracking sound, the stench of the piss . . . and the whole time Freddie's whistling some goofy song, like a goddamn coal miner on his way back up to the sun.

No question, the man had an inner psychopath patiently chewing its way out. Oh, the chicks loved him; he was a big motherfucking teddy bear, and it chilled Dovatelli's blood to see him laughing with some cooing waitress or back-talking stripper, because he'd seen Freddie smile that same broad, farmboy grin while airing out the back of someone's skull, or knotting a chain around some degenerate's throat.

"There is a vast commercial opportunity here," Vince continued, still tirelessly gesticulating, trying to haul in the crowd with outstretched fingers. "The kids are looking for"—here he trailed off briefly, snapping his fingers twice—"cultural inspiration. And this is a vacuum we can fill. Gentlemen, we are in a position to provide no-risk entrée into the mobsta class, to merchandise where no one else dares to set foot."

"Why d'ya keep sayin' 'gentlemen'?" Gina whispered, for the second time.

"Gina, enough already," said Freddie, from across the table.

She stared at him, mouth half open in disbelief at his audacity.

Vince ran a hand through his oiled black hair and flashed his wife a tense smile: *Okay, honey, now hush, okay?* He reached down by his feet and produced an overstuffed briefcase that he laid gently on the table, spinning it around so the latch faced him before looking up to address the table again.

Dramatically pushing back the sleeves of his jacket, Vince slowly, as if defusing a bomb, unclasped the case and raised the lid. "Pass these out, sweetheart," he said to Gina, handing her a stack of laminated pages. "Feast your eyes, gentlemen, on the wave of the future." He paused to wink conspiratorially at Dovatelli.

Wearily, the old man took the proffered page and glanced down at an elegantly designed menu. Under an Italian flag shot up with holes, it read, "Mobstateria: Park It Here If You Know What's Good For You."

Look at this shit, thought Dovatelli, closing his eyes. *My heart is breaking.* There was no denying it anymore; his sixty-plus years had finally started to catch up with him. He was fighting a losing battle just to hold on to his little legacy, the dwindling chunk of territory that remained of his grandfather's once-rambling extralegal empire, and increasingly the temptation was just to swim upstream to Florida and leave it all behind. Dovatelli rubbed his stomach gently and thought: *I do not want to die here.*

"Corleone Cannelloni. Osso Buco Rico," Vince rattled off proudly. "I'm talkin' a whole chain of theme restaurants. The waiters are wiseguys. 'Order the special or else,' that kind of thing."

"'One Pullet in the Chamber'?" read Freddie incredulously. "You kiddin' with this crap?"

"It's chicken potpie," said Vince defensively. "The chamber's the—"

"Shut up, both of you," said Dovatelli, instantly silencing the room's chatter. "A chain of theme restaurants, Vin? That's your big idea?"

A crestfallen Vincent simply sat and stared at the still-yawning briefcase.

"Vin, even people who know how to run restaurants, which we are demonstrably *not,* can't turn a profit," he continued. "We might as well get a contract to build space shuttles."

Somebody snickered at this, and Dovatelli came down hard. "You shut the fuck up." He began slowly circling the table. "In case nobody's noticed, we're getting beat to *shit* out there in the street." He trailed off and glanced out the window, trying consciously to steady his nerves. "Come on, guys. What we need is some real, new business. High margin, low risk, low cost of entry . . . real cash-flow operations. Not this pie-in-the-sky shit."

"I got just the thing, Ronnie," said Freddie. Vince looked up at this, flashing his rival a wounded look.

"Oh, yeah? And what's that?" wondered Dovatelli, exasperation lingering in his voice.

"A *casino*," said Freddie, leaning forward in his seat and smiling darkly, thick black eyebrows coming together like long-lost twins. "Fifty million or more a year, when it's up and running," he predicted.

"Forget it," said Dovatelli, shaking his head. "Too much risk. Every time you get busted, you lose thirty grand in equipment. But that's more along the lines of—"

But Freddie was shaking his head. "Ronnie, excuse me a second here, but . . . I'm talking about a *legal* casino. On an Indian reservation." He looked around the table, meeting only blank stares. "Like Foxwoods."

Vince fake-coughed to insinuate himself into the dialogue. "There's just one slight problem, Freddie," he said with a smirk, extending his hands out to encompass the table. "You see any redskins?"

Dismissing him with a contemptuous sideways glance, Freddie focused instead on Ronnie and leaned into the table again. "There's tribes right there on Long Island dreamin' of Vegas, just waitin' for someone to organize 'em. We got the construction, the landscapers, the union guys, all the equipment. I know a guy who makes the goddamn *tables*. We set 'em up, run the whole operation behind the books, and hand 'em a piece. It's a goddamn money tree."

The silence that followed fed Freddie's confidence; the familiar goofy smile spread across his face. "Ronnie, *think* about it," he said in summary. "A casino that's a stop on the goddamn Long Island Railroad. We could turn Foxwood into a fuckin' *ghost* town."

Vince rolled his eyes at this, but no one was watching him; even the rays of the sun streaming through the blinds behind Dovatelli seemed focused on the old boss. For a long moment he held his silence, contemplating some obscure koan of commerce. Eleven Rolex fakes and one Chanel Le Temps ticked into the vacuum.

At last, Dovatelli spoke. "I'm listening," he said.

Vince squeezed his eyes shut in chained fury, feeling the first pangs of gastric acid eating into the walls of his stomach.

MADISON AVENUE, 9:25 A.M.

"Sorry I'm late," Jason said, cringing outside Halloran's office door.

"Oh, please," said his boss, ushering him inside with a sweep of his cigarette. "Don't get all craven on me now. Come in, come in."

Halloran clicked the door shut behind him as Jason slipped into the room, puzzled and wary. The terse Post-it note ("Jason—See me now. H.") was ominous; in interoffice communication, brevity is the soul of danger. Now, facing a desktop uncharacteristically littered with scribbled notes and Rolodex cards, Jason felt completely at sea, and several moments passed before he realized that his boss was still behind him, lurking in the doorway.

Jason turned to find Halloran leaning back against the door, cigarette held thoughtfully to his lips. On catching Jason's eye, he took a mighty drag and reversed the butt in his hand, staring at the glowing tip as if considering whether or not to stub it into his own nose. As his boss seemed inclined to keep that post, Jason swiveled the visitor's chair in front of the desk and sat down to face him.

"I'm out, apparently," Halloran told the cigarette.

Jason frowned, not comprehending, and the meaning slowly dawned on him. "You're *kidding*," he exclaimed.

"No, I am not," replied Halloran. "I don't even see the funny part."

"What happened?" said Jason, remembering with a bit of horror Nivens' and Walters' earlier, dismissed prediction of his boss's demise.

Halloran frowned and shrugged with forced nonchalance, pacing off half the room's perimeter before seating himself behind his desk. "It's a pretty standard bit of merger financing," he explained. "Sort of a shorthand attempt to help amortize the cost of overleveraging. They've given me a month, but I think I'm just gonna take it in vacation days. None of this is public yet, of course."

Wracked with guilt, his pulse racing with the double agent's fear of discovery, Jason was having difficulty digesting this new information. "Wait a minute, wait a minute," he said, shaking his head. "Overleveraging? What am I missing?"

Halloran looked at Jason with concern as he stubbed the butt into the open smokeless ashtray. "I thought we agreed you were going to start read-ing the paper in the morning."

"Pete, I just walked in."

"The Disney deal went through," said Halloran. "Sixty-five dollars a share. It's worth maybe half of that, of course . . . so they're trimming the soft white underbelly." He picked up a business card from a stack, studied it, relegated it back to the pile. "Isn't it funny how it's always the middle kids who get shafted?"

For a half hour or so, they sat and talked about details of the changeover, and then about nothing at all, while Halloran chain-smoked and Jason's mind roiled and rattled. What had begun so awkwardly quickly became a surreally calm conversation between two people who were suddenly peers. Jason wondered if they'd remain any kind of friends without the glue of their working relationship and the daily contact; he doubted it. But the magnitude of Halloran's misfortune loomed as an operatic backdrop, ren-dering the pleasantries downright silly in contrast.

"So what are you going to do now?" Jason finally asked, tentatively.

Halloran shrugged, now standing. "Well, I've made my little phone calls," he mumbled, "and I'm going to wait to see what happens. That seems to be how it works."

"I still can't believe they fired you," said Jason. "Idiots."

"Well, thanks," said Halloran patiently, completing the catechism. "It's not just me, of course—heads are rolling all over the company. Lots of wailing . . ."

He returned to his desk and sat down again as Jason fought with him-self over whether to come clean about his foreknowledge. "Anyway," Hal-loran went on, "I just wanted to keep you updated. I think you're low enough on the food chain to be out of danger, but you may want to con-sider that résumé upgrade now. I *believe*, although I'm not certain, that Di-ana will be taking over my accounts. But whoever it turns out to be, the pace is going to be stepped up around here. Raises and promotions are go-ing to be rara avis."

"Oh, I can't think about . . . ," Jason trailed off in knee-jerk protest.

"Please, don't be coy," Halloran implored. "We're just friends, now, and

I strongly encourage you to shop around, if you're not already doing it. I know you, Jason, and you are not going to thrive in the new atmosphere." He took a long drag from the cigarette. "You're not what I would call a creature of discipline."

"Diana, huh?" said Jason distastefully, to change the subject.

Halloran managed a weak grin. "You have no idea. Wait until you work with her directly. She'll have a ball-level vise installed at every desk."

◊ ◊ ◊

"What do you mean, you *know?*" Jason demanded into the phone. "I just found out myself."

"You're all over the papers, dumbshit," Nick informed him. "A whole layer of middle-management desk jockeys, chopped down in their prime."

"It's incredible," said Jason. "I'm literally hiding in my office. I don't dare leave the building—I might get locked out."

"I'm telling you, this is the best thing that ever happened to you," Nick replied. "Next to Louisa."

"What are you talking about? Who's Louisa?"

"You know, Louisa."

"Are you actually going to make me say it again?" he asked wearily.

"*Lou-i-sa,*" Nick intoned carefully, as if trying to overcome cellular static. "That sixteen-year-old townie. Wasn't that her name?"

Jason sighed. "Her name was Lori, and she was eighteen, not sixteen. There, now I've told you an even five hundred times."

"Oh, *eighteen,*" Nick scoffed. "Tell me you carded her."

"I can't remember why I called you," Jason mused distractedly. "It can't have been self-abuse. Hold on a minute, that's my other line. . . . Hello?"

He recognized the voice instantly. "How are the slings and arrows of outrageous fortune, my friend?" said Paul, another college friend, a frail and funny unapologetic nerd who quoted Shakespeare and Milton Friedman with equal dexterity. Paul worked with an independent software developer; his current project, modeled on a computer's spellchecker, was designed to seek and destroy trite phrases from text files, the "from the very beginnings" and the "more often than nots" and each and every "each and every."

"Hey, Paul," said Jason, relieved. "I guess you heard the news, eh?"

"Just the *Times'* version. You still employed?"

"Yeah," Jason confirmed, "but my manager isn't, I just found out."

"Really," said Paul, intrigued. "You going for it?"

Jason smiled, wondering how his laid-back friends had managed to evolve this predatory instinct. "I'll tell you tonight; I've got Nick on the other line," he replied. "You're coming out, right?"

"See you then," said Paul. "Tell Nick his mom says hi."

He smiled and flashed back to Nick.

"I hope that was a job offer," said his buddy.

"That was Paul," said Jason. "He says he just climbed off your mom."

Nick ignored this. "Take my advice, Jason. Stop screwing around and start embellishing your résumé."

"Whoa," said Jason. "Why is everyone so anxious to get me out the door? Maybe I'm not going anywhere."

"Well," said Paul, "you'd better figure it out quickly. You've got maybe an hour before everyone else in your office shakes off the funk and starts flooding the market with phone calls."

As he pondered this, his other line flashed again; this time it turned out to be Amanda.

"Hey, it's me," she announced with an encouraging familiarity.

"Hey, you," he replied cheerily. "How's it going?"

"Not bad, not bad. You?"

"Oh, everything's cool," he replied suavely. "Wait, what am I saying? My whole company's gone kablooey. We were swallowed up by Disney or something. I actually just found out my boss was fired as part of the deal."

"That's awful," she said sincerely. "Are you okay?"

"Oh, yeah," he said with forced levity. "But I'll tell you, I wouldn't mind coming into that legacy and putting all this workaday crap behind me. Can you hold on for just one minute?"

"How about meeting me for lunch instead?" she countered.

"It's a little bit crazy today," he replied. "I think I'm meeting a friend to work on my résumé. Guy on the other line, actually."

"So, you *could* still cancel," she said hopefully.

Jason smiled at her brashness. "Now why would I want to do that, sister?"

"Because," she reminded him, "you have a fortune to discover. You don't leave a twenty lying on the street because the nickel might fall out of your shirt pocket."

"Yeah, but how do I know it's a real twenty?" he countered.

"You don't," she acknowledged. "But it's gonna blow away if you don't reach out and grab it. And the nickel won't go too far."

This brought a grin to Jason's face, and though he paused in a last-ditch show of free will, he'd been hooked. "Nice. All right," he relented. "But I'm only going out of respect for your facility with a metaphor."

"I'll take what I can get," she replied. "Where can we meet?"

◇ ◇ ◇

Moments later Jason was back on with Nick. "Sorry about that, Nick," he apologized. "Lunch is off—boy meets girl."

"The chick from last night?"

"Yep," said Jason. "It sounded like her, anyway."

"I take it things went smoothly, then."

"They did, they did," Jason replied, nodding. "I'll tell you all about it tonight."

"I'd like to go on record as saying no good can come of this."

Jason smiled. "Duly noted. Oh, hey, Paul just dropped your mom off for my lap dance . . . I gotta go."

MIDTOWN, 11:45 A.M.

Lurking among the steel-and-stone behemoths that formed the spiny dorsal fin of the New York skyline, the Midtown delis hummed in frantic anticipation. The excitement was almost palpable, like the backstage frenzy of motion and anticipation of off-off-Broadway on a dicey opening night. It was a quarter to lunch, and the salad bars, Manhattan's signature quick-

fix, pay-by-the-pound midday eateries, all bright green awnings and outdoor racks of bunched overpriced wildflowers, made ready to pour out
their cornucopias for the office workers spilling en masse from their skyscrapers like clowns from so many minivans.

Carefully nipped cauliflower and broccoli florets tumbled obediently
into steamers; tomatoes fell into quick, perfect eighths at the touch of
flashing knives. Prepared foods in all shades of brown poured lumpily into
burnished steel pans: a removable feast of sweet-and-sour pork, sesame
chicken, cubed roasted eggplant, and myriad other bite-size delights.

By the time Jason found Amanda tapping a booted heel on the sidewalk outside the Deli Lama's door, the distribution engine was running at
top speed. A steady influx of empty-handed hunter-gatherers neatly balanced an exodus of brown-bag-toting customers, keeping the revolving
door in an almost constant spin cycle. She smiled on seeing him outside,
and extended her hand as they exchanged the requisite greetings.

"It's crowded," she pointed out unnecessarily as they entered, and he
nodded agreement. Hordes of lunchers swarmed about the buffet tables
like cats at the kill.

"Yeah, this is a pretty good place," he said loftily.

Amanda smiled impishly. "I'm sure it's a wonderful salad bar," she said
sympathetically, eyes twinkling. Without awaiting a response, she patted
his upper arm like a consoling coach. "Let's dive in. I'll meet you at the
register."

As they split up to assemble their personal food frescoes, Jason found
himself surreptitiously watching Amanda, ogling her arms and torso
through hazy sneeze guards, ready to avert his gaze into the broccoli pan if
she looked his way. Their comfortable rapport was undeniable, but he
wondered whether the flirtatious humor that had so far characterized their
interaction, the heart and soul of his mating dance, meant anything
deeper at all to Amanda. Ominously, Jason was unable to catch her looking at him once.

"You were right. This *is* a good place," Amanda relented after they had
paid and commandeered a table for two along one wall. "Look—real
jumbo shrimp, not sea legs."

"Don't patronize me," said Jason, and they peeled off rubber bands in tandem, allowing the clear plastic clams that held their salads to yawn open into their paper soup cups.

"You know," said Jason after his first bite, "the salad bar is the perfect model for world peace. Culinary offerings from cultures all over the world, and everything costs the same. You can stick a bagel and a falafel right next to each other on your tray and they won't dispute territory."

"The joy's in the juxtaposition," agreed Amanda. "Look how everyone arranges their food so carefully. Nobody just slops the stuff into the tray. I think for a lot of people it's a brief, shining moment of artistic freedom in an otherwise dull day."

Naturally, this called for a glance at her creation, an impressionistic *objet* where thinly sliced beets and rings of red and yellow peppers danced against a background of subtly shifting greens. Jason looked down with dismay into his own tray: three kinds of sticky fried meat swimming in nondescript Chinese sauces, a side of wilted broccoli, some chunks of ham glumly riding a pineapple ring.

"I'm evidently a Dadaist," he offered by way of apology.

Amanda smiled gracefully. "You're just a starving artist."

"Well, anyway," said Jason, eager to change the subject, "here we are."

"Here we are," she agreed. "Aren't you excited?"

He shrugged. "I've had salad lots of times."

She shot him a withering look. "The way I see it," she began, using her plastic fork as a pointer, "we have a three-step process ahead of us. We have to secure the document itself. We have to prove your lineage—trace an unbroken bloodline back to the ancestor named in the document. And then we have to prove the whole thing in court."

"Do we have time to eat first?"

She blushed faintly. "Am I being overzealous?"

"No, it's nice to see the enthusiasm," he assured her. "I just can't shift gears that quickly."

"Oh," she said. "Sorry. But remember, I researched this for a long time without knowing if you even existed. I'm still on that first adrenaline rush."

Jason smiled. "I have that effect on a lot of women."

"Uh-huh," she said, with a devastating smirk. "So tell me about your boss getting fired. Were you surprised?"

"No, you don't have to do that," said Jason, methodically carving the pineapple ring into trapezoids. "I'm just saying I need more background, if we're going to be . . . partners. How'd you find out about all this?"

The previous night, after her bombshell, Amanda had confirmed Jason's intimation that she was indeed a member of the Manahatas, the tribe that had supposedly sold the land to Peter Minuit and the Dutch settlers. The tribe, she claimed, had dwindled down to fewer than a hundred full-blooded members, and was now so small it was not officially recognized by the federal government. With no land of their own, the Manahatas had long occupied a corner of the Lenape reservation on the south side of Long Island, half an hour east of the city, and there maintained a fierce independence from the outside world and even from the Lenape. Amanda had detailed how she'd finally located Jason, in a newspaper article about his parents' accident (which she proceeded to reproduce in folded photocopy, occasioning in Jason an almost uncontrollable wave of nausea), but not how she'd become aware of the deed in the first place.

Amanda laid a package of Saltines beside her soup and came down hard on it with the heel of her hand, banging the table and making him jump. "I've heard the story, in various forms, since I was little," she replied, picking up the packet and rolling it between her fingers, crumbling the contents. "My people have an unbroken connection to a preliterate past, a rich oral tradition." Tearing one corner, she poured the crumbs neatly into her soup. "So in our culture, legends have the force of truth."

Jason chewed in silence, amused by the perhaps inevitable return of Amanda's passionate, didactic tone from the night before. *She might be crazy*, he mused, *but she is not lying*.

"Some of our oldest stories contain elements of Peter Minuit's infamous island sale," Amanda continued. "Boats carrying white men from across the sea, men bearing gifts and cutting down trees, that sort of thing. In a few, though, there's this one figure, a benevolent, almost godlike man.

He's a white man, but he marries a Manahata and lives among the natives, teaching them the healing arts, protecting them. In our stories, he was sent to us by Manahata himself."

"Wait, wait," said Jason. "Who's Manahata? I thought *you* were the Manahata."

"Manahata is the god of my tribe," replied Amanda, "the spirit of our people incarnate. He also has a geographical dimension: Because we identify ourselves with the island, he is the god of the island as well, its protector. That's why we all share one name—the island, the people, the god. He coexists with the life of my tribe and with the life force of the island. And yet he is independent of all earthly connections; he comes and goes, waxes and wanes like the seasons."

"But you can try him on his cell phone," Jason replied, unable to stop himself.

"Anyway," she continued, "according to the legend, this benevolent white man is eventually called back from the living world, to serve Manahata in the spirit realm. But before he goes, he gives the tribe a gift. The gift is a promise, a promise from Manahata himself, and the promise is this: No matter what misfortunes befall the tribe in the unseeable future, the island is theirs forever." She paused, focusing momentarily on scooping up a reluctant piece of lettuce. "The legend resonates with us, because it affirms the core of our religion—that the people, the place, and the spirit are inseparable at the heart."

"Your tribe's extended relocation must be quite a test of faith," Jason opined.

She shrugged. "You're not mocking me, I hope."

"Absolutely not," said Jason sincerely. "But how do you make the leap from this myth, this children's story, if you don't mind my saying so, to the existence of an actual paper deed?"

"I'm getting there," she promised. "But you're right; for most of the Manahata today, this is a simple foundation myth. Some bitter wishful thinking, perhaps."

"Sure," Jason agreed. "Your tribe traded away the ancestral land, so you soothe the pain of that through myths that imply that the situation is temporary, that it's all part of some grand, unknowable holy plan."

"Well, that's a bit glib," said Amanda.

"It's almost Catholic," Jason decided.

"As I said," Amanda continued, "I've been hearing this story, and others like it, for as long as I can remember. But as I grew older, I came to realize that my mother, who is the sachem, sort of the spiritual leader of our tribe, is quite thoroughly—unnervingly, really—convinced of the story's literal truth."

Jason nodded warily.

"It's uncharacteristic; she's quite a skeptic. I became convinced that she *knew* something." Amanda paused to sip her Orangina. "Some concrete secret the rest of the tribe wasn't in on. But she categorically refused to answer any questions, just kept clamming up, which only convinced me further that I was right about *what* she was hiding."

"This is starting to get tenuous," Jason argued.

"No, hold on, hold on," Amanda insisted. "I was in college by this time, and I had access to libraries and research facilities. I was very busy with pre-law, obviously, but I stole whatever time I could to pore over histories of the time period, dig through old diaries, ships' logs and the like, and to study bits and pieces of tribal legends. And putting all the evidence together, I managed to piece together a rough picture of what must have happened—the story I summarized for you last night."

"Sounds like quite an independent project," he replied neutrally.

"The quest began to take on a distinct symbolic meaning for me," she confessed. "It became sort of a solo rite of passage. I even convinced myself that this was the big test, that I was *supposed* to figure out what my mother knew, independently, in order to take my place in the line of succession and become the next sachem after her. When I presented my case to my mother, and showed her my evidence, she *confirmed* it." She paused, staring at him intently. "Jason, she told me I was *right*."

Jason was suddenly intrigued. "Really?" he said. "About the deed and everything?"

"Well, not in so many words," Amanda admitted. Putting down her fork, she started tallying points on her hand. "She told me that our fate was indeed linked with that of Pieter Haansvoort and his descendants. She confirmed what I had intuited, that some sort of secret information is passed down from sachem to sachem. And she also said the *legend*, the promise that the land would one day be returned to us, was rooted in truth, and that there existed a realistic mechanism for achieving that end, when the time was right."

"That's incredible," said Jason, meaning it literally. "You gonna finish that?" he added, pointing his fork at her salad. It was a joke, he was nearly finished; she, having done all the talking, had taken only a few bites.

But Amanda paid no heed. "I was ecstatic," she went on. "It was like finding buried treasure. But when I tried to press her for details about the deed itself, she refused to speak any more of it. My guess is that she'd been handed a mandate from the sachems before her to do nothing until Pieter's line resurfaced."

"Mm-hmm," murmured Jason nonchalantly.

"That was four years ago," she continued, "and I made it my personal mission to resurrect that line, if it still existed. In the meantime, of course, I graduated from college and enrolled in law school, and basically moved on with my life. I never quite let go of it—it's no accident I ended up here in the city. But it was definitely a dream deferred. Every six months or so, I'd get the bug again, and check the Internet or sift through a Lexis-Nexis search, still trying to find a match. Finally, six months ago, I was varying the spelling of Haansvoort in one of my searches and stumbled on the news report about . . . your parents," she said, injecting a brief sympathetic pause.

Jason nodded, maintaining his composure, and Amanda continued. "It's not proof, of course; we'll need complete documentation of every twig on the tree if this claim's going to have a chance of standing up in court. But when I called you, and you confirmed the spelling change in your name, I knew I had my man."

"And here I am," said Jason, belching surreptitiously into his napkin, disguising it with a cough. "Did you tell Mom yet?"

Amanda nodded. "I called her this morning. She was very excited—said she wants to meet you as soon as possible."

He shook his head, smiling. "Sorry, I never agree to meet a girl's mother until at least the third date."

She laughed. "Well, this isn't exactly a *date* . . ." Suddenly, a look of concern swept over her face. "Jason, I hope I haven't been . . . giving you the wrong impression."

"No, no, of course not," he replied quickly.

"I mean, you seem like a good guy and all," she affirmed. "It's just that . . . that's not why I'm here."

"I flirt with all women," he told her. "It's just my way, I guess. Nuns, hookers—you name it." *Now shut up, please.*

"Are you sure?" she said, smiling.

"Yes, you idiot," Jason confirmed, searching for the magic word that would get her to stop rubbing his nose in it. He was starting to hate this salad bar after all. Now that he'd been spurned officially and unmistakably, honor demanded that he redefine Amanda in his mind, either as a worthy opponent awaiting a persistent conqueror, or as a frigid bitch he was no longer interested in. He wasn't sure which way he was leaning, yet—the wound was still too fresh.

"But, Amanda, here's my question," he began, to change the subject. "Why wouldn't your mother just *tell* you? 'Hey, baby. Our tribe could recover Manhattan, but first we have to find this long-lost heir to the throne'? Why all the mumbo jumbo?" Jason was aware of a new unpleasantness in his attitude—the bitterness talking—but at the moment he didn't feel much like a team player.

Amanda shrugged. "I don't know," she admitted. "She's very superstitious and traditional; maybe she thinks she'll somehow screw up the magic if she doesn't follow the rules."

"But you get my point," Jason continued. "It's hard to see how she's acting with the best interests of the tribe at heart. Also, if the Manahata have always had this deed, why didn't they reclaim their land fifty years ago? A hundred? *Two* hundred? Why did it take so long for your people to call my people?"

This time, though, she was shaking her head before he'd finished. "Because it wasn't *safe*, Jason. I'm sure you're aware that *your* people, as you put it, haven't always been famous for straight dealing with Native Americans. The deed produced at the wrong time would have simply been seized and destroyed. End of story." She paused, as if trying to marshal her own rising emotion. "It wasn't until very, very recently that aboriginal sovereignty began to be upheld in court. I believe the sachems were warned right from the beginning not to let on to the deed's existence until it could be safely proved. That's the whole reason it was hidden in the first place."

"They waited too long," Jason argued. "If this deed *ever* had any legal value, that time is long past. Amanda, you're talking about trying to overturn centuries of land transactions in one of the largest population centers on planet earth. Perry Mason wouldn't touch this case with a fifty-foot pole."

"For a one percent contingency fee he would," she asserted.

"Nope," said Jason, shaking his head. "I see you and me in small-claims court with Al Sharpton and C. Vernon Mason."

Things were degenerating fast, he realized, as he and Amanda shared an icy moment of intimate antagonism. "You're just being perverse," she reproached, picking at her food.

"I'm being rational."

"Okay, look," she replied, making a deal. "Tomorrow's Saturday. Just do this for me—come out to the reservation and hear what my mother has to say. I've got a car, and it's only—"

"*No,*" interrupted Jason, amazed. "Absolutely *not*. Am I speaking Swahili, or something?"

Amanda was visibly crushed. "Why *not?*"

"Because I have a *life,*" he replied too stridently. "Are you aware that I'm probably losing my *job,* here?" He paused when she jerked her head away in frustration.

"Look," he continued, "I'm not saying I'm not interested. I honestly am. For the sheer genealogical interest, if nothing else. I just don't have the time to dive into some extended paper chase at this exact moment in my fucked-up life."

"Jason," she said, turning back toward him, "I know that quite probably nothing will come of this. Really, I know that. But just to have the chance, however remote! How can you hesitate? This is the opportunity of a lifetime."

"You can't expect me to just set my life aside and race off to Long Island because *you* feel some misguided sense of urgency," he replied. "This is what's known in the vernacular as a pipe dream."

"But it's *not* a pipe dream," Amanda insisted. "It's real."

"You don't know that," said Jason, going back to his salad.

"But I *feel* it," she replied, grabbing his free hand, where it lay on the table between them. "Jason . . . there's something else."

He looked up wearily, and waited.

She took a deep breath that served both to calm her and rein in the pace of the discussion. "My mother said she has something to give you," she announced. "*If* you turn out to be who I told her you are, of course."

Jason paused, one elbow on the table, an empty plastic fork locked in a stationary holding pattern just outside his mouth. Amanda shrugged, a sheepish smile tugging up one corner of her mouth.

Her eyes radiated a calm certitude, and her warm hand still enveloped his, and for all his skepticism, Jason felt himself yielding to the irresistible force of her enthusiasm.

"What's that supposed to be," he replied grumpily, "a trump card?"

Emboldened by the slight humor that had returned to his voice, Amanda smiled cautiously. "I swear to God I don't know what it is."

"All right, let me see how things shake out at work today, and I'll *think* about it. Is that good enough? What?" he said, when her smile broadened.

Amanda leaned forward, crouching intimately across the little table. "Can't you feel it?" she asked in a low voice.

He shook his head with exaggerated slowness while keeping his eyes focused on hers, refusing to release her. "No," he confessed woodenly. "Whatever it is, I can't feel it."

"It's Manahata," she whispered breathlessly. "The spirit of the island." She laid her hands out flat on the table like a fortune-teller. "That rumbling you feel under your feet . . . it's the return of a god."

Jason shook his head soberly. "It's the number seven subway," he replied in a low tone. "Times Square to Grand Central and on into Queens, every ten minutes."

Amanda's eyes flashed with devilish amusement. "We'll see."

MADISON AVENUE, 3:30 P.M.

In all the animal kingdom, there is nothing more terrifying than being interrupted in midflight by the syrupy stickiness of a freshly oozed morning spiderweb. Once you feel that irresistible tug on your wings, the elastic snap of dewy webbing, all hope is lost. No more swarming with the gang around trash cans at dusk, no more wonderful, week-old road carcasses, no more wallowing in moist summer dog shit. Never more will you dodge swatters, bump millifaceted eyes into windowpanes, wade in the vertical waters of a cow's eye. Game over; thanks for playing.

You struggle, of course, though you know that your thrashings can only bind you tighter, that each movement jerks a glutinous filament that reaches into the very heart of the spider's lair, a homespun dinner bell. You are about to be devoured alive between the slavering jaws of the ugliest, most pitiless creature on the planet; in the end you struggle simply because there is no other way to occupy the final seconds of your life.

The spider danced across Jason's office ceiling upside down, unaware that she was being watched, her horrible attention focused squarely on her quivering prey. The fear was the tastiest part, mind-numbingly delicious, the prize that made the endless hours of concentric toil worthwhile. She always approached her dinner slowly, exoskeletal legs playing a death knell on the harp of her web. "Fly away!" she'd hiss. "Hurry up—*aaah*, the spider's coming!" And she would laugh and laugh, a horrible grating sound like a torn tin can caught between sliding chalkboards.

Jason placed *Roget's Thesaurus* squarely against the spider's back and squidged it into the unforgiving plaster. Stepping down from the chair, he wiped the book on the lip of the garbage can with a grimace and stood up abruptly. He ran both hands through his hair, as if trying to remove the thick layer of dryer lint that coated his brain.

"This is absurd," he said aloud.

He checked his watch: He'd now officially spent a solid hour wallowing in a paralysis of distraction, creative engines frozen to the touch. He had far too much on his mind for inspiration to get a foothold; being had to spring from nothingness, after all, and his brain was positively jumping.

Clearly I'm not going to shake this funk until I get this line of thought out of my system, he realized. *So here goes.*

He walked toward the window, where he silently observed a pair of po-lice helicopters scooting in low over the park like monstrous dragonflies. *The locusts are coming,* he mused. *We must go and tell Pharoah.*

What if Amanda was right? It was the big navel-pondering question around which all the world revolved. Forget the rational objections for a minute, he urged himself. What if he had, in fact, just hit the biggest Powerball in the history of the world?

Like everyone else in the Western world, Jason had played the what-would-you-do-with-the-millions game a thousand times. In whatever in-carnation—the unexpected inheritance, the winning Lotto ticket, the six-foot check from Publisher's Clearinghouse—that great glittering pot of unearned gold danced in the dreams of every true American, and Jason was culturally incapable of *not* playing. But dreaming was one thing, a properly empty exercise. Considering such a windfall as a real possibility, however slim, was a quantum leap Jason found difficult to make. He'd sim-ply grown up too well-off—the rich don't have to shelter the popular delusion of the lottery as winnable.

What the hell would it all be worth? he wondered, gazing out at the sky-scrapers. The real estate alone, for God's sake. Billions? Trillions? How many zeros? How do you value something that is utterly without context? *Well, Frankfurt sold just last month for eleven-five, but of course it's only three million bedrooms, and it doesn't have central air.*

He wasn't sure why he felt so reluctant to indulge Amanda's little fan-tasy, even just for fun. She'd rejected him, sure, but this resistance ran deeper. Over the past few months, he'd felt a growing urgency to start ac-tively managing his life, particularly his foundering career. The post-collegiate party was winding down; already he could feel his friends and colleagues beginning to define themselves with careers and relationships, or with a maturing sense of purpose, anyway, and it made him feel naked. Galloping around on a lunatic fantasy with a hot young thing seemed just alluring enough to distract him from whatever cheap destiny lay realisti-cally within his reach. If sex with Amanda were an option, it might justify the prodigious waste of time she was proposing . . . but it wasn't, so the case was closed.

The United Nations. The Empire State Building. The New York Stock

Exchange. What about the museums and libraries—would he have any claim to their holdings? The New York Public Library? Dear God: the Met? the Guggenheim? What would the change of ownership do to the fashion industry, to book publishing, to Broadway?

If I could whip up this kind of enthusiasm for anything work-related, Jason thought wryly, *Bill Gates would be wiping my ass with an embroidered hankie.*

What to do, what to do. The temptation to yield to the mysterious turn his life was taking, to simply let the current wash over him, was powerful; surely, hunting for buried treasure couldn't be much more absurd than peddling Hair Peace. Still, Jason resisted abandoning the wheel of reason altogether, trendy though it might be in a world of animal graveyards and Partridge Family reunions. He had evolved by choice into a creature of intellect, and if rational analysis and deduction had never brought him great happiness, neither had they failed him as a source of identity. Faulty or not, they were the steel with which he framed his world.

Jason let out his breath, fell back in his chair, and cast his eyes skyward, where a tiny black grease spot pinpricked the vast whiteness of the ceiling like a feeble pirate's curse. A thousand forgotten flies, avenged at last. *Sic semper arachnidis!*

Just being able to trace back my ancestry a couple of hundred years is probably worth the effort all by itself, he decided. *Nothing says I have to swallow this thing whole.*

He chuckled in amusement at the rationalization. *Jason Hansvoort, reporting for hideous emotional abuse, sir.*

◇ ◇ ◇

"Hello?" came a frail voice from the other end of the line.

"Grandma?" said Jason, as if there were any doubt.

"Yes," she replied querulously. "Who's this?"

That must be something, Jason marvelled, *to identify yourself as a grandma objectively, no matter who's asking.*

"It's me, Jason."

"Oh, hello, Jason. I was just finishing my instaghetti."

He smiled at this. Marguerite was technically his step-great-grandmother, the scandalously young second wife of his great-grandfather. She'd survived her crusty old husband by twenty years and counting, and remained sharp as a tack, thanks to patented reaper dodges like straight lemon juice, ice-cold showers, and a daily tussle with the *Times* crossword puzzle. Grandma (he always left off the prefix "great," which she considered excessively complimentary) was a predictable fan of one-pot meals, and liked to season them with entertaining nicknames.

"So how are you, Jason?" she continued. "You know, I see commercials all the time and I always wonder if any of them are yours."

"Oh, probably not, Grandma—there are so many. The last one I did was for—"

Sweet Springs Douche-a-Day.

"—a motor oil."

Though he loved her dearly, Jason only called Marguerite a couple of times a year. It was hard to feel pressured: The spry old bird gave off such a thoroughly convincing show of immortality that he felt justified in assuming he'd have decades of conversation with her before she succumbed.

"Grandma, I have a quick question for you," he proposed after a few moments of small talk. "I'm trying to do a sort of family tree, and I was hoping you might help me fill in some of the branches."

"Well, you're in luck," she told him. "That's just the sort of thing grandmothers are particularly good at."

Jason grinned. "Well, that's what I thought, too. How far back do you remember Grandpa's family?"

"Oh, let's see now," she began after a moment's consideration. "Well, my husband, Robert, your great-grandfather, he was a merchant, and *his* father, Sam, was a blacksmith. He did the gates at West Point."

Having previously commandeered a blank notepad, Jason began quickly jotting down names, though still on familiar ground. "That's great," he said. "Can you go back any further?"

"Yes, yes," she confirmed. "Sam's mother's name was Ida, I remember that, and she was married twice . . ."

For several minutes long-dead names rolled off her tongue, through the phone system, and onto Jason's little pad. It was a very pleasant distraction, which meant work was almost certain to intrude at some point.

"She called him Adie. Oh, my; she had names for everyone, and some of them not so nice. She was still alive when I was a teenager, but she'd died by the time I married your grandfather. Your great-grandfather, I mean. Good Lord! Adolphus—that's her husband, the first one—was a schoolteacher, and he was a stern, stern man. He was quite feared, from what I'm told. He's buried in the old Haansvoort graveyard."

Jason started. "The what? We have a graveyard?"

"Oh, yes. It's in Tuxedo Park, New York," she replied. "Unless they moved it."

"That's amazing," said Jason. "This is great, Grandma." As if on cue, his other line began flashing.

"Oh, we had a lot of time to talk about such things before the television," she replied.

"Grandma, I hate to do this, but I'm calling from work and someone's trying to reach me on the other line. Would you mind if I put you on hold for just a minute?"

"Okay," she said, "but don't dawdle. I'm ninety-two."

He chuckled. "Hello?"

"Jason, I'm glad you're in," said a frosty female voice. Horror of horrors—it was the great and terrible Diana. "Can you come into my office, please?"

His heart deflated instantly. "Oh, hi, Diana. I'm on the other line with the client—can I come in in a few minutes?"

"Yep," she said tersely, hanging up without further comment.

He retrieved his grandmother. "Sorry about that, Grandma." *Fuck, fuck, fuck.*

"Oh, it's no problem," she assured him. "I feel like a thoroughly modern girl. Anyway, I hope I was able to help you, Jason."

"Well, yes, you have, thank you. But I'm really trying to go back further," he said gently. "Back a *long* way . . . all the way back to when our family came over from Holland, if possible. Do you know if we have any old papers or anything?"

"I'm afraid not," she replied. "There were a lot of old family files we lost in a fire about forty years back. Daguerrotypes and everything. We had an old family Bible that had a lot of names in it too, but it was lost as well. I wonder if anybody ever made a copy."

He checked his watch absently: time to wrap this up. He hit her up for some particulars on how to find the graveyard, made a little more small talk catching up with what was left of the extended family, and began forging an exit.

"Thanks, Grandma. You remember a lot."

"Well, it's a shame you never got much of a chance to talk to your parents about it, God bless them," she said. "A boy should have a father. It was lovely talking to you, dear."

They only died last year, he said to himself.

Hanging up, Jason looked over his notes thoughtfully. *The Haansvoort family graveyard*, he thought, rolling the phrase over on his tongue. Who said nothing good would come of this?

Crap—Diana, he reminded himself with a shudder. *This should be fun.* He took a slug of the now-tepid coffee, wishing he could kick it up a notch with some whiskey, and stared at the phone for a long minute, as if hoping for a reprieve from the governor.

✧ ✧ ✧

The simultaneous dismantling and refurbishing of the office that was now Diana's had produced a number of little undecided islands: squat towers of books perched atop file cabinets, ergonomic plastiform chairs piled high with bound files, and, alone on a librarian's gurney by the door, a forlorn first-generation IMAC, its now-useless plug dangling down over its face like a renegade cowlick. Behind a desk curiously out of parallel with the wall, Diana cradled a phone to one ear and signaled for Jason to *Come in, come in*, in a rushed one-handed semaphore. A van Gogh sunflower print from the Met leaned hopefully against one wall in mute protest at the institutional gray of the room, though whether it was coming or going was anybody's guess.

"No, I don't want to *talk* about it anymore," Diana ranted into the phone. "Every item on that list is necessary and I'm not discussing it again. Do you understand?"

She paused, flashing Jason an openmouthed, *Can-you-believe-these-brain-dead-peons?* expression as she listened to the pitiful miscreant on the other end of the line stammer out a feeble excuse. "Look, just fill the goddamn requisition, *then* send your little messenger up here now, and my secretary will fill out all your little forms," she hissed. "That's all. *Thank* you."

Slamming the phone down with a plastic clang, Diana looked up at last, rolling her eyes in a slow boil of frustration. "Sorry about that," she said. "Thanks for coming by, Jason. You want coffee or something?"

More than life, he was thinking, but declined with a shake of his head; it was at cross-purposes with his goal of keeping this meeting as short as possible.

"Well, I'm going to have some, so don't be shy," she enjoined, gleefully stabbing a button on her intercom. "Janine!" she barked at top volume, as if testing the microphone.

A small commotion in the outer room convinced Jason that Diana's frazzled secretary had just been startled into falling off her chair, or tossing a stack of papers high into the air. Diana continued, without waiting for a response, "Get me, please, a coffee, black, with cream and sugar on the side." She covered the phone with one hand and added, to Jason, "Last chance . . ."

"I'm set," he replied, and Diana released the intercom button. She frowned at a Post-it note on her desk before crumpling it violently.

"Sorry about the craziness," she said insincerely. "Oh, listen, could you shut the door for us, please? That'd be great."

Jason was half a beat slow in rising to oblige; first, because there was a small dignity in such acts of fleeting resistance, and second, because he'd never felt less inclined to seal himself in with another living creature. Diana had always been deeply irritating, a socially graceless politicker of the first order, but it was already clear that her promotion had brought out her inner tyrant. He wondered whether the "us" in "shut the door for us" was meant to include him or not. The subtext of this meeting had begun to dawn on him, and even as he reached for the knob to do her bidding he realized that had the door been closed, she'd have required him to open it.

"Thanks," she offered when he returned, features cringing inauthentically in a *Don't-mundane-tasks-suck?* expression.

"No problem," he replied woodenly.

"Isn't this *exciting?*" she asked, confirming his worst suspicions. "Not my little renovation, I mean the whole . . . transition."

Dear God; how to answer this one. "I guess I'm still a little bewildered," Jason replied, stalling, hoping he could pinpoint what she wanted from him before he made an irreparable blunder.

"Of course, it's unfortunate for certain individuals, obviously," she conceded. "Pete Halloran, for example; it's too bad. But you know what? The ship wasn't exactly being run one hundred percent efficiently, if you know what I mean. I think we'll look back in six months and realize this was the best thing for Y & G."

Jason was horrified: Less than a day into her promotion, and here she was, cheerfully parroting company dogma straight from the peppy in-house newsletter. *This could be the beginning of a beautiful, deep-seated loathing,* he decided. Any residual guilt he'd been carrying around for disliking Diana for no definable reason flaked harmlessly off into the wind.

"But how do *you* feel?" Diana wanted to know. "I know you and Pete were kind of close . . . Do you resent that he was fired?"

Jason's brow furrowed. *"Resent" it? What kind of grade school psychiatrist crap is that?* "Well, I don't understand it, to be frank," he admitted warily. "But I wouldn't say I 'resent' it, exactly. I don't really have that kind of . . . personal investment in my coworkers' lives. It does seem like there must have been better, smarter . . . ways to trim the staff, if that's what needed to be done."

Watch your step, dumbshit, he chided himself. Diana's eyes remained fixed on his the whole time, while her head nodded stupidly—*I see, I see*—a meat metronome.

Suddenly, the rationale behind Diana's uncanny good fortune autofocused into perfect clarity. She'd been promoted not *in spite of* being unqualified, but *because* she was unqualified, and thus utterly beholden to whatever superior had created her. Diana represented the perfect empty vessel: eager to tank up on the new corporate spirit and redistribute it at full strength to the rank and file, to police her fellow inmates in exchange for a seat in the officers' mess.

What I resent, he realized, *is having to treat you as a superior until I decide whether I'm going to quit or not.*

Diana's response was charitably postponed by a double knock at the door, heralding the arrival of Janine. She'd shanghaied an inverted legal pad into service as a wobbly tea tray for a sloshing cup of coffee and a handful of sugars and creamers; her haunted face spoke volumes.

Completing her delivery without incident, Janine turned and was on the verge of escape when Diana, staring coffeeward, called her back. "Oh—could you put that in there for me?" she said, indicating the cream and sugar, scrunching up her face like a little girl. "Jason, this is the best assistant in New York," she gushed, and he was ashamed to find his head nodding and smiling obsequiously of its own accord as Janine quietly, robotically, retraced her steps, tore open the packets, and swizzled them into the brew.

"Anyway," Diana continued after Janine had slunk out to kill herself, "the reason I called you in was to get a kind of an update. Now, you're working on . . . ?"

"Hair Peace," he replied robotically. "For Johnson and Beatrice. It's still in the early stages."

"And how long have we had that account?"

Is that the corporate "we" or the patronizing "we"? Jason wondered silently. "About four months, I guess," he estimated. *Six months, seven months.* "I've only been on it for a couple of weeks."

"Okay," she said. "And what else?"

Jason shook his head, not comprehending.

"Are you working on."

I'm being fired, he realized with a shock. "That's all," he had to confess. "I was on Automatic Static, but Halloran thought I should concentrate on the one."

"Ah," said Diana, rhythmically tapping her pencil on her chin, in a

Morse code that seemed to translate as: *So, how long have the two of you been conspiring to defraud the company?*

Jason started bailing. "It's an unusually difficult project, conceptually," he tried to explain. "Y and G have had . . . a number of false starts."

Diana removed the swizzle stick dramatically, like a sword, and took a tentative sip of coffee. "Well, I'm sorry to be the one to tell you that the glory days of languishing on just one project are over," she informed him bluntly. "Starting in about two weeks, everyone at your level's going to have at least three projects to work on. We're about to become a leaner, meaner, more competitve organization." She took another tiny sip, though perhaps only for the dramatic pause. "It's going to call for a lot of hard work and quick results—no more sitting around for a month here, a month there. I'm not naming any names, you understand, Jason. I'm just talking generalities."

Jason didn't respond; in his head he was quietly lowering his new boss, tied and gagged on a chain, her power suit stuffed with Alpo beef chunks, into a kennel full of yelping, half-starved Dobermans.

"And that's the real reason I called you in, Jason," she continued, cliché piling on top of cliché in a rising crescendo as she prepared her summation. "What I need from you . . ."

Bring me the head of John the Baptist.

". . . is to know whether being a part of this organization is something you're still interested in."

Jason was dizzy with despair. *This is happening too fast,* he protested, *way too fast.* As a rough equal, Diana had simply annoyed him; as a superior, her very presence brought rage to his brain like mercury rising in a thermometer pinned by a ten-year-old's magnifying glass.

"So . . . ," she pressed, uncomfortable with his pause, "what do you think?"

As if from across a canyon, he heard himself reply tamely, "Well, I guess I'll have to roll with whatever . . . the new rules are. But I feel compelled to say that I think putting emphasis on quantity over quality is . . . ill-advised, even as a transitional plan. We're a creative agency; we live or die by the end product."

"Thanks for the primer," said Diana coldly, keeping her eyes locked to his. "But that's not *really* the answer I'm looking for. No one's suggesting that we sacrifice quality for . . . efficiency. The point is that we have to face up to the realities of the new marketplace; we can't continue to produce at the old pace."

Come on, boy: We playin' ball or what?

Diana continued, using strategic pauses to divide her words into separate compartments for easy comprehension. "I need to know, if I, can count on you, to be . . . well, I hate to put it this way, but . . . a part of the team."

The fingers of Diana's right hand flexed and recurled sinuously around the curve of the coffee mug; through some freakish Darth Vader telekinetic transfer, Jason felt the pressure encircle his throat. *This is a goddamn loyalty oath,* he realized. *She's actually going to make me say it.*

"So, what do you think?" she prompted with a mocking little smile, opening her hands as if handing him an invisible book.

But Jason froze in place, robbed of the power of speech. Day passed into night, and night to day; suns rose and set faster and faster, in endless diurnal progression, until the seasons whirled in their passing; the moon spun madly about the earth, and great mountain ranges rose from the plains and eroded away again until finally he stammered out the necessary response.

"Yeah, of course," he said nervously. "I'll do whatever it takes. I mean, I want to stay on, if that's what you're asking."

Somewhere, a cock crowed. Bells tolled and children cried as Jason wandered, bewildered, back to his office. He toyed with the idea of hanging himself in Potter's Field, but decided instead to go on an unprecedented drunk.

LOWER EAST SIDE, 10:00 P.M.

"Excuse me—excuse me, I hate to interrupt," said Becky, knocking three times on the table, next to her beer. "But you guys have *got* to check out what's going on over there." She jerked her head once across the table and toward the main bar area, as if heading a soccer ball back into the crowd.

Seated just to Becky's right and sharing her line of vision, Jason had already independently noticed the object of her amusement, so he instead watched J.D., Paul, and Nick turn as one to plot the trajectory of her nod and discover, at a table along the far wall, the biker couple. A massively bearded road warrior, forlorn and anachronistic in a "Pot for Peace" black T-shirt and a slowly disintegrating bomber jacket, stared in autistic fascination at a similarly leathered female partner who was meticulously sucking on his toes.

"Yeesh," said Nick with a grimace. "Cancel those chicken fingers."

"Now *there's* something you don't see every day," drawled J.D. in his inimitable East Texas twang, grinning and shaking his ponytailed head in disbelief. "That's *great.*"

"Talk about your hoof-and-mouth disease," noted Jason with a wry smile, feeling positively giddy with contentment. This was where he'd longed to be all week, gathered around a crappy wooden table anchored with bottomless pitchers of cheap beer, embarking on yet another episode of this weekly libation ritual he shared with his four tightest friends. Already he felt the tension of the week beginning to leach out through his pores, edged out by fat molecules of alcohol.

"It seems clear she's his 'hog,'" Paul surmised, turning back around to face the table and pushing his wire-frame glasses back from the brink of his nose, a semiconscious tic endearingly familiar to everyone present.

"All right, everyone can stop staring now," said Becky.

"On the plus side," said Nick, "this saves us a trip to the Harley-Davidson Café. What the hell are we doing here, Becky?"

Becky pulled away from the table and threw back her palms in a don't-look-at-me stance. "Hey, this is the part of the world where interesting things happen. If it's too raw for you, go find yourself a Friday's."

A hardened former club kid who'd spent the lion's share of her adolescence trolling for thrills at Tunnel and Limelight, Becky had long ago assumed the role of social director for this little clique. True, J.D., the Southern socialite, had an ironclad grip on the party scene—he was a tireless networker who morphed from job to job with the flipping of his *Maxim* calendar—and Nick or Jason could occasionally swing corporate show tickets or a Rangers skybox. But it was Becky, immersed in the shabby perks of women's magazines, who provided the bread and butter: movie screenings, gallery openings, off-off-off-off-Broadway cast parties. She freely accepted sole responsibility for setting the scene, and generally tried to push the envelope as far as her more conservative friends would tolerate.

"Don't get your panties in a bunch," said Nick. "All I'm saying is, if we're just going to drink beers and sit around talking to ourselves, as usual, we should find a place that doesn't require body armor."

Becky fixed him with a cold look of disdain. "And someday you're actually going to have the gall to tell your kids you lived in New York."

"Ladies, ladies," said J.D., on the far side of Becky. "Have another refreshing frosty beverage and shut the fuck up."

J.D.'s signature TV-speak rarely failed to bring a smile to Jason's face. The lanky Houston boy, an eager and demonstrative performer in social situations anyway, was forever lacing his speech with idioms culled from real or imagined television conversation, describing his omelet, say, as being "full of creamery goodness," or asserting, of just about anything, that "Moms love it." Collectively, the patched-in expressions lent a weird cultural resonance to J.D.'s speech. It was pop culture ground up and sprinkled over everyday banality, performed by a mad method actor.

To J.D.'s left sat Paul, saying next to nothing as usual, bright eyes unerringly following the conversational ball from behind those glasses, quietly gathering data and concentrating the weight of his intellect into brief sardonic bursts. And Nick, already half crocked and belligerent, still dressed for work because he looked better that way; and Becky, with the blue eyes and the bottle-blond hair, with the smooth, fair skin and the generous melons, much too good-looking to be spending every weekend with the same four guys she already knew all too well. She was unconsciously sliding her beer glass around now, smearing a clear pool of condensate into lazy swirls, somehow both deeply dissatisfied and yet, in the moment, sincerely and viscerally happy.

A beery haze was beginning to cloud Jason's concentration. The day's events—Halloran's bombshell, and the grilling he'd received at the hands of Diana—and fielding frequent questions and catcalls had put him squarely at the center of attention, and his friends, as usual, made no secret of their opinions.

"So wait a minute; go back," said J.D. "Y'all *knew* your boss was gonna be fired, and you didn't say anything?"

"No, I didn't 'know' he was going to be fired," Jason clarified patiently. "I'd heard an idle rumor."

At this, Nick laughed aloud. "Define 'idle rumor,'" he said, with evil good humor. "Did he get fired, or didn't he?"

"Oh, leave him alone," said Becky.

"I honestly, honestly didn't believe it," protested Jason. "Shit," he added, half to himself, "I *hate* all this office-politics crap."

"Because you suck at it," observed Nick.

"So are you going to stay?" Becky wanted to know.

Jason shrugged. "I guess so," he said. "For now, anyway." He grabbed the half-empty beer pitcher with his left hand, met it halfway with the glass in his right. "I feel like I'm coming to a big fork in the road," he said as he poured. "I want to keep holding all my options open as long as possible—"

"Because you're a guy," interjected Becky.

"—because I'm a guy," he allowed. "But I think I've reached one of these quantum moments. I have to decide whether I want to really define this as my career with a capital C, or bail and keep looking."

"I'm at the same crossroads," said Becky, nodding. "I'm an associate editor right now, so I do writing *and* editing, and I'd love to keep doing both. But you can't; if I'm going to climb any farther up the masthead, I either have to choose writing or choose editing."

"Well," said Paul, "that's if you accept the assumption that you have to climb."

"Oh, I have to climb," she assured him. "Poverty stops being a badge of honor after about twenty-five."

"But you could go freelance," replied Paul. "Telecommute. Write the Great American Screenplay."

She raised her eyebrows. "You picking up my health insurance?"

"The whole thing just makes me feel sort of . . . I don't know, out of breath," said Jason. He was edging uncomfortably close to a truth he wasn't sure he wanted to state out loud, namely, that he wasn't convinced he was actually *good* at what he was doing. He had enormous confidence in his creative powers, and still felt sure he could propel himself to excellence through sheer focus. But it seemed a long, uphill slog.

J.D. turned back to Jason. "Well, don't have a big midlife crisis on us, pal. There's no hurry."

"There *is*, though," said Jason. "I feel like I can still switch gears now, but it's going to keep getting tougher to escape as a couple of more years go by. It'll be a second career, then. There'll be something vaguely pathetic about it."

"What makes you so certain you're not pathetic now?" wondered Nick.

"Well, that's the nut of the issue, isn't it?" said Paul to Jason. "*Is* this your career, or is it just a job?"

When Jason didn't answer, J.D. filled the silence. "It's *always* just a job," he opined.

Jason grinned. J.D. had held an uninterrupted string of small jobs since college, using a natural handiness and a heaping helping of Texas bullshit to finagle his way into all manner of interesting, but short-lived, posts. He'd refurbished the wrought-iron gates of Brooklyn brownstones, he'd mixed martinis at Lincoln Center, he'd taught English to the toddlers of diplomats. Besides paying the rent, he used the jobs to fund hobbies— photography, computer graphics—that in turn opened up more job opportunities.

J.D. shrugged, smiling. "I think it'd be incredibly boring to do just one thing for the next sixty years, personally. But that's me."

Nick, nodding, replied, "I know, I know. I used to feel that way before I got *my* shit together, too."

✧ ✧ ✧

"Hey, *I* had a date," said Jason, because he wanted to talk about it. "Two, actually."

"Ah, that's right!" replied Nick enthusiastically. "Pocahontas."

"Wait, who's Pocahontas?" said Becky.

"Oh, you know," Nick replied. "She was an Indian princess who—"

Becky froze him with a look of unfiltered disdain. "Was I talking to you?"

Retracing his two encounters with Amanda, last night's drinks and the lunch today, felt oddly liberating. Jason realized that he truly didn't know what to think about Amanda's proposition. The very idea felt slippery in his grasp. Yesterday, it had seemed no more than an intriguing, but implausible, fiction, but their lunch together had gone a long way toward undermining Jason's certainty. Though the bare facts still resisted reason, her inexplicable conviction was proving tougher to sweep aside, and Jason realized he needed his friends to help him put things into perspective.

"Well, how about that," J.D. gushed, when Jason had finished. "Who knew we had such a blue blood in our midst?"

"'Glamis thou art, and Cawdor,'" said Paul.

"I don't know if there's anything to it," replied Jason. "It seems pretty far-fetched, obviously. But I'm certainly willing to play along."

"Oh, so she's *hot*," said J.D., suddenly comprehending. "See, you didn't *say* that."

Jason shrugged. "She's on the hot side."

"What if it's true?" Becky interrupted, unable to contain her enthusiasm. "I mean, what would that mean for you?"

"Him? Fuck *him*," said J.D. "What does it mean for *me*?"

"Exactly," Nick agreed, flashing J.D. an appreciative smile. "*That's* the point. What it means, Beck, is that our friend here owns this bar we're sitting in, and the apartment you live in, and the Korean deli where you get your lemon-poppy muffin in the morning, and all the subway lines and skyscrapers and off-track-betting booths in between." He put his arm around Jason's shoulders. "It means that beers are on him, starting tonight, and right on through the end of time."

"That's what I *thought* it meant," said J.D. excitedly. "You're all right, son."

"I don't know if it means all that," Jason said, smiling, "particularly that last little rider. I'm pretty sure it's just the land itself, not everything on it."

"You just haven't thought it through," Nick interjected. "If I build a house in your parents' backyard without their permission, I don't own it—they do. All these people who built buildings on your land are trespassers, pure and simple."

"You're probably cleared to shoot the bastards," J.D. suggested.

"I don't know," argued Paul. "I'm pretty sure they'd have established some sort of squatters' rights after the first two or three centuries."

"Killjoy," said Nick.

Paul shrugged. "Look, I hate to be the voice of reason," he continued, "but you *do* know this isn't plausible, right?"

"Of course," Jason replied.

"No, she's right," said J.D. "Amanda is, I mean. Indian tribes *are* always winning land-rights and fishing-rights battles and so forth. I read something in the *Times* just a couple of months ago where the British in New Zealand had violated some treaty from the 1800s and the Maoris won back a big chunk of land."

"But we're not talking about a hundred acres of underdeveloped suburb on the outskirts of Bumfuck," said Paul. "This is ground central for planet earth."

"The toast of the globe," suggested J.D. with a dramatic flourish of his beer.

"So let's assume it's real," Paul continued, turning back to Jason. "The deed exists, *and* you find it, *and* you turn out to be the heir in question. What court is ever going to award you the tiniest little corner of Manhattan?" He quickly surveyed the table. "What Alzheimer's-addled judge is going to give you one square foot of Trump's train yards, or Helmsley's hotels, or—"

"Take it easy," Jason protested. "I'm not delusional, I'm just mildly interested in the idea that an ancestor of mine might have had some sort of role in the history of my city."

"Ooh, 'my city,'" said J.D. to Nick, angling a thumb at Jason. "Get him. La-de-dah. All hail the king."

Jason cracked up at this. "I mean the city I live in, you dolt."

"Prepare to be asked to take out a large loan for unspecified 'research,'" warned Paul.

"Oh, lighten up, Nancy," said Nick. "Let a man humor the girl and get laid, willya?"

Becky let out an exasperated little sigh. "I was *wondering* when someone was going to drag the conversation to the lowest common denominator." She looked at Nick. "But I didn't wonder *who* it was going to be."

"Seriously, Jason," said Nick. "In all seriousness, here—" He paused, leaning conspiratorially into the middle of the table. "I'm due about twenty percent of this shit."

"Here it comes," said J.D.

"There's five of us—musketeers to the end, Jason," said Nick. "Don't forget."

"Oh, yeah," Jason laughed. "Pack your bags, asshole. You'll be lucky if I give you till sundown to get the hell off my land."

"How many times have I saved your life?" Nick wondered. "Remember when we were all in that lifeboat, and I said, 'No, no; let's everybody eat *my* leg . . .'?"

"Are you *stoned?*" Jason demanded, grabbing the pitcher and pulling it close to him, dementedly sloshing beer all over the table. "I want it all! All of it, do you understand?" He let out a calculatedly deranged laugh. "It's *mine*, I tell you! *Mine!*"

Chapter Three

The squeal of the garbage truck's brakes went on and on and on in an accelerating blare of elephantine fear, as if it had been skidding sideways for blocks, clearing a wave of haplessly stampeding pedestrians before it. Lying awake in his apartment two stories above the fray, unable to close the window or even cover his ears without an unthinkably energetic muscular contraction, Jason clenched his eyes shut and moaned.

A tentative morning breeze kept picking up and releasing a corner of the shade, widening and contracting a hot triangle of sunlight across Jason's back, at the foot of the bed where he lay, facedown, sprawled in exquisite agony. Outside, trash cans clanged into the back of the truck.

With a melodramatic groan, Jason hoisted his aching face from the fetid bedsheets. Nausea shivered his frame as he encountered his own body's smoky, alcoholic reek, and steel marbles of pain blurred his vision into hazy myopia. *Existence is pain, says the Buddha,* his mind grumbled. Squinting and frowning like a newborn pup, Jason gamely propped himself on one elbow and surveyed the room.

On the floor beside the bed a pair of suit pants had twisted themselves into an awkward tent, one leg inside out. He was still wearing the shirt, a rumpled white Oxford, indifferently buttoned, one shirttail tucked into cotton boxers. He reached up to his hairline, and was immeasurably relieved at not encountering a necktie knotted bachelor-party style around his forehead.

Clumsily, he rolled right and fumbled in the nightstand drawer for a trusty bottle of ibuprofen; he found it by feel, then cursed as he peeled off an arc of fingernail on the childproof cap. *Come on, buddy; hold it together,* he urged with quiet desperation, huddling on the edge of the bed and shaking pills into his hand. Atop the nightstand an oversized Tsing Tao beer, nearly full, had sweated condensation into a ring at its base; he dimly recalled having bought it at a deli while staggering home on autopilot.

"Jesus Christ," he growled, emptying a half dozen pills from fist to mouth, staring dumbly at the beer. "'When,' already."

With a grunt, he forced himself to his feet, socks half sloughed off, and began to lumber toward the kitchenette, pausing en route as another shudder of nausea rippled through him. An archway leading to the tiny kitchen was crowned by an oversize framed print of the *Mona Lisa,* no less, larger than life. A Magic Marker signature in the lower right-hand corner read: "To Jason—handsa offa my wife, ha-ha! XXOO, Leonardo." He patted the side walls as he stepped through, part course correction, part relief at the continued solidity of the material world. *Good wall, nice wall.* The tile floor looked cool and invitingly horizontal.

And then he was squinting into the glare of the refrigerator, scooting aside jars of condiments and a withered carton of Chinese food dating back to some long-dead dynasty—the fridge's total contents, except for one item.

"Ha!" Jason managed in weak triumph, retrieving it: a large, new bottle of V-8.

Elbowing shut the fridge, Jason discovered to his chagrin that he couldn't loosen the lid. He tried again, this time making a conscious effort not to grind his teeth, which magnified the crippling ache in his head. *Here's a setback.* Pausing for breath, he looked at the bottle, lid still doggedly glued shut, and set it down on the edge of the sink to dry his sweaty palms on his boxers. And then disaster struck: The V-8 bottle somehow slipped its perch and toppled into the sink, busting on impact with a hollow pop.

"Fuck!" said Jason aloud, watching seven blended vegetable juices bubble as one into the drain. He looked down at the wide-mouthed juice glass in his hand and dramatically lobbed it into the sink as well, where it shattered satisfyingly. He stared in idiot exultation.

"You see? No God," he said, to nobody in particular.

He turned, defeated, and began to retreat to the womb of the bed, the still-warm bed with the flannel sheets and the rumpled pillow that was right there, a few feet away. A few steps along, already planning the leap, Jason noticed the answering machine light flashing patiently on the nightstand. He paused, sighed, and turned down the volume to a safe decibel level before pressing the replay button.

As the machine rewound, collecting its thoughts, he lay back on the bed wearily and rubbed his eyes.

"Hi, Jason—it's Amanda," said the machine. "I wanted to make sure we were still on for tomorrow morning."

"Fuck off," he barked at the ceiling.

"I assume we're on," the machine continued, ignoring him, "so can we say . . . ten o'clock? I'll pick you up on the southwest corner of . . . call it Eighty-first and Broadway. If that's too early, just call me before I leave."

With growing despair, Jason sat up again and forced his eyes to make the short hop over to the clock radio, where red LEDs blinked out 9:38 in devilish joy.

"I'm not going," he said aloud, suddenly six years old. But it wasn't true. Already his feet were reaching for the floor, his hands rubbing color into his cheeks, his eyes scanning the room bitterly for a baseball cap and sunglasses.

✧ ✧ ✧

Fifteen minutes later, still hungover but with a brown paper bag tucked under one arm, Jason stepped out of H & H Bagels, stuffing change into a front pocket with his free hand in open defiance of the amateur doorman's empty cup. He donned his shades under the awning, shielding his brain from the relentless photon torpedoes that gently warmed the Upper West Side, and braced himself for what was, to people who weren't quite as hung over as he, probably considered a nice day.

Walking over to the literal corner of Broadway and 81st, Jason dropped one foot over the curb and surveyed the shores of Broadway, filtered through soothing Ray-Ban earth tones. Brunchers clustered like bananas around tiny outdoor tables: hot babes in tank tops and ball caps braving the still-breezy April day; college buddies with smoothly retreating hairlines, sipping bottomless mimosas and eating a thousand variants of eggs Benedict. Some languidly read the first half of the Sunday *Times*, the nonessential stuff they release on Saturday because it takes two days to read the behemoth; others, giddy and punchy, dropped silverware and cracked one another up with details from the previous night's escapades.

Enticed by the warmth emanating through his shirtsleeve, Jason uncrinkled the top of the bagel bag and buried his nose in it, drinking in the agreeably doughy smell. Undaunted, a team of Clydesdales thundered mercilessly up the inside of his skull.

Why am I here? Jason asked himself, frowning, even as he turned from the sidewalk attractions to stare uptown into the traffic, eyes peeled for a car to distinguish itself as his ride. *I bought a perfectly good bed for just this sort of situation.*

He remembered discussing going to the reservation with Amanda, but for the life of him, he couldn't remember whether he'd actually promised to go. Probably all part of her diabolical plan. By all rights, he should be at home sitting on the john, with Safire's column spread before him and his cheek comfortingly chilling against the side of his marble sink, patiently waiting for Amanda to get the hint and stop buzzing the intercom. And yet, here he was, manning a street corner with boyish optimism, a warm gift sweating up his hand. She'd told him, in quite unimpeachable English, that she wasn't interested. So why was he here?

Because penises can't hear, said a voice in his head that sounded suspiciously like Nick. *Because despite all evidence to the contrary, deep down you still think you're gonna get your peepee in her tepee.*

Well, it wasn't as if he had anything better to do this weekend. Updating his résumé, for all his procrastination, was a ten-minute affair: one job to add, one date to change, a few vigorous action verbs to reshuffle. It was a matter of control, he supposed. This whole nonaffair with Amanda was too unpredictable for his liking; it resonated uncomfortably with everything else that was helter-skelter in his life.

Just once I'd like to get my hands on the wheel, he said to himself, watching a BMW slam on the brakes to avoid humping the back end of a delivery truck. *Take the world for a little test drive.*

Moments later, an enormous copper-colored station wagon lurched without warning toward the curb in front of him, careening aside at the last minute as if ricocheting off his personal aura. The weather-beaten, lumbering creature, engine bellowing impatience, seemed truly a marvel of mechanics; for all he knew, it was the largest car ever to shave the face of the earth.

"Nice entrance," he said appreciatively, through the now-open passenger window, voice rising to counter the clanking roar.

"Hop in," she invited warmly. "Watch the spring."

Jason lowered himself into the car, executing a quick pelvic thrust to avoid a twisted pigtail of metal that poked menacingly up through the cracked vinyl of the seat. "How's it going?" he asked. Amanda was wearing a tight, short-sleeved white T-shirt and faded jeans; loose hair cascaded messily over her shoulders.

"I feel *great*," she said enthusiastically, gunning the engine and merging recklessly into the traffic before sparing another glance toward him. "You, you don't look so hot."

"Mmm, well," he said, raising a hand to his forehead. "I apparently got caught in some sort of brick storm last night."

She smiled wryly. "I'm glad you could make it, Jason. This is going to be fun—you'll see," she promised slyly.

He shook his head. "Nothing's going to be much fun for Jason today, I'm afraid."

As Amanda steered them through the shifting traffic pattern around the 72nd Street subway station, Jason settled for acclimating himself to the car's interior. The floor at his feet was littered with a mélange of debris: scattered papers and beer cans, fast-food bags, a lone boot, a few battered paperbacks, assorted grimy pens and pencils, a crumpled tampon box. Beside him, the pocket on the passenger door bulged with maps, napkins, and the lid of an old Ho Hos box scribbled with phone messages. A tangle of Mardi Gras beads dangled from the rearview; an actual wad of gum held the car's registration to the base of the dashboard, between his knees.

"You baby-sit monkeys or something?" he wondered.

Amanda shot him a disapproving look. "Now, that's just plain judgmental."

"Sorry," he replied. "Brought you some bagels," he offered, holding up the bag.

With delicate fingers she accepted an onion bagel, still warm to the touch. "Thanks," she said, eyeing it with obvious approval, and he watched as she sank her teeth in. Toasted scabs of onion tumbled teasingly into her crotch.

She had a hypnotizing presence, he decided, meaning it literally. When alone, he could easily dismiss her, forget her gentle geometry, forgive her disorganized brain. Her proximity changed the equation, he realized with a smile as he allowed his gaze to trace her face in profile, skiing lightly off the end of her nose.

"So give me a preview," coaxed Jason as they saw the first signs for the Midtown tunnel. "What's your mother like?"

Amanda studiously kept her eyes on the road. "Yeah, I guess I ought to prepare you a little," she said thoughtfully. "Mom's very . . . intense. An activist, you'd probably call her—very, very into tribal matters. She's the sachem, like I said before, the tribal leader. Our tribe has always been governed by women."

"So . . . is sachem a job, or a title?" Jason replied. "I mean, are there actual duties or responsibilities, or is it mostly ceremonial . . . now?"

She frowned. "It may not have as much practical application these days, granted. But my mother considers herself a living link in an unbroken line of leadership that stretches back more than a thousand years." She paused momentarily. "She's sort of the official keeper of the best interests of the tribe. She speaks for the Manahata; she provides advice and counsel for the whole tribe. That's the nonpolitical part of her job." Here she turned to face Jason. "It's not ceremonial to her, at least," she concluded.

They entered the Queens/Midtown tunnel, rolling downhill along the bottom of the East River and rising again on the far side, off the island. Jason hooked the toe of his sneaker into the tampon box, lifting it off the carpet. "Whose reservation is this again?" he asked. "The other tribe's?"

Amanda nodded. "It's complicated."

"Tell me," said Jason, watching the sights as their highway improbably sliced through the cityscape. "Or we could play 'I Spy'. . ."

"The Indian lands are called sovereign nations," she began, as he settled back, "but it's a little misleading. We're self-governing, but still subject to U.S. federal law. We're . . . more like protectorates. Spain is a sovereign nation."

"I get it."

"U.S. maps don't exclude the Indian reservations, for example, like they probably should. You don't need a visa to go onto a reservation."

But they don't take American Express, Jason thought absurdly.

"So some tribes accept that their reservations reside in America. They're like theme parks, or retirement villages. Most of the Lenape, though, and the Manahata, too, and many other tribes, take a more traditional view. We see all the reservations as linked into one discontinuous territory, whose boundary is tribal rather than geographic. It's that tiny part of the original continent that's left over when you subtract all the European-owned territory."

"The holes in the Swiss cheese," suggested Jason, and she nodded thoughtfully.

"If you ask my mother," replied Amanda, "she'll tell you that your people are not conquerers, but occupiers. That America, as you've been calling it for a couple of hundred years, is really just an extended occupation by an enemy army. My mother firmly believes—like she believes in the sun rising tomorrow—that this will all eventually be restored to native people." She swept a hand across the windshield's panorama.

"Wow," said Jason sincerely. "You're *kidding.*"

Her eyebrows knit into a frown. "Is that funny?" she wondered, palpably shifting the mood in the front seat.

"Okay, maybe it's not funny," he ventured gently. "But come on, Amanda. You gotta admit, we're pretty entrenched."

"Yes, I *know*," she replied. "Don't be a jerk." She said nothing for a moment, and he left the gap unfilled. "My mother believes we were entrusted by our gods with the stewardship of this land, and the simple fact that we *weren't* completely wiped out or assimilated into your culture is proof that the job is still ours."

"Uh-huh," said Jason. The goofymeter was edging into the red zone. "And what about you . . . What do *you* believe?"

Amanda was silent for a long moment, glancing in the rearview as a prelude to passing a gray, graffiti-covered van she'd been patiently trailing for some time. "I'm not sure what I believe," she asserted quietly. "I'm a product of both cultures."

"Well, you *are* allowed to have an independent opinion."

She shook her head. "Not on this issue."

Part of Jason wanted to pursue this, but he was suddenly struck by another line of thought. "So that's why it doesn't seem crazy to you that the island of Manhattan could be transferrable—because you've been raised to believe that this is eventually going to happen everywhere."

"*No*," she said, annoyed, as if he hadn't been listening. "Maybe I've been raised to be more open-minded about it, but the reason I *believe* it is because I can cite all kinds of legal precedent for it."

"Okay," he said, relenting.

"If you think I'm so fucking naive, why are you still here?"

With the bluntness of that question, Jason felt a sudden, irresistible compulsion to come clean with her.

"Because I *dig* you, stupid," he said simply.

"What?" she said, laughing.

"You heard me. That's the only reason I'm here, period. And don't pretend you don't know it."

"Jason, I—"

"No, don't," he replied quickly. "It's okay. Listen, I don't know why I'm telling you this; I know I promised to be good. But that's the truth. I'm tagging along because I'm nurturing this egotistical idea that I can somehow bring you around."

Oh, you fucking sissy, he reprimanded himself as Amanda focused on driving the car, driving the car, driving the car. *Strategic full disclosure. That usually works.* Jason weighed the option of diving for the door handle and madly flinging himself out of the moving auto, bouncing end over end along the roadside like a meat tumbleweed, and decided against it.

"Amanda, I don't want to lead you on," he said. "If my family played a role in New York history, sure, I want to know about it. But that's not why I'm in your car with you right now."

She was nodding, smiling enigmatically. "Okay," she assured him. "I get it. But, Jason . . ."

But she fell silent again, and he had no choice but to return his focus to the highway and free her from the pressure of his gaze. The road was smooth as ice; a few droplets of rain spattered the windshield but couldn't sustain an attack long enough to interest the wipers.

At last Amanda marshaled her thoughts. "I can live with that if you can," she stated carefully, ironing out a contract. Unable to resist, he raised his eyebrows quizzically, but she shrugged him off with a sober shake of her head. "I don't want to lead you on, either, Jason. I need you to help me solve this thing, and I'm still convinced that I can get you to *want* to. But I'm really not looking for any kind of . . . *complication* right now. I mean I—"

"But you'll take what you can get," Jason finished.

Amanda smiled wanly. "Yeah, I guess that's it."

"Devil's bargain," he mumbled, returning his gaze to the outside world, marveling at the turn his life was taking.

✧ ✧ ✧

Somewhere east of Middletown, Long Island, they exited the expressway at last and drove onto a less imposing two-lane street. As the road shrank and the surrounding area crowded with distractions—strip malls, gas stations, diners—conversation dissolved into idle chatter, then dwindled into silence as the road became a dirt road, and the grass on the banks grew increasingly unkempt, and the houses gradually fell away altogether.

At last they came to a lightly wooded area, where a somber-looking sign announced that they were entering the Lenape Reservation. Speed limits strictly enforced; tribal regulations apply, etc., etc. The car lurched unexpectedly over a pothole just inside the entrance, and Jason's heart jumped, alerting him to his own apprehension.

A half mile or so into the wooded interior, the dirt road forked; along the path they chose, occasional clusters of low, squat houses began to appear. The setting reminded Jason of the summer camps traditionally favored by bloodthirsty movie maniacs, but proof of year-round use was in ample supply: TV antennas and satellite dishes; toy-strewn yards; an old Chevy truck with the hood up and one wheel off, standing in a pool of rusty tools. The taut silence between them held, and Jason wondered whether Amanda was ashamed of the obvious squalor.

Amanda pulled up at last before another fork in the road—the place seemed to have no organizing principle—and a not-quite-sprawling split-level cottage of stone and stucco at the center of the fork, a house clearly in better repair than its fellows.

"This is the place," she confirmed, turning off the engine at last. Jason's ears rang in the silence; suddenly there were birds in the air, and the sound of something like a river. Jason looked around weakly as his sense of purpose waned.

"Amanda," he began tentatively, and she paused, door already ajar. "I know I've had three hours to ask this," he continued, "but what exactly are we trying to accomplish here?"

She shrugged confidently, replying, "Fishing, I suppose."

"Should I be witty and charming?"

"Just be yourself, stupid," she advised, swinging out and shutting her door before disappearing around the back of the car.

"Ouch," Jason winced, alone in the front seat. "I'd always kind of hoped I *was* witty and charming." Opening the passenger door, he swung a leg out of the car and tried to exit quickly. Suddenly, he felt a tug and a sharp pain as the forgotten loose spring in the seat seized and ripped the ass of his jeans, digging a stiff metallic fingernail across his gluteus.

"Motherf—" Jason began, but the curse died on his lips as, through his open window, he saw the Indian.

✧ ✧ ✧

The Indian stood, predictably silent and majestic, halfway along the gentle sweep of gravel that trailed from the road to the front door, which now stood open. Jason paused instinctively, halfway out of the car, hand clapped to ass as if holding in a geyser of blood that would otherwise be spurting all over the upholstery. A frame of white-gray hair drifted off and away from the Indian's deeply tanned, middle-aged face, and the loose tails of an unbuttoned blue denim shirt parted like draperies over his oversize, undershirted belly. But it was the Indian's penetrating gaze that riveted Jason's attention, made him forget even the searing pain in his rump.

Amanda, circling around the back of the car, had pulled almost even with Jason's door before she, too, spotted the third party and stopped in her tracks. The Indian's gaze shifted ever so slightly to include Amanda, and then a pair of doors slammed from somewhere behind them. Jason and Amanda turned, surprised by the sudden shattering of the impasse.

Across the road, two men in suits had left a black Lincoln Town Car and were slowly approaching the front lawn. Returning his gaze forward, Jason saw the Indian fix Amanda with a final scowl before striding off purposefully past them, toward the men, hailing them by name as he buttoned his cuffs and tucked in the shirt. Amanda kept her eyes focused on the house as the Indian passed mere inches from her side, but Jason continued to watch, spellbound, as the three men met at the far edge of the lawn, conversed in low tones for a moment, and headed off to the Town Car. A moment later they heard the car start, a smooth, throaty rumble.

"Jason," said Amanda with a sour smile, "meet Dad. Dad, Jason." She trudged up the gravel to the house without further explanation. Jason watched as the Lincoln slowly pulled away, then he turned and followed her up the walk, ass throbbing with real, acute pain.

✧ ✧ ✧

Amanda entered the house after a "Hello?" and a perfunctory knock on the open door, and Jason followed her into a little tiled alcove, where she called out to her mother. From a far-off corner of the house came an incoherent reply and they walked farther in, into an expansive living room. Here, a pair of cats, obese and long in the tooth, held court, a black one stretching its claws into the flesh of a couch, a calico coiled in pillowy slumber on the hearth rug.

"Is something wrong with your ass?" Amanda inquired, noticing Jason's hand still cupping the injured buttock.

The wound turned out to be slight, of course, though not embarrassingly so. Blood had been drawn, and Amanda went off to procure some iodine, leaving Jason alone to inspect the room. White linen curtains, together with broad, dark wood beams that striped the low ceiling, set a tone of rustic simplicity; the wide wooden slats of the floor, indifferently covered with a few area rugs, creaked to the step. Here and there the bucolic charm was interrupted by pieces of modern art: iron and stone twisted into elegantly idealized animal or abstract shapes, and paintings that followed similar themes. It was the home of an artist or aficionado: part living space, part gallery.

As Amanda rifled noisily through kitchen drawers, Jason turned his eyes to the long wall along the back of the house, dominated by an old stone fireplace, where irregular cantaloupes of river stones clustered together beneath a wide, dark wooden mantel. He crossed to it at a respectfully idle pace.

The mantel itself was an asymmetric, rough-hewn slab of soot-blackened timber, the very keel of some ancient warship put to the torch, perhaps, and its horizontal upper surface was festooned with an assortment of knickknacks: an oil lamp, a pair of Remington-style rodeo statues, and, on a velvet pillow, a smooth blue marble globe veined with gold.

Above the fireplace, the broad chimney was sheathed in painted plaster; pinned a few feet upward of the mantel by four concrete nails hung a bare, stretched, mustard-colored skin, roughly two feet square. Onto this had been dyed or painted a map he recognized almost instantly as the island of Manhattan. It looked ancient.

"This is gonna sting," warned Amanda from behind; he turned to find her armed with an uncapped bottle in one hand and a dabbed square of gauze in the other. Her eyes twinkled mischievously. "Drop 'em and bend over."

"Thanks but no thanks, Nurse Ratchett," replied Jason, seizing bottle and cloth. Amanda watched with indiscreet glee as he wincingly attended to his wound through the tear in the cloth.

Amanda's mother, when she appeared, was dressed casually, in a loose black shirt and jean slacks, and surveyed the pair through a pair of rosy sunglasses. She wore her salt-and-pepper hair straight and long, like Amanda, but her face was rounder, having shared in the comfortable middle-age spread of her hips. Smiling thinly, she approached and threw her arms around her daughter.

"Hi, Mom," said a newly cheery Amanda. "Jason, this is my mom, Mary. Mom, this is . . . Jason."

He smiled and offered a hand, which Amanda's mother accepted, still smiling, and they exchanged greetings. "That map . . . it's beautiful," he said.

"The island," she replied in a thick, measured Native accent, inclining her head toward the fireplace. "But it's just a map." She searched his eyes with a hawklike intensity, and Jason found himself mentally plotting the room's exits.

"So are you the one my daughter's been looking for?" she continued at last. "Last child of the Haansvoorts?"

"That's what I'm told," replied Jason, flashing his charmer's smile.

The old woman's lips parted slightly, as if she were about to add something, but she only licked her lips.

"Who were those guys with Dad?" Amanda asked, hooking a thumb toward the front door.

With a dismissive wave, Mary turned and headed toward the kitchen. "Ask him," she sniffed. "They want us to build a casino. Come on, let's have a drink." Without waiting to see whether they'd follow, she slipped quietly across one of the rugs and onto the linoleum of the kitchen floor, with barely a whisper to mark her passing. Jason was surprised to note that she was actually wearing moccasins.

"A casino?" pressed Amanda, two steps behind her mother. Roused from his inertia by some latent herd instinct, Jason followed meekly.

The kitchen was immense, a palace of white Formica, but cluttered and homey, with a card table and chairs by the door, twin sinks full of dishes, knickknack-cluttered countertops. *Like mother, like daughter*, he thought.

"Yes, a damn casino," said Mary, passing the table en route to the far counter. "Here on the Lenape."

"Really," said Amanda, surprised, seating herself at the rickety little table. "Why didn't he bring them inside?" Taking his cue, Jason sat down across from her. It felt cramped and mildly unsanitary: a booth at a low-end diner.

From a cupboard above the sink, Amanda's mother withdrew a handful of assorted mugs. "Because he knows better. Jason, do you drink coffee?"

"Uh, no," he replied nervously. "I mean, yes. Thanks."

✧ ✧ ✧

The three sat together in the kitchen for over an hour, drinking coffee and drifting in and out of lazy conversations. Jason wanted nothing more than to curl up and let the little family visit unfold around him, and for a while, at least, the women seemed inclined to let him. It had apparently been a month or so since Amanda's last visit home, and Jason watched with detached amusement the textbook volleys of mother-daughter interaction.

Intense and confident, Mary enunciated her speech with meticulous care, as if test-driving each word for safety and maneuverability.

Eventually, the conversational wind began to shift, and Jason found himself fielding questions. Mary's gentle inquiries seemed quite innocuous, taken individually, but on the whole, he couldn't shake the suspicion that he was being . . . probed. In particular, he found himself more than once dodging the subject of his parents, which he'd always felt uncomfortable talking about, but never more so than in times like this, when he wasn't physically and mentally running on all cylinders. Jason tried to dismiss his anxiety, but couldn't escape the notion that he'd been led into some sort of trap.

Amanda said little throughout the inquisition, and Jason wondered when exactly she planned to get around to asking for the piece of information or whatever it was she expected to get out of this trip. The extent to which the success of this little enterprise hinged on his presence remained unclear. He was working blind, knowing neither the ground rules nor the objective, and it was starting to make him edgy. Eagerly, desperately, he awaited an opportunity to quiz Amanda, if she could at some point be removed from her mother's watchful gaze.

But it was Amanda who first excused herself, to go to the bathroom, and Jason's mild dread began quickly to escalate in the absence of her mediating presence. Mary's pleasant affability seemed calculated to disarm: the B-movie Nazi interrogator coolly reassuring you that yes, you will of course tell her everything, and then she will find you some soup. His wounded buttock ached sympathetically.

"So," Jason assayed boldly, desperate to change the subject, "why *are* you against the casino? Just out of curiosity."

Mary took a leisurely sip before replying. "Well, it's a terrible notion," she opined, frowning sincerely. "My people have been gravely weakened, Jason, as you may know, by centuries of poverty, alcoholism, and a host of other evils. A casino can bring nothing but further despair to the reservation."

He shook his head. "I'm confused," he confessed. "I assumed your . . . people . . . would own it."

"Well, they would," she confirmed. When he frowned in reply, a maternal smile creased her lips. "You can't be expected to understand, Jason," she explained patiently. "Many of the men of our tribe, the women, too, take their paychecks into town and come back with lottery tickets. Not all of us, but a great number. It doesn't take much imagination to picture what it would be like with a full operating casino in our backyard."

Amanda had returned and caught the thread of her mother's answer as she sat down; she continued to listen intently as Mary turned to face her.

"Those men are from the island," she informed Amanda. "Mobsters, maybe. They want to set the whole thing up for a percentage. Your father won't stop talking to them about it. It's going to be a battle, I'm afraid."

Amanda tapped her mug absently. "Well, they can't do it without you," she replied confidently, though her narrowed look suggested this was a question.

Mary shrugged and smiled, crossing her legs languorously. "Well, remember, this isn't our land," she reminded her daughter. "All they really have to do is convince the Lenape leaders. And there'll be a lot of support once this idea becomes public, support from both tribes."

"What if you could make some sort of a rule," Jason interrupted suddenly, "outlawing the *use* of the casino by the Manahata?"

Amanda and her mother looked at him, then exchanged a glance.

"That way," Jason continued, "you could reap the financial benefits and the employment that a casino could bring, and avoid the—the *costs* to the community."

Mary smiled, but shook her head. "It's not worth the risk, not even in principle," she replied. "We don't need the money *that* badly."

"But you just said poverty was the problem."

"Poverty is *a* problem, yes, Jason," she agreed. "But that doesn't mean money's the solution."

"Well, I'm not sure what that means," Jason responded, ignoring a disapproving look from Amanda. "I mean, this is a tried-and-true formula, here. Do you know how many cities in this country would kill for the opportunity to open a casino?" He paused momentarily, but continued, buoyed by his own momentum. "Think about it. You'd have a steady stream of profits to pay for whatever the tribe needs. Advisers, psychiatrists, lawyers. A new community center, if that's what you want. Guaranteed college tuition for your grandchildren's grandchildren. I mean, these things net hundreds of millions of dollars. No, I get what you're saying," he added, forestalling Mary's objection with an upraised hand. "Money and power can corrupt, I gotcha. But surely you can't be arguing that prosperity itself is bad."

"No," Mary acknowledged. "What I'm arguing against is a pathological reliance on money. I'm arguing that this rush to build a casino implies that we *need* help from the outside world if our tribe is to survive in any kind of meaningful way. It means accepting that our culture is not self-sufficient; it makes an unacceptable statement of dependency. It would be a highly symbolic end to the old ways, to everything that defines us."

"You're assuming your tribe won't be able to handle the temptation of having a casino on the reservation because they gamble now," said Jason. "But if they *owned* the casino, wouldn't they be less inclined toward risk-taking? Rich people don't gamble—poor people do."

"Jason—" cautioned Amanda.

"I just think you should give people a little more credit," he went on. "I'm sorry," he said to Amanda contritely. "I'm sorry. Of course it's none of my business."

"Jason," said Mary, with forced patience, "I appreciate your obviously heartfelt input. But you really have no right even to address the question. You're not a part of this culture; you can't possibly understand the situation."

Now he felt challenged. "Well," he replied, "there's no need to pull rank on me. You and I may not share the same *history*, but we all live in the same culture, now. It's called twentieth-century America. Money's not evil, it's just a medium." Seeing Mary's brow darkening, Jason realized he was going too far. "I'm not arguing you have to have a casino to survive," he went on. "But just to say, 'Oh, money is bad, we must never do anything that's profitable,' seems a little defeatist."

"'The same *culture*'?" Mary repeated, sarcastic and sputtering, no longer disguising her growing anger. "'The same culture'?"

"Mom, hey," Amanda tried to interject, but was ignored.

"It's just infuriating!" said Mary, unexpectedly slamming her coffee mug onto the tabletop and rising to a terrible height. "You take that one-world MTV horseshit back where you came from!"

"Mom!" Amanda yelled, as Jason's eyes widened in shock.

"We are a *conquered people*," her mother practically shouted, leaning over Jason as if she indeed meant to devour him; he could not remember having ever been so terrified. "My ancestors were the children of the earth and sky," she went on, in apoplectic rage. "*Your* ancestors systematically *butchered* us. Shot us and hacked us to pieces, man, woman, and child.

Tore the heart out of our traditions, scattered us, herded us like cattle onto the most undesirable land you could stick us with and left us there to *die*. Now explain to me again how we live in the same culture."

Holy fucking shit, Jason panicked, heart racing. *I'm trapped in a goddamn PC nightmare*. "I'm . . . I'm sorry," he said meekly, looking away. "I didn't mean to offend you."

"Yes, exactly," Mary replied, nodding. "You're sorry that the situation's now uncomfortable, but not for your arrogance or your ignorance." She turned to Amanda. "You hear this? If you can absorb whatever's left of the people you conquer into your own culture, there'll be nobody left to take you to task for your crimes. It has always been the same—always. Well, we're still here, Jason. Out of sight, out of mind, maybe, but still here. We're not just going to blend in quietly and let the world forget what your people did to us. I'm sorry if you find that untidy."

"Ma, take it easy," Amanda urged. "Jason didn't conquer anybody."

"No," Mary agreed. "No, you're right. Jason's only the child of conquerors. With the birthright of blissful ignorance."

Though her anger seemed to be abating, the steely conviction behind it remained. Jason felt he ought to say something, but the risk of reawakening the dragon was too high.

"Let me teach you something they don't tell you in your schools, Jason," she adjured him with mock sweetness. "Hundreds of nations thousands of years old, brought to our knees in a couple of generations. Mass genocide. Outright theft of our ancestral lands. The systematic destruction of our artifacts and heroes and history. Your culture *buried* mine, Jason. Skinned it and burned it alive. It's the most massively significant event in our history—for us it's World War One, Two, and Three all rolled into one. And you don't even teach it in your goddamn *classrooms*. You memorize the goddamn kings of England."

Suddenly feeling intensely claustrophobic, Jason could only sit in agony and try to keep his mouth from swinging open. *It's been hundreds of years*, he wanted to protest. *Time to wake up and join your century*. "I'm sorry," he reiterated in a humble whisper, way past ready to go.

Mary only glared in naked antagonism, silently, as if summoning her forces for another blitzkrieg. Finally, though, she simply scooted back her chair and carried the cups over to the sink without speaking, her face locked in an expression of grim purpose.

So anyway, I was wondering if I could take your daughter to the prom? Jason thought wistfully.

"Amanda." Mary spoke from in front of the sink, her back still turned. "It's getting late. I think it's time your friend went back to the island."

Jason spared a look at the object of his affection, only to find her head buried in her hands.

"I'm sorry my daughter dragged you all the way out here, Jason," Mary continued, turning on the faucet, "but you and I obviously have nothing to talk about."

Suits me fine. "Well, I'm sorry you feel that way," said Jason, rising.

"No, you're not," she replied, shaking her head, turning and squinting at him from across the kitchen. "What a liar you are, through and through! You don't even want to be here. I'm not *reaching* you; I'm only making you uncomfortable."

When he didn't answer, she began walking slowly toward him, drying her hands on her shirt. "Who are you, Jason?" she asked, with a final searching look. "You're obviously not who I thought you were, and so I have to wonder: Who the hell *are* you? Do you even know?"

All he could do was return Mary's stare as best he could. "I know who I am," he replied.

She laughed bitterly. "You're *nobody*, that's who. Go back to your world, boy," she urged, turning away and walking back toward her dishes. "There's nothing for you here." She flicked the faucet on and rolled up her sleeves.

✧ ✧ ✧

The car retraced its path back through the tangle of dirt roads to the highway, the din of its engine uninterrupted by human conversation. Amanda glared at the road from behind the wheel, while Jason slouched in the corner of his seat and pressed his thumbs to his temples, wishing with all his soul that this hellish trip were over, already. *There's no place like home,* he kept repeating to himself, *there's no place like home.*

But the silence was taxing. There's only so long one can play a conversation out in one's head before the need to actually verbalize it overwhelms. When Amanda drew a pair of cigarettes from a pack in the dash, lighting one and tossing the other, unlit, out the window, Jason pounced.

"Why do you *do* that?" he demanded, clumsily breaking the silence: a bowling ball dropped into a glassy pond.

"Why do I do what?" replied Amanda, pouting.

"Throw away every other cigarette. Are you trying to quit?"

She remained sullen. "Something like that."

✧ ✧ ✧

Five minutes later, it was her turn to break the silence. "Okay, so what the hell was that?"

Jason raised one eyebrow, but kept staring straight ahead. "She's *your* mother . . . you tell me," he replied, trying to will the Manhattan skyline into appearing in the distance.

"Why did you—" Amanda began, too softly.

"What?" Jason interjected testily. "I can't even hear you over this goddamn motherfucking bitch-ass space-shuttle engine."

"Why did you try to piss my mother off?" she shouted.

Jason turned to face her. "Oh, that's rich. Are you kidding me?" he demanded. "Look, Amanda. Don't just circle the wagons—you were there. We were having an intellectual debate. It was your mom who took it to eleven, not me." *Circle the wagons,* he thought. *Nice metaphor, Jack. These fuckin' Indians . . .*

"You could have been a little more sensitive, that's all," she replied. "I absolutely did warn you it was a touchy subject."

Jason watched as an ancient Subaru, plastered with college stickers and packed solid with dorm paraphernalia, angled into their lane without signaling. "Let's all remember that I wasn't the one who blew up," he reminded Amanda firmly. "Suddenly I became this Politically Incorrect Poster Boy for daring to suggest—"

"I know," she replied. "But—"

"For daring to have a different opinion about a damn *casino*. And anyway, Amanda," he continued, "you and I aren't boyfriend and girlfriend. Where'd you get the idea you suddenly have the right to edit my conversation?"

"Is this a debate, too?" she wondered. "Because I gotta tell you, it feels like you're picking a fight."

Jason glowered for a moment, determined to outstare her, but she turned away almost instantly; the car's massive inertia required a constant stream of incremental course corrections.

"All right, I'm sorry," he relented after a few moments. "But I'm not a bigot, for Christ's sake. I'm not. I *hate* that crap. It's like, because I'm a white male, I'm not allowed to take part in any argument that involves race, or gender, or anything. Because I'm the Oppressor."

"Well, don't forget, you *were* aligning yourself with those other white guys," Amanda reminded him.

"What other white guys?"

"The ones who want to start the casino," she replied. "Jason, you're never going to have a calm, reasoned conversation about tribal affairs with her. It's *always* politically charged; it's . . . tribal unity's my mom's whole *thing*. To her, if our people just dissolve into mainstream America, then we've been truly conquered, our forefathers forgotten. End of the world. And she doesn't want it to happen on her watch."

"Well, I hate being judged," Jason groused. "I get a little impatient when people let their emotions rule their reason."

"That's awfully condescending," she remarked. "Don't be Ugly Guy."

"I'm not," he replied, shaking his head.

"For you it's just a parlor argument," she continued. "But she's gotta live there if you're wrong. Look at Atlantic City."

"Look at Las Vegas," he countered. "Look at Foxwoods, for crying out loud. All these other Indian tribes are shamelessly raking it in, pulling themselves up and out of poverty. How much hard empirical evidence do you need?"

He paused to gather his thoughts, interrupting her just as she opened her mouth to respond. "I mean, think about this *deed*, Amanda," he said, tapping a finger on the empty seat between them. "If we were to pull it off, haven't you thought for a minute about all the *good* we could do with all that cash?"

"She doesn't want us to find it," Amanda replied quietly, talking to the windshield. "That's what that whole scene was about. Mom was digging to find out what kind of person you are, because it's important for her to know whether or not you're just after the money."

He raised one eyebrow in genuine surprise, turned to stare out the windshield for a moment, then looked back at her. "Think so?"

Amanda nodded gravely. "Doesn't it make sense? She's the gatekeeper. She's not going to just hand over the store without checking out your intentions first."

"See, now I missed that."

A ghost of a smile returned to her lips. "That's because your head's not in the game." She put an elbow up on the window ledge and rested the side of her head against her palm, interlacing fingers in her long hair.

"I felt like prey," said Jason. "I felt like she was going to spit some kind of paralyzing poison on me and swallow me whole."

But Amanda wasn't paying attention. "She *knows*," she said quietly. "She knows where that *freaking* deed is."

$$\diamond \ \diamond \ \diamond$$

As they roared steadily westward, along the Long Island Expressway and into the setting sun, the two fell silent, immersed in private thoughts, and Jason rolled up his window in defense against the chilling breeze. The blocky spires of Manhattan, still distant, began tentatively to emerge out of the burnt orange haze that draped the western horizon, a dream city coalescing gradually at their approach.

At last Amanda spoke. "What do you think would happen," she asked, out of the blue, "if aliens landed a spaceship in Kansas tomorrow?"

Jason frowned. "Why Kansas?"

"Or wherever."

Jason quickly adopted a nasal monotone. "Take us to Stuckey's," he intoned.

"Don't be queer," said Amanda. "Seriously, if you were in charge of the country, what would you do? Aliens just landed."

Jason thought about it for a few moments. "I guess I'd give them the benefit of the doubt and try to communicate with them. Unless they started hauling out laser cannons."

Amanda's face, in delicious profile, was animated by a skeptical smile. "But just because they act diplomatic doesn't necessarily mean they don't have evil intentions."

"I think any race that has intergalactic flight under their belts could probably wipe us out without a lot of pussyfooting around," said Jason.

"But they wouldn't just start blasting away," Amanda objected. "Remember, they'd think of us as aliens, too. They'd want to know more about us, our strengths, our weapons and capabilities, before risking it."

"I suppose," he said, shrugging, wondering where she was going with this.

"I want to paint you a picture," said Amanda, and Jason nodded acquiescence because he felt warm and sedentary, and welcomed the prospect of letting Amanda perform without his being called on to contribute. He closed his eyes.

"Let's say the aliens come bearing gifts," she went on. "Medicine. Technology. New kinds of foods and weapons. I mean, try and think of this in really concrete terms: Aliens land in Kansas and start passing out orgasmatrons and cures for cancer."

"What's the catch?" he said, smiling indulgently.

"Then, after they find out what our strengths and weaknesses are, they give the okay to the rest of the spaceships."

"Hello," Jason interrupted, opening one eye. "When did they become an armada?"

"Well, why not?"

"Wait, I get it," said Jason, rousing himself. "I know exactly where this is going."

"The Manahata used the same word for the ocean and the sky—isn't that something?" said Amanda. "The border, the beyond. It's not far from what space is for us today. We can go out in it, but only for a short distance, with an enormous effort and tons of supplies, and then we have to turn around and come back. Just like paddling out to fish in the ocean. There was no reason even to conceive of another side to the sea."

"And then the first man-o'-wars came sailing in from Europe," said Jason. "I hear what you're saying, Amanda. But you can't assume extraterrestrials would necessarily want to conquer us."

She shrugged. "Exploring cultures always need something—raw goods, new markets—that's why they explore. They'd settle among us, get a good foothold, start quietly trying to find out where we keep our titanium, or whatever it is they're—"

"Why assume that a highly advanced extraterrestrial culture would be motivated by the same kind of greed as colonial Europeans?" Jason argued. "Right now, today, if we sent off a group of scientists in a rocket, they'd be perfectly capable, in principle, of establishing contact with another world and keeping the peace."

"But we don't put scientists in rockets," said Amanda. "We put army pilots in them. All I'm saying is that the more technologically advanced culture always wins the head-to-head meeting, and takes what it wants."

"Okay, sure," he replied.

"And therefore," she went on, "if we *should* ever detect intelligent life somewhere else in the universe, our best strategy is to shut the radio off and pray they don't find us."

"Are you serious?" said Jason.

Amanda shrugged. "We all learn our own lessons from history. Jason, this is the leap of faith I'm going to ask you to make: This UFO invasion we've been talking about is what quite literally happened to my people. We had the same exact . . . *fearlessness* your culture has today, the same unquestioned faith in our place at the top of the world. Losing that—that confidence—is devastating. You can't just assimilate, join the victory party, after that. There's a part of you that's just . . . gone."

Jason just nodded. He felt exhausted, and happily let the conversation fade to black as their car came around to broadside the east side of the island, where the Midtown Tunnel promised a return to the welcome anonymity of the city.

When they cleared the tunnel, Jason blandly offered to take a subway and save Amanda the trip to the Upper West Side, but she insisted on

driving him home. She looped patiently around the one-ways and ultimately pulled up right before his door on 79th. They engaged in a bit of
small talk at curbside, Jason with his door unlatched and slightly ajar,
Amanda turned toward him in the car, one leg curled appetizingly on the
seat.

"So what are you doing later?" she asked.

*For someone who claims to have no carnal interest in me whatsoever, she
sure hates letting me out of her sight,* thought Jason. "Are you asking me on
a date," he wondered pointedly, "or do you just want to root through old
city documents?"

"Come on," she said, smiling sweetly. "I'll go home and dump the car;
you can shower, do your résumé or whatever, and meet me out. I know a
great place."

"I'm not kidding, Amanda," said Jason, shaking his head. "If you want
to go out on a date, yes, I'd like that very much. I could use a big fat drink,
to be perfectly honest. But I'm not digging for buried treasure anymore.
I'm tired."

"What does that mean—'a real date'?"

There, see? he chided himself. *Had to actually slam your weenie in the
door, didn't you?* "Never mind," he said aloud, stepping out of the car.
"Good-bye, Amanda." Shutting the door firmly, Jason crossed the sidewalk, digging for his keys.

Not until he was actually pressing the key into the lock did she issue
her reply. "I'm not going to sleep with you."

Jason turned, slowly, to find her standing on the far side of the car, inside the swing of her open door, looking incredibly uncomfortable. A
maintenance man, walking by, chuckled conspiratorially and gave him
two thumbs up.

"*What?*" said Jason, squinting in confusion.

"If that's what you mean."

"Who asked you to sleep with me?"

Her face fell from brazen resolution to sudden embarrassment. "Well,
I . . . didn't know what you meant," she replied.

Withdrawing his door key, Jason slowly returned to the car. "Amanda,
I don't want to date-rape you," he assured her, shaking his head. "The guy

in me," he explained slowly, tapping his chest, "finds it really hard to accept that you only want me for my bloodline. No, let me finish. All I'm asking is for you to try to meet me halfway, okay?"

She met his gaze, nodding. "Okay. I just—"

"I just want to have drinks with you. Dinner . . . Broadway . . . anything. There's a lot of things to do in this town, I'm told. And then if you're repulsed, you can go home. But I'm holding my DNA hostage until you agree to my terms."

"All right," she said with a little laugh, looking away. "Don't be stupid."

✧ ✧ ✧

Two hours later, they sat across from each other in the middle of a long table, shoulder to shoulder with an audience of strangers at a tightly packed, two-drink-minimum theater club, one giddy friend-of-the-poet table away from the stage itself.

Onstage, a backlit woman in black leotard had improbably assumed a fetal position on a battered stool, head bowed slightly, as if entranced by the mike stand before her.

"You sure about this? These things creep me out," whispered Jason across the table, a little too loud.

"Sshh," urged Amanda. "You want another drink?" She raised an index finger, turned a little circle in the air that brought a waitress over.

"It takes a tough man to make a tender chicken," the poet began without warning, her voice clear and sonorous, stabbing like a searchlight into the darkened room. "Ram tough . . . like a rock. I feel like chicken tonight."

Jason tried to examine the slick program in the dim light—"Elissa Waterston Presents: An Evening of Found Poetry."

Christ, he thought, looking to Amanda for support, but her eyes were turned toward the performer.

"Can you keep a secret?" Waterston wanted to know. "I like the sprite in you. The eye-opener, the original party animal. Made from the best stuff on earth."

✧ ✧ ✧

He sipped his Rolling Rock and wondered if Amanda had chosen this particular show specifically to mock his so-called career. She was shaping up in some ways to be a pretty cool chick, pain in the ass though she was.

As if sensing the attention, Amanda turned. "You surviving okay?" she whispered huskily.

Jason cupped his mouth and enunciated carefully. "I'm still smarting from the ass-kicking your mother gave me."

Amanda grinned at this. "Sorry about that," she replied, wincing sympathetically.

Jason shook his head. "Did you hear her, at the end? 'Who are you? You're nobody.' I mean, no offense, but what the hell's *that* supposed to mean?"

"I know," whispered Amanda, nodding.

"Jesus Christ," hissed Jason with a snort. "That shit hurts."

"If it helps," offered Amanda quietly, "I don't think she meant it in any profound way. I think she was just saying she formally doesn't recognize you as the owner of the deed, as the Haansvoort heir. But you never know; she's forever trying to shape people, and she usually finds the sharpest tool for the job."

"Well, please ask her to restrict herself to a light buffing and sanding," whispered Jason.

She grinned. "Let me work on her."

Beyond them, the poet's opus was reaching fever pitch, and succeeded in recapturing their attention. "I love what you do for me," the poet promised. "It's a honey of an O. It's not small . . . no, no, no. It keeps going and going and going . . ."

"I've got an idea," said Jason drunkenly, too loud.

"Sssh!" said Amanda, still looking onstage. Then she turned. "What?" she wondered, warily.

"Let's go find my family graveyard. I know right where it is . . . where it's supposed to be, anyway."

"Really?" she said, eyes bright.

He beamed boyishly. "Jesus, you're like a ten-year-old. Yes, of course really. I'm hooked. Let's take this thing as far as we can."

"Why ask why?" said Elissa, with heart-wrenching sincerity. "Don't be a paleface, the capitalist tool, totally nuts about payday. It just doesn't ring true. Silly rabbit!"

✧ ✧ ✧

The air outside, after the show, was cold and sudden, a slap in the face.

"Cabinet?" wondered Amanda, bundled in a scarf and a light coat.

Jason looked at her strangely. "What?"

"Are . . . you . . . cabinet?" she asked slowly, bouncing on her toes for emphasis and staggering slightly.

He laughed. "I have no idea what you're talking about, you drunk."

"Are you . . . taking . . . a . . . taxi . . . you . . . stupid . . . idiot," she elaborated.

They shared a cab all the way up the east side, to gallantly drop Amanda off first, and Jason busied himself cracking her up in the back of the cab.

"Same time tomorrow?" she said as they pulled up.

"High noon," he amended.

"Thanks again for coming out with me," she said, smiling indulgently. "Sorry about Mom. Just give me a week or so to work on her."

"Yesterday, you said all I had to do was meet her and then you'd let me go," Jason said drunkenly.

"Yeah, but then you fucked it up," she replied.

"Indian giver."

"Come on," said the cabbie. "In or out?"

With a sneer toward the cabdriver, Amanda suddenly lurched toward Jason with alarming speed, pivot hand burying itself in the cracked seat leather as she planted a big, wet kiss on his mouth. Taken by surprise, Jason missed whatever window of opportunity was there and tried vainly to catch her retreating arm. Their fingers locked briefly as hand slid past hand, but she expertly scooted her tail out of the cab, slammed the door, and was gone.

As the cabdriver peeled out, Jason tried to hold on to the kiss, to paint it warm and wet on his memory. But the impression was already slipping away; a transient taste of candied lipstick died on his tongue as the cab roared into a darkened Central Park, heading for home.

There's plenty more where that *came from,* he reassured himself.

"I'm getting off right up ahead," he said aloud when they neared his place.

"Good for you," said the cabbie.

Chapter Four

The dawn unfurled patiently across the eastern sky, casually dissolving a fleecy field of cloudlets. By the time the sun itself deigned to rise, reflected whole in a million devout faces of glass, it was clear there would be no rain today. No fires or earthquakes, either, no water-main breaks flooding the subways, no mad bombers abandoning ticking U-Hauls in the tunnels, no gutless, wavering would-be jumpers tying up traffic. It was the unofficial first day of spring, and it was picture-perfect. Better still, against all odds, it was a Sunday.

Early risers returned home to shuck long pants and laptops, to fill water bottles and dig out classic reggae tapes and shake roommates awake. By eleven o'clock, virtually all of the city's eight million denizens, instincts honed for the rare public freebie, had poured blinking out of their cubbyholes to soak in the moment.

Already Central Park was awash in dogs and Frisbees, steadily pixillating with color as sunbathers and picnickers staked out square footage. On the Park Avenue side, shaky-limbed doyennes emerged from park-view high-rises in embarrassing sundresses. At Strawberry Fields, the arborial shrine to John Lennon beneath Yoko's Dakota digs, yet another incarnation of the eternal amateur guitarist worked out his "Julia" for a patient crowd. At the bandshell, corporate Rollerbladers bought unexpectedly excellent pot from slack-jawed skate punks and had to sit down under the trees to steady the earth.

Almost reluctantly, Jason stepped off the warm Broadway sidewalk and into the cool, dark cave of Amazonia, a yet-undiscovered Upper West Side brunchery. True to its Zagat's review, Amazonia was a sunken greenhouse thick with thousands of live trees, vines, and plants that had seemingly taken root on every horizontal surface, caressed here and there by gentle billows of steam. The rain-forest walls had the secondary effect of crowding the circular tables tightly into the center of the room, like soap bubbles, requiring waiters and waitresses to scuttle sideways between seat backs. *A little clear-cutting might not be out of place here*, Jason mused as he scanned the room, quickly spotting Becky, then Nick, at a small booth by the door to the kitchen.

"Welcome to the jungle," said Nick as he approached. "We've got fun and games." He was unshaven and a bit haggard, two-hundred-dollar sunglasses notwithstanding. Jason ignored him in favor of a small cheek kiss from Becky.

"What's up, dolly?" he asked, sliding into the seat next to her. Becky, too, looked pale and drained under the lid of a fading MTV baseball cap. When she craned her head to crack the vertebrae of her neck, the limp ponytail that leaked out of the back of the cap lagged behind, as if too exhausted to obey the laws of physics.

"You guys are a wreck." Jason smiled approvingly. "I take it the others are dead or disabled?"

Nick shrugged. "Well," he began slowly, looking at Becky for support, "I think it's safe to say Paul's lying in a pool of his own sick."

"*Stop* it," said Becky gravely. "We ordered you hash and eggs, Jason."

"*Regurgio, ergo sum,*" Nick continued, and resumed construction of a wobbly cheerleaders' pyramid of nondairy creamers. "Paul's an ectomorph, you know," he noted clinically. "His body's not built for stress tests."

"How's J.D.?" Jason wondered.

"Alive and well," Becky replied. "He's entertaining out-of-towners."

"Ouch," said Jason. "Empire State Building?"

Becky smiled, but shook her head. "No, no, it's a couple of friends from high school. You know J.D.—they're probably on the bar crawl already."

Jason laughed. "Yeah, how *does* he do that? He's like an Australian or something."

"You should have seen him last night," said Nick. "He was in top form. He climbed the pole at Hogs and Heifers and put on one of the bras from the ceiling without falling off."

"That's *right!*" Becky squealed, erupting in sudden laughter. "I totally forgot that!"

Egged on by Jason's appreciative grin, Nick launched into a florid tale of the previous day's shenanigans: a twelve-hour Saturday romp that started with curly fries and cheap Rolling Rock pitchers at lunchtime and ended with being thrown out of the Dublin House at three o'clock A.M. Through no small rhetorical effort, the woolly tale seemed perpetually on the verge of mounting to an adventure of epic scope, but ultimately devolved into a series of entertaining, but disconnected, anecdotes: the fight with a bouncer narrowly averted, the dull party heroically escaped, and so on. At some point, Nick and J.D. were taking turns bodily throwing each other into the metal overhead doors that roll down and shield the picture windows of Manhattan stores at night.

"Sorry I missed it," said Jason, and meant it.

"Where were you?" said Becky. "We tried to call."

"Were you with that girl all day long?" said Nick, and Jason nodded. "Did you make ficky-fick?"

Jason responded with a bland look.

"Don't be all civilized on my account," interjected Becky. "Go on, say whatever you want."

Jason nodded. "Well, it was—"

"What kinda titties she got?" Becky interrupted in a gruff, ersatz trucker voice. Nick flashed her a grin.

Jason patiently described the abortive meeting with Amanda's mother, and some of the mini-date after, omitting the good-night kiss as low-end schlock. Somewhere in the middle, the waitress returned with a pitcher of bloodies and platefuls of high-end grub, garnished with suspicious-looking edible flowers. As they ate, Becky was appropriately sympathetic to his trials; Nick was amused, and cracked bon mots that Jason wasn't punchy enough to appreciate, but which tickled the hell out of Becky.

"What a *nightmare*," she exclaimed, shaking her head and painting grape jelly on a triangle of toast. "She blindsided you."

"I've never felt like such an ugly American," said Jason.

"And *she's* the American," Nick reminded him through a mouthful of Brazilian waffle. "That's the kicker."

"Whatever."

"*You're* just ugly."

"I'm actually about this close from packing it in with this chick," said Jason, pinching an invisible grape between thumb and forefinger.

"Oh, you are not," said Becky. "You're practically dating."

Jason smiled. "All right, I'm seeing her again today."

"So you're just blowing through all the warning signs," Nick accused. "Even though you got a glimpse of the mother, the woman she's genetically determined to become—"

"Oh, just stop," Becky reprimanded Nick. "What a frat boy we are today."

Her antagonist smiled broadly, making her point, but she turned back to Jason. "So where are you going?" she wondered.

"A graveyard," Jason replied.

Nick leered at this. "Casanova."

WEST SIDE HIGHWAY, 12:35 P.M.

Amanda's brown bomber tore fearlessly up the West Side Highway, skirting a breathtaking view of the verdant cliffs of the Palisades, across the Hudson. In the northern distance, a misty George Washington Bridge bounded the horizon. Closer at hand, Amanda's tan was contrasting fiendishly with a white sleeveless shirt and red denim shorts; a heavy silver amulet puckered the valley between her twin peaks.

"It's a hell of a view," said Jason from the passenger's seat.

Amanda, unsuspecting, was inexpressibly cool behind opaque sunglasses, wearing a bluesman's smile that shifted constantly, infinitesimally, as if testing its ability to express nuances of emotion.

"You're just loving this day, aren't you?" he guessed.

She grinned broadly. "I am a complete and utter slave to the weather," she confided, tweaking the rearview. She turned to look him over, and her loosely bound hair, caught in the crosswind between the open windows, danced like fire around her head. "You look *much* better today," she decided, and he smiled in response, holding a hand out the open window to cup the breeze.

"So you've never been here, right?" said Amanda.

"Nope," he replied, pointing his flattened hand into the wind, then changing the angle until his palm caught the breeze and jerked backward. "It may not even exist, frankly. We could be chasing an old grandmother's delirium. But she's still pretty sharp."

Amanda nodded. "So then where are your parents buried?"

"They're not," he replied, surprised by the frankness. "They were cremated."

She nodded again, sagely, unaware or unconcerned about overstepping a boundary. "Tell me about them," she urged casually, without looking.

Jason closed his eyes and drew his hand in from the window to rub his forehead, embarrassed by the thrill of anxiety running through him. He hated talking about his parents, had never found a way to do it without reimagining the accident. It was a major roadblock, one which his friends seemed to understand through common, unspoken accord. But admitting his reluctance, now as always, seemed worse than facing it.

"What do you want to know?" he replied softly, in a manner he hoped would sound offhand.

✧ ✧ ✧

Jason's parents had lived a love story far too saccharine for Disney. His father, a stringy eighteen-year-old, worked part-time at a fruit stand in Goleta, California; his mother, also eighteen, was slogging her way through the local community college, and traipsed by the front of his shop every day with her girlfriends, driving the poor guy berserk with her giggling, her apple eating, her book carrying, and so forth. In Jason's mind, the boy stood tall in overalls and a Marlon Brando guinea tee, blond hair slicked back away from slate-gray eyes. When the girls hove into view, he'd hose down the sidewalk in front of the store with redoubled intensity, as if the menial task were a matter of national security, trying vainly to ignore the fruit flies that sabotaged his gravitas by buzzing playfully about his ears.

One day the girl walked by unescorted, and the naked opportunity so discombobulated him that he lost control of his motor functions. Eye contact with the girl had always been minimal; this time, though, he found himself unable to stop staring, garden hose held limply across one hand, water pressure backed up painfully against the nozzle in his other. And then, right as she passed him, he surprised himself by pulling the trigger, and caught her broadside with a blast of water so powerful it literally blew all the books out of her hand. She gave a little yelp and he dropped the hose, terrified. But she said nothing, only stared at him curiously as she picked up her books and ran off, flats splatting through the puddles. He lay awake all night and agonized, quite sure he'd never see her again. But there she was, the very next day, walking by with her now-smiling, blushing friends, and this time she was wearing a full-length raincoat.

They married and had exactly one child; whether they had ever attempted more was a secret that died with them. People weren't supposed to have kids in the mid-seventies, when the world was widely believed to be going to hell. They bandaged his knees and went to his ball games, stayed up with him not just for cough and croup but for test anxiety and teen heartache as well, all the exaggerated agonies of the only child.

They stayed alive just long enough to see him through college, and, the experiment concluded, abruptly left the planet. He'd gotten the call at work.

◇ ◇ ◇

"How well did you guys get along?" Amanda was wondering.

"Pretty well," Jason replied mechanically, bit by bit dragging himself back to her world. "Real well, actually. I supposedly have his eyes and her nose. I know I have his work ethic, his attention to detail. His manners, maybe. He used to pull some wacky shit, but he was charming enough to get away with it. I got a little of that from him, I hope. What else? He was a pretty conservative guy; he wanted to be more liberal than he really was. He always tried to be fair, but I think deep down he preferred order to justice."

"Mmm," she nodded. "And Mom?"

"Well . . . I have her sense of humor," Jason continued. "Mom was one of those late-sixties bedroom feminists. She did the dishes and the laundry, and brought Dad a beer whenever he snapped his fingers. But she always knew how to get exactly what she wanted. I mean, from day one, he completely worshiped her."

"That's sweet," said Amanda softly.

"They were really fantastic, you know." He paused, remembering. "So much in love."

"You're lucky," she said simply.

He put his hand out the window again, felt the breeze ripple across the fine hairs. "I really had no idea just how abnormal it was," he replied dreamily, snaking his hand in and out of the slipstream.

They crossed the Hudson just after one, beetling around the lazy curves of the mighty Tappan Zee, where a blustery crosswind compelled them to close the windows. Amanda was by now enjoying herself immensely. She seemed enormously energized, and kept drawing his attention to this or that roadside attraction in a hyperactive, touristy way. Encouraged and well-rested, Jason swung into full courtship mode, doing his best to crack her up at every turn and succeeding more often than not. If he was being uncomfortably aggressive, she didn't let on.

On the far side of the bridge, they found a town with a tree-lined main street and an agreeably quaint diner and stopped for lunch. Jason performed his smooth urbanity for the parochial waitress, who frowned in confusion at all the right spots. The Hallmark moment came when his "burger with the works" arrived looking suspiciously thin, and he lifted the top bun to reveal a single, pitiful, quarter-size disk of onion.

"I'd better not eat that," he deadpanned. "I might get *a* bad breath." It was a throwaway line, but it tickled the hell out of Amanda, for whatever reason, and she smiled a broad, sly, indescribably intimate smile that kicked the rest of the world out of focus. Basking, Jason caught a knowing look from the old cashier, then a waitress, and it occurred to him suddenly that everyone in the place was rooting for him. He returned a few smiles, nodding in a neighborly way, as if to say: *Don't look at me—I don't know what's going on here any better than you.*

✧ ✧ ✧

"Left of that barn," said Amanda, pointing ahead, through the windshield. "See it?"

"Nope."

"Up on top of the hill?"

"Got it," said Jason. "But your pal at the Amoco said the *third* right."

"But it's *there*," she countered, tapping the glass in the direction of a scattered Stonehenge of gray markers atop a modest little hill, girded by a rambling wrought-iron fence. "How many hilltop graveyards you think there are in this one-horse town?"

With his nod of assent, she nosed the car onto the hardscrabble unpaved road that climbed toward the cemetery gates. Deep, rocky ruts slowed their progress to a frustrating crawl; as they slowly crested the summit, the cemetery gradually revealed itself to be much larger than it had appeared from the valley below, a great circle comprising perhaps two acres of tombstones ringed around a squat brick cottage at the yard's center. Outside the black iron fence that encircled the whole, a handful of actual sheep, startling in their nonchalance, munched peacefully. The road, such as it was, continued right on through the massive gates standing open before them, but Amanda pulled off just outside the fence and shut the engine down.

Jason was suddenly conscious of a large and awesome rural silence, the wind in the grass, some scattered insects buzzing. He could practically hear the chewing of cud.

"Quiet as the grave," he murmured.

Amanda turned to face him. "So, you excited?" she asked, grinning, in a tone that would brook no disagreement. Infected, he returned the smile.

"Maybe."

She shrugged. "Stay in the car, then."

Jason rolled his eyes and unlatched his door, and Amanda needed no further encouragement.

✧ ✧ ✧

The weedy grass grew thick and high inside the spidery iron fence, beyond the reach of ovine maws, rippled with veins of blue and yellow wildflowers, a pretty pastoral picture framed by the impressively ornate gates.

Armed with her camera and his sketchpad, they stepped into the ring and looked around at the boneyard. Beginning ten or twelve feet inside the fence, stone grave markers in grays and browns filled the yard in roughly concentric rings that converged on the cottage at the yard's center, the circles broken only by the single spoke of the road, which led straight up to the cottage, at the absolute peak of the hill. The grass, shorn close in the spiraling six-foot lanes that separated rings of stones, had been left standing between individual graves in each ring, thriving on its unspeakable fertilizer.

The place was deserted, apart from a couple of cars and a single pair of visitors: an old man towing a little boy by one arm and squinting with ancient eyes at the weathered gravestones. The boy, forlorn or just restless, gripped a small novelty American flag by its wooden stick and followed the old man from grave to grave.

In respectfully hushed tones, Jason and Amanda agreed to start their search for Hansvoort graves at the road near the entrance, splitting up to cover parallel rows and gradually working their way side by side counterclockwise around the yard, behind the chapel, and back around to the entrance.

"This is awfully big," Jason noted in a whisper, taking the very outside row. "It's obviously not just Hansvoorts here. But any of these other names could be aunts or uncles."

"Doesn't matter," said Amanda absently, eyes fixed on the old man and the boy, only a few rows off. "The vertical bloodline's all we need, strictly speaking. Let's just look for Hansvoorts and see where that leads us. But if you see anything that strikes a chord with you, by all means jot it down. Might help us fill in the gaps later."

He eyed her ass appreciatively as she turned back to her work. It was just past three o'clock now, and the sun was hot on the back of his neck; as his eyes wandered across the ancient stones, drinking in the weathered record of their dead, he slowly began to relax and lose himself in the experience.

The stones were spaced far enough apart that even a normal strolling pace permitted a meticulous check of each. Jason read the brief histories, where they were legible, with growing interest, the minute chronicles of death and disease, of sundered relationships, of love and loss. Subtracting death dates from birth dates, he lingered, half consciously, whenever a life span was interestingly large or small. He became quite engrossed by the thumbnail dramas, and Amanda began to outdistance him in the tortoise race around the perimeter.

At one point, Jason found an entire row of graves whose occupants had shared a common demise: cholera. *What's* that *like?* he wondered, walking on. He imagined the scene hundreds of years in the future, when generations might gawk at graves bearing then-unfamiliar words like "AIDS" and "Ebola."

"Oh, *yes!*" yelped Amanda, twenty yards away.

Jason felt his heart leap into his throat; sidestepping between adjacent graves, he rushed to her side.

"'Jon Parker Hansvoort,'" Amanda was reading aloud, with positive glee, as he approached. "Born 1812, died 1856. Forty-four years old," she calculated. "One *a*."

"Ho-ly shit," Jason murmured slowly, unable to tear his eyes away from his ancestor's chiseled name. The stone was immense, a heavy white marble number with shallow inset letters darkened by some helpful species of mold. He felt a palpable shift in his mind as, suddenly, the game became undeniably *real*. A car's engine banged into life behind them, and he turned, startled, to see the old man and the child in a battered station wagon, slowly backing out of the yard.

"Jason, meet your ancestor," said Amanda, removing the lens cap from the camera and dropping to one knee.

✧ ✧ ✧

Their search was more fruitful than they'd dared to hope. Before long they were coming across a Hansvoort grave every few minutes or so, and, already conscious of the declining sun, paused just long enough to take photos and jot down the pertinent information. None of the names sounded familiar to Jason, but he welcomed them all, trying, on the fly, to stretch the scant information available into a working mental picture of each, as if doing so might breathe some measure of life back into them.

As they slowly wound their way around the circle, Jason marveled at the remarkable wrought-iron perimeter fence. Eight feet high, black and barbed and baroquely ornate, it locked death in with a fearsome mesh of spears and tulips, a testament to some long-dead ironsmith's otherworldly dedication. Back where they'd parked, the fence rose alone from the grass, but everywhere else it was choked solid from the outside by thick, weedy shrubbery trying to crowd into the yard. Jason mentally sped up geological time and watched the wave of green crash against the fence, which shuddered and held as the grass sprouted unchecked inside, and the gravestones turned bright green with moss, fell over, and sank into the earth.

At the back of the yard, where the hedge was higher than the iron bars and quite overwhelmed it, a large section of the perimeter fence bulged into the graveyard at ninety-degree angles, as if the sheer weight of the hedge had driven a square wedge right into the concentric circles of stones, forcing new walking strategies. It was in one of the inside corners thus formed that Jason found Amanda, after her overjoyed "Bingo!" brought him running.

She knelt happily in the dirt before the last grave in a row, just two feet from the fence, pointing at the name. "'Mary Elizabeth Ha-a-ansvoort,'" she read aloud, elongating the long-awaited double *a* with a satisfied air as Jason crouched by her side. "First of the old guard."

"Amazing," said Jason, shaking his head. "I'm completely fucking blown away."

"Right?" said Amanda, smiling. "Stick with me, kid. I'm going to make you a bazillionaire."

Composed of a reddish stone they hadn't encountered before, Mary's marker tipped forward slightly, and read:

MARY ELIZABETH HAANSVOORT
1720–1734
CHYLDE IS TAKEN TOO SOON FROM US
BUT THE STAR OF HER LYFE LIVES ON
"WHEN PRIDE COMES, THEN COMES DISGRACE
BUT WITH HUMILITY COMES WISDOM"

"Seventeen-twenty," Jason marveled, grinning from ear to ear and thinking giddily that, come what may, this was already one of the most interesting forks his life had ever taken.

"Fourteen years old," Amanda noted quietly. "Poor kid. Doesn't say how she died."

"Could have been just about anything," mused Jason. "Did you catch all that cholera back there?"

"Let's hope not," she quipped.

As Jason glanced around at nearby stones, hoping to luck into another big find, Amanda began clearing away the beard of grass at the base of the stone, revealing the bottom half of a decorative pattern the growth had covered up. It seemed a small, inscrutable act of devotion.

"*Here* we go," she said excitedly, and began feverishly tearing out clumps of the grass. Jason frowned, not understanding . . . then caught a glimpse of lettering and realized what she was up to. He knelt by her side to help, and in less than a minute, they'd unveiled a small motto at the base of the stone that read:

WHAT PROVIDENCE HATH GRANTED
LET CHARITY NEVER FORGET

"Cool," said Jason, scribbling down the words. "Remind me to leave a dollar in the collection plate."

"You can build her a damn cathedral, if we find that deed," replied Amanda.

Elated, they dusted themselves off and continued their search, following the perimeter fence, which here struck back sharply toward the center of the graveyard. Hopes of finding similar stones nearby faded quickly, and

Jason had walked almost twenty yards, squinting into the sun, already starting to decline over the chapel, before he realized that Amanda was no longer next to him. Turning, he found her walking back toward Mary Elizabeth's grave again, running her hands along the fence and peering into the thick wall of undergrowth that pressed up against it.

"What is it?" Jason called out, but she ignored him. He began walking toward her, frowning.

"The fence . . . ," she said enigmatically as he approached, without turning to face him. "It's . . . different."

"Yeah, it kind of angles in here," he said, not comprehending. "I noticed that. We—"

"No, it's a different *fence*," she clarified, pointing. "Look."

Still black and flaking with rust, and nearly obscured by the dark wall of vines and brush squeezing through from the other side, the fence here, it was obvious on a closer look, was of a much more basic, unadorned design than the one they'd been following.

"Hey, you're right," he said, running a cautious thumb along a whorl of flaking iron. "Interesting."

Her smile broadened. "No, think about it. They wouldn't just change the style of fence in the middle of the run. This," she explained, pointing into the hedge, "isn't the perimeter anymore. Look—the fence angles straight in here, then takes a right and continues for a while, then cuts back to the outside. Right?"

Jason nodded, starting to comprehend.

"I'll bet you anything," she continued, "if you walk around the outside of this graveyard, you'll see a smooth, unbroken circle. There's a *space* in there, Jason."

He was nodding. "So what do you think it—"

"I *know* what it is," she interrupted. "It's another graveyard."

◇ ◇ ◇

A quick tour seemed to buttress Amanda's theory. The simpler design continued for all three legs of the square that protruded into the graveyard, reverting to the older style when it rejoined the "normal" circle of the perimeter, after describing an area of perhaps a half acre. But they never came across an obvious entrance, and the wall of brush was too thick at all points for a visual confirmation that there was, indeed, another section of graveyard within.

"Maybe you access it from the exterior," said Jason.

"One way to find out," said Amanda, striking off immediately for the brick cottage that now stood directly between themselves and the graveyard's entrance.

He glanced over his notes as they walked, beginning to realize the enormity of attempting to tie all the names together into a neat tree. Relationships between the deceased were almost never stated on the stones. In most cases, all they'd have to go on were birth and death dates, enough to sort people into rough generations, but not to establish lines of paternity. This was going to be like trying to reassemble a living tree from a pile of firewood.

"Listen," Amanda whispered, laying a hand on his arm, but he'd already heard it, the muted sound of a radio. Turning in the direction of the source, they spied, a hundred feet away or so, a small mound of freshly dug earth keeping watch over an open grave. He looked at Amanda, who shrugged, and together they silently walked toward the sound.

"Is that Korn?" Amanda whispered.

✧ ✧ ✧

Six feet under, a teenage local yokel sat against one wall of the new grave, paperback novel spread open on his lap, the headset of a Sony Discman plugged into his ears. The kid's face was knotted into a menacing frown, and his head rocked back and forth as his lips angrily mouthed the words. A grimy hand turned the page of the book. White-boy dreadlocks oozed out beneath a green John Deere baseball cap; a tattoo on his right arm read simply, "Cop Killer."

Jason and Amanda, peering down into the open grave, were almost overcome with mirth. "This guy's probably the mayor," whispered Jason, plucking the shovel from the pile outside the grave. "Let's bury him."

"Don't!" hissed Amanda, laughing.

Jason replaced the shovel with a mock-penitent look and stooped down. Slowly, he reached into the grave with one hand and waved his fingers, hoping to get the kid's attention without startling him.

The kid simply looked up and pulled the headphones off casually. "Yo," he said neutrally, pressing the stop button on the tape.

"Howdy," said Jason. "You work here?"

The kid nodded.

"We were wondering," said Amanda, "if you could tell us how to get into the old graveyard in the middle, there."

The kid cocked one eyebrow and considered this for a moment. "Whoa," he said. "That's a new one. Sure thing."

Whistling, the kid led them to a shed, about the size of a small garage, which buttressed one side of the cottage. Inside, the sunlight filtered through a thin, corrugated Fiberglas ceiling, giving everything a hot, but not unpleasant, yellow-green glow. The space was cluttered with mowing and weeding equipment, shelves bursting with soils and fertilizers and hand tools, and a solid-looking white pine workbench, where a dusty vise eternally held an ax handle between its jaws. On the pegboard behind hung dozens of lawn-care implements and various other knickknacks—including, disconcertingly, a human skull.

"It's not real," said the kid with a cough, following Jason's eyes. "I mean, it's *real*," he corrected, elongating the word and opening his hands as if holding the object in question. "But it's not . . . a *bone*. You know?"

Amanda suppressed a giggle, and the kid smiled at her in a shyly flirtatious kind of way. "Well, anyway, it's in here somewheres," he said, hiking up his overloose jeans and fishing around in a junk drawer at the bench.

Five minutes later they were following the kid back toward the mysterious old fence, where he began pulling aside vines with agonizing lassitude. A few false starts later, he unveiled a well-camouflaged gate bound by a single Master padlock. Into this he pressed a tiny brass key, and Jason held his breath.

The effort was painful to watch; tendons on the kid's skinny arms stood out like cables as he tried in vain to twist the key in the lock. Minute after minute dripped slowly by.

"Here, can I try?" said Jason desperately. After first glancing around as if unsure he wasn't breaking some law, the teen yielded the key with a shrug, and Jason wiggled it around in the lock. On the third turn, something clicked.

"Cool," pronounced the kid.

With a satisfying creak, and a little more vine-yanking, the door was freed, and swung inward a foot or so into the hedge, just enough to squeeze through.

"Cool," the kid reiterated. "You can just drop the key back on the bench when you're done."

But they were already inside.

✧ ✧ ✧

Contrary to all expectations of cobwebby decay, the hidden yard beyond the hedgerow was literally teeming with life. The eight-foot hedges that had blocked their view from the outside rose up on all sides like the walls of an enormous vault, enclosing a buzzing, chirping world. The wild grass was easily knee high, and all kinds of bushes, vines, and even trees broke through the surface to rise even higher. Birds and butterflies flitted easily around the chamber; as Jason stared openmouthed, a flotilla of enormous bumblebees chugged improbably through the air before him, bloated little lords trotting around through the rarefied air of their private sanctum.

"Whoa," said Jason, spellbound. He glanced sideways to see Amanda positively transfixed with wonder.

"It's a secret garden," she said breathlessly.

"Well, of *dead bodies*," he reminded her, and regretted it instantly when she scowled in reply and bent to start examining stones.

It was easy to sneer at her childlike credulousness, but Jason had to admit he'd never have discovered this inner space without her. Apart from his grandmother, who'd probably never even leave her hometown again, he was perhaps the last person on earth for whom this place held any meaning, and he would have walked right by it if not for Amanda's wishful thinking. Did she discover this graveyard, or did she in some sense create it? Was she actually able to make a more interesting world for herself through sheer force of will?

"Another old-timer!" she said excitedly, just a few feet away.

They ultimately found so many Haansvoort stones in the inner yard that they decided to record all the names, on the principle that since this was obviously a private graveyard, every stone was likely to have some connection that might prove useful.

"Do you think anybody knows they've got graves from the mid-1600s in here?" said Jason, when they were closing in on the last few spots. "This ought to be on the National Register of Historic Places, or something."

"Well, here's my question," said Amanda. "How come the other Haansvoort grave isn't in here, too?"

"That's easy," said Jason. "They ran out of room. This place is packed."

"But some of these graves are from the 1800s," Amanda replied. "Remember that one we just found on the outside, Mary Elizabeth . . . 1720 or so? How come she didn't make the cut while there was still space?"

Jason shrugged. "Maybe the fence went up later."

"I thought of that," confessed Amanda, looking around as if trying to get her bearings. "But look." She high-stepped through the grass to one side of the hedge wall and squatted down between a gravestone and the hedge itself, peeling back some twisted boughs to peer through the fence. "Through there."

Jason followed her eye and saw, through the fence, Mary Elizabeth's grave, just two feet or so on the other side of the fence. "Yeah, it's right here," he acknowledged. "You're thinking if the fence went up later, why would they leave her outside."

"Exactly," she said. "Curious . . ."

✧ ✧ ✧

Two hours later they returned triumphantly to the car, clutching her sketchpad and his film canisters, suffused with good fortune. All told, they'd photographed and cataloged nearly sixty Hansvoort grave markers—thirty-nine of them of the older variety with the abandoned double-*a* spelling.

"Shit," said Jason, frowning and examining the front of the camera.

"What's wrong?"

He shook his head, disgusted. "You never took the damn lens cap off."

"I've got half a mind to leave you here, funny boy."

The sunset was in full swing as their car descended the low hill and began retracing the winding country roads back to the highway, but Jason's mind couldn't rest in peace. It had taken him no small effort to shake the self-pity and redefine himself as a man with virtually no family, to accord himself a hero for making it on his own. Now, all too suddenly, generation after generation of hoary old ancestors crowded in on all sides, clutching at him from beyond the grave. He was a son again, and a grandson, and so on . . . his dead were *grounding* him, somehow, against his will.

Amanda was a raging crackhead of restless energy, and he tried not to let this sober line of thought kill the joy of the moment. Nevertheless, when she enthused about what a chunk they'd taken out of the task, he reminded her of all they had left to do: The earliest Haansvoort birthdate they'd found was something like 1660, and they only ran to the mid-1800s, leaving daunting gaps on both ends. And there was still the matter of finding the deed itself, which they were of course no closer to than before.

"I'm not being pessimistic," he said in self-defense, "just trying to be practical."

"See?" she said, amused. "Progress."

✧ ✧ ✧

"Well, I guess I'll head up, then," he announced as she pulled alongside his apartment, and Amanda nodded in profile, looking sexy as hell with her eyes flashing in the dark and a conversational smile still lingering on her glossy lips.

Without pausing to think, Jason arched his body across the seat and engaged her in a masterful kiss. He caught her right in the sweet spot, that warm, taut triangle right in the corner of the mouth, and the effect was electric, a perfect mesh, warm and soft, and ever so slightly pneumatic, and he knew by the way she kissed him back that she had been falling for him after all, that his charm had not failed him. Which meant there was something else, some barrier to be addressed later . . . but no matter, not yet. There was no sound or motion to disturb the moment, just the perfect heat of her flesh on his face. And then they separated, opening eyes and wordlessly untangling fingers that had somehow gotten entwined.

"O-kay . . . gotta go," said Amanda too quickly.

"Let's hang out."

She frowned. "I would definitely like to. Unfortunately . . . oh, man . . . tonight I have a, kind of a prior commitment."

Jason nodded and waited politely, but the confession was over. "Okay, well . . . ," he began with forced awkwardness, "call me at work tomorrow," he suggested. "Want me to get that film developed? There's a place right by my—"

"No, I can—" she began quickly, then stopped and blushed when she saw his smile. "You know I'd only have to call you every ten minutes to see if you'd done it yet."

"Yes, I know."

He lingered on the walk after her car had pulled out of sight, watching her go, tracking the car as far as he could.

CARROLL GARDENS, BROOKLYN, 10:30 P.M.

"If the guy you're dealing with is not the owner of the land, then you're talking to the wrong guy—it's that simple," said Dovatelli.

But Freddie shook his head. "It ain't like that, Ron. I'm telling you, this guy's the chief, and they have a perpetual lease on the property. Yes, they gotta kick back part of the profits to the Lenapes, but it all comes out of their half of the sandwich." He plowed another impossible forkful of ziti into his maw.

A broad smile settled across Dovatelli's face, and he took a sip of the wine. "Well, maybe you got something after all," he said. "Pass me that bread."

The four of them—Dovatelli, Freddie, Vinnie, and Gina—sat around a small table at Leone's, a dimly lit, white-linen Sicilian restaurant on Court Street. Dovatelli's darling daughter was pretending to pay attention, but couldn't keep her eyes off the next table over, swarming with a pack of noisy kids making a hell of a mess. Vinnie was just eating, not that it ever put any weight on him.

A grandkid or two would be a kick, Dovatelli thought, looking at Vinnie and wondering if the little bookworm had it in him.

"Details," he said, motioning for Freddie to go on.

Freddie shrugged his big shoulders, poured the last of his Peroni into the glass. "I took Carmen and little Frank out to the reservation and we went over the numbers. It's gonna happen."

"You sign him?"

"Not yet," said Freddie. "There's one small holdup—the guy's wife is balking. And there's a couple of percentages to work out here and there . . . usual shit. We're meeting with a few of the—"

"His *wife?* Gimme a break with that shit," Dovatelli interrupted. He watched Gina smile at a little boy making a goofy face at her from the other table. "Fuck's his wife got to do with it?"

"Nothing to worry about," assured Freddie. "Just a minor pussy-control issue. Sorry," he added insincerely, nodding to Gina.

"Maybe we should talk to one of the other tribes out there," Vinnie piped up. "Sort of a backup in case this falls through."

Freddie shot him a malicious stare. "Enough from you."

"All right, shut up," said Dovatelli, peeved. "Freddie, please explain why the wife is a problem."

"She's not."

"You brought it up."

Freddie wagged a half meatball on a fork back and forth. "Well . . . this Indian likes his booze. Two hours in the bar and he started spilling some shit. She don't want the casino. He says she's got some kind of . . . well, some kind of treasure map."

Dovatelli snorted. "Get the fuck out of here."

"I'm just telling you what he said," Freddie replied defensively. "She's got some old map that leads to a fuck of a lot of money."

"So she's like a lady pirate," ventured Vinnie mirthfully, trying to catch the wave of his father-in-law's skepticism.

"You disrespecting me, you little shit?" said Freddie.

"That's *enough*," Dovatelli barked. "Freddie," the old man continued, "skip the bullshit. What does this guy want to close the deal?"

"He don't want nothing," said Freddie. "Like I said, the casino's not a problem. I think she gets a vote or something . . . might have to find a way to lean on her. Maybe she's afraid we'll dig it up if we build there. I know it sounds crazy, but this guy's awfully damn sure they're sitting on a *shitload* of buried treasure."

Or just a shit load, thought Dovatelli, glancing over at Vinnie, in an all-too familiar pout. Christ. He'd give half his money to see his spineless son-in-law haul off and clock his tormentor just once. Freddie would kill him, of course, which would hurt his daughter in the short run, but might not be such a bad thing over the long haul.

"All right, whatever," he said dismissively. "Are you telling me you wanna strong-arm this guy's squaw?"

Freddie drank his beer slowly, pacing himself. "I'm just telling you what I heard," he replied. "Maybe there's nothing there . . . maybe something. I'll smoke it out." *What I should have done*, he was thinking, *is shut my trap, get the map, kill the bitch myself, and cut all you stupid fucks out of the deal. How's your pasta?* He smiled for the table and sucked down the rest of his beer. *Still not a bad plan at all, when you think about it.*

It seemed pretty clear to Freddie which way the wind was blowing. Dovatelli had one foot out the door already, and the clock was ticking. *Sorry, old-timer*, he thought, gazing across the table at the once-formidable don crumbling into a dusty old man right before his eyes. *But if you think I put in the hours so I can kiss Vinnie's ass after you bug out, you're all in for one big motherfuckin' surprise.*

Chapter Five

Jason squeezed through the subway turnstiles just in time to miss the number 9 train. The steel doors slid shut, but the train hesitated at the platform, mired in some sort of mechanical uncertainty, and so he hustled to claim a spot within pouncing reach in case the doors relented and slid open again. He felt no need to rush. It was a Monday, and there was nothing waiting for him down in Midtown but the first day of Diana's sure-to-be-hellish new regime. But missing the train meant losing in the very first challenge of the day.

The transit gods, pleased with Jason's token sacrifice, spread the doors halfway open one final time. Not one to waste a boon, Jason wedged briefcase and ass into the gap and popped painlessly inside, and the train, satisfied, creaked into motion.

Forcing himself to don work clothes had been a real trial this morning. If he'd been ambivalent about his job before, today it filled him with nothing but dread. *I actually hate going to work, now*, he realized. *It's come to this.*

As the train rocketed through its dark tunnel, a peripheral awareness of something amiss came into focus, and he saw with some curiosity that several passengers were watching something at one end of the car. Trian-

gulating their gazes, he saw a bit of motion in a small pile of wretched refuse beneath one of the seats. He stepped a few feet closer to satisfy his curiosity.

A single plump, juicy green grape was rolling around between a candy
wrapper and a broken wedge of Styrofoam cup. As the train's acceleration
breached some last restraining coefficient of friction, the grape rolled up
and over the wrapper and took off on a jaunty, end-over-end race toward
the back of the car—free at last. Jason grinned at the heroic little struggle,
wondering how long it'd been amusing the passengers. Almost immediately, the train began to slow for the 72nd Street station, and the grape
was forced into wobbly retreat.

Why do people stay at jobs they hate? he wondered. It can't really be fear;
even in a crappy economy, there's always *something* out there for anyone
with half an education and a dash of Puritan work ethic. Maybe a hundred
years ago it made sense, when unemployment translated into actual
hunger. But now? How could anybody keep going back to the actuary office, knowing that a block or two away somebody was testing video games?
The doors whooshed closed, ushering in a moment of reverent silence.

"Come on, fella," said a dreadlocked passenger in a heavy Jamaican accent. "Ya con make it."

The train lurched into motion, and once more the grape, compelled by
physics, resumed its eccentric rush to freedom, hopping and rolling in an
eerily anthropomorphic way, picking up speed. Jason grinned as it passed
him; it was impossible to avoid imagining the grape as a conscious agent.
By now enough of a critical mass was watching to keep the train car spellbound; tennis shoes and Bruno Maglis stepped out of the way when the
grape's meandering brought it too close. Passing the midpoint of the train
for the first time, the grape wavered, between the doors, as the train settled into a constant speed.

"I think he's trying to get off," Jason suggested.

The deceleration at the 59th Street station had just begun when the
grape, launching into its longest return trip yet, improbably broadsided
one of the floor-to-ceiling support poles at the car's center, dispersing its
energy in a profitless spin a few feet away from the doors as the train
slowed to a stop. "Yes!" cheered someone at the end of the train.

"He's gonna make it!" said Jason, jubilant.

The doors slid open, and at the head of the surging crowd, a steel-jawed corporate type, folded-back newspaper in hand, swept grandly into the car, his left shoe squashing the grape like a grape into the floor of the train. Within moments, the tiny green pancake of flesh had been shredded by a stampede of other soles.

"It's a tough town, dey say," said the Jamaican.

"Oh, *fuck*," said Jason, leaping up and lunging, too late, for the closing doors.

MADISON AVENUE, 9:45 A.M.

"I'm not angry, Jason," said Diana icily, from behind her desk, not even trying to make it believable.

The receptionist had warned Jason that he was a wanted man, and the terse note on his computer—"Jason—see me immediately. Diana"—had confirmed it. He'd been prepared to be admonished for being tardy, but not with this goofy degree of gravity. He watched, horrified, as his new boss painstakingly applied a shocking-red nail polish, bristling her fingers with bright power, like a cat preening its claws.

"Um . . . good," he said noncommitally. *You see, there was this grape . . .* He shifted in the unforgivingly stiff chair.

Behind her desk, Diana was laboriously painting a dangling thumb, a gladiator's death sentence. Taking a long breath, she let it out in a clownishly serious sigh. "I'm not mad because you're late," she clarified. "I'm upset because you don't seem to *care* that you're late. This office starts work at nine-thirty, and you have to start respecting that."

"Diana," said Jason gently, hoping the thin veneer of respect cloaking his disdain would hold, "we're talking about fifteen minutes. I work at least nine or ten hours a day, sometimes on the weekends. What can you possibly be concerned about?"

"I am *concerned*," she said too loudly, "because if people straggle in at all hours of the morning, this office doesn't coalesce properly, and nothing gets done before noon."

As he watched her return her attention to painting her nails, it finally occurred to Jason that he was just being hazed—that this was all about confirming hierarchy. "Well, not everyone's a morning person," he suggested simply, sure it would be taken as a challenge.

"Why do creatives always try to get away with that one?" Diana said smoothly, patronizingly, focusing cross-eyed on the lacquer. "This is about personal discipline. You have it or you don't."

"I just don't think that—"

"You need to start getting in by nine-thirty," she interjected busily. "That's all."

"Fine," he replied, washing his hands of the argument. "Is there anything else?"

"No—that's it," she said with calm finality, and hit the intercom button with the heel of her hand, sparing the wet nails. "Marci," she called, "I'll take that coffee now."

Thus dismissed, Jason rose from the chair to go find some Maalox, shouting down the voices in his head urging him to quit, to torch that bridge just to watch the gory conflagration.

"Where's Janine today?" he asked blandly, not really caring about Diana's regular assistant, just blurting out conversation to relieve the pressure of holding his peace.

Diana didn't speak for a few moments, then looked up, annoyed. "Well, Janine's no longer with us," she said pointedly: a warning. "Goodbye, Jason."

His thoughts whirling, Jason forced his feet to march out of her office, pausing just outside her open doorway to get a look at the new girl, a hot little number in a soft-looking wool skirt and sweater combo, ladling sugar into a coffee mug. He pictured Janine outside somewhere, running through a breezy wheat field in a sundress, laughing and tossing fresh-picked flowers into the sky.

From behind, he heard a grumpy "Is there anything else, Jason?" and realized he was still darkening the beast's doorway. Marci glanced up at him with new-gal curiosity, but Jason's eyes were transfixed by the coffee in her hand—steaming and impenetrably dark, a black hole at the fixed center of his vision, slowly swirling, sucking in the light of the world.

Marci waited, confused—he was now officially blocking the door—and Jason breathed in deeply, inflating his chest with a feast of cool oxygen.

Slowly, he turned and stepped back into Diana's room. "Yeah, there is one more thing," he said.

"And what's that?" said Diana, not looking up.

"I'm going to start leaving at five-thirty."

Because he was watching her face intently, Jason caught the exact moment when his words took effect. "What?" she said, recovering quickly. "The *hell* you are." Her voice was naked with hostility.

"Listen," Jason replied, "if you're going to start requiring that I get in at nine-thirty, I'm leaving at five-thirty, too. We either go by the book or we don't—you can't have it both ways."

"Oh, no, no, no," she said in haughty disbelief. "We are *so* not having this discussion." She rose from her seat, absurdly outstretched fingers absently drying themselves through the air. "You work for me. If you don't like the rules, you are more than welcome to take your sorry butt to another firm."

But Jason was already gone. "Well, then," he replied, "I suppose this is the part where I invite you to pucker up and kiss my hairy ass," he said, savoring the words like individual bonbons. *My God*, he thought, watching real shock, and something like fear, spread across her face. *That felt every bit as good as I hoped it would.*

Diana was visibly shaken. "You absolutely *cannot* talk to me like that!"

"Oh, but I *can*," he replied. "I quit, Diana. And I'm quite sure I won't be the last." Adrenaline had turned his arteries into fire hoses.

Diana made a very visible attempt to recover her vanished dignity, one that began by closing her mouth. "Very mature, Jason. Very professional."

"Well, you know us flighty creative types."

"Just get out," she said calmly, suddenly the voice of the company. "We'll mail you your last check, prorated to"—here she checked her watch—"nine-fifty today."

"I have a bit of career advice for you," he continued, trying to prolong the moment.

"Marci, get security," she screeched.

Marci poked her head into the room, correctly read the firestorm in progress, and wheeled back out again, stammering, "I don't . . . uh, do you know the number?"

"*FIGURE IT OUT*," bellowed Diana.

Jason smiled. *No point in leaving any napalm in the chopper, right?* "Here's the career advice, Diana, so listen carefully."

"Get out!"

"You . . . are . . . a . . . secretary."

CENTRAL PARK, 10:35 A.M.

Two hours ago, I was an ad executive, thought Jason, languishing on a bench in the park, the tongue of his discarded tie flapping out of his shirt pocket, as if coughing for air. The realization aroused nothing but amusement, and he shook his head in surprise at his own lackadaisical reaction. He was unemployed and literally on a park bench, and while his considerable savings put him a long step from homelessness, his career was officially in shambles. But he searched his soul high and low for the panic that ought to be there, and found nothing but elation.

Why does quitting always feel so good? he mused. Is it just the brief taste of a life of permanent leisure? That was part of it, surely. Quitting temporarily lifts the curse of Cain, luring you with the prospect of no more toiling in the dust. For the moment, he felt as carefree as in his college days, though he knew remorse and responsibility would have to set in at some point, if only to keep hunger at bay.

Another reason quickly suggested itself: We love to leave a job for the same reason we like to be the one to break up a relationship. Nobody wants to get dumped. Quitting is a way of declaring superiority to a job, even a career, a shorthand way of saying: *I don't know what I am yet, but I am better than this.* If you were not committed wholly to an enterprise, you didn't have to take full responsibility for failing at it.

This postcollege freedom wasn't all it was cracked up to be. In fact, the responsibility of figuring out how to spend your own working life was almost too much to bear. Was there any avoiding becoming a washed-up old man? he wondered. How could you possibly do the same thing, whatever

it is, for fifty, sixty years and not grow to hate it—and hate yourself for doing it?

His eyes drifted to the passing joggers, bicyclists, and Razor scooterers,
but his mind was miles away, back at Princeton. With graduation looming, Jason had applied to ad companies on the idle suggestion of a voca-
tion counselor whose name he'd forgotten; he'd taken this job because it
was April and he'd wanted to sew up his first job quickly, so he could get
down to the business of enjoying the rapidly burning wick of his senior
year of college.

And then, the summer of disaster.

Jason looked at the beautiful, suddenly obsolete briefcase he'd set on
the bench next to him. Money, at least, wouldn't be a problem, if he decided to drift awhile. Being exactly twenty-one at the time of his parents'
demise, Jason had had no trouble accessing the funds they'd left him. In
the bank he had rent and fart-around money for a couple of years, and
that was ignoring the big account: six figures' worth of untouched pre-
mium from a double life insurance policy. He shuddered; he'd eat his own
frostbitten toes before he dipped into that particular nest egg.

An insane woman sauntered by, an old black hag with horrible teeth
and two different shoes, lugging a clear, torn trash bag from which a horrible cornucopia of cast-off items threatened to spill. She was shaking her
head and laughing, or crying, and he watched with great trepidation.

Jason was as hardened to Manhattan's permanent itinerants as the
next guy, with their wild-eyed babbling and the dried, cracked skin of
their heels and their acrid stink. But when he was alone, and an encounter loomed, the enormity of the great cosmic inequity sometimes
overwhelmed him. *What if there is a God, but it doesn't make any difference?*
Suddenly feeling very alone, he roused himself from his stupor and pulled
out his cell phone. Time to go public.

✧ ✧ ✧

"I'm proud of you," said Nick.

What does it say about our culture, Jason wondered, *when everyone's first
response on hearing that you've quit is to congratulate you?*

"Thanks, Pop," Jason replied. "You free for lunch?"

"Not a chance," said Nick. "The Pacific Rim's in a tailspin. But come out to Barleycorn's tonight. I'm taking a couple of clients—steak, scotch, and cee-gars. Come on, it'll be just like the eighties. We'll celebrate your good fortune."

"Maybe," replied Jason. "Are they good guys?"

"Complete and total assholes, both of 'em," said Nick. "No kidding; I guarantee you'll want to punch them in the mouth. But make it count, 'cuz it'll cost me about ten thousand bucks apiece."

"I don't think so, pal," said Jason. "That's in Brooklyn, right?"

"We're taking a car. Look, aren't you going to be eating in a lot of soup kitchens now? Take the free meal."

Jason smiled. "Well, that's a point."

"Scotch older than you, stinky cigars, crappy company, and steaks that melt in your mouth—"

Jason smiled, in spite of himself; he realized he was being wooed like a client. "All right, I'm in," he said.

He started to put the phone away, then thought better of it and stabbed in another series of numbers. He really didn't feel like eating alone, and if landing a lunch date was now the most pressing problem in his life, at this, at least, he was determined to succeed.

SOUTH STREET SEAPORT, 12:15 P.M.

The South Street Seaport, a painstakingly re-cobblestoned acre of turn-of-the-century marina between Battery Park and the Brooklyn Bridge, was the city's only theme park, and it had a tourist-trappy, wall-to-wall-gift-shop inauthenticity about it; the "restoration" had rendered the area about as similar to a real seaport as Disneyland's star-spangled Main Street, USA, is to the real small-town experience. Pockets of tourists gamely shouldered into the scrimshaw shop; Styrofoam flotsam battered the hulls of proud reconstruction schooners in the harbor; imitation fish-wives ladled out bowls of lukewarm oyster stew quietly imported from some coast where oysters still thrived.

An authentically restored seaport, Jason mused as he looked across this one's spotless esplanade, would be swarming with black flies. Wharf rats as big as your brain crawling in and out of greasy barrels of spoiled fish, gout-wracked old rummies and prostitutes crippled with syphillis crabbing around in the horseshit and fish heads. An end of town to be avoided at all costs.

And on the very spot where rough pirates had once tumbled ashore, spilling pieces of eight on rough plank bars to exchange pubic lice with the local whores, now rose the squeaky-clean mizzen of Blackbeard's Brewery, a microbrewery where many a manly broker quaffed a subtle single-barrel bourbon and bunged his pie hole with pepper-crusted filet of monkfish with a red-pepper remoulade.

"To new beginnings," said Amanda, offering her cherry pilsener up for a high five.

"Cheers," echoed Jason, in the seaside chair, bemusedly watching the nippy sea breeze whip her hair around.

"So, are you happy with your big move?"

"I am," he said simply.

"Good," she replied, sipping her beer. "That job never sounded quite right for you."

In and around the ordering process, he gave her the morning's play-by-play, reveling especially in the details of the final scene in Diana's office. She seemed genuinely shocked and impressed.

"Good for you," she said finally.

"God, it felt good," he replied.

Amanda nodded, seemed about to ask a question, then thought better of it. "Law school's wearing thin on me, too," she confided, leaning back in her chair, and Jason smiled at the gesture of camaraderie. "It's tough being cooped up all spring."

"So why don't you leave?" he asked, a newly minted anarchist. "What do you really want to do?"

"Eh," she replied, dismissing the idea with a wave of her hand. "I've got thousands of dollars invested in it. I want the degree, at this point. Plus, there's a lot of it I really do like. Arguing cases . . . the complexity of individual battles. I still get off on that."

"You do love to talk," observed Jason.

"Maybe," she admitted with a smirk. "I hate the paper chase part of it. Poring over journals, comparing precedents, all that mechanical legwork. So much of the business is about small print and proper forms—it makes you crazy. If I could do old-style Solomon adjudication, I'd be happy as a clam."

"What about *being* a judge?" said Jason. "Could you do that?"

Amanda smiled. "I'm on the road. But come on, back to you," she continued, a wave of her hand preemptively setting aside any objections to her course change. "What are you going to do now?"

"Nothing, for a little while," said Jason, watching her sip her beer; he'd thought about this question all the way downtown. "I'm happy to chase this deed for a few weeks while I get my shit together."

"I like that plan," she said, smiling broadly behind her glass.

"Good timing, huh?" he said with a grin.

Amanda responded with a knowing look. "You think it's a coincidence, do you?"

He laughed. "You think I quit my job because I subconsciously wanted some free time to scour New York for this deed with you?"

Amanda shrugged. "I don't believe in accidents, that's all."

Jason nodded soberly. "Well, I do. The laws of probability demand them."

She looked amused, but fixed him with a searching look. "Well, are you familiar with the Heisenberg uncertainty principle?"

He nodded. "Sure—from physics, right?"

"It has to do with how the tool you use subtly compromises any measurement you're trying to take. That's my philosophy: The way you choose to view the world changes that world. You create your own reality."

"No offense," said Jason, "but that's bullshit. A rock is a rock."

"Sure," said Amanda, "but whether it's a doorstop, or a building block, or a weapon depends on what you bring to the table."

He shrugged. "Still hurts if you drop it on your toe."

She settled back in her chair again. "You're not going to like this, Jason," she began, and he grinned, intrigued. "But here goes. You exist only because I *need* you to exist. I mean that very literally," she continued soberly, trying to quell his rising amusement. "Think about it. I haven't got a shred of evidence that you existed before I needed you to help me secure this deed. So when you tell me you quit your job, and it just *happens* to free you up to devote more time to my search, how can I accept that as a coincidence? Why *you* think you quit may matter to you, but it's completely irrelevant to *my* world."

He smiled and nodded. "Very entertaining theory."

"Now you know why you quit, anyway."

"So why are you telling me all this?"

"Because you're the type of person who just lets life happen to you, and I can't have that in a partner. I need your full attention; I need your will to power. You act like you have no control over your world—you're just wandering around trying not to let anything too heavy hit you in the head."

"Now you're just insulting me."

She shrugged.

"And changing your attitude about reality is *not* the same thing as changing reality."

"Are you so sure there's a difference?" she queried.

"Yes, there's a difference!" Jason replied, incredulous. "All your believing can't create the deed if it isn't already there. There's either a piece of paper at the end of this search, or there isn't."

"But we're not *at* the end of this search," she replied, with a mild karate chop into the table for emphasis. "Jason, if you're going to be any use at all, you've got to stop saying, 'Well, if there really is a deed,' and so on." She brushed the hair back from her face. "This is the long shot of all long shots, you're right. It may never happen. But if we don't play to win, it *definitely* dies with us."

Pausing, Amanda took a long pull of beer as he sat back in his chair, munching tiny oyster crackers thoughtfully. "We can only preserve what slim odds we've got by really believing and operating as if we know this thing is real. That's all I'm saying."

"You have a very screwy philosophy," said Jason.

"I want to show you something after lunch," she continued, "if our food ever gets here. You game?"

He leaned back and laced his fingers behind his head. "Why not? I've got all the time in the world."

"I don't see it," said Jason.

"Keep looking," Amanda instructed. "Try not to focus so much. Let your mind wander a little."

They were standing at the northeast corner of Broadway and Fremont Street, facing north, having traced a wiggly westward path from the seaport following some map in Amanda's head. Three corners of the intersection were pinned down by stately brick office towers; a fourth featured a pointlessly small corporate park. *Here, peasants—have a tree.*

"Look uptown," she suggested.

"I *am* looking uptown," he replied. "I need a hint."

"Don't look so hard. What do you see?"

"I see taxicabs and limousines," he said. "I see pedestrians, traffic lights, skyscrapers."

"That's it," she said. "Now put it all together."

"Manhattan."

"Well, no," she chastised. "Zoom in a little."

He shook his head and folded his arms. "I don't care what it is anymore."

"Come on. What do you see?" she coaxed slowly, as if speaking to a child.

"I see Broadway," he said, annoyed.

"*There* ya go," she replied, following his gaze uptown. "See? That wasn't so hard."

Jason glanced upward from the busy street to the crooked line traced by the tops of the tall buildings on either side, revisualizing Broadway as a deep canyon cut through skyscraper blocks.

"This is the oldest street in Manhattan," said Amanda.

"I thought you said Water Street was the oldest street."

"No," she replied patiently, "I said that was the first street built by the *settlers*. Broadway is an old Native American warpath—it predates the white settlement by hundreds of years. Maybe thousands. Come on," she said, as the light changed, taking his hand and leading him south across the street.

"I love that Broadway was a warpath," said Jason.

"Know what that means?" asked Amanda. "Tribal lands in this part of the country tended to be laid out in east-west swatches," she explained. "Roads that went from east to west, within one tribe's domain, were called paths of peace. North-south paths crossed into different tribes' territories, so they were called paths of war."

A few more turns and a little more small talk later, they came across a part of town he did recognize. As they neared the corner, he could see the New York Stock Exchange two blocks uptown. "'Wall Street,'" he read off the sign. "Financial capital of the world. Lots and lots of cash."

"Do you know anything about Wall Street?" she asked.

"I think that unless I blurt something out," said Jason, "you can safely assume that I don't know anything."

She pouted. "Don't get testy; I'm trying to make this fun."

"It is," Jason assured her. "It's very fascinating."

"Well, we're not just surveying your property; I'm trying to prepare you for the detective work to come. So anyway, Wall Street."

"Didn't there use to be an actual wall here?" he remembered suddenly.

"Good," she said. "It was put up by Peter Stuyvesant, New York's famous one-legged governor, after this or that native uprising. The Indians would come down Broadway"—here she turned uptown—"with furs, and be let in through the wall, where they'd trade them with the Dutch for seeds, pipes, guns, et cetera. Anyway, I'm very sure our transaction happened before this wall went up, in 1650."

"Because the island was starting to matter to the Dutch?" suggested Jason.

"Right," she said. "Plus, more specifically, Stuyvesant would *never* have signed the island away—he'd have eaten his other leg first. He's the one who wanted to fight the whole British army by himself to keep it, remember. No, I think our man is his predecessor, Kieft. He was notoriously awful and corrupt."

Jason watched the noon traffic, letting her monologue flow over him.

"Try to imagine what this must have looked like three hundred and fifty years ago," she cajoled him. As Jason complied, she held his shoulders from behind and gently turned his body uptown. "Ahead of you is a couple of cornfields, then virgin forest—Indian land. Wild and untamed, and just the leading edge of a vast green continent, millions of square miles of uninterrupted forest, grasslands, rivers, prairies. You're peeking over a five-foot wooden wall at the primeval planet."

"Gotcha."

"Behind you is your fort, a few hundred skittish Dutch and a handful of soldiers. The typical gun of the time takes about two minutes to load and fire, bare minimum. You've got a wooden ship or two, anchored far out in the harbor—no docks yet—and beyond that, the unthinkably vast sea, with the rest of your world and everything you've ever known—civilization itself, to your way of thinking—on the other side."

He nodded, entranced, as she continued.

"Now put yourself on the other side of the wall, looking in."

BATTERY PARK, 2:00 P.M.

Several minutes later, after a winding tour of the canyons, they were standing in Battery Park, a subway stop that spilled out into a backyard-size green at the southern tip of the island. Here, great sweeping postcard views unrolled before them: Brooklyn to the east, New Jersey to the southwest, and in between, off in the mists to the southeast, the spidery Verranzano-Narrows Bridge, a distant but majestic span that kept Staten Island from floating off to Jersey.

"This is where we originally sold you the island," said Amanda distractedly. "A clearing in the forest, a dozen tribal leaders, Peter Minuit, and maybe twenty or thirty Dutch. Your ancestors versus mine."

"Right here?" said Jason.

"Close enough," she said. "Nobody knows for sure, anymore, of course."

"Pretty wild," he said.

"What we're looking for is somewhere between here and Washington

Heights, at the northern end of the island . . . twenty-four square miles of real estate."

"No problem," said Jason. "We'll sweep the city. You take the east side, I'll take the west."

She gave him a withering look, and he put his arm around her.

"I know you think there's no way it could have survived," she said. "All I'm asking is for you to rephrase the thought: If it *did* survive, where would they have had to put it?"

They sat down on a nearby park bench, scattering seagulls from a treasure trove of bread crusts.

"There can't be much still around that was here in 1650," said Jason, playing along. "Central Park?"

Amanda shook her head. "Central Park's not a preserve—it was artificially created in the 1800s. It was mostly farmland before that."

"Just a thought," said Jason dejectedly.

"I've thought about it a lot, as you might imagine," said Amanda.

"So where do we start?" said Jason. "I'm assuming you checked the obvious, rare-book rooms and all?"

She shook her head. "There are a thousand tiny libraries and museums on Manhattan. Plus I don't know what I'm looking for. It could be tucked into an old survey, or something. It could take a couple of lifetimes of searching."

"That's encouraging. What about churches?" said Jason. "If you're trying to set something aside for a couple of centuries, that seems like a good bet."

"Absolutely," said Amanda. "Trinity Church is the oldest—that's right down here by Wall Street. Then there's St. Paul's, and St. Bart's on Park Avenue, St. John the Divine in Morningside Heights . . ."

"This is going to be like finding a needle in a million haystacks, isn't it?" murmured Jason.

"It doesn't even make sense to worry about it until we find out whatever my mother knows," said Amanda. "We've simply got to narrow the search. That's why I'm going to see her tonight."

"You want me to come along, stir things up a bit?"

She laughed. "No thanks—go have your drinks with your friend. Mom's a tough old bird, but she's got a vested interest in this, too."

"And you're certain she's got something useful to contribute."

"We can't find it if she doesn't, so yes," she replied.

"You may not want to hear this," said Jason, "but I think it's a big assumption that this thing's still on the island. What's to keep it from being hidden in the false drawer of some old rolltop desk in a Massachussetts antique shop?"

Amanda shrugged. "'The page and the land are one,'" she said quietly.

"What's that?" said Jason.

She shrugged. "Just an old saying."

UPPER WEST SIDE, 5:00 P.M.

He reached her at her apartment, barely a half hour after they'd parted company in the subway station.

"You've gotta come up and see this," he repeated. "Quit wasting time."

"It really can't wait? What is it?" she said into the phone.

"Just come over," replied Jason, ear pinching the phone to his shoulder as he paced inside his front door, repeatedly sidestepping the hastily discarded UPS packaging at his feet. The book lay in his hands now, heavy and thick and impossibly old, its triumphantly pure white leather cover lovingly embossed with a giant gold cross.

"I'm all the way on the East Side, pal," she said, already weakening. "This'd better be important."

He smiled at this, picturing her reaction. It was a King James Bible, splendid and ancient, its hide tarnished only by a blackened trail along the spine, where some old fire had ventured a taste. The note was on a flowery piece of personalized stationery inside the cover: "Got to looking and realized I had this after all, Jason. Thought you should have it. Love, Grandma."

He ran one finger lightly across the overleaf, inscribed in old ink: "William Haansvoort, anno Domini MDCCL."

"Hellooo . . . ," she said impatiently. "Jason, what is it?"

He beamed. "I think I just found Jesus."

156

✧ ✧ ✧

He gazed down over the railing, into the eye of a tornado of circular stairs, watching Amanda lumber upward in a slow spiral, puffing under an unwieldy stack of books.

"Need some help?" he called down, his attempt at a macho tone undercut by the tinny, half-assed tenement echo.

Amanda, two flights down, raised her face to the sound. "I know—it's ridiculous, right? I really only meant to grab a couple."

He stepped out into the hall, relieved her of her load, and waved her past, into the apartment.

"Thanks," she said breathily, peeking inside from the doorway. "This is nice."

Jason stepped in behind her and stole a glance at her exquisitely flat belly when she pulled her sweater up over her head and the shirt went partway along for the ride; he ignored her navel's one-eyed disapproval.

"So," he said, "you want to rent a movie or something?"

"Oh, for Pete's sake, just show it to me!" she demanded happily.

✧ ✧ ✧

The grave, imposing book overflowed Amanda's straining, upturned palms like a monstrous bar of white gold. It was more than a foot tall and almost as wide, and thicker than a Coke can. The leather of the cover was disconcertingly pliable, like a well-worn coat, with a gently scalloped border that fell in toward the pages as if trying to envelop them completely. The page edges had once been gilt, and some hardy flakes of gold still clung here, and to the blocky, weatherbeaten cross embossed into the cover, beneath the wholly unnecessary "Holy Bible."

"Now, *that's* a Good Book," said Jason.

"My God," said Amanda, agape. "It's beautiful."

"She dates to 1750, if my Latin still holds," said Jason as she turned back the cover to see the illuminated overleaf. "Flip to the end."

She carefully turned the book onto its face in her left hand and peeled up the back cover with her right. A few loose pages, the last gasps of Revelation, momentarily rose, too, then slid back dramatically to reveal a two-page spread of handwritten names, a compendium of changing pens and penmanship beneath a single, monolithic, totemic word: "Haansvoort." All the names below were followed by a small H to the power of t and a date. The last date was 1856; the first, one Adriaen H^t, was born in 1685.

"Ohh," Amanda breathed from her diaphragm, a mystical syllable of total sensory satisfaction.

"It's not complete," he warned with a grin. "I mean, I've just taken a glance—it doesn't have all the relationships spelled out, and some of the dates are spotty. But—"

"But together with what we learned from the gravestones," she finished for him, "we ought to be able to connect the dots."

Jason grinned. "A *monkey* ought to be able to connect the dots. Put it this way—if we can't, we don't *deserve* this thing. Assuming it's all correct, of course."

"We can carbon-date the pages and the ink," said Amanda professionally, eyes still drinking in the page, "but I'm sure it's right. These things are sacred, you know."

"Yes, I know." He smiled, amused by her abject wonder, reveling in her mood.

"It's just such a beautiful . . . thing," said Amanda, and together they watched the pages uncurl as she slowly flipped backward through the ages: the letters to the churches, the Acts of the Apostles, Jesus' death, and birth, then the prophecies of his birth, and so on, right back toward Creation. Glimpsed snatches of text—the quaint King James stylings, folks begetting other folks, going forth unto another place, and so on—here seemed gloriously in tune with the ancient parchment that was their vehicle. It was like peeking into a cathedral and spotting medieval clerics at their matins.

"I don't have to leave for about an hour," said Jason. "You wanna sit down?"

✧ ✧ ✧

It took them most of that hour, but by the end a family tree of index cards had flowered across his apartment wall, with the Haansvoort direct line down the center and spouses and siblings tailing off to the sides and down like the arms of a wilting cactus.

When all the cards were up, Jason and Amanda sat back on the couch to survey their work.

"We are in *such* good shape," said Amanda.

"Aye, lass," said Jason. "Not one hundred percent there, but we're pretty close." He felt energized by her exhilaration.

Amanda pointed at the last name—"Robert Haansvoort, born 1902"—without speaking.

"My great-grandfather," he told her confidently. "My great-grandma remembers him, obviously. I can fill it out from there on down."

"Cool," she replied, shifting her attention to the top. "We need a card for Pieter, the original benefactor," said Amanda, "and one for his son, also Pieter."

"How do you know that?" said Jason.

"Oral tradition," she replied, "confirmed with a ship's log from Amsterdam. I had a copy faxed over from the Rijksmuseum. Our legend says Nahoti bore him a son—which must be true, of course, because your last name survived—and that she named him Pieter, because her husband had already died before his son was born."

"Perfect," he said confidently. "So that just leaves this little nightmare," he continued, stabbing a conspicuous hole three cards down from the top.

Amanda nodded; they'd both been avoiding this one. It was worse than a mere gap of information—what little evidence they had seemed to thwart any possibility of connection. Just above the break, Richard and Abigail had borne three children, Mark, Louisa, and John, in the waning years of the seventeenth century. Then came the gap; the next card down was William, born in 1750, fifty-one years later. There was clearly a generation missing . . . but which child had continued the line? They discussed the options. Louisa was out, as her children would have taken her husband's last name. Mark had died fighting pirates in the Caribbean in his early twenties, old enough to have kids, but there was no record of it. And John and his wife had only a girl, Mary, who died at fourteen.

"Either Mark fathered a son before he went to sea . . ." said Amanda.

". . . or John and his wife had a son, too," Jason continued. "How do we know he only had the girl?"

"The gravestone called her their only child. Remember?"

"Maybe they had another one after she died," suggested Jason. "Empty-nest syndrome. You wouldn't go back and change a gravestone."

Amanda nodded. "Here's something else. It may just be a coincidence, but this missing link occurs at exactly the same time your relatives stopped being buried in the old graveyard. Remember? Mary's stone was the oldest one in the outside yard."

"That's right," he said appreciatively. "Good call."

Together they stared at the wall. "What child is this?" he mused, tapping the empty space. Everything seemed to hinge on the answer.

◇ ◇ ◇

"You okay with us not figuring it out tonight?" wondered Jason as she poked her head back into the sweater, momentarily revealing that enticing swath of torso again.

"Yeah, it's fine," Amanda reassured him. "I've still got to get out to Long Island tonight, remember? Speaking of which, you want a ride to Brooklyn? It couldn't be more on the way."

He shook his head. "Thanks . . . I'm being picked up by a limo, apparently."

She smiled. "Must be nice."

"Tell your mom I said hi," he said wryly.

"At least I have something to tell her, finally," she said at the door. "Hey . . . can I show her the book?"

The quick innocence of the question moved him; only through an intense effort was he able to keep his head from nodding stupidly of its own accord. But this seemed a little much to ask.

"Ooh," he said, with ill-disguised discomfort. "Really?"

"Well, you have to admit, it'd be a damn good visual aid for proving you are who we think you are," she replied, then continued in a slightly hurt tone. "Jason—you do trust me, I hope."

"Of course I trust you," he said dismissively. "It's just . . . well, this thing's my only heirloom."

But even as the words left his lips, Jason knew he was going to give it to her, and that Amanda probably knew it, too, because that was the way the world worked. The only question was how long he'd be able to drag it out before coming around.

Chapter Six

Jason sat alone, bellied up to Barleycorn's old oaken bar just off the main floor with a small crowd of other patrons, sipping an icy martini and trying to get a bead on the place. Already it was clear that this joint lay a few bills north of Jason's usual standard of living, but it seemed quite agreeable so far. The beefy, smoky stench of the place had him fired for a memorable dinner, which it would be indeed if this aperitif were any judge, this absurdly delicious martini, smooth as sin, colder than a witch's tit.

It oughtta be, he reminded himself, *for eight bucks*. But that was only the ghost of prudence. Drinks were free tonight, even this preliminary tie loosener, as Nick had made clear when he'd called, unavoidably delayed as usual, to urge Jason to head on over without him. That was Nick: reliably unreliable.

He watched the tuxedoed bartender shave ice into a scotch as if carving a figurine, his client a bald, jowly tycoon either mesmerized by the process or already too sauced to look away. The place was lousy with testosterone, from the stately waiters who strolled impassively by to the suited Wall Street regulars in various states of repose.

As Jason sat and sipped his second drink, he felt his tension physically unraveling. Amanda and her quest were already a memory, left outside the door; his job—his old job, he gently reminded himself—a half-remembered dream. God*damn* this was a good martini. Jason slid gently down, down the inside of the glass, the silky fluid slowing his fall to a dreamlike trickle, until he bumped silently against the bottom of the tri-angle, legs sticking awkwardly up the far side, the olive curled up like a cat in his lap.

He managed to conjure up Amanda's face, then lost it again. The New Yorker in him, all ruthless efficiency, wanted to use this waiting time pro-ductively, to work at solving the nagging genealogical puzzle that would put them on the road to eating at places like this every night. But screw it. He sipped the martini again, losing its chill as the cone of clarity shrank toward its apex, and tried to picture Amanda naked. But the image that arose in his mind composed itself from memory, not fantasy: sex on a pool table with a now-forgotten girl back in his old eating club at college, a passable sexual experience amplified to *Penthouse* Forum heights by its perfect anecdotal setting.

"Welcome, fellow Beefeater," said a sudden voice to his left. He turned slowly to find Nick there, a grinning gargoyle perched on the stool next to him as if he'd been there all along, hair slicked back in a hundred parallel ebony streaks, a seesaw of wedgy little sunglasses balanced across his nose.

"What's up, buddy?" Jason smiled, clambering back to reality.

They exchanged small talk for a moment or two, then Nick checked his watch. "We should go up—the guys are probably upstairs already. I just wanna grab a drink. What kind of gin is that?" he wondered, indicating his friend's nearly empty glass.

Jason shrugged. "Ya got me."

Nick stared at him for a moment before speaking. "Jason, no well drinks tonight, you got it? These assholes are here to blow an enormous wad of dough on me, so you'd better start helping me. *Capiche?*"

Jason laughed. "Yeah, I *capiche.*"

Nick nodded sagely. "Okay then. Let's try the Sapphire," he suggested, snapping a finger in the direction of the bartender. "*That's* a martini."

✧ ✧ ✧

Kyle and Louis, their hosts for the night, were indeed upstairs, in a paneled private room, reached after a long and disorienting trek through the interior of the club, across parqueted dining rooms, past bars and rest rooms, up two half flights of stairs that bookended a golden little cigar lounge.

"Are women even allowed up here?" wondered Jason as they crested the last landing, shouldering their way through a small crowd of tuxedoed gents apparently just off the *Titanic*.

Nick shrugged. "Strippers are women."

At last Jason and Nick reached a warm oaken chamber, fitted with a table and four chairs and a small sitting area in front of a quietly roaring miniature fireplace; the head of an eight-point buck projecting over the hearth provided the room's only decoration. Fatigued and discombobulated, and scraping the bottom of his martini, Jason was elated at the room's promise of total relaxation.

Kyle, an Aryan classic with patrician good looks and the height to back it up, stood half a head taller than his partner. Louis was stocky and square-shouldered, a textbook tug-of-war anchor; as he and his partner stood to exchange greetings with Jason and Nick, Louis unleashed exactly the booming voice his beast chest implied. He quickly proved excitable and demonstrative to the breaking point, infusing the most trivial statement with curious import. Their jackets were already on the backs of their chairs, and they extended right hands in greeting, drinks sloshing around in their lefts.

"Oh, brother," said Louis, hearing that Jason had been waiting downstairs. "I wish we'd known—you could have come up."

"Don't worry about it," urged Jason.

"Crossed wires," said Nick definitively, putting an end to the conversation with an easy abruptness that reminded Jason that his friend was the client, and that these two would be picking up the tab. It was an exhilarating prospect, an evening of being wined and dined like a four-star client, and getting to watch Nick perform into the bargain.

"You guys get a waiter yet?" said Nick.

"I'm on it," said Kyle, reaching behind him to press a small buzzer on the wall behind him. "The garçon button," he said proudly.

"Why do I get the feeling you've been here before?" said Nick with a wry smile.

A waiter appeared at the door within moments, and was entrusted with drink orders. "And let's get a pitcher of Sapphire martinis for my friend," said Kyle, eyeing the drink in Jason's hand.

Jason opened his mouth to protest, but stopped short, wondering how the hell Kyle had guessed the brand of gin, and the moment slipped away.

So they make pitchers of martinis, he said to himself. *Wonder what happens when I drink one of those?*

He suspected he was about to find out.

◇ ◇ ◇

Most of the conversation left him, frankly, in the dust. Nick, Louis, and Kyle lived in a testosterone-drenched world where sports, business, new electronic gizmos, raunchy jokes, the fortunes of various international businesses, and tales of improbable sexual conquests combined in unthinkably complex combinations. He had the impression at first that the three were mutually trying to impress him at some rarefied expert level, but the conversational dance was so seamless and spontaneous that it quickly became clear this was their lingua franca. Unable to take more than a step or two into the maelstrom, he dutifully fielded the questions that were politely lobbed his way and accepted congratulations for quitting his job—a universal good, apparently. And he was otherwise ignored, which suited him fine, as he was beginning to suspect he didn't live on the same planet as these guys anyway.

Louis and Kyle were currency traders; they worked for rival firms but were fraternity brothers who had gone to Brown together. Nick was apparently some kind of broker, a guy who put deals together between folks like Louis and Kyle. In the grand casino of Wall Street, which took bets on quarterly reports and corn futures rather than on the turn of a friendly card, Nick's job seemed to be roughly equivalent to putting together high-stakes poker games. These two were the modern equivalent of foppish dandies itching to find The Game.

The waiter appeared again in the doorway, with an expectant look that led Jason to understand he'd been summoned.

"When the meat arrives, we're going to need a bottle of the best scotch in the house," said Kyle, with only a backward glance at the waiter.

"That would be our—"

"No, no," said Kyle abruptly, waving off the details without looking up again. "Don't spoil the surprise. Just bring it out."

The waiter nodded, with a nervous, effeminate little chuckle. Jason felt embarrassed for the poor guy, being ordered about by brats at least fifteen years his junior. "Oh, and send the captain back, please," Kyle continued as the waiter nodded and left.

"Ostentatious," said Louis, grinning approvingly.

"That's *all* we need—a fag waiter," groused Kyle. "That'll really make the evening complete. The fine aroma of dick breath."

"Shut the fuck up," said Louis, laughing.

"Kyle has some *issues*," said Nick to Jason, trying to draw him in. But Jason only grinned noncommittally.

An overdressed maître d' arrived moments later, or at least his head—bottle-brush hair and a neatly trimmed beard and mustache like a sea captain—popping around the corner of the doorway. "Everyone who orders a three-hundred-dollar bottle of scotch gets a personal visit," he said, grinning, by way of introduction.

"Robert, thank God," said Kyle, brightening at last. "Listen, we've got a first-timer here tonight," he said, indicating Jason. "Tell Marco to put some elbow grease into it."

"Sure thing, boss," the captain replied.

"And one more thing," said Kyle as the other turned to leave. "Would it be possible to get a different waiter?"

After the barest pause, the captain smiled and replied, "Not a problem, sir."

✧ ✧ ✧

"This guy goes into the men's room," said Louis, after a fifty-something waiter with the mannered poise of an Old World butler had taken their dinner order. "He's taking a piss," Louis continued, "about to whip it out, when he happens to look over at the guy next to him and he sees the guy's got no arms. Big dirty army jacket, two flapping sleeves."

Helping himself to another martini from the bottomless pitcher, now pearled with condensation, Jason smiled involuntarily. Clearly Louis was a veteran joke teller, the type of guy who warms up his own crowd, whose jokes you can't get quite right the next day. He was flying high on a gin buzz; the amber lighting and tight space gave the room a cocoonlike feel, an effect only amplified whenever the door opened temporarily, letting in fresh drinks and a little background noise.

"So he's trying not to stare," Louis continued, "but he's thinking, 'How the hell's this freak gonna even unzip?' And sure enough, just as he's finishing up, the guy with no arms turns to him and in the most pathetic voice you ever heard, says, 'Hey, buddy—help me out, here, wouldja?'

"So what can he do? I mean, the guy's *crippled*. So he reaches over and carefully, trying not to cringe, unzips the guy's fly. He tries to leave again, but the guy says, 'Thanks, buddy, but, uh, now could you . . . could you pull it out for me?'"

"This is a true story, right?" said Nick.

"So now the guy's really depressed," Louis continued. "He looks around, and there's nobody else in the men's room, so he's, like, *Oh, what the fuck. This guy's got a shitty life, the least I can do is help him out a little.*"

"Give him a hand," suggested Jason.

"Right," said Louis with an appreciative nod. "So he reaches in and pulls out the guy's cock. And it's the most disgusting, filthy schlong you could possibly imagine." This elicited grins, and Louis pressed the point home. "I mean, it's lumpy and green, and it smells like bad cheese, and it has knotted bristly hair and—"

"Oh, for Christ's sake," said Nick. "Get on with it."

"Right," said Louis, but everyone was cracking up already; he owned the room. "So anyway, it's too late to back out now. So he holds the guy's evil, diseased, greasy proto-penis with the tips of two fingers while the guy takes a leak. I won't even tell you what the piss looked like."

"So it *is* a true story," said Kyle.

"And when he's done, the no-armed guy of course asks him to put it back in and zip up for him. So he does, even though what he really wants to do is lean over and puke in the urinal. And finally, the guy says, 'Thanks, man. I know it took a lot of courage for you to help me, and I really appreciate it.' 'No sweat,' says the Good Samaritan. 'But, buddy, I gotta ask you: What the fuck is wrong with your johnson?'

"And the no-armed guy does this little contortion, and pulls his arms from around behind his back and out through the sleeves of the jacket, and he says, 'Fuck if I know, but *I* sure as hell ain't touching it.'"

Jason erupted in laughter, but Nick only rolled his eyes. "You got that out of *Martha Stewart Living,*" he accused.

✧ ✧ ✧

It was a porterhouse steak, tall and proud, branded with a perfect cross-hatch of grill marks, running with juice, in fact still audibly sizzling. Amazed by the sheer beauty of the thing, Jason wanted to touch the meat with his hands, to dig his thumbs into it, to rub it on his chest. A small pile of forlorn, wilted vegetables rode shotgun, but Jason knew they'd be sailing back to the kitchen untasted, next to a big greasy hole where the perfect steak had once been.

Pierced with a tentative fork, the meat gave a little hiss, and Jason effortlessly carved off a wedge, like a spoon through gelato. He suspected he could have cut it with the napkin. The bite fell away like a sheared cliff, splashing into a shallow pool of rich blood grease to reveal an obscenely pink middle. And then, without delay, into the mouth. The beef was silky and smooth, like some sort of dessert meat, lightly crispy at the edges, bursting with juice. Amazing. One bite and he knew with absolute certainty that he'd never eat another salad in his life.

"Well, fuck McDonald's," he said aloud, to scattered chuckles.

The joy of dismantling the steak helped revive Jason from his opium-like trance; his buzz retreated to a more comfortable level without dispersing altogether. *This is what it's all about,* he was thinking. The best food money can buy, an endless supply of liquor, no hassles. The good life.

Jason had been brought up, as are most people, to believe that money didn't matter in some important cosmic sense. But he was starting to see the idiocy of that concept; it was a simplistic frame of mind available only to the sheltered young or the willfully enchanted. Wealth allowed you to work less and enjoy life more. Maybe it was true it couldn't buy you happiness, but it seemed awfully suspicious that only poor people ever said so. It could clearly buy you sensual pleasure, prestige, insurance against future spells of rotten luck . . . happiness sure seemed a damn sight easier with it than without it. He tangentially wondered whether adulthood was a simple process of being able to absorb increasing amounts of cynicism into your philosophy.

"Jason," said Nick, again, and he turned, with infinite slowness; the grins of the three were upon him.

"He's zoned," said Louis good-naturedly.

Jason grinned sheepishly. "Yeah, I guess I am; sorry. What?"

"I want to tell them about your deed. And the Indian chick. Is that okay, or is it still a state secret?"

Jason rolled his eyes. Amanda had warned him to keep the whole thing quiet, but her concern seemed paranoid and girlish in the present context, and, in any event, the sea of expectant faces would brook no refusal. "I don't care," he said, shrugging. "It's not that interesting."

But it was. Nick launched into a colorful rehashing of the events surrounding the mysterious deed; at every point, his enthusiasm seemed about to carry him over into the first person. Jason abstained from correcting his friend on minor points; for the purposes of this dinner, this might as well have been a fictional anecdote. Perhaps it was. But no, he corrected himself, he didn't really believe that anymore.

"The deed to Manhattan," repeated Louis appreciatively. "That's classic. You gotta get me into rent control."

"The girl's a lawyer?" said Kyle.

"In law school."

"It's gotta be bullshit, right?" he went on. "I mean, I can't believe there's not some law on the books declaring all deeds that haven't come out yet are null and void."

"Agreed," said Nick. "Our ancestors screwed the Indians out of this land fair and square."

Memo to self, thought Jason, *try to get Nick into the same room with*

Amanda's mother sometime. "Well, the argument *for*," he said aloud, "is that Indians are winning these battles, on a much smaller scale, of course. A deed's a deed forever—that's why you have title insurance."

"This is a scam," said Kyle. "She's scamming you."

"How is she scamming me?" he replied defensively.

"All scams start with the same basic strategy," said Kyle. "If you want someone to part with X, lead them to believe they stand to win ten X."

"Or in this case, a million X," said Nick with a grin, clearly enjoying the little social game he'd set up.

"For one thing," Kyle continued, "the government can just take any property it wants by eminent domain. There's the first hole in the plan."

"But they do have to pay you market value," piped in Louis.

Jason smiled appreciatively. "I could live with that," he said. "I was actually trying to compute it the other morning. There's a lot of zeroes."

"This thing could go to the Supreme Court just on entertainment value," continued Louis, an unexpected ally.

"Ah," said Nick, "but can the Supreme Court adjudicate a deed that's older than the Constitution their authority derives from?"

"I've actually wondered that myself," said Jason. "If the deed predates the country, what's the proper jurisdiction?"

"The United Nations?" suggested Louis.

"Perfect," said Nick, breaking into a broad smile.

"Why?"

But Jason was able to field this one. "Because the UN headquarters is situated on my land, and I'm fully prepared to evict the bastards if they don't rule in my favor."

"If they don't rule in your favor, you won't be evicting shit," said Kyle, reentering the fray. "Has this chick asked you yet for any old papers, family heirlooms, that kind of thing?"

Frowning at the general direction in which this was going, Jason was tempted to answer no, but the intimacy of the room evoked honesty. "Just a family Bible," he replied quietly. It felt like a betrayal.

Kyle grinned triumphantly. "Mm-hmm. But you didn't give it to her, right?"

Jason paused momentarily; it was all the opening Kyle needed. "You *did?* Sweet—the game's afoot!" He took a sip of his drink. "Hope it wasn't worth much."

Jason shook his head. "You're barking up the wrong tree."

Kyle's smile broadened. "Is it old? Valuable?"

"No," said Jason. "I mean, yes. But she didn't even know about it. *I* didn't even know about it." Peripherally, he couldn't miss Nick's shit-eating grin; he wondered if he could paste it with a forearm without taking his gaze away from his more immediate antagonist.

"A hundred bucks says you mysteriously haven't been to her apartment yet," said Kyle, obviously enjoying himself immensely.

"Let me get this straight," said Jason, taking the offensive. "You think she concocted this elaborate plan just to steal a rare book? Spent a whole day in a graveyard, another carting me back and forth to Long Island? And her mom's in on it? There's got to be better ways to earn a living out there."

"See, it sounds stupid when *you* say it," said Louis, still on his side.

"I'm not saying she's after your Bible," said Kyle with thinly disguised mockery. "It's obviously more complicated than that. Maybe she returns it to you as proof of her trustworthiness, to soften you up for later. Or maybe . . . ," he said, trailing off momentarily. "Maybe there is a deed, but it's in her name, not yours. Have you thought of that? Maybe she just needs your records to help her establish *her* claim."

Jason shrugged, disturbed, but not moved. "Then why not just tell me the truth?"

"Because you'd extort her for millions, of course. Wouldn't you?"

"I trust her."

"Oh, you trust her," said Kyle, looking around the table with a smug smile. "Have you even fucked her yet? Not that *that* means anything."

"I'm officially dropping out of this conversation," Jason replied.

"I wanna do business with *you*, man."

Nick finally stepped in to help. "Maybe there's something to it," he said. "If you found out someone stood to make a pile of money, wouldn't you go make nice with them?"

"Well, that's it exactly," said Kyle. "What's her motive? It's great that you trust this babe, but ask yourself what she's really in it for. Does she think if you get the island you're just going to hand it over to her people? 'Here you go, enjoy it, kids, I'll be back slaving away at my day job.'"

"I think it's cigar time," said Nick, in a transparent effort to disperse the ugly mood that had begun to creep up on the gathering.

"I'm for that," agreed Louis, and Jason nodded dumbly, his confidence shaken.

"Super," said Kyle, rising to his feet. As they gathered coats and filed out the door, he paused to take Jason's hand in a hearty handshake. "You know I'm just kidding around, right?" he said unconvincingly. "But it's true that you won't know a thing till you do her. You know that, right?"

◇ ◇ ◇

Entering the pool room was like walking into a cigar: tight and brown, and full of the thick, roasty stench of old tobacco. There was even a fire at one end. Despite a sizable loitering crowd, an open pool table proved easy to claim, and Jason wondered if this, too, had been arranged. He reached in his pocket for quarters, but Kyle was already procuring a rack and he realized there was nowhere to put any money. The last trace of guest responsibility fluttered away, and Jason sat on a seat to drink his drink.

Nick and Jason teamed up to take on the interlopers, and Jason didn't argue, deferring without dishonor when his partner strode toward the head of the table to break. He wondered how his drunkenness would affect his game, whether the confidence boost could master the coordination gap.

"Before I die," said Nick dramatically, as he lined up his shot, "I want to kill somebody." With that he fired, punctuating the announcement with a loud crack and the usual chaotic rainbow of rebounding and dispersion.

In Nick, the normal male drive to be the center of attention was absolute and biological, a matter of identity survival, and his efforts to establish social dominance by fiat aroused, in Jason, enthralled amusement tinged with something like pity. *My friend is a walking cry for help*, he thought.

"Who do you want to kill?" Jason replied blandly, accepting a cigar from Louis. As he rolled it in his fingers, awaiting a light, he wondered how much it was worth.

"Don't be condescending; I'm serious," said his friend, expertly chalking his cue with a wrist twist as he strode purposefully around the table, sniper's eyes fixed immovably on his next target. "A stranger. I'm not talking about some messy crime of passion. Three in the corner."

"You don't gotta call 'em," reminded Kyle.

"Admit it, Jason," said Nick. "Aren't you dying to know what it's actually like?"

"The murder, or the twenty-to-life?"

"Don't give me all that pussy ramification nonsense," Nick admonished. "I'm talking about the immediate act, the pure, physical, irrevocable taking of another human life. What it's like to look into someone's eyes as you choke out their last breath? Tell me there isn't a small part of you that wants to know what that's like."

"Keep shootin', Kaczynski," Louis complained.

"I'm in," said Kyle, seated.

The billiard light overhead bathed the table in bright fluorescence, but reflected up and into the faces gathered around, it lent them a shadowy, flashlight-at-the-campfire demonic quality; the room's smoky haze, and the bright points of fire and smoke, conspired to turn the game into a feast of fiends.

"Too rich for my blood," said Louis. "I got no inner Son of Sam."

"That's where you're wrong," Nick accused, poking him lightly in the chest with the butt of the cue stick. For the first time, it occurred to Jason that these guys had to be getting drunk, too. "You're a natural-born killer," Nick continued, forgetting the game. "You have canine teeth carefully honed by natural selection for gnawing flesh. You have fingers for choking and nails for clawing. For millions of years nature has painstakingly crafted you into a fabulous killing machine. You can't just repudiate that with an act of will."

"I repudiate it thus!" shouted Louis, menacing Nick with his own cue, then snapping it over his knee with a loud crack. Kyle laughed out loud, and Louis beamed, holding the pieces aloft, triumphantly. Jason was amazed at the utter lack of self-consciousness; when a concerned goon from the club headed over, Kyle's quick hand motion, scribbling on an invisible pad—*Put it on my tab, pal*—was accepted as hard currency.

"Let's not forget," said Jason, trying to rescuscitate the discussion, "that we killing machines later climbed down out of the trees and invented farming and civilization and so forth."

"Oh yeah," said Nick derisively. "I forgot you were a shepherd."

Jason shrugged. "I don't want to kill anyone," he reiterated. "*You*, yes; a stranger, no."

"Me neither," said Louis.

"Thank you," said Jason.

"Now, *rape*—there's something I could sink my teeth into," Louis deadpanned. "It'd be just as intense—plus you get laid!"

"You are one sick fuck," said Nick, grinning.

Kyle laughed. "Someone's inner child needs a serious spanking."

"Oh, *now* everybody's outraged," laughed Jason. "But murder's fine and dandy."

Nick finally missed on his third shot, handed the cue to Louis, and took a seat next to Jason. "It's not as if humans are an endangered species," he said under his breath. "A loose cannon here or there isn't going to do any harm."

"Oh, my God—are you still talking about it?"

"I just want to kill *one person*," Nick continued impassively. "Is that a crime?"

"I'm not sure I like the way you're looking at me," said Jason.

"I also want to go to the Guggenheim," Nick said, sitting back. "I mean, what's the point of living in the city if you don't visit its cultural treasures, and all that crap?"

"You blowhard," said Jason. "Stop trying to be outrageous."

"Eat me."

MASSAPEQUA, LONG ISLAND, 7:00 P.M.
The house lights dimmed momentarily, as if an electric chair had gone into action somewhere in the building, and a fusillade of funky, staccato horn blares kicked off the disco euphoria of Foxy's "Get Off." But the

dancer, when she emerged from the back room, was even more disappointing than the last, with a bright green bikini pasted over rock-hard silicone towers and an unappetizingly roomy lobby below. Resolutely, the girl hooked her thumbs in her G-string and did a fast butter churn to the beat, causing her freakishly protruding pudendum to jut out alarmingly over the listless crowd.

At their ringside table, Freddie smoldered disconsolately. "So help me, Vin," he shouted over the music, "if a cock pops out of there, I'm gonna shoot you myself."

Vinnie, already giddy and stupid on a couple of doubles, laughed until scotch threatened to trickle out of his nose. "Don't worry, don't worry," he slurred, palms clearing an invisible windshield between them as he spared a sideways smirk at the silent third member of their party. The Indian continued silently watching the girl and pouring straight bourbon down his throat like Coca-Cola.

Gazing rightward at their blithely distracted partner, Freddie tried to decide whether the Indian was entranced or simply bored out of his skull. He fancied himself a good reader of men, and to his eyes the way the Indian had dressed up tonight—starched white button-down, cheap, but dry-cleaned suit, skinny tie—made it all too plain he was eager to deal. The knowledge should have given Freddie a leg up in the negotiations, but his dipshit partner's amateurish, frat-boy antics now threatened to undermine everything. As he fixed Vinnie with a reproachful stare, he could feel something beginning to give way inside him, some ropy bond of loyalty that was too old-fashioned, or had been too often tested, or had simply outlived its useful life. The emasculating claustrophobia of this shitty little strip club had brought him to the brink of rage; his heart pounded in his wrists and forehead, more or less synchronized to the disco beat, and it was all he could do to keep his huge hands from clenching into wrecking balls.

"Come on," he hissed at Vinnie. "Fucking get on with it."

"All right, yeah, fine," said Vinnie, chuckling with a casual superiority that very nearly had him taking the rest of his life's meals through a straw. He tapped the Indian on one shoulder, lurched over the table toward him, and smiled idiotically.

"So let's talk turkey," he shouted hoarsely over the goofy bump and grind.

✧ ✧ ✧

The purpose of the meeting, ostensibly, was to begin turning the casino idea into a working plan. In practice, it played out more like an interrogation, with Vinnie, all sodden enthusiasm, badgering the Indian on a million and one trivial points, each new question following so closely on the heels of the last, and bearing so little relation to it, that it soon became clear he was trying, through sheer swagger, to cow the Indian into accepting a submissive role in the deal.

Dovatelli had made it clear: he wanted Freddie to stay out of the negotiations. So Freddie had spent most of the evening plotting the future. For years now he'd been keeping one eye peeled for the big score, an escape route, a clear path to something loftier than the tin-pot organization he'd been scrabbling around in here for most of a decade, like a cockroach caught in a smooth-walled spittoon. Working for Dovatelli had once been promising, but the old man had taken over the business too late in life, and had been overwhelmed by strange distractions: nieces and nephews, playing the stock market, and now his own fading health. Dovatelli was already half out of the game, and the business was crumbling away. The fact that he was looking for leadership from below spelled certain doom. When the big dog starts asking for help mounting the females, you know a sea change is coming.

Privately, Freddie no longer even *wanted* to run the organization. Truth be told, there just wasn't anything to it anymore. Ten worthwhile guys, maybe seven or eight million in revenue if everyone paid their bills, which they didn't, and a mountain of overhead in column B. And the constant risk of the whole operation being blown wide open, meaning jail or death, a risk magnified by trigger-happy idiots and this ludicrous confessional age. The thought of someday running this show had once inspired him to greatness; today it felt more like a small inheritance promised by an eccentric uncle only after fulfilling some abominable condition, a tainted treasure not quite worth the effort of acquiring it.

An old-school pragmatist, Freddie understood steel and unions and head-busting and bullets. That, to him, was business, and he felt a disgust for paperwork that was honestly akin to the nausea others feel, he'd heard and had no choice but to believe, at the sight of a corpse in the trunk of a car. The casino Vinnie and the Indian were haggling over was a rock-solid concept, and in the old days Freddie would have insisted on involving himself, would, in fact, have already sent Junior out for a pizza and closed this deal himself, and Dovatelli be damned. So why did he feel so . . . bored?

The half-overheard discussion was fading away, and Freddie felt his perspective shift in an ecstasy similar to déjà vu. There comes a moment, more often in Freddie's line of work than in most, when you become aware of a deeper reality underlying the seemingly simple situation you *thought* you were in—that moment when you suddenly realize your boss has decided to have you killed, or that the waitress is a cop. Having a good nose for this sort of thing, as Freddie did, could save your life, and he was beginning to feel that itch right now.

"Freddie, help me out here—I can't explain it any better to him," said the Indian, eyes darkening. "It's Lenape land as far as the federal government is concerned. But my people have an agreement with the Lenape for the territory we're talking about. It's our property."

"Yeah, I get that," said Vinnie dismissively. "I know they're not going to object. The point is, do you have the legal standing to do a contract with us, or do we have to get them to sign off?"

The Indian polished off his drink, spared a glance at the dancer who'd wandered into their vicinity, strutting her stuff just above eye level, and slowly turned back to Vinnie.

"Let's talk about the deal," he said gravely.

Freddie, now wholly reengaged, poured the rest of his tequila and OJ down his throat and eyeballed the antagonists, handicapping the battle to come.

Vinnie was losing his cool. "But do you understand the problem?"

Christ, thought Freddie. *Enough's enough.* "We run the daily ops," he interjected steadily, ignoring the sudden, angry dart from Vinnie. "Your people get twenty-five percent of the book as a host fee. That's extremely generous. How you split that is up to you. Parking and concessions we split fifty-fifty. You pay taxes and building and grounds maintenance; we handle construction while it's being built and the payroll after."

"But wait, wait," interjected Vinnie, desperate to remain central. "Before we discuss any of this, we need to have some assurances that your tribe owns the land, and that you are the guy who can—who has the authority to negotiate for them. I mean"—he switched his attention to Freddie—"are we talking to the right person or aren't we?"

At this, caught up in his own rhetoric, Vinnie swayed to his feet, lurched, and tried to grab the table. But the hand still had his drink in it, and he busted the glass into the table's edge. "Whoa," he said, staring at the table, then his hand, which had miraculously survived uncut.

"Come here a sec," said Freddie, rising and walking Vinnie over to one side; the Indian resumed watching the show.

"It's just a glass," said Vinnie.

"Why'n't you slow it down a little with the sauce."

"I'm fine," Vinnie replied. "I just got up to drain the lizard. You just keep Dances with Hookers occupied."

❖ ❖ ❖

"John," said Freddie, taking his seat again as Vin staggered off toward a men's room, "he's the boss's son. Fuck him, and fuck the boss. You and I have more important things to discuss." When the Indian remained impassive, Freddie added, "'The treasure map,' that's your phrase, not mine."

The Indian looked up, met his eyes. "I was drunk. I misspoke."

Freddie chuckled. "Yes, you were drunk," he said amiably. "And that's how I know you weren't shitting me. The fact is, John, you *did* say something to me—so *that* tells me you could use a little help. If you could land this one yourself, you would've done it already. I'm not going to ask you if I'm right, because I *know* I'm right. And so do you. So why bullshit each other?"

The Indian was silent; he drank a great draft of his liquor and let his gaze drift back to the dance floor.

"Hold on a second," said Freddie, seeing Vin staggering back toward them. He got up and peeled a twenty off the wad in his pocket, handing it to Vinnie as he approached.

"Injun Joe wants to treat you to a lap dance," he whispered conspiratorially. "I wouldn't say no, if I were you."

Vinnie looked over Freddie's shoulder with a touch of concern, then smiled. "Well, business is business. Which girl?"

Freddie shrugged. "Player's choice."

✧ ✧ ✧

"Now, I know you're on to something, and I don't know what it is," Freddie continued, retaking his seat. "But it's big, that's obvious. The way I look at it, the only reason you said shit to me is that you correctly recognized that I'm the type of guy who can help you get it."

"I was drunk," reiterated the Indian, still focused on the dancer.

"You're drunk now," said Freddie, and the Indian laughed, turned away from the stage at last, and matched Freddie's intense gaze.

"How do I know you can help me?" said the Indian.

Freddie nodded, happy with the turn of conversation. "Let me tell you who I am," he said slowly, leaning forward. "I'm a problem solver. I make sure whatever is supposed to happen happens. When people have to go to jail, when nice restaurants need to burn down, when people have to get their hands broken or their heads kicked in or go bottom fishing in the Hudson, I'm the guy who sees to it that it happens." He gave a cheery double thumbs-up sign to a grinning Vinnie, being led to a couch at the wall by an inhumanly busty blonde. "There is absolutely no trouble I can't get you out of," Freddie continued, "there's nobody I can't get to, and there's nothing that has to be done that I can't get done. *That's* who the fuck I am."

The Indian remained silent for a moment, drinking. Freddie marveled at the sheer quantity of crappy well liquor he'd downed . . . he put it at even odds whether or not the man could stand up.

"This has nothing to do with the casino deal," said the Indian.

"Yeah, I know," said Fred. "For the record, this is also not about the people I work for, or that drunk dipshit over there, or your bitch wife—no offense, but you told me the score—or anyone else. This is about you and me. You know what the score is; I'm going to make all the roadblocks disappear." He paused. "Come on, I'm Old World. You have my word, we're partners. Let's figure it out together."

The Indian slowly turned his eyes stageward again, where a somewhat prettier brunette, already down to a thong and a prayer, was thrashing entertainingly to the crashing percussion of Vicki Sue Robinson's "Turn the Beat Around." Freddie wondered if he'd somehow lost him, as the Indian remained silent, watching the flesh spin. Finally, though, he spoke.

"It *is* a treasure map," he confirmed in a low tone, and Freddie leaned forward in his chair.

✧ ✧ ✧

Just two dozen steps away, but completely out of hearing range thanks to the din, Vinnie observed their conversation with something like despair, helpless to intervene. The stripper, now completely nude, had straddled his lap and was busy whapping him in the face with her 44DD breasts, one after the other: left, right, left, right, to the beat.

"Okay, okay, sweetheart, that's *enough*," he ventured again between blows, craning his neck to try lip-reading whatever the hell was going down. "Come on, no shit—cut it *out*."

She paused the action, sulking. "It's part of the whap dance," she pouted.

"Well, I don't *want* it," said Vinnie, straining to look past her. "Now couldja shut up a minute?" *Shit, shit, shit,* he thought.

"Fine," she replied, angrily pasting him one more time in the jaw with her right jahoobie. "Fag."

She lifted one leg casually off his lap, disembarking with petulant slowness; for Vinnie, this was the last straw. "Okay, just *get off*," he hissed bitterly, trying vainly to clear his line of sight by giving her upraised pelvis a gentle shove.

"BAD TOUCHING!" she shouted at the top of her lungs, poking him in the chest. Within seconds a scowling, squinty-eyed meat mountain of a bouncer was plowing through the sea of guys toward Vinnie, like a bloated great white homing in on a tiny, bleeding piece of chum.

LOWER EAST SIDE, 10:30 P.M.

Torrents of rain pelted the taxi as it slid left to right across the puddled tarmac and gently into the curb, bumping Jason awake as it shuddered to a stop.

"Where are we?" he asked sleepily, trying to peer out through the raindrop-crazed window.

"Second Avenue," replied Nick, to his left, leaning forward to hand a crisply folded bill through the Plexiglas gate in the bulletproof driver-passenger firewall. "Receipt, please," he said, unlatching his door.

"Why are we stopping?" Jason wondered, rubbing his eyes and trying to shake off the foggy buzz.

"I thought we'd get one more drink," Nick replied, accepting his change. "The night's still *kinda* young, anyway."

"I don't know; I'm pretty toasty," said Jason, but Nick was already lurching out of the street side of the cab and into the rain; as the door slammed shut, Jason watched his friend do a half-crouch hustle across the street, an upraised arm protecting his perfect hair from the downpour until he could disappear into a doorway.

"Fuck," he said, and fumbled for the latch on his own door. He stepped out of the cab and into a shin-deep puddle, where his legs failed him and he stumbled hard to his knees, throwing up a majestic splash mirroring the burst of pain that flared in his brain.

"Oh, for Chrissakes," said the cabbie. "Couldja close the door?"

Leaning on the taxi for support, Jason staggered to his feet, slammed the door, and hobble-hopped across the street, soaked to the bone already and no doubt bleeding and fractured. At the far side, he followed his friend's still-steaming trail through a wall of beaded strings and into the dry haven of the Rastaria.

The Caribbean-themed bar was one of their regular stops; Jason had been here literally dozens of times. The colorful, hole-in-the-wall first-date joint featured fine music, impressively overpriced drinks, and enough of a freak factor to coax blazing conversations out of the tiniest spark of commonality. Rastaria's bar and restaurant were separated like island from water by a long, low "bamboo wall" of painted plaster, and only the funked-up, first-generation reggae—Bunny and the Wailers, Echo, some Marley for the tourists—bridged the two worlds. To the left as you entered, waitresses in bikini tops and Bermuda shorts buzzed around circular tables with thatched umbrella roofs; to the right, a room-length tiki bar rode along the long wall, whereupon curling plastic monkeys, little rubber whales, and other Hong Kong trinkets topped great goblets of red and orange flaming or frozen concoctions no Jamaican would be caught dead drinking.

It was along the bar, unsurprisingly, that Jason spotted Nick, now joined by Becky and J.D., drinking up a storm.

"Hey," said Becky, spotting his approach. "Congratulations!"

"What's this—a party?" Jason grinned.

"I took the liberty of inviting a few friends," said Nick, casually dangling a twenty out over the bar, in search of service.

"What's the occasion?"

"You quitting your job, dumbbell!" gushed Becky, obviously thrilled by the sheer decadence of declaring this worthy of celebration.

"Welcome to unemployment hell, my friend," said J.D., turning from the bar with two tequila shots and handing him one.

Jason grinned at the familiar drawl, even as his heart sank. He was far too inebriated for the partying to proceed at this pace; already he was haunted by the ghostly image of his head framed by a toilet seat later.

This is going to take sound buzz management, he realized, reaching for his glass. "Thanks," he said, eyeing the oversize shot. "I guess I don't exactly have to get up early tomorrow."

"That's the spirit," said J.D. "Come taste the smoldering heart of old Mexico." He drained his shot glass in a single smooth movement, an old West gunslinger, and set the empty upside down on the counter with a satisfying click.

"Paul's here, too—he's trying to get a table," said Becky. "So, Jason, I want to hear all about it. What are you gonna do now?"

"I have no idea," Jason replied, stalling his own shot. "I just know I don't want to think about it tonight."

"Amen to that," said J.D. "I think that tequila's aged quite long enough, my friend."

Taking the hint, Jason took a deep breath. For all his weariness, he felt socked in and ecstatic.

✧ ✧ ✧

They secured a table after a half hour or so, and it was there that Jason finally consented to recap the events of the morning, at his witty best thanks to the solid baseline buzz energizing his brain. He marveled at his crowd's unexpected enthusiasm, knowing full well it wasn't his expert storytelling. No matter what the job is, everybody cheers when you leave it.

"What a wench," said Becky, of Diana. "I had an editor like her once. She'd gotten the job because she knew all the right people, and it was clear from day one she was in way over her head. She was just such an idiot, and she knew everyone was just yessing her to death because they had to, so she developed this weird aggression to cover it up."

"'If they won't respect me, let them fear me,'" paraphrased Paul.

"Yeah," Becky confirmed, "she gave herself a total personality makeover."

Nick, shifting in his seat beside her, grinned. "You're in such a pretend industry," he said fiendishly.

"What's that supposed to mean?" Her eyes narrowed.

Nick smiled, placating. "Well, you and your fashion-mag gal pals just kind of sit around and decide what trends are hot this month, and whether blue is the new black or not." Ignoring the middle finger, Nick went on. "In industries where actual *work* gets done, managers without talent find it a little harder to survive."

"That's grade-A bullshit," opined J.D. "*Every* industry has managers without talent."

"Thank you," said Becky, still stung.

Gallantly, Jason joined the rally. "*Complete* bullshit," he echoed. "In fact, it seems pretty clear positions of power attract boneheads."

"Oooooh, everybody hates Nick," said Nick.

"Well, don't be such a dawg," J.D. replied. "You can't just insult some-one's passion like that."

"Hey, it's not my passion," said Becky. "It's just a job."

"Oh," said J.D. "Well . . . Nick, you can't just insult someone's casual, temporary, piece-of-shit job that they don't care about like that," he cor-rected, sipping his booze. "That shit ain't right."

✧ ✧ ✧

As the place began to fill up with late-night revelers, the noise and the bustle made tabletop conversation increasingly problematic; after one of many trips to the men's room, Jason returned to find that his friends had abandoned their claim altogether, leaving the table to be resettled by four sweatshirted NYU students and *their* fruity rum drinks.

He discovered the gang after a quick look around. Nick and Paul were in the back, taking on the old untiltable *Terminator 2* pinball machine. Becky was trying to squeeze some edge out of the very classic rock juke-box, and J.D. had returned to the bar—no surprise there. The empty beer bottle in his own hand settled Jason's indecision, and he headed for Texas with a purposeful stride. The beer, Jason noted with some surprise, was go-ing down with dangerous ease; he'd reached that free-fall stage of the evening where any further alcohol he consumed was irrelevant to his buzz.

J.D. smiled at his approach, having known all along the path Jason would choose. "I know this isn't a real birthday party, or nothin'," he in-toned over the crowd as Jason drew near, "but it is sort of in your honor, so I, uh . . . well, I got you a little something."

"Uh-huh," said Jason, immediately wary. "What is it?"

J.D. frowned with comic gravity. "I ain't gonna lie to you. It is, in fact, another shot of tequila."

In spite of himself, Jason grinned. "You really, *really* shouldn't have," he replied. "Really."

"I know," said J.D. "But what can I say? I love you, man."

"Did you honestly buy me another shot of tequila?"

"It's right behind me on the bar. Don't look," J.D. added, shifting his

185

shoulders to block Jason's view. "You've known me for a long time, Jason, and I think you know you can trust me on this one."

"You know I actually already had one, about twenty minutes ago."

J.D. nodded, still deadpan. "Yeah, I know."

"I'm actually pretty ripping, fucking, stinking drunk already, if you have to know the truth," said Jason.

"Then one more shot won't make a lick o' difference," reasoned J.D. "Wait'll you see it. Little bitty thing."

"I'm just not sure I can do it justice, that's all I'm—"

"Okay," J.D. interrupted. "Now close your eyes . . ."

⋄ ⋄ ⋄

By the time the bartender returned with his beer, Jason had determined to put some distance between himself and J.D.'s liver, and he wandered to the back of the bar with a sense of victory, the tequila still burning in his chest. *What doesn't kill you makes you stronger.*

Nick was furiously rocking the machine back and forth, to a chorus of angry electronic tilt warnings he knew he could ignore. Paul looked on, introspectively sipping his big-bowled rum drink.

"Put Bally in," said Nick after a high-scoring series, and Paul laughed.

Jason was out of the loop. "In what?"

"Paul and I are starting a mutual fund," Nick replied, expertly passing the ball from one flipper to the other, then rocketing it back to the top.

"I'm impressed."

Paul shrugged. "It's really more of an investment club and a deal with a trader."

"You'll get a prospectus," Nick assured him.

"We're predicting the specifics of the new industrial age by researching the financial history of the last one and scoping out parallel patterns," Paul explained. "Think of your computers as cars. Chip companies are the new Big Steel and Big Oil, broadband is the railroad, et cetera. We're picking the blue-chippers for the next generation by metaphor only."

"Wow," said Jason. "How's it going?"

"We made two million dollars in pretend money last month."

"Bought myself a pretend Porsche," said Nick, slapping flippers madly to save an out-of-control ball. "Drives like a dream . . . literally. Fuck *you*," he added for the machine, then stepped aside.

"So how does one go about setting up a mutual fund?" said Jason.

Paul considered his response before taking up a position at the helm of the pinball machine. "I don't think I'm going to tell you," he replied, cocking the plunger. "It's very complicated."

"Try me," said Jason.

"Nope," Paul replied. "The way I see it, it's highly unlikely that your desire to know outweighs the pain in the ass of me telling you."

"Come on," Jason protested. "I'm not a complete moron."

But Paul shook his head gravely, watching his ball ping-ping-ping like lightning between two bumpers. "Let's not take that risk."

Jason laughed and waited, but heard nothing but pinball chirps and beeps. He turned to Nick. "He's seriously not going to tell me."

"Doesn't look like it."

"Now you're both just making me feel stupid."

Paul nodded. "Let's just chat about current TV shows and stuff."

"I'm going to tell J.D. you dare him to a chug to the death," said Jason. "Nick, *you* tell me how this thing works."

"She's here," said Nick, whose attention had been caught by something behind them.

"Who's here?"

"J.D.'s new hog," said Nick, pointing toward the front entrance. "That Century Twenty-one realtor by the door."

Jason followed the sight line from Nick's pointing finger to a pixieish girl in a bright red corduroy jacket.

"Just what we need," said Nick. "A girlfriend hanging around making J.D. do even stupider things than he already does. Look at that haircut and tell me she's not an idiot."

"What a couple of sassy girls you are," said Jason. "I'm hitting the john." With that, he stepped toward the gently beckoning light of the men's room, rubbery legs threatening to give out at every step, thanks to the diabolical mixed-liquor brew sloshing around in his guts. Slowly, the light grew closer.

Severely underestimating his inertia, Jason missed the turn into the doorway and ran smack into the wall, catching his balance with a spastic lunge and knocking a painting cockeyed with the effort. The painting was of a slave galley battling a storm at sea, and in its new orientation the ship seemed to be climbing the crest of an unimaginably huge wave.

◇ ◇ ◇

In the bathroom, Jason conducted his business and checked himself in the mirror. He was relaxed and jubilant; he could be happy hanging out in this moment, with these guys, forever. He was acutely conscious of how unique this was, this twilight happy hour between the juvenalia of college and the inevitable onset of adult concerns. With a frown, he raked his fingers through his messed-up hair.

Moments earlier, watching Becky chatting up some random guy, he'd found himself picturing them together, peeling each other's clothes off. They were destined, all of them, he supposed, to pair off eventually, and in the heady adolescent one-night stands going on, he could glimpse the diaspora to come. As close as they all were right now, would they even know each other's names in ten years? he wondered.

Jason thought about Amanda, for the first time in hours; tried to decide whether she was soul-mate material or just a passing fancy. Tough to tell; all that held them together at the moment was a single thin, quite possibly imaginary, piece of paper. He laughed at himself for coming back to the deed after all, on his night off, as if some dedicated problem-solving center in his mind couldn't rest, searching subconsciously for a solution that danced just out of reach.

Taking a deep breath, he plowed back into the fray.

Chapter Seven

THE MEATPACKING DISTRICT

The balding right-front tire of the garbage truck bounced heavily into a pothole on Little West 12th Street, splashing into a stagnant puddle and spraying a corner mailbox with unspeakable filth.

The truck was northbound, happily beating feet out of the Meatpacking District, a small maze of streets squeezed into a rough triangle south of 14th between Hudson and the West Side Highway. It was an old and weary corner of the city, bleak and shadowy even at high noon, a theme park of bricked-in windows, rattling overhead corrugated metal doors, and crumbling concrete facades. No residences, no retail stores to speak of, no visible police protection. No color, even, apart from the ribbons of graffiti scattershot all over the walls and doors, and the varicolored crack-vial caps that frosted the gutters in a candy-sprinkle rainbow.

In another hour or so, the morning light, strained into great shafts of gold by the vertical sieve of the cityscape, would begin to knife into this lawless western reach, scattering the last of the ratty night people. By breakfast, scant evidence of the wee hours' sex-bazaar commerce would remain. No receipts, no W-4s—just telling little circles of cigarette butts, the odd unfinished malt-liquor bottle, a straggling school of latex jellyfish bobbing down the mighty Hudson.

With dawn already on the move, the real meatpackers were lumbering into action, unlocking freezers, sniff-testing fatty haunches, throwing open wide-mouthed delivery doors. The streets would soon be lousy with well-marbled men in blood-spattered aprons ambling around, dangling cigars from fat lips and drinking in the rich, bloody aroma, talking of coarse grinds and last night's sitcoms. But for now, only the diesel roar of the lone garbage truck split the silence, a last machine sadly rumbling the empty streets after Armageddon.

Creaking and groaning in saurian claustrophobia, the garbage truck reached 14th Street at last, where the crazy quilt of southern Manhattan gives way at last to a navigable grid, and turned right. Then a quick left up 8th Avenue, past a doughnut store that used to be a different doughnut store, and it was gone.

"Okay," said Freddie as the truck disappeared—leaving himself, in the passenger seat, and Vinnie, at the wheel, alone again. "Now turn the car off."

"Why?" sighed Vinnie, dog-tired and petulant, comical in his raccoon's black eye. "What the hell are we doing here?" His head was aching; all he wanted on earth, swear to God, was to drive straight home, climb in bed with his wife, and sleep away this whole horrible night. But Freddie had insisted they drive here first and then refused to explain why, which scared and irritated him.

"Do it," said Freddie, gazing out the passenger's window, and Vinnie shook his head with a sigh and turned the key. The engine wound down and expired, perfecting the silence.

Freddy rolled his head slowly left and eyed his compatriot with barely concealed contempt. *Good a spot as any,* he thought.

"I'm really fuckin' tired, Freddie," whined Vinnie, jerking his head around nervously. "What's happening? Why are we here?" A seagull cried in the distance, like a voice from a dream.

"Open your mouth," said Freddie absently, still staring out the passenger window.

"What the f—?" Vinnie began, choking off his own protest when he saw his partner withdraw a Glock from his coat pocket.

It took only a split second to pin Vinnie to the seat with his left hand

and thrust the piece up to the smaller man's quivering lips. Freddie knew it wasn't the mere *fact* of the gun that had paralyzed his companion, it was partly the impressive gun itself; a huge, jet-black, hand-finished mother-fucking Glock that looked, even in his big strangler's hands, like a god-damn cannon.

"Oh, God! Fuckin' . . . Freddie," blubbered Vinnie, trying to keep his lips pursed against the invasion of the gun barrel. His fists were curled up insect style behind the massive forearm crushing him back into the leather, as if his very arms were withering in terror.

"Shut up, Vin," said Freddie coolly, the voice of reason, not even both-ering to look around, knowing with perfect certainty that they were quite alone. "I'm asking you *exactly one last time* to shut the fuck up." With tiny, practiced movements, he slid the barrel of the gun up under the smaller man's tented upper lip and tapped it twice against the front teeth. "Open."

Vinnie nodded dumbly, head shuddering, eyes alternately squinting and staring. A small moan escaped his lips as they closed around the bar-rel of the gun.

Freddie smiled broadly, deeply gratified at staring once again into the face of abject, total fear. This was so much easier than it looked, he thought; that was, of course, the secret. Now he spared a glance out at the deserted streets; there was nobody in sight.

"I *hate* like *hell* to do this," he said with gravelly drama, fixing his gaze on Vinnie. "I want to make sure you know that, Vin. This is dirty work, and I don't like it."

His victim's eyes widened. "Wh-wha?"

"You're out, Vin. End of the line."

"Wh-what? Wait, wait, wait," he murmured, panicking.

"Please do not *fucking* struggle," said Freddie, slamming the other's suddenly lurching body back to the seat, irritated now. "I don't like this any better than you. I don't make the rules; I just try to do right by the company. End of story."

"Okay," murmured Vinnie, on bizarre and shaky ground here, trying to focus on subduing his blind panic.

"Maybe that's where *you* got into trouble. Who knows?"

Vinnie wrenched his mouth away from the gun. "Freddie, I swear to

God I don't understand," he babbled. "I swear to God I don't. Freddie, wait, you gotta talk to me, man. What's this about?"

"Open your mouth, Vinnie."

"Freddie, please, you gotta fucking talk to me; don't *do* this, Freddie, look at me; what the *fuck* are you doing?" His speech was cranking up in speed and pitch; mad flecks of foamy spittle whitened the corners of his mouth.

"Don't make this harder than it has to be," said Freddie. "This is tough as it is. Please, just open your mouth."

Vinnie was shaking, now, sweating hysterically, practically crying. "Freddie—"

"Open your mouth," the big man cooed. "Open your mouth and be quiet now, okay?"

Lips quivering violently, Vinnie complied, and Freddie poked the gun gently inside.

"When I heard that this had to be done, I volunteered," said Freddie. "Nothing personal, I swear, I just didn't want anyone else doing it but me. Now that's the truth, Vin, okay? I wanted you to know that."

Vinnie's body was racking with spasms, and his eyes pleaded silently, loath to break the order of silence and touch off the gun, but choking to death on unreleased terror.

"I am truly sorry, Vin," said Freddie as he curled a finger around the trigger. "It's just . . . business." Vinnie squeezed shut his eyes and emitted a last, gasping canine whine.

"BANG!" yelled Freddie, loud enough to scare a pigeon off the adjacent curb.

Vinnie squealed and clicked his teeth so violently on the barrel of the gun that Freddie almost did fire the damn thing. He slid the barrel out of Vinnie's mouth and grinned madly.

As his target stared woodenly into the steering wheel, Freddie smiled and closed his eyes, sublimely happy and at peace with himself, even as the unmistakable stench of human piss violated the airspace. "This isn't complicated, Vin. You answer to me now," he said coolly. "You got it?"

A brief pause, and then Vinnie nodded, broken and wordless.

"Come on, get this car moving," said Freddie. "We got some recon-
naissance work ahead of us today. We'll take care of the old man later."

The car left the curb slowly, shakily, and he tucked the gun back in his
shoulder holster, then rolled down his window to take in the cold morning breeze.

The world was lookin' *big*.

UPPER WEST SIDE, 8:30 A.M.

Somewhere in the ice-choked depths of his mini-freezer Jason had discovered the butt end of an old joint, and he proudly finished it off on the
way into the shower, breathing in the smoke and eagerly anticipating the
thousand liquid fingers of pleasure poised to leap out and massage his
body. Standing outside waiting for the water to get hot, he inhaled deeply
one last time, held his breath, and set the tiny roach on the edge of the
sink, where it instantly tumbled off onto the floor, the still-glowing cherry
decapitating itself on impact. Amused but in control, he coughed just
once and pulled the curtain aside.

He considered the billions of individual droplets packed in behind his
showerhead and down the pipe to the basement water heater and out to
the street. They'd survived a long journey, each drop preparing for that
shimmering kamikaze moment when it would burst briefly into open-air
freedom, ricochet once off his skin, and swirl down into the drain again,
to mingle with sweat and soap and alligator feces and God knew what else
in the sewers on its long, dark journey back to the sea.

What an absurd little career, he thought. *Maybe they all are*.

Jason's head was still pounding a bit when he stepped out twenty minutes later, but the hangover was definitely in retreat. He left the bathroom
dry, nude, and imperial, and surveyed his domain.

His regal eye fell quickly on the stack of papers holding down the coffee table in the living-roomish end of his studio apartment. Sauntering
over, feeling quite a bit stoned now, he picked up the top page of the
graveyard sketches, pulled out of the book. He let his eye drift to the note-
card family tree still hanging hopefully on the wall. The blank break in

the middle stood out, in his heightened state of awareness, like a light-house beacon.

Flipping through, he found a sketch at the bottom, a rough overhead map of the graveyard, which Amanda had apparently drawn. It looked like a supercharged Stonehenge, the circular yard filled in with concentric rings of tiny Xs in black, red, and blue. A rash of red dots inside the squared-off secret inner yard solved the color coding: red for the two-*a* older Haansvoort stones, blue for the one-*as*, black for the rest.

All thoughts of a Hot-Pocket breakfast fled as the thrill of the chase overtook him. "We're gonna sort this out right now," he said aloud and sat down to work, naked but determined.

Setting the chart aside, he picked up the grave rubbings and began placing them on the table, absently orienting them side by side in accordance with the overhead drawing. The process triggered a higher sense of order, and he picked them all back up again and began moving furniture around, clearing a section of floor large enough to replicate the map on a larger scale.

Meticulously, he placed the rubbings around the floor, tiptoeing gingerly between them as he dipped in and out of the design to tweak their proper placement. *Look at me: I'm the guy who builds the mashed-potato mountain in* Close Encounters, he thought. Bending over on all fours to place one rubbing, he suddenly became aware of his dangling balls, and the notion struck him as so funny he had to collapse, laughing, on the couch. He looked down at his handiwork. Amazing!

He wondered whether Amanda had gone through this same exercise in her apartment, minus the pot, of course, then wondered whether she'd even have *thought* of doing this. Shifting perspective across scales was a telltale stoner strategy. Might he not, in fact, pretend to be a giant clomping around in this tiny graveyard, making Godzilla noises and terrifying the villagers? And so he did, for a long, long minute or two.

A sober moment came when he recalled, for no good reason, the previous night's conversation with the guys, and the offhand way they'd warned him not to trust Amanda's motives. It was as disturbing in retrospect as the first time around. Just male bonding, probably, but the dart, however casually thrown, had stuck. *Could* he trust her . . . really? Jason wondered. With such a prize at stake, what *wouldn't* someone do to secure whatever help she needed?

He shook his head, trying to dispel the line of thought. He really, really liked this girl—his heart, brain, gut, and cock were in rare agreement on this. Surely he had to be able to trust his own instincts. Or was that a sucker line of reasoning?

Jason wrenched his attention back to the floor pattern, now an exact replica of Amanda's scrawly map, but on a more suitably impressive scale. He stepped up onto the couch for the aerial view, staggered once in its springiness, then caught his footing.

It was impressive. The sketches retrieved his memory of the stones themselves, and he felt a sense of vertigo, as if unable to convince his brain that he wasn't enormous and towering above an actual field of stones. Staring at the masking tape he'd used to indicate the fence dividing off the old graveyard, Jason tried to think of a more wall-like replacement to complete the sense of reality, then correctly recognized this as the leading edge of a black hole that would, if indulged, kill the rest of the morning. He shrugged it off without much difficulty.

Staring beyond the graveyard at the relatively distant family tree on the wall, he could pick out no detail but the glaring gap toward the top. It occurred to Jason that he and Amanda had one unknown—the mysterious middle of his descendancy line—but two equations, the family tree and the map. Combining them should let him solve for the unknown, shouldn't it? It seemed reasonable, anyway.

He began correlating the names on either side of the family-tree gap to their grave sites, on the hunch that a geographical clue might emerge, suspecting even as he did it that there was a tiny flaw in the logic here that would become obvious later, when his head was clearer.

But he was wrong. Almost instantly, the experiment yielded pay dirt.

There was only one double-*a* Haansvoort grave out in the main graveyard, poor fourteen-year-old Mary, buried right up against the fence. Robert, the first of the single-*a* Hansvoorts, was also just outside the fence but a little farther away, in the same concentric circle as Mary. The old inner fence corraled all the old Haansvoort stones apart from Mary's, and none of the new ones. And it was after Mary, on the wall map, that the trail went cold.

There simply had to be something here. He wanted to call Amanda, but she'd still be out at the reservation with her mother, he had to assume, and if she had a cell phone he didn't know about it yet. It was a frustratingly primitive problem, this business of not being able to reach somebody whenever you wanted. Balancing on the couch, hungry for further insight, Jason turned back to the treasure map on his floor.

And made a new discovery.

There had been a gap, he now realized, between the girl's gravestone, close to the fence, and Robert's grave, six or eight feet away in the same circle. On Jason's floor, this was represented only by five inches of immaculate oak flooring. But on Amanda's drawing, a small black scribbled-in circle stood between his grave and hers, like an errant standardized test entry. Searching his memory, Jason recalled the phenomenon the scribble represented, a small unmarked mound they'd both dismissed that day as the spot of a removed tree. Now, Amanda's map made it clear that the spot lined up perfectly with the concentric circular grid of gravestones. He wondered if the fact that she'd bothered to include it meant that this had occurred to her, too.

The mound between Robert's and Mary's stones was a grave, clear as day, an unmarked grave that corresponded exactly to the gap in the family tree, if it could be deciphered. He felt another wave of vertigo, as if the apartment were rolling away beneath his feet.

Catching his breath a little, he stepped off the couch and walked gingerly into the graveyard, rustling the dead as he slipped past, and lifted up the two critical sketches, Mary's and Robert's, for a closer look.

Robert's was simple:

ROBERT MICHAEL HANSVOORT
1765–1810
DEVOTED SON AND FATHER
AND SERVANT OF OUR LORD
JESUS CHRIST

Crowning the stone was the same three-leaf pattern found on Mary's stone—another parallel, one he remembered noticing, but not investigating, back in the graveyard.

Mary's stone, more than seventy years older, read:

MARY ELIZABETH HAANSVOORT
1720–1734
CHYLDE IS TAKEN TOO SOON FROM US
BUT THE STAR OF HER LYFE LIVES ON
"WHEN PRIDE COMES, THEN COMES DISGRACE
BUT WITH HUMILITY COMES WISDOM"

WHAT PROVIDENCE HATH GRANTED
LET CHARITY NEVER FORGET

He smiled, remembering Amanda's elated discovery of the weed-obscured line at the bottom and their mutual efforts to clear it.

This is all the clue you get, Jason told himself. *Time to try Amanda's crazy logic: Start from the presumption that the line's important, and work it backward. Imagine there's a reason that that line . . . revealed itself to us. Pretend it wanted to be found.*

"What Providence hath granted, let Charity never forget."

He looked at the rubbings in his hand, peered at the wall, mentally subtracted dates. Thirty-one years between the girl's death at age fourteen and Robert's birth.

Let Charity never forget.

Suddenly, his jaw dropped, and he sat down on the couch. Could it be?

Mary had died at fourteen, putting an apparent end to the line. But it hadn't ended, clearly, and the only possible explanation, however improbable it might seem, had to be the right one.

Mary had been pregnant, and had died in childbirth.

He glanced at the clock as he leaped up to race for the door. "Fantastic!" he shouted, amused by just how close he'd come to actually opening the apartment door before remembering he was buck, raving naked.

Jason threw on his boxers and fell to the floor pulling on his pants, thumping his ass on the hardwood and scattering ancestors helter-skelter. He began laughing uncontrollably at his piteous state, then somehow got himself dressed and jammed the two critical sketches in his pocket. Ten minutes later, he was out the door and hailing a cab. First stop: Chase Manhattan for some cash. This was going to be the longest cab ride of his life. But money was no object.

Charity was a *person*.

LONG ISLAND, 1:45 P.M.

In his addled state, haggling over a fee with the cabdriver had proved excruciating beyond belief. But by the time they'd left the Long Island Expressway and begun the steady downgrading of roads leading to the reservation itself, Jason's buzz had worn down to a manageable level. He proudly plotted, for the cabbie, the exact route to the reservation; his mind was ideally hardwired for the stone logic of streets, and new ones, once sketched into the ever-developing atlas in his head, tended to stay firmly put.

They dipped down at last off the end of the paved road, and Jason smiled in anticipation. A half mile inside the reservation, just short of the house itself, the car came to a lurching halt, as if fatally intimidated by the moonscape of undercarriage-eating potholes pocking the path. He fished out the monstrous fare and stepped outside.

Even as Jason's euphoria wandered and reason, with a reproachful glare, politely took up the reins again, his belief that he was on to the truth only continued to crystallize. And all the evidence he could bring to bear, he considered as he walked the final half mile to Amanda's mother's house, only buttressed the hypothesis. Mary gets pregnant at fourteen, dies in childbirth. No surprise there. She's a Haansvoort, of course, so as an unmarried teenager, she takes her maiden surname to that early grave. Her parents name the baby Charity, maybe for the simple fact that she survives; for lack of a legal father—did they ever even find out who he was?—Charity keeps the Haansvoort name as well.

So far, so good.

But why is Charity's grave unmarked, and her identity struck from the family Bible—evidence of an organized effort to wipe out her entire existence? There were indications of no small familial distress here, it seemed to Jason, and while he had to allow that his theory from this point on flowered into wilder speculation, still Jason thought it stayed within the bounds of logic. Charity would have been born out of wedlock—could a girl be a "bastard"?—and an orphan, effectively. Difficult enough today; no doubt unthinkable in the days of witch-burning and so on. She would have been an outcast from day one.

Whatever had happened to her next was buried in that unmarked grave. But would it have surprised anybody if Charity had grown up to repeat the sin of her mother? One way or another, by the time Charity came around to bearing her own child, Robert, there was again no husband in the picture to give the boy a new last name.

And just so, the Haansvoort name had survived.

Jason crossed the lawn, climbed the unpainted steps of the porch, and pressed the bell. He felt a thrill of accomplishment about to come to fruition: the clever boy bringing a term project to school at last. But his elation was mixed with a little of the unease he'd felt the last time he was out here, now spiced with a dash of stoner paranoia. How would Amanda's mom react to seeing him again . . . and would this, plus the family Bible Amanda had brought earlier, be enough to get her to cough up her secrets? Most important of all, did she know where the deed was, or not?

Jason had already depressed the buzzer again when he heard footsteps shuffling on the other side of the door, too late to stay his hand. He smiled sheepishly, loading up a casual apology to deliver to Amanda or her mother, whichever one answered.

But it was Amanda's father who pulled back the door, framing himself darkly in the opening, and the shock thoroughly disabled Jason. He stood drowning on the doorstep, honestly trying to remember why he'd come.

The big Indian was less overtly hostile than in their first encounter, but still presented a terrifying figure, his linebacker build augmented by a completely unfair six-inch height bonus courtesy of the step-down porch. As in their last encounter, he spoke not a word, merely assaulted Jason with an evil *You-bangin'-my-daughter?* glare. His rough-and-tumble appearance—unshaven, one shirttail hanging out—helped humanize him, diffusing the terror somewhat. He'd slept on the couch, maybe . . . but the potentially humorous observation couldn't compete, in Jason's mind, with the image of a whistling tomahawk sending a hairy pizza of scalp flipping gracelessly off the top of his head.

"Hi, I'm . . . ," began Jason, suddenly a fourteen-year-old selling newspaper subscriptions. "I'm Jason," he continued. Behind him he heard the cab's undercarriage scrape as it backed up onto the pavement, and part of him wanted to turn and sprint for it, knees pumping like a racehorse, and try to leap in through the open window, *Dukes of Hazzard*–style.

"Amanda's not here," said the Indian.

Caught unawares, Jason started, felt his mouth drop open. *Here's a cog in the works*, he thought, struggling for a plan, not remotely ready to face an absurd journey back to Manhattan empty-handed. "Do you have any idea where . . . when she's coming back?" he managed weakly. *Because maybe we could just watch the game together or something while we wait. Dad.*

Again the Indian said nothing, and Jason marveled at the man's complete lack of civility. It occurred to him to wonder whether he knew anything at all about the deed. If he did, how did he feel about Jason's role? About an ancient mother-to-daughter succession structure that left him to bake cookies in the kitchen while the womenfolk talked business?

I could see where that could make a man edgy, Jason decided.

But that clearly wasn't the whole answer; there was something else here. Amanda's relationship with her dad had soured long before any of this deed nonsense; or her knowledge of it, anyway. This silent, antagonistic soul, Jason reminded himself, was the guy who'd first defined men for her. Food for thought.

Perhaps conceding that his burning stare wasn't tumbling Jason backward off the step, Amanda's father relented and slowly hooked one thumb rightward, indicating a spot in the woods behind his house. "They're out by the sound," he said.

The sound? "Thanks," said Jason, confused but gleefully seizing the opportunity to beat feet. He'd know the sound when he heard it, he decided, turning on one heel and leaping sideways off the stoop like a rabbit having finally chewed through his ankle and slipped the trap.

The door latched behind him without incident.

✧ ✧ ✧

As crappy an excuse for civilization as this godforsaken housing tract was, Jason felt sorry to leave it as the trees closed in around him. By the time he'd gone a hundred paces downhill and into an indifferently wooded gully, glances behind him no longer caught any corner of the houses, the lines of sight intercepted by trunks of unnaturally thick birch trees. For the first time, he began to doubt whether the profundity of his discovery was really worth coming all the way out here. This apparent triumph of instinct over reason unsettled him at a deep level; he felt a sudden need to take care of his business quickly and head back to the firmer ground of Manhattan.

It had rained here—this morning, apparently—and in the spaces between his own mushy footfalls and the brushing of his jeans in the uncannily long grass he could still hear occasional droplets slapping onto foliage. Jason paused and did a full three-sixty to check out the surroundings. The quick little breeze into which he was sailing upturned the leaves' matte green underbellies; above him loomed a brooding, billowing sky. There was an eternal sort of grandeur to this intimate dance of the elements; it occurred to Jason that he was alone in what was perhaps one of the last untouched areas of forest on the Atlantic seaboard.

Tracking Indians, no less, he reminded himself.

He continued tramping through the mulchy underbrush as the land fell away toward the ocean. *Toward Long Island Sound,* he corrected himself with a sudden grin; suddenly Amanda's father made sense. The trees were heavy with water above him; the same wind that inhaled him steadily down the hill occasionally shook out a sprinkling cascade from branches above, gradually drenching his hair and shoulders.

Still warm in the afterglow of the pot and focused by the solitude, Jason thought he could see something holy in this untouched chunk of forest, where statuesque trees stretched fat, lazy arms in every direction amid chattering stands of saplings. *Beautiful,* he thought, then shook his head; the word seemed cheap.

Maybe this was why Amanda's mom was so resistant to the influence of the West, for all its advantages. To voluntarily subvert your power to the

wild magic of the natural world, instead of yielding to the human temptation to assume ownership of that world, was to loiter forever in childhood,
to refuse to accept the awesome destructive powers of the adult world.
There was comfort in that. The earth would always be there, and voluntarily submitting to its rule let you cleave indefinitely to a parent who
would never desert you.

The sea hove into view at last, choppy and laced with foam, the horizon nearly invisible between the twin grays of sea and sky. An instant later
he'd broken free of the trees, and at last saw Amanda and her mother. The
women, huddled against the cold, formed a small pocket of color atop a
breathtaking little sandy cove right at land's end, where the last of the forest turf, undermined by the ceaseless undercut of the waves, had been
scalloped into high dunes.

Mother and daughter sat on a rocky overhang by their discarded shoes
some forty feet away, dangling bare feet over the ocean, and though he
didn't say a word, they turned to face him as abruptly as if he'd stepped on
a Model A's oogah horn. Amanda's quick shock mellowed into a confused
little wave; her mother just glanced over, then back at the sea. With a
pang, Jason wondered whether he was intruding into a sacred spot: Ac-
taeon surprising Artemis and her huntresses, and about to get torn apart
for his troubles. But he pressed forward with a confident wave of his own,
buoyed on by his mission.

Cut the shit, lady, he said to himself. *Don't you know who I am?*

✧ ✧ ✧

Throughout the inevitable exchange of pleasantries and the satisfaction
of the women's great curiosity as to his mystical appearance here, Mary remained mostly silent, nodding and tossing off a syllable or two where required, watching Jason intently. Amanda, though, made no secret of her
delight at seeing him, though she'd waved warily when he first walked up,
as if his approach might magnetically repel her mother off the dune and
into the sea. He wondered if he'd by chance shown up at just the right
moment to interrupt a conversation about himself.

"Why am I here?" he repeated the question, when Amanda had finally gotten around to asking him, freeing him at last to roll out the speech he'd played out during the cab ride. "I'm here to claim my birthright," he continued, looking past Amanda to her mother. "Mary, I apologize for everything I said the last time I was here. You were right, I really didn't know who I was."

Amanda self-consciously backed up a step—they were all standing, now—evening up the legs of their conversational triangle.

"But I do now," said Jason. "My name is Jason Hansvoort, son of David, son of Elwood, son of Robert, son of Sam." He grimaced briefly at the treacherous little cosmic joke trying to undercut his solemnity, then soldiered on. "Son of Hendrick, son of . . ."

He trailed off here as a look flitted between daughter and mother. "I've made all the connections," he summarized. "I can trace my lineage back directly, right back to Pieter Haansvoort. There was one jump in the middle but I've solved it: an unmarried girl in the mid-1700s named Charity."

"Charity," said Amanda wonderingly, tasting it on her tongue.

"Yes," he replied, excited. "'What Providence hath granted, let Charity never forget.'"

Amanda was nodding, eyes closed, feeling the truth of this wash over her. "She stayed a Haansvoort because she never married."

"Bingo," said Jason. "And I know what you want," he said, redirecting his attention to Mary. "You want to know that I'm not in this thing for the money; you want to know that I can see the big picture, that I'm . . . here with my ancestors, and not just for myself . . . you want to know that I'm also part of a family."

She said nothing, as he'd half-expected, so he continued. "Well, I'll tell you exactly where my head is, and you can decide whether you want anything to do with me or not. I think that Nahoti, your ancestor, must have saved mine—or maybe just made his life worth living. There had to be a damn good reason he put his neck on the line to stand up for her tribe . . . your tribe. And in return for whatever she gave him, he gave your people a future. Saved them too, maybe . . ."

He stumbled for a moment, having become aware that he was on the verge of dissolving into stoner tangentiality—becoming more and more right but less and less understandable. "Put it this way," he tried to simplify. "This deed doesn't exist apart from your people; I understand that. Amanda's resurrected it as surely as if she'd written it herself. Without me, it's just a piece of paper. But without you, it doesn't exist at all.

"Mary, I know you take the long view historically, so it's hard for you to trust a nice white nice guy like me. That's essentially what you're waiting for, isn't it? A white man you can trust?" He looked away, briefly scanning the horizon for the answer, listening as a handful of oversize raindrops began scattering velvety fingertaps into the sand. "All I can do is assure you that I know I'm a pawn in this . . . in the history-altering event going on here," he continued. "I have no pride anymore. Too much has happened here that I can't explain, too many coincidences. I recognize that I'm being pulled along by the . . . by the tide, here, as much as you are." He took a breath. "But I'm not just any white man. I'm the descendant of the man to whom your ancestor devoted her life and entrusted the fortunes of her people. That's who I am."

A smile slowly broke across Mary's face. "You've made some strides since we last spoke," she said.

"Hmm . . . well, don't start talking down to me again, or I'll take it all back," Jason replied. Amanda grinned in relief, then looked skyward when a large raindrop bounced a small sheaf of bangs down into her eye.

"I won't promise you anything, Mary," Jason continued, ignoring the shower that was coming on fast. "I know you wouldn't accept it if I did. But whatever this thing is that's now officially taken over my life, I'm going to see it through."

He paused now, waiting for a response. Mary studied him, but her eyes were sparkling. "Ooh, I like you much better this time around," she said at last.

"I claim the deed as my birthright," Jason added: a coda.

He exhaled in relief, satisfied with his ending, but Mary was shaking her head.

"The deed is lost," she said.

✧ ✧ ✧

They followed her back through the wettening woods; as soon as it became clear that Mary didn't intend to say another word until they'd reached shelter, Jason hung back to exchange a few words with Amanda.

"Your father's at the house," he said as a warning. "Freaked the holy hell out of me."

"He was out all night," said Amanda, watching her shoes traverse a muddy puddle. "He's just hung over, that's all."

Feeling a little shut out, he fell silent.

"If he's still there, don't mention the deed or any of it, okay?"

"How come?"

She shrugged. "My mom doesn't trust him."

"Good enough," agreed Jason, nodding. But it was a moot point; even as they began to crest the final hill and the house came into view, they heard a car kick into life and drive away.

✧ ✧ ✧

They entered the house single file: Mary first, kicking off her wet shoes, Jason politely following suit, Amanda bringing up the rear.

"It's somewhere on the island," said Mary, as if crossing the threshold had freed her to break the silence. "The last person who knew where it was died almost a hundred years ago."

Jason, still in a crouch to remove his wet shoes, felt a chill as Amanda pulled the door closed behind him. He watched in amusement as she shucked her light jacket, eyes narrowed on her mom like a tiger on its prey.

"But there's more," Amanda prodded.

Mary only raised her eyebrows mysteriously and headed out of the entry hall. "Amanda, why don't you get us some coffee?" she called out, halfway to the living room.

Jason grinned at this. "Just sugar for me, sweetie. Thanks."

Amanda flipped him the bird, then stepped quickly into the kitchen.

He followed Mary's trail into the living room, but she'd already disappeared somewhere farther into the house, leaving him alone to glance around. The two housecats were here again, positions only trivially changed since his last visit, little mismatched lumps of kinetic art.

"Your hair looks good wet," he said when Amanda entered with a coffee tray.

She sneered in a cute way, then blew a straggling cowlick up and out of her eyes with a quick Popeye lip whistle. Crossing the room to him, she set the tray down and sat on the couch, and he lowered himself into an easy chair next to her.

"So, son of Elroy . . . ," she said, eyes twinkling.

"Elwood," he laughed. "Don't start with me, woman."

"Seriously, nice job. I'm impressed."

Jason smiled; *bring it on, baby.*

"No offense," she said, eyes twinkling, "but did you really come all the way out here because you were so proud of yourself for figuring that out?"

"Well, *someone* had to kick this search into gear."

"Sure," said Amanda.

"Oh, *I* get it," said Jason, enjoying himself immensely. "You think I came all the way out here to see *your* drippy ass. Is that it?"

She laughed. "Puh-lease."

He smiled automatically at hearing her now-familiar laugh; something in their relationship was shifting.

With that, Mary swooped back into the living room, holding a small, dark wooden box. "I'm going to tell you everything I know, but I warn you, it's not much," she said grandly.

She sat down beside her daughter on the couch and placed the box on the table and ignored it, despite their silent pleas. Instead, she turned to the coffee, tediously adding sugar and cream, stirring and stirring as if trying to dissolve the spoon in the liquid.

"There we go. The deed's resting place," she said at last, tapping the spoon on the edge of the cup, "has been a jealously guarded secret since it was given to us. In every generation, I suppose, there's been a faction that wants to expose the deed and stake our claim. But it can only be done once, of course. Since the very beginning, it's been the job of the sachem . . . my job . . . to decide when the time is right to make our bid. I really believe," she said, looking back and forth between Jason and Amanda, "the time is now."

Jason nodded and peripherally saw Amanda do the same.

Mary accepted this with a slight regal bow of her head. "But there's a problem," she continued. "Keeping this secret, generation after generation, has meant restricting its knowledge to a very few. Only two people at any one time were ever meant to know the location. The sachem passes on the knowledge to her successor once that successor has proven she can handle the task. When the old sachem dies, a new successor is chosen, and the cycle repeats."

"And somewhere along the line, someone died before they could pass on the location," said Amanda.

"Apparently," Mary said, nodding. "But I'm just guessing. I know that your great-grandmother, who was sachem before my mother, never knew where it was. But I don't know if she's the break in the chain or if it happened before her."

"Didn't it ever occur to anyone that the secret could die with somebody?" said Jason.

She frowned. "Yes, Jason; we aren't idiots. We decided early on to keep a written record of the deed's location . . . but something cryptic, that couldn't be deciphered by a layman. It was more of a set of clues that, ideally, only the sachems, the deed's intended stewards, should be able to figure out. That way, as long as there was a tribe and a leader—in other words, as long as the deed had any meaning—the location could be recovered, if lost."

"So figuring out where the deed is could be a test of worthiness to be the next sachem," said Jason thoughtfully. "Like a koan."

"That's insightful, Jason; it's very likely we used to do exactly that. It's different now, of course," said Mary. She then turned to Amanda. "But that does bring us to you, darling."

"Knew it," said Amanda. "The pressure's on."

"You can do it, if it can still be done," said her mother. "You know the stakes here—the rest is up to you."

Jason pointed to the box, confused.

"That's just a gift for you," warned Mary with a smile. She slid the box across to meet his outstretched fingers; unable to reach it from the chair, Jason slid forward and dropped to his knees in front of the table.

About ten inches long, intricately carved and blackened with age, the box seemed hand-cut out of a single brick of wood. Reverently, he lifted the top piece completely off, like the lid of a hatbox, to reveal, inside, a long, crooked, carved pipe.

"It was his," said Mary quietly. "The box, too."

"Whose?" Jason replied, figuring it out even as he said it. "Oh, wait—his?"

Mary nodded sagely. He caught a glimpse of Amanda's dumbstruck expression and realized it mirrored his own.

"You're telling me this pipe was owned by my ancestor in the early 1600s," said Jason.

"It is unquestionably his. The box, too, as I say. It's a tribal heirloom, but it isn't really ours, now that you've been found. Take it as a gesture of good faith."

"Mary, this is so far beyond cool it's . . ." Jason began. "Thank you. I don't know what else I could possibly say."

"Just will it back to us if you die without an heir, okay?"

"Mom," said Amanda.

"I'm overwhelmed," said Jason, fondling his pipe. "Seriously." He ran a finger around the rim of the bowl, resisting the temptation to put it to his lips. "This whole thing is so *unreal* . . ."

"The clues, Mom—the clues," said Amanda.

Mary smiled and drained her coffee, then looked hard at Jason. As Jason and Amanda exchanged a long glance, she walked over to the fireplace, stepped up onto the hearth, and unhooked the old parchment map of New York that Jason had noticed on his first trip here.

"No *way*," said Amanda.

"I *knew* there was more to that thing," said Jason. "I swear to God I did."

"You told me you made that," Amanda accused.

"We did—all of us," said Mary, and held the parchment out toward her daughter. "This is yours now, my dear; it's the legacy of our people."

Amanda nodded solemnly as Jason rose again to get a better look.

With a last searching glance at each of them, Mary slowly turned the map over. The flip side contained several paragraphs of tiny little characters frozen in mid-scrawl, like bugs transfixed by the sudden exposure to light.

"What language is that?" said Jason.

"The old language," Mary replied. "I'll write up a translation for you."

"It looks like poetry," Amanda ventured. "Is that significant?"

Mary considered her answer carefully before continuing. "I don't think I'm going to pass along my own conjectures. We already know I couldn't figure it out."

Methodically, patiently, she launched into a speech she must have been working on for some time. The time of her people, she said, and indeed of all Native Americans, had passed, rendering them shadows, or ghosts. And the function of ghosts, she explained, was to advise the living. She sipped her coffee languorously as she spoke, relaxing into eccentric tangency now that the main order of business had been concluded.

Mary believed, she said, that the Creator is never casual, that as trivial a role as her people were currently playing in the machine of the modern world, they did have a purpose still—as a living conscience for the Western world, which otherwise, she seemed happy to say, had none.

As he listened, Jason fought the desire to rise to the defense of the West, knowing his propensity to let his argumentative nature lead him into trouble. He distracted himself by trying to appreciate what a momentous occasion this must be for her, handing over the keys to the kingdom after three hundred years of waiting. He respectfully listened to her every sanctimonious word, tried to hear her as the calm, reverberating voice of an all-but-extinguished race of people.

And here sat Amanda in rapt attention next to him, her fortunes inextricably bound with his in this crazy, preordained partnership racing toward some cosmic conclusion. It felt almost as if her mother were blessing their union, with the island of Manhattan as the dowry.

LONG ISLAND EXPRESSWAY, 3:00 P.M.

"It's unfathomable to me," said Jason playfully from the passenger seat, "that you haven't torn into this thing yet."

Amanda smiled and kept her eyes glued to the road. The rain had abated for the time being, but the car's twin wipers still arced gamely across the windshield, swishing in absolute synchronicity. The map and Mary's translation lay on Jason's lap, his pipe and Bible secure in the back-seat.

"It's crazy," she replied distractedly. "Now that we have the answer in front of us, I'm almost afraid to start."

"Makes sense to me," said Jason, looking over the translation Mary had provided. "Before, this was an intellectual exercise. Now it's about proving yourself."

"What are you talking about? We don't have to prove ourselves."

"'We'?" said Jason. "What do you mean 'we,' kemo sabe?"

"What is it with you and all the Indian jokes?" she said.

He winced. "Sorry. What I mean is that for me it's still a game, but for you it's about proving your worthiness to be the next sachem."

"Oh, please."

"This is the rite of passage you've been waiting for," he goaded. "But it puts the pressure on. It's not enough that *we* solve it . . . *you* have to solve it."

"I don't think of it that way," she said softly.

"Bullshit," said Jason, smiling. "Don't worry. I promise if I figure it out first, I'll sandbag and drop hints until you figure it out."

She turned to fix him with a stern gaze. "Okay. A, you're not going to figure it out before me, and B, don't you dare delay this thing by even a minute. We figure it out together. Partner."

"Okay, partner," he laughed. "But seriously, if I get it first I'll keep my mouth shut."

"No, *don't*," she said firmly.

"Okay, I won't," he replied. "But I will."

"You're such a dick."

He laughed and went back to scanning Mary's translation of the ancient text.

"Well, read it out loud at least," she said, annoyed, and he did.

> *I am the hard shell of a tough nut*
> *At the hub of a wheel of fire and death.*
> *Your forests hold back the wind*

But I am the land itself, rolling toward you.
My walls enclose the blue sky itself
Keep soaring spirits bound to earth.
They come to live, who die at the gates
I sleep outside, above the first to fall.
Now earth and sky wall in the ocean
A mountain of water rides a sea of land
The city's blood imprisoned; life entombed in death.
I hold the doorway keeping back the flood.
The red god rises straight and tall
Straining to touch the yellow sun
He is the land, he watches over all
I dream beneath the red god's fire.

"That shit is just bristling with clues," murmured Jason. "A god rising from the earth to kiss the sun—a skyscraper?"

"But which one?" said Amanda, puzzled. "A red god."

"Well, we know it's been hidden at least since the late nineteenth century, so it's probably made out of bricks, right?"

Amanda's face lightened. "Good," she said. "It's probably not even what we'd call a skyscraper anymore."

"We should get a list of all the tallest buildings by year."

"I have all that stuff at my apartment," she replied excitedly. "Reference books, old New York history—the works. We can get started as soon as we get back."

Jason shook his head. "I'm busy tonight," he said. "Are you doing anything tomorrow?"

He loved how predictable she was; the shocked look on her face was perfect. "I'm kidding, Amanda," he reassured her. "I didn't chase you all the way out here to pencil you in for next week."

She grinned reluctantly and craned her head around to check the blind spot before making another ill-advised lane change to scoot past a short line of slow cars in her mad dash for the city.

They both fell silent for a while. To all appearances Amanda seemed focused on the road, but when she asked for a rereading of the translation it became clear where her mind was. After complying, Jason picked up the original and began idly looking it over. The poem itself being indecipherable, he scanned the page for nonverbal visual clues, then flipped it over and visually traced the contours of the map with one finger, trying to find a pattern. He held the page up to the windshield and watched the white light bleed through the frail old parchment.

"I wonder if there's any kind of interplay between the words and the map?" he said aloud. "If we knew which of these words meant what, we could search the map wherever key words lie on the—"

Suddenly, Amanda slammed both feet on the brake, which instantly locked up on the rain-slicked road. Jason lurched forward, flailing out one arm to protect the documents, and looked over the dashboard, where he saw red taillights coming on fast—they were rocketing out of control toward a square white wall of truck parked improbably in the fast lane, flashers flashing.

Amanda wrenched the wheel to the right, and he rolled his head around to see if her intended lane was clear. Not even close. There was no escape; either they'd plow into the back of the truck or, if their hard-turned and skidding wheels caught, they'd nose into the next lane, to be creamed by an oncoming Expedition. "Jesus Christ," he squeezed out, as their brakes struck up a chilling death wail.

The glowing red taillights spread across the drizzly pane in hideous close-up, and Jason became suddenly aware of himself drifting forward in slow motion. Somewhere in the midst of Amanda's desperate "Fuck! Fuck! Fuck!" he heard, rather than felt, the wheels find traction, and the car lurched right, missing the truck's bumper by the width of a couple of fingers. Jason scrunched his face in preparation for the next-lane impact, but the Expedition had somehow managed to brake in time, horn blaring indignation.

As they shot past the semi, Amanda astutely laid off the useless brakes and resumed speed, now safe in the other lane.

"Holy *shit*," said Amanda. "Sorry about—"

"Pull over," Jason mumbled, head between his knees.

"No, we're okay now."

"Could you please just *fucking* pull over?" said Jason, catching the note of real fear in his own voice.

Amanda eased the car onto the shoulder; before it rolled to a halt, Jason was already unlatching the door and hopping out. Seconds later, he was leaning over a guardrail, violently puking.

He stood there for what seemed like hours, feeling the rain pelt the back of his head and run around to his chin, where it dripped onto the roadside mess he'd left for some lucky dog.

"You okay?" she called tentatively from the car, and he realized he'd left the door open; he kicked it shut without turning.

A few moments later, a discreet wipe of mouth on sleeve, and he was ready to face the car's interior again. "I'm sorry about that," he said, pulling in and closing the door. "That wasn't a critique of your driving."

"Oh, my God, don't apologize. I nearly got you killed."

"I get queasy in cars sometimes," he explained.

She put the car in gear and pulled back onto the highway with exaggerated slowness. "That's fine."

"No it's not, it's stupid."

"Lots of people get carsick," Amanda offered halfheartedly.

He shook his head. "It's not carsickness," he said. "It's . . . I don't know what it is. It's like my stomach's empty, and it's trying to suck the rest of my body in. Do you ever have fear like that?" He ran his fingers over his scalp, brushing back his newly slicked hair. "I just sort of suddenly become hyperconscious of the fact that I'm hurtling at sixty miles an hour down the road, and that there are other cars racing just as fast toward me, and there's nothing between us but—"

"Hey," she said, before he could finish. "Hey, you okay?"

A nod. "Yeah, I'm fine."

"I'm really sorry I did that to you," she said.

He smiled weakly, wondered whether she'd already put two and two together. He realized he was tossing around clues because he wanted to talk about it, because he was monumentally sick and tired of keeping it all to himself all the time.

"Where did it happen?" she asked politely.

He felt fear knot up in his chest. "Do we have to talk about this?"

"No," she said. "Of course not."

But, of course, they did.

◇ ◇ ◇

Jason didn't speak for a long time, tried to watch the road and think logically about what he wanted to say. But each passing moment of silent anticipation lent more and more weight to the revelation to come, and so in the end he just started talking, let the words escape like fireflies out of a jar, thought after disconnected thought.

Losing his parents had been a terrible blow; losing them at the same time had been incomprehensible. He'd never really been able to grieve for them separately, couldn't extricate their charred hands from each other in his mind. Even now, it was still hard for him to picture them separately.

"Isn't that strange?" he wondered. "I have lots of memories of each of them separately, of course. But my memories are like photographs. I can't picture them solo without drawing on a specific memory. Whenever I'm trying to imagine them just . . . just *being* there, as themselves, they're always together."

Encouraged by a long pause, Amanda spoke cautiously. "Well, there's a kind of beauty to that."

He shrugged. "It's not very satisfying. I want to be able to miss just my dad. To dream about walking by a river with him, or playing catch. And then I want to imagine hanging out with my mom, and talking about things. They should still be individuals. They should be people."

"Maybe it's a way of shielding yourself," she suggested. "Like, if they're together, it's not as bad, somehow. For them. They've got each other—you know?"

"No, no," he protested. "It makes the whole thing too surreal. It's just . . . just loss. I can't reconcile it." He was staring out the windshield, watching the wipers battle the remains of the rain. "Two people should never die at the same time. Death's too enormous a concept to be multiplied."

"I totally agree with that."

"It paralyzed me for a long time, I guess," he acknowledged. "I still, to-day, don't feel really compelled to do anything. Succeed, or whatever. Even make basic choices. House or apartment? Cable or satellite?"

"Please, I can't even—"

"And yet, at the same time," he interrupted, to steamroll over her well-intentioned attempt to empathize, "I feel like I'm hitting that stage of my life where I really, really need to get my shit together and figure out what it is I need to do. What I *want* to do. Who I am."

Amanda changed lanes with deliberate, penitent caution, and Jason became distracted, losing his line of thought. When she broke the silence herself, the words seemed wholly disconnected from everything that had gone before.

"Do you think maybe," she ventured carefully, "maybe you're worried that if you start doing what *you* want, you'll be betraying them some-how . . . leaving them behind?"

The rain had dwindled to a light sprinkle now, and the Manhattan sky-line splayed across the horizon ahead of them, deceptively distant and golden in the afternoon sun, like a postcard propped casually against the sky.

"Or should I just keep my big fat mouth shut?"

"Let's just keep driving," he replied.

UPPER EAST SIDE, 5:30 P.M.

"It's kind of a mess," Amanda warned.

"Holy fucking Christ," said Jason, in the doorway, truly astonished.

Amanda's was a good-size apartment by New York's shoe-box standards, but the space was fatally compromised by the clutter. Floor-to-ceiling bookshelves lined most of the walls, spread haphazardly with vertical, horizontal, and spread-open stacks of books in a ragged riot. The comic disarray played itself out on every horizontal surface, from couch to floor to fish tank; it was as if the apartment itself were composed entirely of books, with the occasional laundry bag and empty juice bottle thrown in for spice or contrast.

"So this is kind of a tornado-versus-the-Library-of-Congress decorating scheme going on here."

"Whatever," she said, discreetly snatching up a bra on her way out of the room. "You want a Coke?"

The apartment was roughly square, with archways leading out from either side and the entry door in the middle of a third wall. Amanda had disappeared into one of these arches, apparently the kitchenette; the other was dark, and he crossed toward it, stepping gingerly around the flotsam, to satisfy his curiosity.

He'd expected a bedroom, but found instead a small stretch of hallway, where stood a little table just inside a rather ornate pair of French doors opening out onto an amazing little half rooftop, an unexpected open space she'd cluttered, predictably, with all manner of plants. Flowers, ferns, and even small trees, in a hodgepodge of pots, were drinking in the steady rain that spattered the Astro Turf.

"This is cool, Amanda," he called to the kitchen. "I dig your roof."

The hiss of a bottle opening, the clink and gurgle of carbonated liquid drowning ice cubes. "Open the doors," she suggested.

He followed her suggestion and instantly the smell of the rain billowed into the apartment with a cool rooftop breeze.

"Here," she said, suddenly beside him.

"Very cool," he reiterated, accepting the soda and sitting down at the little drop-leaf table. "You've got your own secret garden."

"It's a big bonus," she agreed. "This is a corner apartment; the layout's kind of strange."

"Yeah, I was wondering where your bedroom is."

She took a sip, peering at him over the rim. "Don't get cocky."

✧ ✧ ✧

By six o'clock the sky was already darkening. They decided to work on the puzzle until hunger or exasperation overtook them, then either make dinner from the fridge or order in, as the mood took them. A poor excuse for a plan by Jason's standards, but it was all Amanda would agree to be held to, here on her own turf.

She cleared a place for them both on the couch, then a space for the parchment poem and her mom's translation on a rickety-looking wooden coffee table. As he seated himself, she headed to one wall of the room and began cherry-picking individual books she hoped would help their cause.

"Here's one problem," said Jason. "Any place we'd have access to is also accessible to twenty million other people a day."

"And yet it hasn't been found," said Amanda. He didn't say anything, and she paused in her search to look at him. "Remember, we have to assume it hasn't been found, or we've got nothing."

"There's a proof of God's existence that goes something like that."

"I know you think it's stupid," said Amanda in a patronizing tone. "Just remember, Jason: Two weeks ago you were secure in a rational little world, plugging away at that horrible megacompany and hoping that someday, somehow, things were going to get better. All you had to do was widen your perception a little, and look what's happened to your life."

"Well, no," he protested. "I think it's the reality that's remarkable here, not my perception of it. Amanda, you've gotta admit stumbling onto a four-hundred-year-old deed is pretty unique." His own tone sounded antagonistic in his ears, and a warning bell went off in his head. This was how he got himself in trouble, by succumbing to his natural inclination to argue without regard for consequence. He determined to reel it in a bit.

But this time, at least, she was up to the challenge. "Is this really unimaginably unique for you?" she said. "Is the world such a dull place? Maybe the quarters clinking together in your pocket were bag mates in a bank twenty years ago. Maybe the author of this book," she continued, thrusting a tome at him from across the room, "taught geometry to my grandfather. I think coincidence is a basic building block of the universe, that it's no accident that the veins on a leaf look the same as the branches of its tree, or the tributaries of a river. Whenever we come across a really mysterious phenomenon we're blown away, we see the hand of God in it. But that's just the busy lives we lead, blinding us little by little to the truly mind-blowing complexity of the world."

He was impressed. "Okay," he conceded with a smile, stealing a glimpse at her slacks tightening around her exquisite ass as she plumped down triumphantly beside him. "Then let's do this for real. If the deed still exists, then it necessarily must also be hidden really well. Not just where it can't be found, but where it won't even be noticed."

"That's the spirit," said Amanda. "All we're assuming, really, is competence on the part of the hiders of the deed. And some luck."

"A lot of luck," he added, as a parting shot. They both looked over the translation again without speaking, and several minutes passed.

Announcing that she was going to get a couple of notebooks, Amanda rose and disappeared into the kitchen—*why the kitchen?*—and his eyes expertly tracked the fluid motion of her body as it passed. Critically, he eyed the fold-out couch beneath him, surreptitiously testing the bounce.

She glided back into the room and dropped a pair of half-used yellow legal pads between them. "Let's do it," she enjoined, innocently stoking his impure thoughts. Silently, they read together:

> *I am the hard shell of a tough nut*
> *At the hub of a wheel of fire and death.*
> *Your forests hold back the wind*
> *But I am the land itself, rolling toward you.*
> *My walls enclose the blue sky itself*
> *Keep soaring spirits bound to earth.*
> *They come to live, who die at the gates*
> *I sleep outside, above the first to fall.*
> *Now earth and sky wall in the ocean*
> *A mountain of water rides a sea of land*
> *The city's blood imprisoned; life entombed in death.*
> *I hold the doorway keeping back the flood.*
> *The red god rises straight and tall*
> *Straining to touch the yellow sun*
> *He is the land, he watches over all*
> *I dream beneath the red god's fire.*

They bent silently over the translation for a few moments: Amanda trying to prise out its secrets through laser focus, Jason's loyalty torn between the noble quest and the fair princess, his resolve undermined by the emanating warmth of her, the way the couch beneath him torqued when she shifted her weight, and above all her deliriously wafting woman-scent, woody and flowery and dangerously amplified by the torturous proximity.

"It seems to be buried near a building," said Amanda, tapping a key phrase on the page. "It's the land itself, it sleeps outside the gates, it dreams beneath a fire."

Jason took a hormone-dousing swig of his Coke. "This whole thing sounds too general to be a useful practical guide," he replied. "I was kind of hoping for a 'Then take three paces and turn left; now art thou stepping on it,' kind of thing."

Amanda shrugged. "It's an old riddle structure. The conceit is that when you have something you want your listeners to guess, you pretend you *are* that thing, and describe yourself. Everything has a spirit, so you're speaking in the voice of the thing's spirit."

Jason nodded.

"It was big in medieval Europe, too," she continued with a shrug.

"So who's the 'I' of this poem?" he wondered. "In the beginning, it's 'I am the land itself, rolling toward you.' Then it's buried, and dreaming, as if it's the deed itself."

"Probably both," said Amanda. "For one thing, we're reading this in translation, so who knows what's been lost? But remember, it's poetry, not prose. Multiple meanings are possible. The god and the land are one; the page and the land are one."

"Is Manahata this red god?" said Jason. "Does that sound familiar? Is he a bloody god of war, like Mars?"

But Amanda shook her head. "The total opposite. He's the peace that's always there in the background, the constant presence that makes war temporary, and thus bearable."

"Like the last three hundred years?"

"If you like."

Jason ruminated, drank some more soda. "Maybe he's the embarrassed god," he mused. "Or the wheezing, asthmatic god."

"Yuk, yuk." She leaned away from him and began animatedly riffling through one of her books, on to something. Jason pursed his lips in competitive chagrin.

Outside, the thunder rumbled loudly and ominously, vibrating the glass of the open porch doors.

"I am a loud and gray and puffy thing," said Jason grandly. "Shitloads of water dump I on your city."

Amanda smiled without looking up.

They both remained silent for a few minutes as Jason picked up the translation again and Amanda, apparently not finding what she was looking for, switched books and continued leafing through dog-eared pages.

"It's hard to see what this *doesn't* include," said Jason, reading the translation. "It's touching the sky; it's between walls; it's under a fire . . . confusing."

"These things always go heavy on the metaphor," said Amanda.

"I still think the skyscraper's our best bet," he went on. "A red god touching the sky—that's got to be a tall brick building of some kind. What else is red? 'I am the land itself rolling toward you,' 'my walls enclose the blue sky itself,' um, where is it . . . 'I hold the doorway.'"

"I'm trying to find that list of tallest buildings by year. It's here, somewhere."

Jason nodded absently, setting down the translation page and running his hands through his hair. "Maybe it's in a cornerstone," he suggested, brightening. "You know, like a time capsule—"

"Wait a minute," said Amanda, flopping over the book she was looking in and setting it facedown on the couch, and snatching the translation out of his hand.

"What?" said Jason, mildly affronted.

She ignored him for a minute, and he watched her pupils flit as her eyes worked the page like a high-speed typewriter. "There's a *pattern* to this thing. Look," she said, stealing the pen from his hand with even less ceremony and making four horizontal slashes between lines of text. "Here's the logical division," she declared. "Four stanzas."

He stared at her work for a few minutes, then nodded; the logic was inescapable. "Right. Yeah, that's definitely right."

The page now looked like this:

I am the hard shell of a tough nut
At the hub of a wheel of fire and death.
Your forests hold back the wind
<u>But I am the land itself, rolling toward you.</u>
My walls enclose the blue sky itself
Keep soaring spirits bound to earth.
They come to live, who die at the gates
<u>I sleep outside, above the first to fall.</u>
Now earth and sky wall in the ocean
A mountain of water rides a sea of land
The city's blood imprisoned; life entombed in death.
<u>I hold the doorway keeping back the flood.</u>
The red god rises straight and tall
Straining to touch the yellow sun
He is the land, he watches over all
I dream beneath the red god's fire.

"We've been focusing on the translation," Jason pointed out, "which your mom wrote out for us all at once. But if you look back at the original, you can see the handwriting's subtly different between stanzas."

She was bubbling over with excitement. "Haven't you figured out what this means yet, Jason? It's been *moved*."

"What's been—" he began, then broke off as the truth started to dawn on him.

◇ ◇ ◇

Amanda was kicking herself, and wouldn't let it go. As Jason pointed out, and a closer look at the original confirmed, the handwriting, and even the ink color, changed slightly along the fault lines Amanda had drawn. This clue had been there, in a sense, all along. Divided into quatrains, the poem became much more digestible, with a more or less obvious sea change between stanzas.

She was taking the oversight too hard, he thought. They had both blithely assumed the deed had been put in one safe repository for all eternity. But that assumption betrayed a European bias, she now recognized, the notion of founding something in one place and trying to maintain it there forever, like a cathedral or a college. Her people had been nomadic, which was the very point of the deed, of course; it was only natural they'd have moved the deed to keep up with the changing city, so it would remain safe in every era.

His pity was tempered by amusement, but he tried to maintain focus. "So each of these stanzas defines a separate place," said Jason, trying to coax her out of her funk with the bait at hand. "Maybe that's another role for the sachem—to figure out where the last generation put it, then hide it all over again for the next generation."

"Maybe," she replied.

"On the plus side, it does narrow the search," he continued. "We only really have to figure out the last stanza. What?" he added when this brought an unexpected twinkle to her eye.

"Typical guy," she said. "Jump straight to the payoff."

Jason raised an eyebrow. "Let me get this straight. You want the *foreplay* of solving the nonessential stanzas?"

"Maybe there's some sort of helpful progression."

He decided to let it go. "Okay, then, let's go back to the 1600s. Your people get the deed; they're trying to keep it someplace secure."

"Some concrete expression of permanence," she agreed.

"Well put," said Jason. "Only there can't have been many choices in the early days, right?" said Jason. "So they chose a wheel of fire and death."

"The fort!" she yelped, then blushed. "Of course. Fort Amsterdam was laid out in a rough circle . . ."

"Man, is this easy," said Jason. "Fire and death."

"It's 'at the hub,'" said Amanda. "I wonder what was at the exact center of the fort."

Jason shrugged. "No offense, but who gives a rat's ass? It's not there anymore."

"Spoilsport," said Amanda. "Okay, you take the second stanza; I'll take the third."

"Why don't we keep doing them together?"

"Because I've already got mine," she said excitedly, jumping up and heading for her bookshelves.

He was amazed. "Bullshit."

"I've had it all along," she said, quickly seizing a fat encyclopedic tome; she flipped pages furiously, back to the index. "It was my original guess for the whole thing, but it didn't square with stuff from the other stanzas."

He reread the stanza she was solving as he waited: the mountains and sky enclosing water, a doorway keeping back the flood. The rain pounded the deck outside in sympathetic harmony as he watched her thumb riffle the pages like a Vegas dealer, then jam itself rudely into a break.

"The Croton Reservoir," she announced at last, bubbling over with glee as she returned to plunk herself back on the couch and summarize from the book splayed open on her palm. "Built in 1840. It was a twenty-million-gallon aboveground reservoir at Sixth Avenue and Fortieth, on the site of an old mass graveyard. It was a whole city block long. Here, look."

A veiny woodcut showed an imposing windowless fortress taking up an entire tree-lined city block. Period line-drawing families strolled by, unconcerned.

"It was torn down in 1902," she continued. "It's where Bryant Park is today."

"Nice work," he said. "Food break?"

"Look at you!" she replied, highly amused. "You're jealous!"

◇ ◇ ◇

Amanda's delivery menus, a photocopy tour of the world's delivery cuisine, packed the kitchen's junk drawer like uranium in a warhead. But Amanda hankered for regular-old Chinese, and Jason was far too hungry to argue.

"Ain't I smart?" said Amanda as Jason chivalrously dialed the number. "A four-hundred-year-old puzzle, and we're halfway there."

"The unimportant half," he reminded her. "What do you bet your mom figured the whole thing out years ago, and this is all just part of your test?" he said. She stuck her tongue out.

He fed their order into the phone, repeating the difficult parts to the thick but patient restaurant gal on the other end of the line; meanwhile Amanda drifted back and forth with plates and forks and so on, setting the small table by the doors to the rooftop porch, which the rain was lightly drizzling now. His eye wandered to the doors themselves, open and spilling a little water inside the apartment; he suspected she didn't care. She interrupted his view with yet another kitchen-to-hall run, this time carrying nothing but napkins; four trips so far that could have been accomplished, with the tiniest bit of forethought, in one.

"Mmm. *Smell* that rain," she said. "Sit down; let's have some wine."

The hanging, heavy stench of the rain was all out of proportion to its volume; the light sprinkle dusting the porch barely seemed capable of keeping Amanda's garden moist. It put him in mind of the spray mister in a vegetable aisle.

Amanda appeared again in the kitchen doorway, this time carrying only a wine opener, and he smiled from his seat, amused by just how far away she apparently kept it from the wine itself. As she passed, he surreptitiously inhaled her sweet scent.

"Do you realize I met you about a week ago?" he called after her. "Isn't that insane?"

"It's happening fast," she admitted from the other room.

"It's happening *really* fast," he replied, eyes distracted outside, where a sudden increase in the rain had been followed by an almost imperceptible glow of heat lightning.

"You know, I saw you almost get hit by that cab," Amanda confessed, bringing wine and glasses at last—*hallelujah!*—and taking the seat opposite.

"Whatchoo talkin' 'bout, Willis?"

"That first day I called you," said Amanda. "You almost got hit by a cab, at Columbus Circle."

"Could be," he said. "That shit happens to me all the time."

Amanda uncorked the bottle and poured their glasses too fast and too full, passing one to Jason.

"Seriously, Amanda," said Jason. "Think about how improbably quickly this has all come together."

"What's your point?" she wondered. "That it's not really happening?"

"I don't know what my point is anymore," said Jason.

"Then shut up and drink," Amanda replied, raising her glass in toast. "Here's to stanza four."

◇ ◇ ◇

By the time they'd strewn the small table with chopsticks, duck sauce, and little white pagoda boxes, the storm had begun in earnest, sounding its approach over Amanda's battlements in a rumbling overture heavy on the bass. Reflected white lightning slivered the half-open windowpanes and thunder rolled in answer, a long, ponderous cannonade of a hundred celestial bowling balls marching sloppily down a flight of stairs. Then came the wind, and behind it the first glassy marbles, bright with the reflected light from the moon and the kitchen, spattering into the parched plastiblades of Astro Turf on her porch. A happy, wet-dog smell blew in through the open windows.

"Phenomenal," said Jason, meaning the food. Amanda nodded, entranced by the storm, her pretty mouth chewing without her. The rain battered the porch mercilessly, skittering up and down her little stretch of rooftop in a mad frenzy, as if egged on by its own maddening sound. Beyond Amanda's exquisite shoulder the downspout coughed out a steady trickle.

Viewing the deluge from inside the open doors, Jason felt a primal sort of apprehension. He was Cro-Magnon man in the mouth of a dry cave, wondering how he could have angered his horned penis gods enough to get the cosmic coffeepot emptied into the lap of the world. The sheer decibel level of the thunder, when it cracked, seemed to trumpet his insignificance.

"I feel like we should be gathering up animals, or something," he murmured, and Amanda smiled politely.

Between the storm's interruptions and their appetites, no small-talk conversation would kindle. When even a long pause to retrieve and uncork a new bottle of wine failed to break the silence, Jason sighed and capitulated; there was obviously only one appropriate discussion.

"You said the reservoir was built in 1840?" he said.

Amanda nodded, filling their glasses.

"We may as well start putting a rough time frame in place," he replied. "If we're right on all counts here, the deed was hidden in the fort in, say, the mid- to late 1600s, then moved somewhere else at some point, then moved *again*, this time after 1840, when the reservoir was built. When did it get torn down?"

"Just after the turn of the century," she supplied, her reply absurdly punctuated by a terrifyingly loud thunderclap.

"Let's call it 1900, for the sake of argument," said Jason. "That's the latest it could have been moved on to its final resting place, cataloged in the elusive stanza four."

"Which you've figured out, right?" she asked wickedly.

"Nooo . . . but I think the place in stanza two is a church," he replied, hoping to surprise her, and jumping up to retrieve the translation. "'My walls enclose the blue sky itself,'" he read on the way back. "What other buildings had big airy spaces before we had big ugly corporate lobbies? And that part about people dying outside—every church you've ever seen has a graveyard out back. So far we've got a fort and that reservoir, which looks for all the world like a fort. That got me thinking: What else looks appealingly fortresslike? And a church—especially in those days—would definitely do it."

"That's excellent, Jason," said Amanda appreciatively, looking over the stanza in question. "'I sleep outside, above the first to fall.' Buried under the oldest gravestone in the churchyard—that sounds perfect. But which church?"

"Well, again, I don't suppose it matters now," said Jason, "if we're right and the deed's not there anymore. Maybe Trinity, on Broadway at Wall Street? Seems nice and symbolic."

"It burned to the ground during the Revolutionary War," she said matter-of-factly.

"Not my problem," said Jason. "If it was buried under a gravestone, it would have survived, right according to plan."

"You're starting to scare me," Amanda said, grinning.

He nodded. "And that brings us to the last stanza."

They read it together:

> *The red god rises straight and tall*
> *Straining to touch the yellow sun*
> *He is the land, he watches over all*
> *I dream beneath the red god's fire.*

"The only thing I've been able to come up with so far is a firehouse," he intoned after reading it aloud.

Amanda continued chewing, but her eyes waited for more.

"I picked up on an elemental progression in the four stanzas—land, sky, water, and fire," said Jason. "So I started thinking, could the red god be fire itself?"

"I don't know," said Amanda. "That four-element thing is a European concept."

"Well, I didn't make that up—it's in the poem, like it or not," he said.

She shook her head. "But remember, we're theorizing that this wasn't written all at once. Some guy wrote a paragraph, and a generation or two later someone added to it, et cetera."

"Just . . . let me finish my firehouse defense," Jason argued. "Firehouses are pretty solid buildings you could reasonably expect to last. They're usually red, and made out of bricks. And if the thing you're trying to keep safe is a piece of paper, wouldn't you put it in the place least likely to burn down in the entire city?"

She paused in her chewing, considered this.

"Okay, maybe."

❖ ❖ ❖

On the couch after dinner, armed with the last of the wine, they discovered another pattern. The three stanzas they now considered more or less solved, if they were correct, traced a progression up the island: from the fort, down in Battery Park, to Trinity Church at Wall Street, to 40th Street in Midtown. Though it made him feel a bit curmudgeonly, Jason felt duty-bound to point out that the deed's gradual move northward made sense even if it wasn't by design: The city had begun at the southern tip and gradually developed in a northerly direction.

"There's not much in the way of old firehouses north of Forty-second Street anyway," Amanda warned. "Only fifteen or twenty more blocks before Central Park."

Jason shrugged. "Probably just a red herring. Get it?"

"Central Park," Amanda repeated.

"What?"

"There's a castle in the middle of Central Park," she said, frowning. "Did you know that? It's called the Belvedere, I think. Just north of the Great Lawn."

Amanda rose and crossed toward the door as if leaving, then bent and began digging through a stack of books. After three or four false starts, she stood up.

"Here it is," she said, crossing back toward him, finger pinning open the book. "It was built by Frederick Law Olmsted, the architect who built the park itself. It went up in 1854."

"The timing works," said Jason, reaching for the page she was pinning open for him. The washed-out watercolor print showed a small, almost childlike yellow castle rising two or three stories against the park's familiar spiky cityscape curtains.

"It's not red," said Jason. "That's the only thing."

"Maybe it was," she said hopefully. "Get your shoes—let's go scrape some paint off right now."

"You're kidding, right?"

She grinned. "I could do tomorrow morning."

✧ ✧ ✧

The rain continued to batter the porch, a fierce counterpoint to the pleasant haze the wine had draped over what was left of the conversation, and Jason began to grow acutely conscious that it was just the two of them, alone in her apartment, and now after eight o'clock. Time for the start of the "So am I staying?" conversation. His brain was alert and buzzing, having caught the scent of the hunt.

There was a general sense of relief once they'd settled on the Belvedere castle solution; it was as if a wave had crested. He and Amanda had traced back his bloodline, and now had possibly solved the riddle, and if that was true then all that remained was to follow the clues and try to find the actual deed. Could they really have taken a step closer to holding the paper in their hands? Either way, there was nothing else they could do tonight. Nothing decent, anyhow.

Jason ached to bust some kind of a move, to spin this moment out for all it was worth and turn her adrenaline thrill to the dark side. And there she was, for all her obvious excitement, sitting quietly now on the couch just a few feet away, deep in private thought or just peacefully listening to the rain.

The storm winds howled in ghoulish encouragement, and he had just begun rifling through his mind for the proper segue when Amanda put her hands on her knees and stood up. Unable to scramble the words that would hold her, he reached out instead with his foot and stepped lightly on her foot. But momentum had the upper hand, and his similarly unshod foot caught only the toe of her sock, yanking it off her retreating foot.

They both stared dumbly at the shrunken sock curled under his big toe like a shed skin, and then at her naked foot, smooth and adorably knobbly and extremely vulnerable. Jason looked up to find Amanda already looking at him, transfixed by an unspeakably sexy look. If ever there'd been a now-or-never moment in his life, this was it—and so he closed the gap between them at the speed of light, catching her by the shoulders just as she reached toward him, locking up her gently parting lips with his own.

And then her hands were burrowing through his hair, and the thin crinkle of her clothes was failing to mask the warmth of the body beneath, pressing in now at too many points to defend. Maybe it was the wine, maybe it was the MSG, but Amanda was responding with pure animal passion, and Jason found, to his surprise, that he was doing the same, reacting without thinking, squeezing her to him and pressing her head to his as if devouring her whole were the next natural step in their courtship.

Jason fought hard to keep sensory awareness from busting up the dream. He'd always had trouble abandoning himself in these moments;

even at the point of orgasm, his brain was always thinking, agitating, wondering what came next. He brought one hand around to the front of her waist, a warm base camp from which to launch a northern expedition, and decided he was thinking too much about it. He tried tipping her back on the couch, and met some resistance, a struggle to keep her body vertical. Crap. He tried again, unable to believe her stomach muscles could somehow not be in on the game plan, and Amanda abruptly broke off the kiss.

From below his waist, he could practically hear the tiny shout: "Oh, *tell me* somebody up there fucked this up."

"You okay?" he asked her. "Is this . . . too . . . ," he stammered, desperate for answers but loath to give her any ideas.

"I have to move my car," she murmured.

"What?" he replied, incredulous. "Screw your car. I'll buy you a new one."

She giggled. "Alternate-side parking rules. I'm so sorry, but I just remembered. They'll tow it, Jason. Have you ever been towed here? It sucks like nobody's business."

"But . . . right now?" he protested. "Can't we move it in five minutes? *Twenty* minutes?" he corrected, smiling weakly.

She grinned, but dropped her hands from his neck. "If we're ready to move it in twenty minutes, you won't be staying, my friend," she said, snatching up the wayward sock and yanking it back onto her foot. "Seriously, I have to move it before midnight, then I can bring it back sometime before eight in the morning."

"Oh, this fucking city," he said. "I don't even want it anymore." He watched in despair as she snatched up her shoes. "Gimme the keys; I'll move it."

She shook her head. "It'd take me too long to guide you to all the safe spots," she replied, rising to her feet. "But it's very Sir Galahad of you to offer."

He nodded, still frowning, and followed her to the door. "Lancelot," he replied. "Galahad didn't care much for the ladies."

"Lancelot, then," she accepted, already stepping into shoes in the doorway and slipping out of his grasp.

"Run," he adjured her.

She smiled, threw her arms across his shoulders, and planted a superlative, brain-blackout of a kiss on his lips that, even while it was going on, he knew he'd remember the rest of his life. A wave of feverish anticipation welled up from within and washed over him, pebbling his skin with goose pimples.

"Jesus Christ," he said, as Amanda pulled away, winked, and headed for the stairs. "Run!" he demanded again. "Run like the wind!"

"I *will*," she promised, and disappeared.

✧ ✧ ✧

"That her?"

Through the windshield, Freddie followed Vinnie's pointing finger to its object, the girl leaving the building across the street, sweater and jeans, clutching her elbows for warmth. "Yeah, that's her," he confirmed, checking the photo on the dash. "Go."

"Where's her coat?" said Vinnie. "It's pourin' out there."

Freddie boxed him hard in the ear. "Will you fuckin' get out there? Don't lose her, you little dipshit."

"Ow," said Vinnie, fumbling for the latch. "What about him?"

"Don't worry about him," said Freddie. "This guy's going nowhere."

✧ ✧ ✧

Alone in Amanda's apartment, Jason was flipping madly through her CDs, unsure how much time he had, trying to find something to reestablish the mood after her bout with the elements. But it didn't look good. The first disc he found was actually a collection of Sousa marches: good for the climax, maybe, but not much help in getting there. A lot of bad top-forty stuff, a few halfhearted stabs at popular hip-hop, nothing romantic that wasn't cheesy.

"We have such a long way to go," he said aloud, staring at a Vanilla Ice CD.

He settled for tweaking the lighting—turning off the odd little central chandelier and clicking on a dimmable lamp in the corner. It occurred to him that he wasn't exactly *prepared,* in the sexually responsible sense. But he let the worry evaporate away—she'd have something. Hopefully. He could always run out, if the need arose.

A loud buzz startled him; coming quickly to his senses, he bounded to the doorway and pressed the button releasing the downstairs door. Not until a moment later did it occur to him, in a flash, that it might have been someone else at the buzzer down there, that he could have just let in some homeless vandal, or worse. He stood, poised but unarmed, at the door, hoping he was ready for whatever happened next.

And then the doorway opened and she exploded upon him, bedraggled and beautiful, engagingly wet and cold. They joined in a pneumatic kiss that felt as if she were actively trying to draw the heat from him, a kiss that outlasted the kicking off of shoes, the slamming of the door, the driving home of the deadbolt that let relief wash over him. They did a Siamese crab walk back toward the center of the room, a face sandwich with too many legs, and Jason had to suck in his belly hard if his fingers were going to make any headway unbuttoning her sweater.

Grabbing both his hands, still maintaining the kiss, Amanda promenaded him slowly back past their dinner nook and toward the last unexplored door, the one that had no choice but to be the bedroom.

"I thought you said the couch folded out," he whispered.

She shrugged. "Fine, stay on the couch."

As they passed under the arch, a stack of books on an end table nearby, bumped in the passing, tipped over as if trying to seal the doorway behind them.

✧ ✧ ✧

Moments later, they were spooning and cupping and squeezing and disrobing all over her unmade futon in a bedroom that, predictably, was a rumpled mess of cast-off clothing, open drawers, and other residual typhoon damage. It was oddly endearing, in the current carnal crisis.

The girl's dark eyes stayed open, sparkling in the scant light that stole into the room, the faint yellow glow from the main room and the white city lights peeking in under the window shade. Out in the hall, the doors to the patio still stood gloriously open, and the rain's patter joined with the moody lighting to lend a cinematic sheen to the slowly unfolding scene.

For long minutes, the pure act of making out satisfied them both. Jason had had a thought, back in the living room, that the thing to do was to throw her back on the bed, to playfully bind her hands with one of his and ravish her like a drunken Viking. But all his strategizing had fled in the presence of this awesome reality; he could barely move, let alone ravish. How the hell did the Vikings do it?

He'd ended up beside her in the bed, face-to-face with a gorgeous, if clothed, statue, and he wonderingly let his free hand (the right was pinned beneath her) slide up and into her bra from below, every inch a teenager stoned on Cuervo behind a 7-Eleven. The bra came away in his hand, surprising him. Somewhere in the course of their proto-rutting she had unclasped it, or he had.

The sensation was indescribable. Her breast felt taut and smooth, magically chilly against the hot flesh of his hand. As his fingertips slowly circled toward the peak, he became aware of her own hands subtly working the buttons of his 501s. What a truly wonderful world! He sucked in his gut as discreetly as possible but had to bend his mind to something else, anything; if she touched him now, even through denim and boxers, he was done for; his little armada was setting sail without him.

Sum, es, est; sumus, estis, sunt, he recited to himself. *Bo, bis, bit; bimis, bitis, bunt.*

His right arm was now quite insensate beneath her; the welcome weight of her shoulder had pinned it at precisely the pressure point an Eagle Scout would bind with a tourniquet. His left hand, free, was having the time of its life, and he dismissed the dead arm as superfluous, already half-forgotten, an external appendix to be chewed off at some more convenient time.

Amanda rolled tantalizingly onto her back, eyes closed, shirt open. For a century or two, he could do nothing but stare at the feast, worried that his voyeurism would freak her out if she opened her eyes, but utterly unable to act. Would she be offended or complimented? Then he looked down to see his loyal hands already caressing her legs, covering for his momentary brain paralysis. He tried to allow himself to stop worrying. It was going to be okay.

Cozying up closer, he slid his fingers along her gloriously flat abdomen and down into the waistband of her jeans without pausing, as if the slightest deceleration might trip some defense mechanism. His knuckles skirted elastic, then soft cotton; effortlessly, he popped the button of her jeans with a sideways move of his thumb, elated at having pulled it off so suavely. The zipper below inched down a teasing half inch or so on its own; a nudge of the tiny bar eagerly widened the V.

Veni, vidi, vici, he repeated to himself. *The quick brown fox jumped over the lazy dog.*

Amanda murmured something, some sort of vague approval, and he tried to work her jeans off with the one hand, alternating tugs from hip to hip; they were still making out passionately. "Shoes," she reminded him softly, and he bent to take these off her, soles wet from the walk outside, then rolled off both her socks at the same time and threw them back over his head into a sea of dirty laundry already surging against the sides of the futon.

Amanda chose this moment to pounce on him, literally, knocking him over backward; he laughed as she dragged his jeans off with a few simple motions. He quickly recaptured her and began trailing kisses from the perch of her lips right down to the promised land.

Soon only one article of clothing remained between the two of them as he paused above her just long enough to record the scene. Closing his eyes, he hooked his fingers into the baby-soft fabric at her hips and began sliding it down against her smooth skin, and she arched her hips upward ever so slightly to make it easy, and he thought that this, this was surely the greatest thing in the universe, this business of a beautiful girl actually helping you debauch her, the sublime eternal moment where innocence takes experience out for a spin.

Honeycomb's big: yeah, yeah, yeah. It's not small: no, no, no.

A moment later, parts perfectly machined by nature came together and the rest of the world fell away. The fit, the rhythm, where their smoothly straining faces ended up in relation to one another—everything was perfect. Amanda wrapped her legs around him and they rode the experience together, as if it were a physical thing between them.

And then, and then . . .

Her delicious moaning was building in intensity; the moment was approaching. Suddenly realizing the imminent danger, he whispered, "Amanda, we can't . . . I don't have . . ."

"Yes we can," she purred. "It's okay."

The angel on his right shoulder wanted details, but the devil on his left launched his pitchfork and hit the whiny thing right at the base of its skull. The steady pulse of their horizontal dance transitioned into a berserker frenzy; they left their bodies and swam for the light more or less at the same time, and fell back down to earth entwined together, hair slick with sweat, hearts thundering, with real thunder clapping on and off outside the door like celestial aftershocks.

"Holy shit," said Jason a few moments later, when the power of speech returned.

"Mmmm," was all she could muster.

"Wow," he reiterated. "We—"

"I know."

"It was like a . . ."

"But then it . . ."

"That was really . . . something," he finished, feeling delirious and stupid.

"Exactly," she said, and they both laughed.

✧ ✧ ✧

"I lost her," said Vinnie, out of breath and dripping with the rain, clambering inside the car. He squeezed the door shut against the downpour. "Whoever she is, she's good."

"She's back in the apartment, you numb fuck," said Freddie. "She came back five minutes after you left." Lightning flashed.

Vinnie looked bewildered. "I watched her drive away."

"Well, she's here," said Freddie, profoundly irritated, reclining in the passenger seat. "Nice work, Sherlock. Just take the first watch; wake me up if you see either one of 'em. Don't take your eyes off that door or it's your ass."

A moment of silence, then, "Can't we get some doughnuts or something?"

Freddie ignored him, closing his eyes and folding his arms in front of his chest, a position that naturally placed one hand an inch from his shoulder holster.

Vinnie rubbed his black eye, still swollen, and turned and stared longingly out through his rain-drizzled window at the apartment entrance, the standard-issue iron-girded concrete stairway spilling straight down from big oak doors.

"People gotta eat," he mumbled, not quite loud enough to be heard.

✧ ✧ ✧

Jason and Amanda lay side by side on their backs, bodies cooling under a single sheet, his right foot thrown possessively over her left to maintain the link.

"You probably want a couple of cigarettes," he said.

She shook her head. "No, don't get up. Don't go anywhere."

"I'm not going anywhere," he reassured her, and gave her ear a little bite. For a while they lay quietly, listening to the rain on the porch, smelling the breeze.

"You never did explain that bit with the cigarettes," he reminded her. "Breaking one in half every time you smoke. That's about trying to quit, right?"

"Nope," she said. "Good guess, though."

Jason waited, but she remained silent. He rolled toward her. "You're really not going to tell me?"

"Maybe someday," she said playfully.

"That's cold."

"It has to do with my last boyfriend—my only boyfriend, if we're going to be brutally honest here. I needed to get some control back in my life."

He watched the ceiling for a few moments as a sideways gust scattered a sheet of spray across the bedroom window like a drum roll. "I don't get it."

"It's not important."

"You've really had only one boyfriend?"

"That's right," she replied. "Why, how many have you had?"

He gently brushed a wisp of hair away from her forehead and turned to look out the window with a sigh. "I've never had a boyfriend," he said wistfully.

"Hardy, har har."

He cast his mind back. "Well, it's been a long time, that's for sure. I went through a big one-night-stand phase after my parents died. Nobody serious since then."

Amanda didn't reply, and he felt compelled to continue; her serene silences had an odd way of driving him to dig deeper. "When I look back now," he confessed carefully, "everything I've done seems designed to sort of freeze things, kind of—keep everything just the way it was when they died."

Still she held her silence, and he considered his words; this was new ground for him. "I don't mean not moving the stuff out of their closets. I mean . . . committing myself to anything. Seriously, I can't even hold down a hobby; I just lose the fascination with whatever it is after a couple of months and try something else." He paused, rolled toward her again, demanding a response.

She frowned. "Not very encouraging for me, is it?"

He nodded soberly; no point in denial. "Well, at least I'm talking about it," he replied. "*That's* new."

She returned his little display of affection, running a fingertip across his forehead. "It means a lot to me," she said.

At a loss for words, he kissed her again, and she responded passionately. His heart was soaring; it felt as if they'd been together for ages.

They made out like crazed teenagers for a luxurious fifteen or twenty minutes, punctuated with occasional bits of conversation. He was in existential heaven, marooned on this strange island of an apartment with Amanda, his past happily dissolving behind him, the future bright, if still out of focus. Past experience made him leery of rocking the boat unnecessarily, but one thing bothered him enough to override his weak internal-warning system.

"You are on the pill, right?" he said warily, in a lull. "Please tell me I didn't misread that signal back there."

"Yes, my little worrywart." She smiled warmly.

At this Jason relaxed a little. "Cool. So just out of curiosity, what turned the corner for you tonight?"

A frown. "The corner?"

"Why did you finally succumb to my many and obvious charms?"

"I don't know," she replied, simultaneously shaking her head and shrugging in a complex, exasperated little move. "I guess I just felt ready. Is that so strange?"

Jason shook his head. "No, it's *fantastic*, obviously. It's just that . . . well, you've been sending pretty clear signals that you're not interested in me for a week, and now here we are. It's just funny how it's all working out at once—the pieces starting to come together on the deed, you coming around . . . what's the matter?"

He'd felt, rather than seen, her posture stiffen; her eyes locked on his with an almost audible click. In a heartbeat, the dreamy postcoital stupor was gone; he'd misstepped somehow.

"I'm just wondering what you're implying, exactly." she said curtly.

"Nothing," he offered lamely; the mood was slipping away fast. "I'm not implying anything. I'm just—"

Amanda sat up abruptly, setting up a defensive position, and he had no choice but to mirror the motion. "Well, if you're afraid to put it into words, I will," she offered helpfully. "You think I'm sleeping with you just to make sure you'll stay with me, now that there's some light at the end of the tunnel."

"That is ridiculous," he said, and meant it. "Weren't you here when there was all this mind-blowing sex going on? Weren't we *connecting*?" Confusion and despair wrestled for his soul; he wanted badly to brush this aside, or at least distract her—*Hey, look out the window—isn't that the Goodyear blimp?* But he had zero skills for extricating himself from this sort of thing; in fact, his argumentative nature nearly always found a way to make things worse.

"But the thought's occurred to you," she pressed. "That I'd have sex with you to make sure you stayed interested—to reaffirm our partnership."

Of course it had—but was honesty the best policy here? Suddenly there were mines all around him; he couldn't even backtrack without blowing off toes. And that moment's hesitation damned him; Amanda rolled her eyes and leaned back on her hands.

"I cannot *friggin'* believe this," she said, leaving her mouth hanging half open.

"Yes, okay, I've *thought* of it," he confessed, aggressive now, starting to care more about truth than consequences. "I look at everything from every possible angle. That's who I am. But it doesn't mean I *believe* it."

"So just how long have you been sitting there wondering whether or not I would fuck you just to make sure you stayed in the game?"

"Amanda, whoa! That's *not* what I—"

"That's why you asked about the birth control, isn't it? Were you worried I might want to produce a little descendant of my own?"

It was all unraveling now, but there was no way he was letting her get away with this one. "Amanda, you are completely off the deep end here," he affirmed. "You're being paranoid and"—there was no way to soften it—"ridiculous."

"Oh, my God," she wailed, falling backward onto the futon from her seated position. "I'm actually doing it again. You're just like every guy I've ever met."

"I absolutely am not. Amanda—"

"No, Jason. I just want to ask you the same question you asked me. Why do *you* think I had sex with you tonight?"

He paused, weary and dejected, the adrenaline starting to wear off. "I don't know, Amanda. You've been treating me like . . . like I'm gay or something, for a week, and only after I sort of 'prove my loyalty to the quest' . . ."

Her shove, when it came, took him wholly by surprise; he rolled all the way off the futon and onto the floor with a tiny thump. "Amanda, what the—?"

"Just get the hell out," she ordered, livid and raving, eyes brimming with hot tears. "Go!"

Chapter Eight

The storm continued to pour out its dazzling fury, sandblasting the side-walks in a shower of glassy sparks. Rain pounded the already raging gutter streams, glittered brightly in the steam of reflected headlights that dis-creetly hazed the gaudy lights of Broadway. Great rolling booms echoed up and down the avenues and ricocheted across the short blocks of Mid-town, where skyscraper walls bound the streets into sonic canyons. White lightning, in jagged freeze-frame, split the heavens again and again, just a half step ahead of its thunder now, backlighting the deluge in momentary splendor. The rain seemed relentless and infinite, incapable of slackening, as if the city were caught in the tidal embrace of a jealous moon bent on scouring away all Times Square's ancient sins in one terrific night.

A few bedraggled passersby still scampered across the streets, heads bent into the gale, or hustled between points of cheap shelter along the sidewalks, pulling themselves uptown or downtown awning by awning. The city traffic pulsed slowly in and out with the dumb cycle of impervi-ous streetlights. Maimed umbrellas littered the slick, ghost-town streets in wretched skeletal heaps, a cold trail of yuppie spoor.

Jason stared straight up into a curious infinity of falling droplets, white with reflected light, starbursting in perfect symmetry around the vertical axis. Then he tore his gaze away, so as not to fall; he was running as fast as his heaving lungs and the tequila bottle cradled in one drenched arm would allow.

A headlong race up Broadway, splashing amphibiously through flooded low spots, cackling at the anarchy of it all. He was soaked and exuberant and drunk as an ox, and though his leg hurt as if the thighbone itself had popped out through the flesh to say hi, he no longer remembered or cared where he'd logged the injury. As if on cue, he tripped awkwardly over a curb located exactly where you'd expect a curb to be and fell heavily, skidding on the wet concrete.

His hair an unwrung mop drizzling icy rivers into his ears and eyes, wet clothes plastered to his freezing body, Jason rose and took inventory: The bottle was fine. He staggered forward a step or two, found his rhythm, and began running again. The downpour was more than welcome, if only for its ability to drown out so much else; he drank it in with cartoonishly outstretched arms. *Sweet, sweet water: the universal solvent.* He wanted to wallow in this pickling process, this self-preservation, and to that end he clutched the Cuervo, already half its weight. And the night so very young . . .

The current window of lucidity had opened with a crystal moment a half hour earlier, four blocks south, at 38th Street. Jason had heard the strange, undeniable peal of a bell singing out from high atop the Herald Square war monument, a bright, unexpected bit of whimsy instantly demolished by a startling crack of thunder. It was then that he first realized he was running, and adjusted his flight so as to head at least in the general direction of home, in case the next waking blackout came.

It had been a long time, a year or more, since Jason had drunk alone, and he wasn't sure he'd ever been quite *this* wasted. He tried to force his brain to remember the right way to end it: aspirin and water, bucket by the nightstand, a spread-eagle sleeping pose to pin the diabolically spinning bed. And the morning after: pain, nausea, and that odd disassociated hangover guilt.

But God, it felt good the night before. Already the passion and the frenzy of the past week—Amanda's bitchy self-righteousness, the humiliation, all of it, the sheer waste of freaking *time* his life seemed intent on devolving into—was slipping into delirious, who-gives-a-fuck oblivion. All that remained of him now was this urge to erase himself, to let this truly remarkable once-in-a-century rain scrub him from the face of the planet.

Jason's perilously thudding heart hauled in the reins at last at 42nd and Broadway, Times Square proper. Thoroughly winded, he collapsed against a streetlamp and took in the visuals, marveling that he had managed to end up here, at the very heart and groin of the city, as if drawn by cultural gravitational attraction.

He recalled catching a cab away from Amanda's place, out of the female-friendly Upper East Side and into the welcoming sunset of the Wild Wild Upper West. Remembered ringing up friends in unsuccessful bids for companionship, then coercing J.D. at last, the easy mark, into some cocktails. Ditching him mercilessly when they'd both become too drunk for anything but more drinking.

All this running, though, was a mystery. Toward something or from? He couldn't remember. It seemed important to know, a puny polar dilemma any three-year-old in similar straits could solve. Yet memory failed him.

"It is to laugh," he panted thickly, and he did laugh, long and hard, sincerely. Life was simple again, finally.

His eyes were drawn upward to One Times Square's slowly revolving neon news ticker. ESCAPED FEDERAL PRISONERS STILL ON THE LOOSE, SAYS FBI . . . SIXERS UPEND KNICKS, 79–68 . . . U.S. MINT TO PLAN NEW QUARTER . . .

Then lightning blazed once more over Sodom, seeming fainter here when viewed through the jungle of neon, and Jason took another swig of firewater, swaggering invincibly across the street, through the unrelenting torrent.

He found a surviving porn movie house and stepped under its welcome awning, reveling to find himself in a dry cube surrounded by a showery curtain. He looked around at the signage in the dim light. The old playhouse was currently featuring *Scamlet, Titties Andronica,* and—a nightcap—*The Shaming of the True.* An intellectual spot, then, perfect for a quick picnic. Angry droplets pinged impotently on the metallic rooflet as

Jason shook his hair dry and treated himself to another pull-grimace-shiver from the tequila. He sat down by the wall, ass landing harder than expected.

His mind went back to a night during his first week of college, when he'd gotten so spectacularly wasted that he'd passed out on a sheetless laundry-day mattress and not regained consciousness until noon the following day, awash in a stew of his own vomit. The rude awakening had terrified and fascinated him. *That* close to death, he remembered, pinching an invisible marble. He'd walked out of his room invigorated, a conquering hero.

"Fuck *you!*" he shouted aloud to the mostly empty street.

Amanda's freak-out, the stress of the last week . . . it had all fermented, ounce by ounce, block by block, into a shimmering rage.

Women have an awesome, spellbinding magic, he conceded, one of the truly great motive forces on the planet. *Look at what this one girl, dimly glimpsed, has made me think and do and become in the course of a week*, he reminded himself. *I quit my fucking job, for starters*. Not because he thought he'd inherit New York, but because he wanted to set up camp in her pants.

What a house of cards.

Jason took another slug of tequila and dug deeper. Was he being honest with himself? Fact is, he really *had* thought he might inherit New York. Seemed like there was a possibility, anyway. She'd sidled right through his defenses, brought him to the brink of buying her whole curious tale. Why had he allowed himself to believe his life would be anything but ordinary? That she'd converted his cynicism so quickly was amazing. Almost made you want to take a hacksaw to your balls so you could fucking think straight.

"Am I insane?" he asked aloud, and the sound of his own gravelly voice amid a percussive chorus of raindrops seemed to shift the question disturbingly away from the rhetorical.

The thunder roared, low and long, but the imperfect echo of the overhang gave it a cheap, hollow ring—it was not the wrath of the plague-raising, temple-toppling god of Moses, but that of an impotent post-Biblical God, a drooling, retarded God armed with a handful of crappy parlor tricks, growing ever more irrelevant with each passing year.

From his perch, Jason could still see the news ticker through the rain, a more oblique angle now. NATHAN HALE GRAVESITE DISTURBED BY TEEN VANDALS . . .

The New Year's Eve ball drops from the top of this building, he remembered. Near midnight on any December 31, this area would be wall-to-wall drunken revelers, literally tens of *thousands* of them, from all over the globe, massing around the square like lemmings. Every year, *on* the year; a farsighted, slow-moving race of aliens could set their cosmic watch by it. Times Square was one of the few places on earth where you could actually look a fair distance into the future or past and accurately predict the scene.

It was something like being in an early prototype for a time machine. And while he still wasn't sure how or why he had come here, Jason recalled, suddenly, that he'd just been swigging tequila and wandering in and out of Times Square all night, returning to the mecca of sensory lust whenever he strayed too far into its dark and dirty backstreets. For all its showiness, this was in fact a dangerous neighborhood, Disney or no Disney, but he didn't care. He was waiting for something—anything, really—to happen.

BRYANT PARK, 1:00 A.M.

He stood spread-eagled against a twelve-foot chain-link fence, fingers hooked through the links as if preparing to be frisked and cuffed, eyes staring upward and blinking into the rain. Bryant Park was sealed off for renovations, as it had been for many months; but here had once stood the Croton Reservoir, a fortress of water that had also held, if his and Amanda's reasoning was correct, his deed, and the fact that he'd run across it in his drunken wanderings had to be significant. Didn't it?

He wondered what was to stop him, apart from the nausea of course, from scaling this fence. Nobody could possibly be watching. Could he in fact wander around inside, root around in piles of unearthed dirt and rock, see if the renovation had *just happened* to unearth some crusty ancient chest?

But he knew, looking up, that he didn't have the strength left for the fence. Even if he did somehow scrabble his way to the top, he reasoned, he'd probably snag his crotch on the way over and get stuck, dangling there by his bleeding nuts until the rescue crew could overcome their hilarity long enough to bring him down.

He tried to superimpose the mental picture he'd copied from Amanda's book onto the empty park block. The Croton Reservoir had been a square stone monolith, only a story high and slanting gently inward and upward on all sides, like the base of an eventual pyramid, containing all the water for the city. At the other end of the block, the part facing 5th Avenue, they'd later built the New York Public Library, and he knew the library had miles and miles of stacks underground that extended all across Bryant Park, under his very feet. Any chance the foundations of the reservoir had been incorporated into the library's underground walls?

But no, he reminded himself, *this is foolishness; the deed's moved on from here, if it ever was here.* His brain was too muddled to work properly; he threw in the towel with another long pull from the tequila bottle. It was starting to feel distinctly foolish, this drinking and wandering around in the rain, but he held on to the bottle, just the same.

Jason continued west on 40th Street and was just rounding the corner to head up 6th Avenue when the nausea that had been shadowing him all night overtook him at last. Immediately on his right he saw a cute little stone atrium inset into the wall, as if set there by God himself for just this dark purpose, and he leaned gratefully over it, freely donating the contents of his stomach. *Whatever else happens tonight,* he promised himself, wiping his lip, *no more of this running shit.* He looked at the disgraceful mulligatawny he'd left behind, already thinning in the ceaseless downpour, and let his eyes glaze out of focus.

◇ ◇ ◇

"Well, whatever else happens," J.D. had drawled, "at least you nailed her. No one can ever take that away."

"I don't get it," said Jason, dipping a shrimp, a half beer hovering expectantly in the other hand. "Why do you always have to watch what you say? I mean, isn't that the point, to try to find a girl you don't have to be on your guard with?"

J.D. shrugged. "Well, you *did* call her a slut. Women don't take that shit lightly."

"I didn't call her a slut."

"You suggested she had ulterior motives for sleeping with you," his friend reminded him. "It's exactly the same thing as accusing her of banging the football team. Don't you read your manual?"

"Whatever," said Jason.

J.D. grinned. He was smoking already, a habit he indulged only while drinking. "I'm telling you," he said through an enigmatic haze, "if you call a woman insane, or a Communist, she'll squint and look at you funny. But if you call her a *slut*, she'll slap you. Why? Because the idea's not strange to her. It's one of the two things any woman will believe about herself." He waited, but Jason didn't bite. "The other one is that she's fat."

"Okay, can we drop this now?" grumbled Jason, amused nonetheless.

And more drinks came, and still more after that, and they sat there checking out the local talent and shooting the shit like lords. And when they got tired of picking at the shrimpiest shrimp at the bottom of the basket, they relocated to an old pinball machine near the front door. J.D. flavored the corner with clovey white smoke, and Jason pounded beers in desperate double time until he began to feel power welling up within him, until he caught the leading edge of a wild euphoria and rose above the thick buzz of the crowd. Slowly he began to dominate the gravity game, coaxing and cajoling the ball from bumper to bumper with divine authority, stoned and invincible.

Outside, the storm, having abated somewhat after the scene at Amanda's place, had gathered new strength, and spirited gusts banged the flimsy screen door partway open and closed, open and closed, providing intermittent percussion for the analog bells and clanks of the old machine.

The slamming disturbed Jason every time, a recurring unexpected jolt that kept cutting through the welcome numbness. He could have stopped it with two steps and a hand motion, but didn't dare consciously register the annoyance, for fear of breaking the spell of his buzz. And slowly, the escapist dream of the night started to unravel. He tried to watch J.D.'s ball pinging and knocking around like a legless questing beast, but the notion that his life was at some sort of crossroads, that his full attention was required for an important decision or two, kept freedom at bay.

Bang, went the door, again and again, contributing to his growing feeling of being trapped by everything in his life.

And the more Jason watched the pinball darting from the flippers, and shuttling madly between bumpers, the more it ate away at him, like a time-release capsule of angst. His earlier, heady joy began to drift into restlessness; he found himself second-guessing his own conversation with J.D., and even becoming exasperated by the inability of his friend's slow drawl to keep up the pace. Slowly but surely, the slap-slamming of the door started to feel like a call to action, as if it were reminding him it was there if needed.

The moment came, finally, when J.D. was in the bathroom and the door slammed again, no louder but more poignant in the lull of activity, and Jason, drunk and determined, left a business card on the machine and staggered out.

Trading the weight of the crowded bar behind him for the clean, open air felt like shedding a skin. The storm pelted him in the face with everything it had as Jason cleared the building's eaves and turned uptown. It felt fresh and inspiring, and Jason began to run, trailing glassy footprints in the pooling rain.

◇ ◇ ◇

The memory brought no guilt with it. Jason knew his friend would understand, would in fact take the act as an expression of the closeness of their relationship—they did this crap to each other all the time.

The farther he got into the bottle, the better the tequila tasted. At first it was just medicine to be sneaked past the gag reflex, but as his mind numbed, it became first easier, then almost pleasurable. He smiled at the progression: wine with the lady, then beers with a pal, then the hard stuff, all by himself.

Amanda. It was becoming clear that neither of them would ever quite be able to trust the other. Did she honestly feel betrayed, or was she playing him—maybe testing his loyalty again? Both solutions seemed equally plausible; Occam's razor had twin blades for extra smoothness. Either she was totally good or totally evil, and there was simply no way of knowing. Making decisions under these conditions seemed an article of faith parallel to believing in a divine being—the answer was all yes or all no, with eternity in the balance.

It was foolishness, this forbidden reaching for the Big Apple. He wondered how much the sperm backup had clouded his reasoning. Why *was* he here, really? Maybe now, with a clearer head, he'd be able to get up the mental scratch to solve the mystery.

This is the first place I ever bought pot, he recalled with a little thrill of nostalgia. Actually, he'd been more of a bystander, visiting the city as a freshman under the wing of a few upperclassmen. They'd taken a cab to Bryant Park, having heard that was where you went, and had poured out of a taxi, all fearful and suburban, and the con artists had eaten them alive. Twenty dollars apiece for a tiny plastic bag of something just north of pizza topping.

A police car drifted slowly by, hydroplaning at the gutter's edge, and Jason's heart did a guilty little flip. He smiled; time was starting to play tricks on him. He decided to head back toward Times Square one last time and catch the subway home. *Maybe that's why I keep looping in and out of this block*, he realized. *I keep forgetting I'm trying to get the hell out of here.*

CHAMBERS STREET, 2:12 A.M.
Jason awoke, sluggish and disoriented, to the hiss of the opening subway doors. Groping for comprehension, he opened his eyes and stared at the yawning doorway, sitting up with a start as he realized time had elapsed. *Can't fall asleep*, he told himself. *That's how nice boys wind up dead in the South Bronx.*

Chambers Street, he read on the post outside, as the doors slowly shushed closed.

A moment later he realized his error; he'd mistakenly hopped the southbound train. "Shit," he croaked, and tried to rise, then sank back, an error of mechanics. He laughed at his own drunken ineptitude, and the train rolled into motion again, taking him farther south, away from his ever-receding bed. "Shit, shit, shit."

Down, down, downtown. Jason was still quite loaded, he realized, as his turn in the seat to check out the wall map combined with the train's acceleration to activate a dizziness that temporarily paralyzed him with nausea. Recovering, he dragged a guiding finger down the red line to the Chambers Street stop. Almost at the southern tip of the island; a few more stops and then the train would head all the way back uptown. Perfect. Sitting down again, he realized for the first time that he had the car to himself, a safety bonus, and he felt his eyes creeping closed again, trying to pull a fast one on him.

He tried to shake off the malaise, but already his body was shutting down nonvital functions. *So many blocks to go . . . no need to worry . . .*

Looking beside him for inspiration, he found José in the next seat, the squat little bottle only a quarter full now but, having idealized its center of gravity, riding as proudly as if it had paid its own fare.

"Hey, buddy!" he smiled, patting its teeny little head.

◇ ◇ ◇

A foul reek assaulted Jason's nostrils, prying open his eyes. Clearly he'd fallen asleep again, because the car was partly filled with people: nose-pierced high-school kids, old rummies, and other night folk straight out of central casting.

How long had he slept? he wondered. There were no clues to be glimpsed out of the windows, no sound above the gentle hum and clack of steel wheels on an infinite rail, the groans of metal twisting around turns. He felt disoriented; he shook his head, but couldn't clear the cobwebs.

The odor was unbearable. Directly across from his seat, a filthy homeless man sat buried in layers upon layers of shabby rags, slouched back in the seat but with chin on chest, asleep or in some sort of drunken stupor.

Catching a whiff of his own tequila breath, Jason spared a smirk for the irony, but continued staring intently at the slumbering man. What life events had brought this creature to this sad state? Jason had lived his life and arrived on one side of the car; the other had encountered vastly different circumstances, yet had somehow wound up a mirror image, right there across from him. He silently willed the filthy creature to lift its horrible head, so he could glimpse the face.

As if on cue, the man awoke, apparently, and slowly lifted his head with a broad smile, a stewbum's nothing-to-lose leer. Jason was thunderstruck; his jaw literally unhinged and dropped open.

"Hello, son," said the bum.

Jason forgot to breathe, choked back an unexpected sob.

"Dad?"

✧ ✧ ✧

"Don't use your brain, Jason," his father warned, leaning forward. A fat lady eating an apple looked over with casual disdain, chewing slowly, her sagging ruby lips framing a slowly pulsing trash compactor. "If you use your brain," his old man continued in a conspiratorial undertone, "I'm out of here. No choice in the matter."

"I'm dreaming . . . ?" said Jason, a question.

"Don't finish that line of thought. Stare directly at the sun and you go blind."

Jason grinned at the familiar cadence and tenor of his dad's voice, willed his mind away from any thought that might disrupt this most excellent reverie. He fought to keep awareness itself at bay, content to live by whatever rules would keep this image before him. His father's old eyes twinkled from deep inside that wrinkled mask; it was a wonderful bit of magic, and Jason had a sudden fear that the vision would collapse under the weight of its own improbability if he didn't say something, anything.

"Where's Mom?" he blurted out.

His dad shrugged. "She's dead," he replied. "Don't be absurd."

Jason smiled, still staring. "You, too, I guess."

His dad chuckled a little. "Well, I've been better." He fingered a silver-dollar-size hole in his filth-encrusted jeans. "Jesus, look at this getup."

"I miss you something fierce," said Jason.

His dad looked troubled, paused for what seemed an eternity before speaking. "On Albert Einstein's deathbed," he said, "he started speaking in his native German. Of course, the nurse couldn't understand a word he was saying, and by the time she could run off and find someone who could translate, the great man was dead. Everyone went a bit nuts that the world's greatest physicist's last words were lost to history. But what did they think? That he'd suddenly sorted out superstring theory or invented the microwave? He was probably begging for a fresh bedpan."

"I already know that story."

"Of course you do," said his father. "The point is, my last words weren't 'Make us proud, son,' or 'I love you, Jason.' Your mom and I just whipped around the corner and there was a car, in our lane, headed right for us. I probably said, 'Oh, FUCK,' or just 'AAAAAH!'" He paused to let this sink in a little. "Jason, I'd love to be able to tell you I left you a videotape full of great advice and the secrets of life. But who knew I was going anywhere?"

"I've got a million things I've always wanted to ask you," said Jason.

"I won't know the answers."

"I know," he replied. "I get it; I'm sort of putting you together from the memories in my head. But don't all those memories have to add up to *something*?"

His dad shrugged. "You tell me."

Jason racked his brain; already time seemed to be growing short, and he had no way of knowing if he'd ever be here, in this place, again. "I'm tired of *doing* things," he said. "Working, playing, buying food, taking a crap . . . all of it. I really don't want anything for myself except . . . except what I can't have."

"Jason, what do you think I would have given for one more day with you?" his dad replied. "Your mom, too. You already *know* that's true, Jason, which is why I can say it. We just got stolen away, and that's all, the simple, brutal, unfair, cosmically stupid truth. Until you're a parent, you can't understand the way the love for your child obliterates everything else. So don't bother trying. But listen: Before there was you, your mom and I were just these two stick bugs crawling around on the surface of this planet who found each other. We were so in love, we rejected the rest of the world and all our other possible futures to lash our ships together, come what may. That was an affair to remember, let me tell you, quite enough to head off into eternity with. And yet, when we had you, we gave all that up and poured everything we had into you. It didn't even require a conscious decision."

Jason was nodding. "I felt that."

"You'd better have," said his dad. "It's a hell of a stupid sacrifice, otherwise. But, Jason, as big as that was, and as much as we loved you, you were still just a part of our story. Our roles in each other's life, yours and ours, were always destined to fade, because that's the way of things. Sooner or later you were going to marry and move away, drop by for Thanksgivings and to show off your kids and cars. Your story was always meant to take off on its own, without us, anyway." He paused, and poked a dirty finger into Jason's chest. "And if I know that, it means *you* know that."

Jason smiled at this. The subway car was empty again, rattling along the rails, and the piercing smell had returned to wrinkle his nose. Sensing such impressions beginning to intrude on the sanctity of the scene, Jason tried desperately to hold on to the moment. "But how do I know where to go?" he said.

His dad's gaze narrowed. "Use the force."

"Excuse me?"

"Just kidding. Just pick something and turn your wheel toward it."

"What if it's wrong?"

"Then you'll know something about yourself you didn't know before. It beats drifting."

Jason noted with alarm that the speaker was starting to look less and less like his father; except for the piercing blue eyes, the guy sitting across from him, gravelly voice echoing in the now-empty car, could have been any old drunk.

"I think I gotta go, Jason," his dad continued. "But here's one thing to take with you. We all find lots of ways to sabotage our own potential. We put sixty-percent efforts into our jobs, our friendships, our marriages. It gives your ego a fallback position. If you *really* give it everything you've got, then it's a personal failure if you don't win. But there's a real cost to your soul each time you slack off, and in the aggregate the cost is tremendous."

"Why?" said Jason into the pause, and the question seemed obvious, preordained by the pause itself, as if the dad persona was melting back into his own mind, and he was asking and answering his own questions.

"Because the *distance*," his dad continued, "between who you are and who you could have been always widens over the course of your life. Nobody will ever know just how far apart they are but you . . . and that distance, I promise you, Jason, is the true measure of a man."

The finality was inescapable.

"I love you, Dad," said Jason, speaking straight from his soul.

His dad, or what was left of him in the twinkling eyes of the strange rummy across from him, smiled and nodded indulgently. "Fag."

Jason laughed out loud, and drifted into a clear and dreamless sleep.

SOUTH FERRY, 2:15 A.M.

He woke up in shadowy darkness and blinked three or four times, as if testing a faulty light switch. A primal fear sank into his gut with the return of cold, total awareness, as the buzz that had formerly consumed him now only loitered sheepishly at the edge of his consciousness. He was freezing; it was dark; he was still on the train, deep underground. But the train was darkened now and not moving, in some sort of mechanical limbo. A smattering of white noise echoed down the tunnel, muffled by distance, exacerbating the otherwise total silence.

There was a little light, he realized as his eyes finally adjusted to it. He turned and peered out through the window behind him. His train was on some kind of siding; the lights were station lights, but oddly distant. His track was no longer next to the station platform; he was out in the middle of some vast underground train yard. Mentally he calculated the risk of hopping off and scrambling across, but that infamous "third rail" had enough juice to drop a rhino, and he had no idea how you identified which one was the hot one.

"Oh, you fucking idiot," he chastised himself, slamming his hand on the orange plastic seat. His body was still drunk, but the adrenaline had focused his energies; now the nausea and unsteadiness just seemed like annoyances. He leaped up and stood before the doors, tried to push them apart to no avail. "Tell me this is going to be all *goddamn* night," he lamented bitterly.

The clang echoed strangely, too far away and an instant too late. For the first time he wondered whether or not he was alone on the train. He realized he was sweating, despite the chill.

And with that the animal fear swept over him utterly. *This is the combination that gets people killed,* he chastised himself. Drunk underground in the middle of the night, trapped on a beached train. If there *were* anyone else on the car, he'd be easy pickings.

The clang rang out again, louder and closer, then another in short order, and Jason suddenly placed the sound: the end doors of subway cars opening and closing. Someone was at the faraway end of the train, moving toward him; he'd hear actual footsteps any minute. Another clang, infinitesimally louder, steady in its progress.

His eyes had adjusted to the point where he could see dim outlines of things, and Jason decided to risk a look at the new arrival. With much trepidation, he peered through the window at the end of the car, which combined with all the others in a long, cloudy telescope that ran the length of the train. Through the window, three or four cars away, he saw a large black man in shabby clothes striding purposefully through the cars, toward him.

Jason watched his approach, entranced, as the nearing subject picked up more and more detail. Hooded sweatshirt, muscular build, sleeves rolled up to reveal massive forearms, dark sunglasses, all of it rolling steadily toward him like a juggernaut.

Heart racing, with no idea what to do, Jason stood paralyzed as the man cleared the next car and the next. He fled the window and returned to his seat only a moment before the door to his own car opened, and there he waited in dark silence, hoping absurdly that the guy would walk on through the car on his own business, without stopping. And for a moment it seemed it might happen just that way; the stranger was nearly abreast of Jason before he paused and turned slowly toward him with a diabolical smile.

"End of the line," said the stranger.

✧ ✧ ✧

"I don't have any money," said Jason, trying to sound confident but humble, wondering if it was true. To his surprise, the stranger laughed, a deep, booming Barry White laugh.

"Man, I don't have any money either—ain't that a bitch?" the man assured him. "The *train*, my young friend—this is the end of the line."

Jason smiled weakly, then realized the smile wouldn't be seen in the dark. "Sorry," he said. "I'm a little—"

"No need to apologize—I'm the one interrupted you," said the man, and continued on his way. "You take care, now."

The man had almost left the car—*going where?*—before Jason decided the companionship was worth the risk. "Excuse me," he called out. "What . . . what happens now?"

The man turned and walked back toward him. "Well, we set here awhiles until they turn the lights back on, and then we set some more, and then this train kinda curves around in a circle and heads back uptown again. First stop's right here at South Ferry if you wanna get off." He sat down in the seat directly across, dispersing the last of Jason's father's ghost. "My name's Jones—Dow Jones," he clarified, and laughed at his own joke.

"I'm Jason."

"Well, Jason. You mind if I have a shot of your sodey pop, there?"

✧ ✧ ✧

Jason sat quietly while Jones polished off the tequila, wiping lip on forearm after each big gulp. "Ohh, top shelf," was his only comment, but he said it twice, just the same way.

Jason wondered if he was going to get rolled after all; he'd give a lot to have the lights go back on. But Jones seemed harmless enough, for his bulk. He wondered if the man was homeless or just shabby, wondered if it made much of a difference.

They made a little small talk, with Jones doing most of the gabbing. Jason was flustered by their different status, and couldn't formulate even the simplest question that didn't seem insulting or condescending on some level. *So what do you do? Where do you live?* But Jones quickly proved himself clever, confident, and possessed of a broad sense of humor that belied his obvious condition. And he took a dim view of Jason's advertising career, fully justifying the reluctance with which Jason had confessed it.

"Now what a silly, stupid thing to be!" said Jones, triumphant.

Jason frowned, then smiled. No need to be defensive about that anymore. "It does sound stupid when you say it like that."

Jones guffawed. "I don't think it's my delivery, son."

"Well, everyone's gotta do something, I guess."

"You know what you should do, Ad Man? You should carve yourself a spoon. Out of wood."

"A spoon?"

"A spoon's a useful thing," Jones explained. "All you need's a flat stick, about a six-inch stick or so, and a whittling knife. And then after you carve it, you'll own this spoon that you yourself made out of a stick."

"Mm-hmm."

"And then when you die, and the angels ask you if you did anything in your life that was worthwhile, why, you just whip out that spoon!"

The lights came on in short order, and the cars creaked into slow, rolling motion. Jason welcomed the sound, though he was warming to his companion, chattering now about sports and current events.

Painstakingly, the cars followed one another around a broad, dark curve. "Here's where I get out," said Jones as the South Ferry northbound station came into view up ahead. He smacked his lips. "Much obliged for your hospitality."

"Pleasure's mine," said Jason, feeling oddly as if he shouldn't let him go. "Jones, can I . . . can I ask you something?"

"Shoot."

"Are you homeless?" he asked bluntly.

Jones looked him up and down. "Is it obvious?" he said sadly, paused, then cracked up laughing. "What a bold question. Finally. Yes, I am indeed rootless, my friend, if that's what you mean."

"No offense."

"None taken. But why do you care?"

"What's it like?" said Jason.

The car sidled slowly into the South Ferry station, and Jones rose. "Well, why don't you try it out for an hour or two? Come on with me."

Jason laughed and shook his head. "No thanks," he replied, and declined the proffered hand. Behind Jones, the doors slid open wide and hung there. Jones shrugged, still staring at him. The offer was still open, and the doors seemed in no great hurry to close.

"All right, let's do it," said Jason, surprising even himself.

Jones beamed. "Glad to hear it, boy. Maybe there's something to you after all."

SOUTH FERRY, 3:15 A.M.

They were walking side by side along a broad avenue between rows of trees, a brisk graveyard-shift breeze at their backs. Behind them, the city was well lit but silent; above, a canopy of stars beamed through fast-moving, but patchy clouds.

"So what do *you* imagine it's like?" said Jones. "Being homeless."

Jason pictured all he'd ever heard: the crowded, filthy shelters, being awakened by the smack of a nightstick, relentless cold and filth and hunger. "To be honest?" he said. "It sounds like hell."

Jones smiled. "Well, 'hell' is a mighty strong word. There's upsides." He tossed the empty Cuervo bottle into an open garbage can. "You do get to do what you want—don't answer to nobody. You don't call no man boss, ever, and that's a powerful thing. You walk where you want, say what you want, do what you want, all the time."

"Within the limits of your budget," said Jason.

"Well, everybody's got a budget," Jones replied. "It don't take long at all to get used to living without fancy clothes and dessert."

They emerged from the trees and came up to the old Battery fort, facing the Hudson, as it had done for hundreds of years.

"It's nice right now," said Jones, looking at the stars. "Spring is the good season. Look at the two of us, out and about with no coats. Now, winter's the worst. You can't imagine what winter's like. You ever been real, real cold, Jason?"

I used to think so, thought Jason. "No."

"Well, let's see . . . Imagine going out in your underwear to get the mail on the coldest night of the year. Only when you get back with the mail, there's no house there."

They crossed the plaza, skirting the great circle of the fort; from here Jason thought he could hear the waves lapping against the shore beyond. It occurred to him that it had stopped raining.

"So . . . does it balance out?" Jason asked tentatively, hoping the question wouldn't offend. "The freedom versus the . . . the discomfort?"

Jones laughed. "How cold would you have to be to wrap a smelly, piss-stained, ratty old dog blanket around you all night?" he asked. "How tired would you have to be to try to sleep on the floor of a bus station men's room? How hungry would you have to be to beg people for food money, knowing they're paying you just to get you the hell out of their sight?" He grinned. "No, Jason, it don't quite balance out."

✧ ✧ ✧

Rounding the far side of the fort, the pair made their way down a paved, handrailed esplanade that capped, more or less, the southern tip of the island. The indifferent starlight revealed only the whitecaps against the dark sea, but the sound was soothing, eternal. The World Trade Center towered behind them, lit up like a postcard; it was a sight to behold. Looking out across the water they could see other night lights: the Verrazano-Narrows bridge, Governor's Island, New Jersey. It was a 360-degree panorama of dizzying beauty.

"I come down here a lot," said Jones.

"This is incredible," said Jason. "Look at those lights."

"That's Governor's Island," said Jones, pointing it out. "Governor don't live there anymore, though."

"This is really something," said Jason appreciatively. "Look, you can see the Statue of Liberty."

"Liberty Enlightening the World," said Jones.

"How's that?"

"That's her full name," said Jones. "Patron saint of the homeless, you see."

Jason nodded silently, watching the tiny green figure and its pinprick torch, keeping eternal watch over the harbor. "'Give me your tired, your poor, your huddled masses yearning to breathe free,'" he recited, feeling competitive.

"That's it," said Jones. "See, now that statue *means* something to me. I reckon I'm living as free as a man can be."

"But you pay a price."

Jones rubbed his palms on his stubbled cheeks. "Well, here's my theory. I figure a fella's born about as happy as he's gonna get. Your circumstances don't change that. You can win the lottery and still feel like killing yourself."

"True."

"So if you're a naturally happy person, you go through life finding reasons to be happy. And if you're naturally unhappy—"

"You'll always find something to complain about," Jason supplied.

"That's right," said Jones. "Now me, I get beat up a lot. Kids, cops, all kind of crazy fuckers. Bad, sometimes. I'm in a hospital two or three times a year."

Jason was staring out into the bay, elbows on the handrail. A long barge was slowly knifing southward through the dark waters, trying to find its way out of the harbor.

"Sleeping's the tough end," Jones continued. "You go to the shelters, someone steals your shit. Or you catch the TB. You lay your weary ass down in the wrong place, and you get moved on, or some drunk kids might light you on fire. And the worst of it, by far, Jason, is that people hate to fucking look at me. Can you imagine that?"

Jason turned to look at him. "No, I can't."

"On the other hand," Jones said, smiling, "when I wake up in the morning, I got nothing to do, nobody to answer to, no place I have to go. It's like all Creation just rolls out in front of me brand-new every day."

Jason nodded, returning his eyes to the bay; the ferry was almost out of sight now. "Where I come from," he replied, surprised by his own voice, "there are just laid-down ways of doing things. You go to high school, and then you go to college, and you find a wife and you get married, and you have kids, and that's just how it seems to go. Nobody ever really asks: *Do I want this?*"

"The things of the world are very alluring," said Jones. "It's no sin to want them. You can always choose my way, you know."

"It would be tough to leave it all," said Jason. "I'm not the ascetic type. If I were home right now, I'd have aspirin, a glass of juice, a warm bed waiting for me."

"Come on, cast aside your worldly things and follow me!" said Jones, laughing. "I am freedom, Jason. I'll show you the ways of the street and the art of survival. Bright white guy like you would *thrive* out here. People'd be falling all over each other to give you their hats." He laughed. "I'm just kidding, of course. You stay put, son."

Jason nodded; he was checking out Lady Liberty again, pale green against the night sky, in a bay awash with stars. *Liberty or prosperity—which do you want?* he mused, with just a touch of bitterness. *Make your selection at any time.*

Seeing the object of Jason's view, Jones nodded slowly. "I think of her as kind of a fertility symbol, her being green and all. She represents the land of milk and honey."

Jason shrugged. "It's the corrosion," he said absently. "She wasn't meant to be green. Maybe that's a symbol of corruption."

"What's that now?"

"That's why the statue's green," said Jason, intentionally fuzzing his vision, blurring his focus until he could just see the torch, flaming like another star in the sky. "It's made out of copper, only it's been corroded by the salt in the—"

He fell silent.

"The sea breeze?" suggested Jones.

"Holy *shit*," said Jason, putting both hands to his mouth.

"What's that?"

"That's where it is."

"Where what is? Boy, what in the holy hell are you talking about?"

Jason was giddy with sudden delight. "The red god's fire," he said excitedly. "Jones, I'm sorry . . . I . . . I gotta go."

"What? You kiddin' me? We were just gettin' friendly."

"I'm truly sorry, man, I just . . . Oh, my God, it's such a long story. I wouldn't know where to start. I'll find you again, somehow, I promise. Here," he said, fishing out his wallet. "You want some money after all?"

"Now you're just insulting me," said Jones, waving him off with a hand. "Where you running off to?"

Jason grinned. "I gotta go wake up my girlfriend."

Chapter Nine

Bells jangled hard against the glass as she walked in through the door of the coffee shop, and Jason smiled in spite of himself. The flannel shirt and sweats, presumably what she'd worn to bed, looked soft and inviting, and he felt another pang of regret. But it was all going to be all right now.

She found him easily, as he was the only customer, and ambled over warily, her face stony and impenetrable, emotions at bay. That she'd come at all told the whole story anyway. An oversize leather bag swung from one shoulder, as he'd requested.

He imagined what he must look like to Amanda: soaked to the bone and shivering, wet jeans squeaking on the cracked vinyl of the bench with every weight shift, slick hair raining beads all over the Formica. He raised the coffee to his lips—bitter and awful, some of the worst he'd ever tasted, but still an improvement over the puke and tequila on his palate—and drew in its warmth as she walked over.

"Thanks for coming," he said with a flash of B-movie cool, then cleared his throat as Amanda wordlessly dropped the leather bag on the table and slid into the booth across from him. His excitement threatened to burst all the stops; he had to fight to remain appropriately somber.

Amanda reached into her purse and quietly withdrew a box of cigarettes, tapped the box into the heel of her hand until two bounced out into curled fingers. "No small talk, okay?" she said at last, laying the smokes out carefully on the table.

"Don't still be mad," he replied. "I'm sorry."

"Sorry for what, exactly?" she said a little too easily: a test.

But he was ready. "I'm sorry for leaving when you told me to," he replied. "I should have demanded that you let me stay so we could work it out. I'm sorry for letting you think for a minute that my interest in you was casual enough to be dismissed like that. Let's see. I'm sorry for the mess I must look and smell like to you right now. Most of all, I'm sorry for being a general dickhead control freak who loves hearing himself talk so much that he doesn't know when to shut up." He shrugged. "That's all I can think of right now."

A ghost of a smile creased the corner of her lips, and he knew he had her; her eyes flickered once toward the cigarettes on the table, then back to his eyes. "Not bad," she said. "You must find yourself apologizing to women a lot."

He dipped his head in supplication.

"But you *did* forget 'sorry for dragging you out of bed at four in the morning.'"

Jason shook his head, allowing himself a moderate grin. "*That* I'm not sorry for. If you still feel that way in five minutes, I'll go away and you never have to see me again, I swear."

Amanda turned, tried to make eye contact with the waitress. "Can we get—" she began, but he put a restraining hand on her arm.

"I took the *liberty* of ordering for you," he said. "You and I have a ferry to catch."

She protested weakly, hating the loss of control, or perhaps just loath to let him escape justice so easily. But this, too, he'd foreseen. Her pride, though considerable, was no match for her curiosity, and they both knew it. In all their time together, he'd never been in charge like this; everything was falling together exactly as he'd imagined. She even looked just as he'd pictured: sleepy and warm, soft sweats encased in an exoskeletal rain jacket, lips partly open. No bra, from the looks of things . . . right out of bed at a dead run, then.

And so he gently coaxed her back into the comforting fold of the mystery, not to assure her participation—he already had her—but as a gentlemanly gesture to help her justify setting aside her righteous anger. He described the preceding night, that curiously backward chain of events that started in her bed and ended with a wrong-way subway ride to the wrong end of the island—as having been the most amazing night of his life. He painted the tale boldly but with surreal swirls, all the while conscious of time melting away; they had less than an hour to get downtown, and still a stop to make. But it had been a long time since he'd felt so in control, and he frankly didn't feel like rushing.

"I have a proposition," he offered. "What do you say we agree to set everything between us aside, just for six hours? We'll know what we've got by then, and we'll have the rest of our lives to be pissed at each other."

"Fine," she said, nodding acquiescence. "So what's your theory?"

He took a last sip of his coffee, daring himself to drag it out a bit to protect the secret, the revelation of which might sap his newfound strength. But his internal tussle was pathetic; he simply couldn't deny those impatient almond eyes that clearly weren't going to look away until they saw what he'd seen.

"It's in the Statue of Liberty," he said abruptly. Glancing around self-consciously, he saw the waitress headed toward them with their food, packed in to-go bags as he'd requested. "Up in the torch."

"No, it isn't," Amanda replied, irritated: *We've gone over this.* "It's got to be somewhere on the island."

"Says who?" he shrugged. "I'm gonna prove it to you. Can I see the clues, please?"

Amanda reached into her bag and withdrew both the map and her mom's translation, as he'd instructed, in a distracted way that made it clear her mind was racing. She held them out and flipped them over and back, looking for direction as to which side he wanted up, and he set the map faceup on the table with the translation on top.

"'I dream beneath the red god's fire,'" he read. "That's the red herring, you see. Imagine if it had said 'green god's fire.' You'd have said, 'Oh, Statue of Liberty. Got it.'"

"But it *isn't* red," she replied slowly, not sure which one of them was the idiot.

Jason smiled. "It *was*," he replied. "That statue's pure copper. If they'd had color photography at the time, you could see a picture. Probably took years for the salty sea air to green it up."

He could see the truth starting to dawn on her. "Amanda," he went on, "you always said you thought it would be on the island, and I believed it, too, right from the beginning. You were right about so many other things. But it makes sense, doesn't it? You don't keep the deed to your house *in* the house—you find a safe external place."

She was staring at the table, digesting this, with one hand over her mouth in a way that exaggerated whatever shock his theory had legitimately excited in her.

"Let me lay it out for you," he said gently. "It's important to me that you be as convinced as I am."

She looked at him again and nodded assent, taking a long, slow sip of her coffee.

Jason rubbed his hands together. "Okay. Let's think about where we think the deed's been hidden. The old fort, the church, the reservoir building." As he spoke, he tapped the relevant spots on the map. "These places are about more than just keeping it safe—your ancestors could've stuck it behind a brick in the Columbia University Library and never risked moving it. But they didn't. Why? Because these places are also symbolic places of strength, pillars of the city. You with me so far?"

She nodded, and he went on. "Those symbolic pillars of strength keep moving as the city changes. A pain in the ass to keep moving the deed, but that's the game. Now picture what the Statue of Liberty must have looked like going up in the 1880s," he said. "To your people. The headdress. The masculine face. Honestly, Lady Liberty's the most *unladylike* statue you ever saw: strong jaw, no tits. I think that whatever the statue meant to my people, to yours it must have looked like Manahata himself."

He paused; the leading edge of her coffee cup was on the verge of dripping onto the map. Softly, without breaking eye contact, he tilted her hand and cup back up to horizontal.

"Picture your great-great-whatever-grandmother, watching that statue go up," he continued, rolling up the map for safety and to hasten their departure. "It's clear it's going to be there permanently, watching over the city, and it's obviously hugely symbolic. It's liberty, freedom—everything your people lost. It's what recapturing the island would return to them, right?"

He'd never seen her at such rapt attention, and he smiled, remembering their very different roles at their first meeting. "So to recap, an enormous, glistening copper-red statue of an Indian figure rises in the harbor, right about where white men first appeared to *her* ancestors. For someone who felt her race had been kept alive specifically to watch and wait for the return of her God, this would be one hell of a sight, no? How could this construction *not* have been ordained by Manahata himself? It certainly seems to symbolize the fulfillment of his promise."

He paused to drain the rest of his coffee, now quite lukewarm, and awaited her response.

"Okay, it's good," she said at last, picking up one of the two cigarettes off the table and rolling it around in her fingers.

"You bet it is."

"But that doesn't mean it's *there*," she said, snapping the cigarette in half. "Everything you've said would make just as much sense if it isn't there."

"But it *is* there, Amanda," he replied. "I know it with every fiber of my being. I know it's there just in the way it was revealed to me, if nothing else. I'm telling you, something happened to me last night, something . . . extraterrestrial. Gotta have some faith, here."

The waitress poked her head in. "Anything else?"

Get this, thought Jason, looking around at the empty diner, *she needs the table*. "No, we're going to get out of here. Thanks."

The waitress shrugged, and walked away.

"She's pissed," said Amanda.

"Wait till she sees her two-hundred-dollar tip," he said, grinning, standing up to peel the bills out of his wallet.

Amanda finally cracked a smile; he'd breached the wall, and he could see the old enthusiasm rushing in like a torrent. "Jesus Christ, Jason. You really think you've got it."

"No, *we've* got it," he corrected.

"We need my books," said Amanda. "We need to see what the statue looks like inside."

But Jason shook his head again. "We can get all the info we need off the Internet. My place is closer, and we need some tools. You print while I pack."

"What's the big hurry? It's four in the morning."

"Haven't you ever been to the statue?" he said, grabbing his coat and handing her her bag. "I went with my mom and dad once. You and I are going to be standing in line literally for hours. And if we don't catch that very first ferry, we'll never make it up the steps—we'll have to go back to-morrow," he continued. "And I don't think either of us wants that."

UPPER WEST SIDE, 5:00 A.M.

"There's a complication," said Amanda, at the computer.

Jason was in the bedroom end of the apartment, staring into the empty hull of a flashlight and trying to figure out which way to load the batter-ies, wishing he had another flashlight with which to peer into the murky depths. His briefcase, disemboweled of papers, lay open on the bed; he was haphazardly filling it with a selection of tools. "What's that?"

"The torch is closed to tourists," she replied. "Arm and everything. Has been since 1916—traffic-flow problems."

"I know that," said Jason. "In fact, I'm counting on it. And we're not tourists, anyway—we're the owners." Suddenly realizing he'd been ago-nizing for minutes over a problem with only two solutions, he picked an orientation at random and dropped the batteries in. *Sleep would help*, he said to himself.

The soothing thrum of the printer accentuated the relative silence. "So, how are we going to get into the arm, MacGyver?" she called. "It's sealed off."

"I won't know till we get there. But when I do get in, at least I know I won't have tourists crawling all over me." He tested the plastic slide but-ton: *Let there be light*.

Amanda's clicking and clacking resumed. "There are one hundred and sixty-seven steps in the pedestal," she said after a pause, "and another hundred and sixty-eight from her feet to the observation platform in her crown."

"Print, don't read," said Jason. "And call us a cab, too." *Crescent wrench, hammer, screwdriver.* "You get the ferry times yet?"

"The ladder has fifty-four rungs. Not yet."

He made a final check of the briefcase, but it was absurd; he had no idea what he'd encounter, if he could even get in there. He whirled through the room, evaluating possible additions on the fly. The Swiss Army–style utility knife from his top drawer? Definitely—one of those twenty-seven tools ought to be good for something. Map of New York? Sure, why not. Remembering something else, he headed out into the main room.

Amanda was staring into the printer, trying to coax out the last page. "Here," said Jason, tossing her a bundle of cloth, "borrow a real sweat-shirt." He knelt at the coffee table and unzipped her bag. "I'm gonna hide your mom's map over the microwave for safekeeping, if that's okay," he continued.

"You're just trying to get me to come back to your apartment," she accused.

He allowed a smirk as he crossed the room toward the kitchen, map in hand.

Shutting down computer and printer, Amanda swiveled in the chair and pressed the fluffy, clean sweatshirt into her face, drinking in the freshness. He reentered and caught her in the act.

"It's clean," he claimed.

"It's ridiculously clean," she said. "Your mother would be proud."

NEW YORK HARBOR, 6:00 A.M.

A cold dawn was breaking over Brooklyn as the ferry plowed through the choppy harbor. The ship's rapid passage accentuated a biting sea breeze that had sent most of the passengers scuttling below, view or no view. But Amanda and Jason walked around the upper deck, braving the chill and the light spray for the unthinkably majestic panorama.

Behind them, the World Trade Center's looming twin towers formed the southern bookend of the famous Manhattan skyline, thick and tall like the very legs of Atlas, stubbornly refusing to recede in the distance as the ferry chugged along. A clockwise tour of the upper deck revealed first Brooklyn, hazed to the east, then a flat and deserted-looking Governor's Island floating in the foreground to the southeast, and beyond it, the long sweep of the Verrazano-Narrows Bridge, connecting Brooklyn and Long Island with Staten Island, funny uncle of the five boroughs. And dead ahead, to the south by southwest, stood a tiny green statue, expanding ever so slowly in their sights.

"This is where it all started," said Amanda, momentarily ignoring her wind-whipped printouts, fifteen or twenty pages of all you could ever want to know about the Statue of Liberty, clutched in one hand.

Jason nodded. He'd been thinking the same thing, picturing that unimaginably momentous point of first contact between the Europeans and the natives, the collision of worlds. What must those first tall ships have looked like to the barefoot natives standing agape on the shore?

Seagulls keened in the air above, chasing one another's vapor trails across the steely sky.

"So what's the deal with the cigarettes?" Jason wondered.

She shrugged. "You mean why do I smoke?"

"No, I do not."

Amanda broke into a grin and reached into her bag for a pack of smokes. "Okay, Jason, but this is very personal and symbolic, so keep your amazing wit in check, please." As she spoke, she drew out two cigarettes, replaced the pack, and pulled out a lighter, all with the one hand, fingers in constant, fluid magician motion. "It's to honor the path not taken, whenever I make a choice," she explained, carefully resting her elbows on the gunwale.

"Every time my father flips a coin," she continued, "he throws the coin away. The idea is that every significant decision you make really means closing off all doors but one. We make these choices all our lives, and every time, we radically limit our billions of possible futures. You can still be a great businessman, Jason, but you can never be a rock star or an

Olympic athlete or say something to your parents—those paths are no longer open to you.

"There's no way around it, but it's hard. People like to keep their options open. But you can't get anything done that way—you just become Hamlet. So to be at peace with my choices, I try to take that one moment to acknowledge and respect all those other possibilities"—here she took a drag from the cigarette she'd lit and held the other in front of his eyes—"and then repudiate them forever in one blow, like this." The cigarette tumbled, end over end, into the harbor.

"No regrets," said Jason, nodding.

"That's it," replied Amanda.

"So what'd you just decide?"

She drew in a deep drag of the remaining cigarette, but ignored him. "That's about the only thing I took away from my father," she went on. "And I've never told anybody what I just told you," she continued.

He closed his eyes and nodded serenely, enjoying the intimacy.

"Now will you leave me alone about it?" she said with a smirk.

He laughed. "Well, Amanda, you can't just do a very odd public thing and expect not to be asked about it," he replied. "Imagine if I put a slice of cheese on my head every time I got irritated, say."

"Don't push it, Jason. I can still turn around and go home."

He smiled. "Can you?"

She fell silent, watching the waves, and he instantly regretted his reply; his mouth was driving him into danger again. He and Amanda had clearly entered some heightened state of awareness where everything was charged with meaning, and he wondered if he'd ever break through that particular wall, and find her where she walked when she walked alone. In the truest sense, for entirely different reasons, neither of them could ever go home. Was that the only thing bonding them, after all? He had to wonder.

"Thar she blows," said Amanda, and he followed her pointing finger.

The Statue of Liberty stood, torch arm upswept in the world's most famous welcome, greenly gracing her tiny island, with all the New World at her back. Already, even at this distance, she looked massive, stately, and permanent.

"She's huge," said Amanda.

"You're used to seeing her as a six-inch paperweight, that's all."

"Guess so. Jason, I . . . there's something I want you to know," she continued, not looking up. "My dad didn't want any kids. I was an accident. But my mom did, and I think she . . . I don't know . . . *sprung* me on him, I guess. I believe he never touched her again."

It was such a bolt out of the blue, Jason didn't remotely know how to respond. "Did your mom tell you that?" he asked lamely, feeling an intense pressure to say *something*.

"Yes," she said. "I can't believe she really thought about what it would mean to me, knowing."

"Well, I'm very glad you told me," he said, putting up a hand to cup her cheek.

"I don't know why I did," she said, looking genuinely disturbed. "I think I feel—unlucky. Like we're fading away, or something."

He brought up his other hand, held her face tenderly. "Hey, Amanda," he said, soothingly. "Don't think that. Do you want to do this a different day? Even if it's there, the freakin' thing's sat there for a hundred years, it'll—"

But she was shaking her head. "Nope, nope. You were right; we have to know now. It would just burn me up inside." She thought of something, riffled through the pages for a moment, and put her finger on a passage from one of the sheets.

"'Send these, the homeless, tempest-tossed to me,'" she quoted. "'I lift my lamp beside the golden door.'"

Before the blunt prow of their ship, the Statue of Liberty slowly grew and grew until it towered over the sea and the island, blocking out everything else.

LIBERTY ISLAND, 6:20 A.M.

They disembarked to the screeching of scrap-hungry seagulls, and let themselves be borne by the crowd, many of whom were already jockeying for line position with a quick trot, out onto the great plaza at the base of the statue's massive pedestal. Two ragged lines of tourists, hilarious in their plumage, already stretched a hundred yards or more from the base: one line to ride the elevators to the base of the statue, the other, longer one for the athletes who'd determined to brave the circular iron stairway all the way up to Liberty's crown. Jason found comfort in the queue. Measuring as it did the exact distance between himself and his future, its extravagant length let him breathe easy. He let his eyes drift again of their own accord to the statue towering above them, dwarfed from this angle by its seven-story pedestal. Layers upon layers of cold, windowless stonework gave the whole affair the distinct look of a mausoleum—the final resting place of liberty, if his calculations were correct. The looming physical symbol did not hurt his faith in his theory one bit.

"Check this out," said Amanda, excitedly reading from one of her pages. "The entire arm, torch and all, was put on display all over the country as a publicity stunt to raise money to build this pedestal."

Jason nodded, intrigued. "Cool. All kinds of opportunity to sneak something inside."

"No question," she replied, eyeing him curiously.

He looked over at her, then glanced up along the statue's majestic height again.

"So what happens to us, Jason?" she wondered.

He shrugged; it was a big question. "If it's there? I have no idea. I haven't thought it through beyond that point. It's still too *out there* to think about. A fairly massive party, I guess."

She smiled wanly. "Actually, I meant what happens if it *isn't* there."

"Oh," he said. "Wow. I really don't know. I don't think I could just go back to the drawing board again."

She shrugged. "It'd be a major blow," she conceded, and, thankfully, left it at that.

At seven o'clock, the doors opened and the line surged forward with a liquid bolt of adrenaline.

◇ ◇ ◇

Twenty minutes later, Jason and Amanda had oozed with the crowd into the main room of the pedestal, a large square chamber chockablock with small artifacts, wall plaques, and photos detailing the building of the statue and other historical trivia.

"This way," said Jason, tugging her hand toward the stairs, up which the main body of tourists was already flowing.

"Wait, Jason—look at that," she said in a worried tone, pointing across the room to the right.

Jason's following gaze met with an arresting surprise: the top half of the torch, green and massive and unmistakable. He wrinkled his brow; this didn't make sense. They wandered over warily, like dogs investigating an unfamiliar odor.

He was amazed by how small the torch was, less than twenty feet across. No more than a dozen or so people could stand comfortably on its balcony. The flame, a cloudy orange glass crosshatched by a bright green, overly thick grid of copper bands, splayed out in a crazily horizontal limbo dance: Liberty buffeted by gale-force winds.

"This is the original," Amanda whispered, reading the plaque beneath it as the crowd flowed around them. "It was corroding. They put up a new one with an updated lighting system in 1985."

He tore his gaze away from the hypnotic torch itself and watched Amanda take a few steps around the railing, eyes glued to the flame, as thoroughly hypnotized by the sight as he. "It could be right *there*," she continued.

"I'm going to guess no," replied Jason after a moment. "The top of the torch was always designed to be a high-traffic area—the deed would have been safer in the arm, on the way up."

"But everyone who made it here had to climb the arm first."

"True, but people are *moving* on a ladder," he reminded her. "Fifty-four rungs, remember? They're not standing around catching their breath and looking for something to do. Plus it's in the dark. That's where I'd have put it, anyway."

"We're in wild-speculation land here, aren't we?"

He shrugged. "Search here if you want—I'm going up."

✧ ✧ ✧

They climbed and climbed, joining the heaving mob in a relentless circular cattle drive to the top. The clatter of footfalls on iron reverberated through the structure in constant cacophany; Jason, feeling hemmed in and claustrophobic, felt the echoes as physical vibrations, bat-radar warnings of walls creeping closer.

The tourists craned their necks as they rose, staring up through the iron-mesh floor treads, eyes straining for the observation platform and journey's end. Jason and Amanda alone, it seemed, turned their gaze perpetually toward the outside of the stairs. The winding had him hopelessly turned around, and he knew he'd have no idea on which side the arm would appear until he saw it.

At last it appeared, unmistakably: a small white door off to one side. Two or three more orbits up around the vertical axis and they'd be there. He squeezed Amanda's hand in a prearranged signal, and they stopped traveling together; he went on several steps ahead, where he'd listen for her action before making his move. He let himself be carried by the throng, stared at the unassuming little door whenever their winding brought it back into view. There was a handle, but no obvious lock on the door, though there was no real way of knowing. He wondered whether he could bust the latch with a hard enough shoulder slam. Was the door frame wood or steel?

He heard Amanda's small fainting cry behind him, seemingly too soon, and for all the mission-critical importance of exact timing, he couldn't help turning to look. Amanda had fallen dramatically back into the crowd, twenty or so steps behind him. Her faith in the absolute predictability of mass behavior proved justified: Some tourists caught her, others stumbled and created a general clatter, and various shrieks of alarm brought every eye in the vicinity her way.

Time for action. Jason wrenched his eyes away and covered the remaining twelve feet to the door, now passing the shocked faces of tourists staring at the scene behind him. He tried the handle; the door was indeed locked, but without any apparent dead bolt. He spared another glance back, but could no longer see Amanda in the press; at least nobody was looking in his direction. Now or never. He threw his weight against the door, snapping the strike plate out of the doorway, pushed open the door just wide enough to slide inside, and shut himself into the arm's eternal midnight.

✧ ✧ ✧

There he waited, heart racing, for what must have been several minutes, eyes bugging in the blackness like the wasted orbs of a blind cave fish. The metal door (for it *had* been metal, his already sore shoulder informed him) muffled the commotion below into incomprehensibility, increasing the likelihood of total, underwear-wrecking surprise should some hawkeyed authority burst in after him. He had no idea whether he'd been seen, and no way of finding out. Jaded New Yorkers wouldn't bother disrupting their day by turning him in, of course, but the population here was all gentle Midwesterners and well-meaning international types. As each second ticked by, he fully expected the door to swing open, but couldn't focus his racing mind long enough to clap together a simple alibi.

Claustrophobia and paranoia were spiraling into panic, here in the impenetrable dark—he had to keep moving.

"'To be or not to be,'" he muttered, and the space was so small that even this whisper echoed, adding unwelcome detail to his growing sense of being locked in a cold copper coffin.

He retrieved the flashlight with a minimum of fumbling; its pathetic glow revealed a closetlike space centered around a simple black-iron ladder stretching up into shadow. It was surprisingly narrow inside Lady Liberty's arm, less than five feet or so across even down here at the meat of the shoulder, and tapering off, with the ladder running straight up the middle, into a darkness his puny beam couldn't begin to penetrate.

Jason took a deep, whistling breath and felt his jacket pocket, making sure the spare batteries were there. If he were caught, the college-kid-on-a-lark excuse was going to fall pretty flat, considering the fat wad of destructive tools he was sporting. No, it was all or nothing.

Gripping the ladder halfheartedly with one hand, Jason played the light along every inch of the walls, as if hoping to expand the space through sheer photon pressure. He could feel anxiety tugging at him, begging for audience. Here, as out in the main part of the statue, the copper skin that stretched smoothly across the contours of Lady Liberty's musculature was held in place with a mesh of iron reinforcing bars. His high beam gamely chased darkness out of corners, and threw crazy diagonal grids dancing all over the interior whenever it crossed the ladder.

"Right," he said aloud, to calm his nerves with the familiar sound of his own voice. "Like it's going to be taped to a wall right here." But the echo unnerved him, and he fell silent.

Fifty-four rungs, he reminded himself. He began laboriously to make his way up the ladder, flashlight and briefcase compromising his handholds. He wondered idly how many people were looking at the statue's arm at this very moment—from the air, from the sea, from cars on the New Jersey Turnpike, from the line outside the statue itself. Five thousand? Ten thousand? It was one of the most obvious focal points of planet earth, and not one of the viewers could know there was a man inside here, inching his way up the inside of the arm like a blood clot on the move.

He passed the elbow, his only landmark; on a whim, he paused, pinned the briefcase to the ladder with one knee, and shone the light straight up. The vertical tunnel closed in even farther, tapering off toward Lady Lib's shapely wrist—already he could reach out and tap the flashlight on any point of the interior wall, and it was only getting tighter. Dimly, he could see the top of the ladder, where it bumped up against a small Alice-in-Wonderland trapdoor: the torch proper.

He was checking his watch by the flashlight when the ladder suddenly swayed under his legs and he nearly fell. He clumsily threw his off-balance torso back into the ladder with such a jolt he almost lost the pinned briefcase, then nearly dropped the flashlight in his spastic grab to save it.

Holy shit, he thought. *This simply cannot be allowed to get worse.* He pictured the flashlight eluding his grasp and clattering down, down, down all the way back to the base of the ladder, putting out its eye on some stupid rivet and leaving him in total blackness.

"I am really out on a limb, here—no pun intended," he said aloud, feeling his heartbeat vibrate his body on the ladder. He wondered how good the oxygen flow was in here, wondered if the dizziness he felt were real or psychosomatic.

Back to work, back to work. He looped one hand around the ladder—
now stay still, *ya hear?*—and painted the inner walls with light again. The
skin seemed smooth and contoured; he didn't come across any anomalies
that would suggest a likely spot for a hidden document. Some bundle of
arteries—power cables for the torch, no doubt—ran through a series of
metal hoops along the arm's upper side; he made a mental note to avoid
them.

Jason reached the tiny door at the top of the ladder without finding
anything. He knew with absolute certainty that the deed wasn't out
there—this was the part of the torch that had been replaced in the eighties. Still, here he was . . . He reached up, turned the latch, and flopped the
door up onto the torch platform. Sunlight poured in like bathwater. A
moment later he was outside.

The torch rose imperially above him, in a sea of dazzling blue sky. The
claustrophobia dissolved instantly, but the vertigo hit him like a hammer.
He set down the briefcase on the metal platform, clicked off the now quite
useless light, and steadied his nerves before heading to the iron rail that
girdled the platform.

The view was truly, literally breathtaking, the swaying of the arm terrifyingly pronounced. Every gust of wind seemed to bend it four or five feet
out of whack. Far below, across the blue ribbon of water, Manhattan's skyline glittered fantastically in the morning sun, like a slumbering steel
dragon.

"Hello, my people!" he shouted aloud.

A little despair intruded on his exuberance; he'd found nothing, and
for the first time since his epiphany of the night before Jason allowed himself to wonder what it would mean if the deed wasn't here after all. He
could all too easily see himself crawling sheepishly out of the lower door
empty-handed. And then what?

Maybe it was for the best, anyway. If he *did* find the deed, could he ever
be totally sure of Amanda's affection? It would have to change them, one
way or another . . . and frankly, he liked things just the way they were.

Funny, he decided as he looked over the city. In the beginning they'd
absolutely needed the deed to hold them together, and now that they

seemed on the edge of discovering it, it had become a sort of threat. Was this a partnership or a relationship?

He knew which one he wanted, and time was wasting. Reluctantly, he drank in the once-in-a-lifetime view one last time, then picked up his briefcase and headed for the door. *I can handle this*, now, he told himself as he looked down the length of the ladder, this time taking advantage of the illumination streaming in from above. And the extra light turned the tide—suddenly, Jason saw the answer.

It was the bottom of the torch, revealed by the light from above as a little hollow cup dipping below Lady Lib's curled fingers around the shaft. That was it—had to be, if it was here at all. There was no question that this was the safest spot in the whole arm/torch assembly, the only place that would never be brushed on the way past by tourists' hands.

Briefcase in tow, Jason clambered a few steps down the ladder, craning his body to one side so as not to block the light. As he approached, filled with excitement and dread, the torch bottom took on the shape of a copper octagon, nearly a square but with nipped-off corners, the whole of it no more than a foot and a half across.

Okay, he reassured himself, stretching one foot off the ladder and testing his weight on the iron superstructure. *This, then, is the stage on which my madness is going to play itself out.* He was literally in Lady Liberty's hand now, kneeling inside a finger and reaching into the well-lit recess of the torch bottom. He ran one hand along the edge of the copper seam, then stared at the black ring of ages-old dust on his fingers. *What's here?* he wondered. *A speck from a Rockefeller's boot? The dandruff of a king?* He wiped it on the ass of his pants, cracked open the briefcase, and plucked out a regular screwdriver.

"This isn't what it looks like, Officer," he said aloud, voice echoing eerily as he forced the screwdriver into the seam, midway between two thumb-size rivets. "Yes, I suppose technically I am desecrating a national monument. But you see, I met this girl . . ."

He hit the screwdriver with the heel of his hand, leery of risking the noise of the hammer; the copper, defiant but thin, tented up agreeably at the wedge. It was slow work, digging little channels around the rivets. But at least his efforts weren't opening up a hole to the outside—this was, in-deed, a false bottom, and that alone was grounds for optimism.

After five minutes of frenzied work, he'd broken the panel away from the rivets along only two walls of the square, not the three sides that would allow him to peel back the whole sheet, but enough to try turning one corner back. He took a break to check his watch and discovered he'd been in the arm for nearly fifty minutes. *Christ—tempus fugit.*

Replacing the screwdriver in his briefcase, he yoked pliers and monkey wrench together at the single freed corner and tried to fold the copper back on itself. It proved more resistant than expected, a difficulty com-pounded by the lack of leverage in the narrow space. He kept tugging, and succeeded in pulling up the edge a couple of inches, and then the copper would not budge farther. He'd gained just enough space to reach a hand inside.

It would have to do.

He pictured Amanda waiting somewhere below, being fanned back to health by a concerned Ohio couple, and wondered if he was doing the right thing. He could just turn now and walk away, tell her there was nothing here . . . couldn't he?

"If I don't reach in there, it's not there," he mused aloud. "But is the re-verse true?"

It's probably some access panel or something, his brain warned him. *You're going to electrocute yourself in the freaking arm of the Statue of Liberty.* But there was no turning away now; he'd never even make it to the bottom of the ladder without finding out for sure. Mentally crossing himself, he closed his eyes, flattened his hand into a shark fin, and slid it sidewise into the hollow.

✧ ✧ ✧

He found her milling around near the ferry dock, watching a crowd list-lessly board.

"Eureka," he said, surprising her from behind.

She whirled around. "Oh, my God," she said, instantly catching the fire in his gaze. "Tell me you found something."

Jason silently pinned the briefcase tight between his feet and whipped off his windbreaker, turning it inside out.

She shook her head. "What are you *doing?*"

"Disguising myself," he said, slipping his arms through the sleeves and wrapping them around her. "Quick—kiss me, hard."

He planted his lips on hers and closed his eyes. Her kiss was amazing, warm and soft in the chill of the buffeting sea breeze, a perfect movie kiss. He held her there for half a minute of pure paradise before letting her pull away.

She glanced over his shoulder. "There's nobody after you."

He shrugged. "Who said there was anyone after me?"

"Did you find something, you bastard, or not?"

"Come on—we've got to catch this ferry."

She looked at his briefcase, pointed. "Is it—"

Grinning like a madman, he tugged her hand toward the loading ferry. "Come on!" he enjoined her. "Come on, come on, come on!"

SOUTH FERRY, 12:30 P.M.

In the twenty minutes it took for the ferry to return to the Manhattan side, they spoke in furtive whispers, penned in as they were by blissful peacock tourists.

It's a big piece of parchment, he confided, tapping his briefcase, barely speaking. *In a crumbling leather bag.*

Let's at least look at it, she begged.

I don't know about you, but I'd feel pretty stupid if the damn thing blew into Hudson Bay after all that.

All right, all right, she allowed. *But the instant we hit shore.*

Seriously, I might have been tailed for real, he replied. *I came out more or less right in front of a security guy. I'm pretty sure he saw me. I don't know if he left his post or sounded any alarm or not; I didn't dare look back.*

She looked around their deck, couldn't pick out any park police. *You're being paranoid,* she said, and he shrugged.

I hope so.

He couldn't believe it—it was right here in his bag, the answer to questions and the key to futures. For all his show of patience, Jason was every bit as anxious to see it as she was, to hold it and pore over it in some safe place where they wouldn't be disturbed. He looked over and wondered what thoughts were going through her head; wondered if you ever got so close to another person that you knew, really knew, what they were think-ing. A stony silence had sprung up between them; he didn't believe either of them could screw up the energy for small talk, with so much in the offing.

The World Trade Center loomed again in the foreground, literally scraping the sky, twin fortresses of almighty commerce. *My babies*, he said to himself, gazing up their dizzying height as they drew closer.

They docked and unloaded at last, disembarking with a jostling crowd surge that worried him enough to cause him to pin the briefcase closer to his chest.

"Your place or mine?" Jason said aloud as they cleared the dock and the crowd started to disperse in all directions.

"Oh, no, you don't," she replied. "We find a bar or something. If you *even* think I'm sitting still for a ride uptown . . ."

"That's far enough," said a stern voice behind them. "You two, step this way, please."

✧ ✧ ✧

Jason's heart sank; he turned slowly toward Amanda and then back. Two grave-looking men filled the space immediately behind them: sunglasses, charcoal suits, trivial variants of some basic undercover-cop style. Jason could see Amanda's shoulders visibly slump beside him; running seemed utterly out of the question. The smaller man flashed some sort of badge, as his beefier partner smirked without humor and pulled a cell phone from his pocket.

"Come with us, please," said Badge, replacing his wallet. "Don't make any trouble, okay?"

"Look," said Jason, contrite. "This isn't what it looks like, Officer. I can—"

"Not in front of the tourists," said Cellphone calmly, fingers poised above the keypad. "If you make things hard for us, I assure you we can make them very hard for you. *Very* hard. Could you please come this way?"

"But we haven't—" piped in Amanda.

"You have the right to remain silent," Cellphone interrupted in a deeply sonorous, no-nonsense voice. "I strongly suggest you use it."

Fighting an almost overwhelming urge to run, Jason looked around at the crowd breaking around them, felt the tourists' curious glances at the demi-scene unfolding. Had they tracked him all the way from the island, or called ahead? It seemed so pathetic now, in retrospect, he thought with embarrassment. What kind of hubris had let him think he could really vandalize a crowded national monument in the middle of the day without repercussions?

The muscular officer had stepped to one side and was speaking low into the cell phone while his partner watched over them with a wary eye. Suddenly Jason found a ray of hope—this had to be about the trespassing, or at worst, breaking and entering. The police would of course have no reason to suspect he'd removed anything from the statue, even if they'd inspected and found the damaged copper inside the torch—something there simply hadn't been time for yet anyway.

"You think we should cuff 'em?" Badge called back to his partner, never taking his eyes off them. There was a touch of nervousness in his voice.

Cellphone shook his head dismissively. "No, we don't need to cuff 'em—they're gonna play nice. Isn't that right, kids?"

Shrouded in silence, Jason and Amanda were led toward a nondescript black unmarked four-door idling some twenty feet away. Jason took a deep, rattling breath and stole a guilty glance at his girl, where he met a brief but expectant stare before self-consciousness drove both their gazes earthward. He didn't know how to read Amanda's look, a bitter reminder that he'd only known her for a week after all.

He felt dizzy and light-headed, anchored only by the weight of his parents' briefcase and its cargo as he and Amanda were led around to different doors. After installing them in the back of the car, the cops climbed into the front; the beefy one, driving now, pressed the button that locked the four doors and they headed out onto the streets of southern Manhattan without exchanging another word.

It was all spiraling out of control now. Jason could feel the adrenaline that had buoyed him for so long begin to drain away as his body suddenly remembered the lack of sleep, the stress and activity, the world-class excessive drinking from the previous night. A wave of guilt helped diffuse his burgeoning nausea. He couldn't help feeling that he'd betrayed Amanda again, with the recklessness of the last few hours—irredeemably, this time. Had he subconsciously rushed the endgame too fast, squandering his invaluable revelation in a cheap ploy to win her forgiveness?

The car angled right—avoiding the Peter Minuit plaza, Jason noted wryly—and turned onto Water Street. He glanced over at Amanda. *It's not supposed to end this way,* he tried to will his gaze to convey, but her head was down.

Then don't let it, said a voice in his head, quite as distinct as if it had been heard rather than imagined.

The cops were mumbling in the front seat, conversing in secret. He looked into the rearview and caught the reflection of the smaller cop looking at him, then quickly looking away. There was something odd about all this . . .

Suddenly, he had it.

Jason glanced over at Amanda again, and this time she slid her hand over to meet his. It was warm and wonderful . . . and he squeezed her palm once, twice. On the third time, she raised her eyes to his, curious.

They're not cops, Jason mouthed.

Her brow wrinkled. *How do you know?*

He shrugged. *I recognize them. They're your dad's goons, the casino guys.*

Her eyes widened and she nodded. It had been like that for him, too; the comprehension was total, when it came.

The car turned left again, heading north now, onto some larger street. *All we have to do is escape,* he continued, *and we're free.*

She nodded, eyes alight, and mouthed something he couldn't understand. He gave her a questioning look, and she repeated it: *liberty.*

He smiled and nodded.

But we're locked in.

Jason shook his head, pantomimed the simple reach forward that would unlock the driver's door and, presumably, all the locks.

Beneath eye level, Jason pointed in quick succession to Amanda, then her door, then himself and his door. *Columbus Circle*, he mouthed silently. *Meet me there as soon as you can.*

A few agonizing minutes later, the car slowed for a yellow light turning red up ahead. Jason felt uneasy not knowing where they were, exactly, but they had no choice but to move . . . who knew what the next minute would bring?

Amanda recognized this, too; as the car slowed, she smiled and mouthed: *I love you.*

He pointed to himself and made a peace sign—*me, too*—as the car halted. No time for hesitation. He stealthily slid his hand in alongside the driver's shoulder and popped the lock. Four door locks leaped up with a loud pop and Jason, hand already pulling the handle, threw his shoulder into the door, wincing with pain.

Suddenly there was activity in the front seat; hearing Amanda's door open as well, Jason pressed the driver's lock back down—excellent touch, he thought—and half-fell, half-climbed out of the car, scrambled to his feet, and raced between the stopped cars for the safety of the sidewalk, briefcase smacking his side, desperately trying to keep his footing in a very real race for his life.

Behind him he heard the angry shouts to halt, the front doors opening at last with the pursuit that would be just a little too late. Hitting the sidewalk at a dead run, Jason saw bystanders backing away and clutching purses, and he realized that to the crowd, he and Amanda, wherever her escape route took her, would look like criminals. *No*, he corrected. *In fact, we are criminals.* Some do-gooder might even trip him up or try to take him out with a clothesline. But the farther away he drew from the scene, the less interested the crowd seemed in the reason for his hurry, and by the time he made it to the next corner and stole a glance back, the car was gone. With nobody tailing him, he slowed to a sustainable jog.

He had to check his elation when it occurred to him that if they weren't chasing him, they were certainly chasing her. He wanted to go back . . . but then the document would definitely fall into their hands. Better to secure it and trust to luck.

Ten minutes later he was sliding into a number 9 subway car, panting for breath, scanning each disinterested face with paranoid intensity. Satisfied that he was safe for now, he sat facing the still-open doors and tried to slow his breathing. He stared silently at the briefcase, on the seat beside him. *Got the deed . . . lost the girl.*

Did Amanda get away? There was no way of knowing until 59th Street/Columbus Circle, still many, many blocks away. Jason could only watch helplessly as the sliding doors opened and closed, opened and closed in their perpetual foolish dance.

Hope was treading water, but in his heart Jason knew, with terrifying certainty, that she wouldn't be there.

UPPER WEST SIDE, 5:00 P.M.

Jason took the stairs three at a time—lungs gasping involuntarily, every muscle crying out in pain—flagellating himself for having let things get so out of hand. All he could think to do was hurry, as if moving closer to the speed of light would keep time from elapsing, put off disaster indefinitely. The briefcase swung heavily from one hand as he jammed the other in his pocket, somehow squeezing out the keys between floors.

Fumbling with the lock, he dropped the keys and stopped, leaning heavily on the wall, forcing himself to concentrate. The silent, dead air of the stairwell felt like a judgment.

He'd waited at the rendezvous point, in an agony of indecision, for nearly an hour.

Jason had no idea what to do next—who to call, where to go. His buzzing had gone unanswered at Amanda's apartment, and so he'd returned home partly on the off chance she'd headed there instead, partly as a logical base of operations for whatever was to come.

He clearly couldn't call the police without telling them everything— and if he did that, and she really *had* escaped but had simply been delayed, all their effort would be wasted. On the other hand, if they'd caught her, her life was surely in danger.

Pushing through the door, he set the briefcase, unopened, on the coffee table. He felt a pang of guilt, acknowledging that a curious part of him still wanted to check out the document—what could it hurt at this point?

But it would have been the worst kind of betrayal. He'd already resolved not to so much as look at the damn deed until Amanda was safe, a promise the harried last hour had hardened into a blood oath. He wound his way to his phone, where he saw the blinking message light.

He approached warily, homing in on the tiny beacon and pressed Play, bracing himself for the colossal absurdity of the mundane message sure to follow.

"We know you want this all to work out between us," said the caller, and Jason gritted his teeth, recognizing the voice. "You know what we're looking for—bring it over to the Brooklyn Bridge at seven o'clock tonight if you want to make an exchange. At the underpass at Pearl Street, on the north side. Come alone or you're going home alone."

Silence.

Jason sat down heavily in the chair by the phone, twirling the pen he'd grabbed off the phone pad, knowing he wouldn't need to use it; the key information was burned into his forebrain like a brand. His eyes wandered to the table where his briefcase sat, plump with promise. So close . . . the goddamn deed.

Would they actually harm her, if he showed up with the police? Would they kill her? Really? *I have no idea how to deal with this*, Jason realized. From what his movies had taught him, gangsters used acts of violence mostly so the *threat* of violence would have teeth. On the other hand, lots of people got shot and killed every day. And there was a hell of a lot of money at stake here, potentially, which surely multiplied the danger.

It was amazing, he thought suddenly, just how laughably easy his entire life had been right up to this point.

He stood up and clapped his hands together, trying to call himself to action.

How much did they know? They must have found out about the deed through Amanda's father, obviously. He wondered if the man knew, or cared, that he'd put his own daughter's life at risk. But did they somehow not understand that the deed wasn't transferable—that it was only useful to him? Or did they want to hold it hostage for cash, extort some kind of concession, sell it to a third party?

Maybe they could be reasoned with. There were plenty of millions to go around, if all went as planned; logic screamed that they ought to be able to strike some sort of devil's bargain. But maybe that only worked for small fortunes you could get your brain around. Maybe a pearl beyond price naturally inspires treachery without bounds. It was suddenly clear, he thought, how curses attach themselves to priceless objects—by their very nature they attract the world's greediest desperadoes, and the violence they bring with them, like flies to the zapper.

He checked his watch, and realized with despair that it was already time to start heading to the rendezvous, so as not to risk getting stuck in afternoon traffic. But still, cops or no cops? Was this a call to reason, or to heroism?

Of course he had to go to the police, and of course he couldn't, and both absolutes were so strong Jason was dizzy with the dissonance. One hand was reaching for the phone, the other physically restraining it. He looked over at the briefcase again, tried to rack his brain for some kind of plan.

"I am in *so* far over my fuckin' head," he said aloud.

THE BROOKLYN BRIDGE, 7:00 P.M.

The giant pilings rose like skyscrapers of their own from the muck of the East River; the mighty span blundered halfway onto the island before deigning to circle back and attenuate down to street level. For a hundred years, New Yorkers had walked on water right here, watched square-riggers slice through the whitecaps below; seen magnificent fireworks outshine, for seconds only, the dazzling city lights; walked and driven across to see the Dodgers take the field at Ebbets. The southern, Brooklyn-bound side of the bridge still bloomed with commuter taillights, but here on the Manhattan-bound side the traffic was much reduced; only an occasional car came along to disturb their wait.

The men were outside the car, but keeping a watchful eye on Amanda, sullen in the backseat. "What if he brings cops?" said Vinnie, leaning on the railing.

Freddie, pacing up by the hood, shot him a deprecating stare. "Would you?"

Vinnie shrugged and fell silent, finally, and ashed his cigarette into the side of the railing. It was starting to get chilly; he wished he hadn't left his coat in the car, but it seemed stupid and weak to go back to retrieve it. He looked over anyway, saw Amanda sitting still in the middle of the backseat, a bitter frown spoiling her hot little mug. *Gotta keep an eye on that one.*

Freddie had no such worries; he'd already spoken to Amanda alone, and that was that. He was quite certain there'd be no trouble from her end—she would not be leaving the car until he told her to. People were quite reasonable, he'd always found, once things were put in perspective for them.

Son of a bitch pulled a fast one on me, he thought again bitterly, as he let his gaze splay out over all the possible approaches, watching for his man. *It won't happen again.* He'd chosen this spot carefully: lots of exits, and virtually no chance of being surprised. When Jason appeared, strolling down Pearl Street right on schedule, Freddie saw him coming from blocks away.

"Showtime," he said quietly.

✧ ✧ ✧

Jason saw the car up on the bridge and the two men beside it long before he could make out their faces, but their identity was never in doubt. No sign of Amanda . . . in the car, he could only hope, though he couldn't see through the windows yet. The off-ramp, reached from a U-turn at the end of the bridge, crossed back above Pearl Street, down which he was walking, and sloped gently back down toward the East River, pouring out its traffic into the city and onto the FDR Drive. He tried to record the whole scene: About twenty feet from where the two men stood by the car, an iron stairway led down to the sidewalk in front of him. Either he'd be going up or they'd be coming down.

You're a salesman, he reminded himself in a mostly vain effort to calm his nerves. *So sell this thing. Get them to deal.* He glanced down at the briefcase and tried not to think about what a tough sell it was.

Jason stopped at the foot of the stairs, unsure whether to climb up and join them.

"Where's Amanda?" he said aloud.

"She's up here," said Freddie, nodding sideways at the car. "Come on up."

"I want to see her," he said boldly.

The man grinned, nodded to the other, who stepped back and obligingly opened the car door. Amanda emerged bedraggled and beautiful and furious; his heart leaped at the sight. Everything he wanted was right within his grasp, if he could only sort out how to secure it.

"Come on up," the man repeated, a slight shift in intonation indicating that this time it was an order.

$$\diamond \; \diamond \; \diamond$$

"That's far enough," said Freddie, when Jason had set foot on the bridge, now twenty feet from the car. "Now show it to us."

Jason set the case down and unlatched it, reached inside and pulled out the tattered brown leather bag. Holding it in one hand, he looked up, a question, but Freddie shook his head, not yet satisfied. Jason reached in reluctantly and carefully withdrew the ancient parchment, shielding it with his body from the ripping breeze off the water.

"Why don't you let her go?" said Jason. "I'm not going anywhere."

"That's right, you're not," said Vinnie from the far side of the car.

"Listen," Jason replied, gently pinning the parchment against his chest with one hand, not looking at it. "Do you even know what this is? It's useless to anybody but myself and her, I swear it."

"Put it back in the bag," said Freddie.

"Let's work something out," said Jason, keeping his eyes on Freddie as he obediently replaced the parchment in the bag and latched it in the briefcase. "She and I are the only people in the world this is valuable to."

"You still talking? Toss it over."

Jason paused. "How do I know you'll let her go?"

Freddie laughed at this. "You don't. Now toss it the *fuck* over."

Jason scrambled furiously for a solution, some alternative to giving up his bargaining chip. It was impossible to read Amanda's expression from this distance, but he couldn't give up this easily.

"Not until you let her go," he said brazenly.

Freddie looked amazed. "You hearin' this unbelievable shit?" he said to Vinnie, then turned back around. "This isn't a game, you little dipshit."

Jason laid out his palms in what he hoped would be a placating gesture. "All I want—"

"No, no more talking," said Freddie, grabbing Amanda with one hand and reaching into an interior pocket of his jacket with the other, drawing out a gun. "I'm going to be as clear as I can. You're going to toss that bag the *fuck* over," Freddie continued calmly, "or I start blowing off fingers."

The gun was a machine Jason had seen in operation ten bazillion times, all of them fictional, and now it was the most real thing he had ever seen, an inescapable black hole at the center of his vision—he literally couldn't wrench his gaze away.

"You and I both know," Freddie was saying in slow motion, pinning Amanda's hand to the rail in front of him, "that after I have to shoot off one of this lady's thumbs, you're going to get religion fast and toss that bag over here." He smiled broadly. "So we're really just haggling over how many fingers it's gonna take, aren't we?"

Jason saw the raw terror in Amanda's eyes, and spared a glance at Vinnie, who was nervous as a cat, shifting from foot to foot. Now he didn't know *what* to do. Two or three odd cars had drifted past them down the off-ramp in the last few minutes, ignoring them absolutely, and Jason knew there was no help coming. *Never a damn cop around when you need one, is there?*

"If you could just please, please listen to me for a—"

"I'm going to give you a standing five count," Freddie continued smoothly, unperturbed. "That'll give you lots of time to think about what you want to do. But if I get to 'five,' the very next sound you hear is going to be a gunshot."

"One . . ."

◇ ◇ ◇

The impossible gravity of the moment slowed time to a crawl. On some level, Jason was aware that his brain was operating in some rarefied synaptic hyperdrive. He'd seen enough cop shows to know that if you gave the bad guys what they wanted, you always lost in the end. Was this man really capable of such violence? He talked a good game, and maybe it was a bluff—but hell, who knew? He turned his head slowly and the lights of the city left ghostly white trails, like a time-lapse photograph. Looking hopefully out over the edge of the off-ramp for help, down at the mostly empty street, he realized that stalling was pointless. He was in this thing alone.

✧ ✧ ✧

". . . two . . ."

✧ ✧ ✧

His primal impulse was to run, to find a way to escape and defer this thing to another day. It meant leaving Amanda behind and that was unthinkable. But of course they wouldn't *really* harm her—she was their only bargaining chip, as surely as the deed was his. They'd still have her and he'd still have the document, and they'd be in the same predicament, but maybe he could buy time to think of a solution, or find a way to get the police involved. The alternative, to simply hand over the bag, was to entrust her safety—and his, for that matter—to the mercy of mobsters . . . mobsters who'd been recognized. It would be a pointless squandering of his one asset. No, the smart move was to take the money and run—nobody shoots a woman on a bridge in broad daylight—and find a smart way to buy her safety later on. What would it take to get these goons to let her go? A million? Ten million? He had it, now; there was no way they'd risk killing a golden goose like that, now that they apparently knew what was at stake.

✧ ✧ ✧

". . . three . . ."

✧ ✧ ✧

And then he saw Amanda's terrified face, a veneer of defiance speedily coming unglued, and he knew he couldn't possibly leave her, knew that no amount of pragmatic reasoning could possibly hold up in the face of her raw need. He had no free will at all, really, only the tantalizing illusion of choice. In her dark eyes he saw everything that mattered, and knew instantly that he would hand over the goods even though it was no guarantee of her safety, even though it demonstrably imperiled them even further. His only option was unconditional surrender, and he opened his mind to it.

Then, just as he changed his grip on the bag, preparing to toss it over, he heard the rumble, rolling toward him like an angry storm front.

It was a strangely familiar noise, and yet somehow, in the cocoon of the here and now, truly transcendental. Even as he turned north to face the wave, felt the wind of its coming on his cheek, he recognized the sound, and smiled.

It was the footsteps of a god.

✧ ✧ ✧

". . . four . . ."

✧ ✧ ✧

Manahata rolled noisily into view, and the mundane incarnation he'd chosen did nothing to dissuade Jason of the belief that he was staring into the face of the godhead. And suddenly his choice was clear, and everything was okay. He smiled.

And as his hand cocked back to toss away the briefcase at last, Jason felt a deep serenity wash over him, a carefree security he hadn't known since childhood. Suddenly he was fourteen and free, with his parents' death and all the pain and stress of life far ahead of him. Dawn was breaking and he was racing his mud-caked Huffy down a narrow alleyway, skidding to a diagonal halt at the end of Mission Lane. Turning into the wind, he checked his watch. The instant the second hand dragged its lazy ass across the twelve, he released the hand brake and the race was on. His feet pedaled furiously and his long hair streaked back from his face and out of his eyes; pimple trauma and the slights of teenage bitches scattered before the fury of his ride.

The first house was the toughest, a slim four feet of porch set far back from the road, with windows on both sides. This called for strength and skill; you practically had to land it on the mat. Come on, Jason, he cheered himself. You've done this a hundred times before. One hand on the handlebars, one eye on the sidewalk . . . He took aim and launched the newspaper, watching it arc gently end over end over end . . .

✧ ✧ ✧

". . . five . . ." said Freddie reflexively, but he was already watching the briefcase in flight.

The garbage truck trundled slowly down Pearl Street, scooting under the Brooklyn Bridge and continuing its moderate downtown amble, quite oblivious to its new passenger.

"Oh, you little fuck!" said Vinnie, looking over the edge.

"Go get it," said Freddie, releasing Amanda's hand and aiming the gun at Jason. "Not smart. You sit down." Jason backed away from the stairs and sat down.

But Vinnie was pointing over the edge, even as he jogged for the stairs. "Freddie, it went in the truck!"

"What?"

"That garbage truck! Come on, it's going slow, we can catch it!" Vinnie squealed, clambering down the stairs.

"Stay *here*," Freddie hissed, but Vinnie had dropped below the level of the bridge. Freddie looked back and forth between Jason and Amanda, undecided.

Gunshots sounded from the street below.

"Fuck!" screamed Freddie, kicking a sizable dent in the side of the car. He took off toward the stairs, still training the gun on Jason. Jason stared into the barrel, seated and motionless, a semi-serene Buddha trying to save his life by not smiling.

"I oughtta cap your fuckin' ass anyway," hissed Freddie, dripping with malice. And for an agonizing second, it appeared he was going to, then another shot rang out from below, and he was off and down the stairs at a dead run. "Stay where you are!" he shouted back.

"Sure thing, pal," muttered Jason, clambering to his feet as Amanda sprinted toward him.

"You idiot!" she said. "Did you think they were really gonna shoot me?"

"You want to be saved or not?" he said absently. His eyes were still over the bridge, entranced by the scene below.

"My hero," she said wryly, tugging at him. "Come on, let's get out of here."

"Run the light, run the light, run the light."

"What?"

"I'm talking to my truck."

The men had closed the distance to ten or fifteen yards, and the traffic light went yellow, half a block ahead. Vinnie fired another shot in the air.

"Stop shooting, you asshole!" they could hear Freddie yell.

"For Christ's sake, please run that light," said Jason again.

The light turned red, but the truck driver, spooked either by the shots themselves or the reflected view of two gunmen racing toward his side mirror, kicked it into gear and sped through the light, horn blaring like a wounded animal.

"Kiss me," said Amanda.

"Are you nuts?" he said, turning his attention to her at last. "First we escape, then we kiss."

"Come on," she said. "You'll never have another moment like this in your life."

He knew she was right, and so he kissed her, for as long as he dared. They looked down over the railing to see the gangsters jogging purposefully back toward them, still a block away.

"Run," he said. "No, this way."

"One minute," she said, racing back over to the car and slamming open the driver's-side door. Reaching in awkwardly, she yanked out the car keys, hauled back, and launched them off the far side of the bridge as far as she could throw.

"Damn," she said, racing back toward him. "I really thought I could hit the river."

He grinned broadly, and they picked up the pace in unison and together raced back down the ramp to where it merged with the rest of the inbound Brooklyn Bridge traffic.

Jason glanced over at Amanda as they ran, then at the road, then back to her. He felt buoyant, as if he could easily win a marathon. It was easier running without the briefcase, but harder, in a way; he couldn't escape the distinct notion that he was leaving something important behind.

"My hand feels empty," he confessed aloud, turning up his palm to inspect it.

"Here," she said, slipping her hand in his, and together they ran as if their lives depended on it, due west, down the hill of the off-ramp and into the heart of their city, into a blazing sunset.

Epilogue

The seagull cried and swooped in a lazy helix high above the bay, crazy with the worms in its gut and the stink of the sea. Seconds later, an infinitesimal guano grenade exploded into a smear on the rust-iron hull of a garbage scow steaming a line across the gray-blue ocean. In the ship's wake lay Manhattan Island, dusky gem of the East, a rocky, bridge-bound glacial outcropping overrun to ecological insupportibility with just a few species: rats, cockroaches, pigeons, and a certain annoyingly tenacious hairless ape.

Dead ahead in her sights sprawled the docks at Fresh Kills, Staten Island, the world's largest landfill and a mound of waste that was already taller than the Great Pyramid of Cheops; a project of such unthinkable mass it was scheduled to be closed in just a few years, lest its bloated bulk sink its host island below sea level.

But not today. Behind the barge, another was already loading up on the Manhattan side in a more or less continuous flow of waste disposal. Talk about Flushing, New York. The seagull skimmed along at the waterline, gamely pounced on a bit of sea foam, then flapped angrily up, up, and away, into the brooding sky.

UPPER WEST SIDE, 8:00 P.M.

A man slouches in an easy chair, moves not a muscle as a heavy bump and grind kicks into gear. He is intently watching something behind us, outside the camera's range. A woman's voice, a husky soprano, begins shadowing the melody, throaty and pleading, a latter-day Billie Holiday. The man's head begins bobbing gently in time to the music, as if he's nodding yes, yes, yes. A smile, lecherous but playful, steals across his face. Still we don't see the object of his attraction; his body remains motionless in repose.

And now the music creeps toward some sort of crescendo. The man's smile broadens and the inane bobbing stops. The camera tightens on his face, then slowly pans around. The point of view rotates and rotates—first bare wall, then a door creeps in at stage left and makes its way out stage right, and you're going crazy with trying to find out what's got him so turned on. Then more bare wall and a corner—and suddenly, half a circle too soon, we find ourselves looking at the man again: It's a mirror.

Watching him in reflection now, we see him grin lustily; he reaches up to touch his hair. The crescendo peaks; the woman's voice becomes a wail as she belts out a message of heart-wrenching sluttiness that makes your knees buckle. The man's eyes remain fixed, entranced; the camera pans down too quickly, as if falling, from his shit-eating grin to the lime green bottle on the counter beside him, focusing in tight on the label itself: "Hair Peace."

"Who cares about that crap?" said Nick. "Tell us the rest of the story."

Jason shrugged, tossed back the last third of his beer, and glanced around the table at his rapt little audience. "I already told you, there's nothing else to tell. She went home, I went home."

"And you never got a chance to find out if it was the real thing or not," said Becky.

"The document?" Jason smiled wryly. "Well, it wasn't in English, I can tell you that much."

"It was probably some old parts list for the statue," said Paul, feigning a French accent. "Feefty-thousan' rivets, *oui oui.*"

"I'm sorry, but that's *amazing,*" said Becky, drawing out the middle syllable in rank disbelief. "You guys went through all that together, you rescued her from *kidnappers,* and she sent you home alone?"

"What's romantic about that?" said Nick. "He lost the Maltese falcon."

"She didn't send me home," Jason replied. "We were both exhausted. And we've each got our own issues to sort out, I reckon."

"Tell me something, Beck," said Nick. "Why do gals always find it romantic when a guy throws away money?"

"We don't, you imbecile."

"Let's take the diamond ring, as another example. Why does a guy sinking all his savings into a tiny rock spell 'This guy's a smart provider'?"

"It seems awfully suspicious we've never even met the girl," interrupted Paul.

"Couldn't agree more," said Nick. "There's some kind of an elaborate hoax going on here."

"You'll meet her someday," said Jason. "I think so, anyway. She's coming over"—he checked his watch—"later on tonight."

"Here?" said Becky hopefully.

He smiled. "Sorry."

"Oh, bring her by," said Paul. "We'll be ready for her."

"Yeah, right," Jason replied, pushing the hair back on his forehead. "I'm sorry, does it say 'stupid' up here?"

J.D. returned from the bar and sat in the last empty chair, depositing a round of shots on the table before him. The odor gave it away instantly.

"Oh, you and your tequila," said Becky. "It's eight o'clock, for Chrissakes."

"Did you know that a tequila shot is technically better than finding out you're the richest person in the world?" said Paul, looking at Jason.

"I'll bite," said Jason. "How do you figure?"

His friend shrugged. "Well, *nothing* is better than finding out you're the richest person in the world. But a tequila shot is better than nothing." He paused for effect. "Don't you think?"

✧ ✧ ✧

Amanda waltzed restlessly around his apartment, sipping the Rolling Rock he'd handed her at the door. Jason sat down next to the coat she'd shucked on the couch and quietly watched her white denim shorts and loose V-necked cardigan move. There was an uneasy silence between them, as if the events of the preceding week had drained them of all ability to communicate.

"So, you want to rent a movie or something?" he said, meaning it as a joke.

"It's on Fresh Kills, you know."

"Oh, Christ, Amanda—leave it alone," he replied, touching a bruise the size of Rhode Island on his hip. "Who wants this polluted piece-of-shit city, anyway?"

"That's where all the municipal garbage goes—they don't do any ocean dumping anymore," Amanda continued, now talking directly to her beer. "We probably have a window of maybe a week to halt dumping there."

"Halt dumping? Did you actually say 'halt dumping'? I'm not picking through ten thousand tons of bagel chips and dog poop," said Jason. "I made my choice."

She plumped down next to him on the couch, defeated. "Do you really think that guy would have shot me if you hadn't been so damn clever?"

"I have no idea," said Jason. "But it seems to me that if you're the kind of person who'd go to the effort of buying a gun and carrying it around, you probably don't have a lot of scruples about using it."

Amanda took a long draft of her beer, swirled it around in her mouth thoughtfully. "We had it in our *hands*. I haven't told my mom yet. I don't know how I'm gonna do it."

"What are you going to do about your dad?"

She was silent, and he let it go.

"I have a question for you, too, Amanda. Do you truly, honestly think this thing would have held up in court?"

She considered this for a long while. "Oh, probably not," she admitted. "But maybe, sure. A fatalistic part of me wants to say of course not, that it was a pipe dream from the beginning. But everything that should have been impossible just kept coming up roses."

Jason nodded. "Well, on the bright side, it's on top of the heap, in a good sturdy bag, and Fresh Kills is closing in a couple of years. That puppy could conceivably last another thousand years."

He saw the hope light up her eyes. "You think so?"

"Yes, I do," he said. "In fact," he continued, narrowing his eyes and fishing a folded square of paper from his pocket, "I took the *liberty* of writing the next stanza."

"I think I'm depressed enough right now, thanks," she said.

"'I snuggle under mounds of discarded crap,'" read Jason. "'Cold banana peels are my bedding/An old man's diaper beneath my head.'"

"How can you possibly joke at a time like this?"

"Because I saved the princess. Let's not lose all perspective, sweetheart."

"Yeah, well . . ."

"Come on," he said, grabbing her hands and pulling her closer. "Tell me it's not over just because the game's over."

She let her hands lie in his, but stared at him gravely. "Jason, all my life, all I've ever had was that deed," she said. "I've spent most of my adult years chasing it down. All that wasted time . . . it's not easy for me to swallow." She put her forearms on his shoulders. "I can't promise anything." She paused, searching for the right phrase. "But I'll try. I want to try."

Going to have to be good enough, he thought as their lips took their cue and found one another; she caressed his hair as they fell back into his couch. If Amanda's love for him was still conditional, still derivative of her philosophy, it seemed like as good a starting point as any.

"So you wanna dance, or something?" he wondered.

"Something," she murmured. "Do you have anything at all to eat?"

He laughed out loud. "I thought you'd never ask." He brushed an imaginary hair out of her eye as an excuse for preserving the moment. "Look in the cupboard right over the microwave."

"Those are your dishes," she said matter-of-factly.

"Whose apartment is this, yours or mine?"

The creak of the floorboards, then a cabinet door; muffled sounds of rooting around. "Plates," she said.

"Second shelf, behind the glasses," he said, rising from the couch. "Just keep looking; you'll find it." Carefully avoiding the squeaky floorboard, he padded over to the kitchen archway to watch. When she whirled around, eyes wide, with the document in her hand, he was right there, grinning.

"Did you find something to chew on?" he said.

"You total bastard!" she said merrily, socking him hard in the arm. "You said the game was over!"

"It *is* over. I didn't say we lost."

She was bewildered. "But how—?"

"Your mom's map is gone, I'm afraid," said Jason. "When those guys had you, I was sitting here in the apartment frantically trying to decide what to do when it occurred to me that they had no way of knowing we'd already solved the puzzle. They were still after the map—so that's what I gave 'em."

"I can't breathe," she said, holding the stiff, heavy page up before her and running a finger delicately over the dark lettering. The ancient script was still easily legible, though in some very old Dutch neither of them could decipher. In fact, the only two words they recognized comprised the oversize signature at the bottom, under the big wax gubernatorial seal: Pieter Haansvoort.

Jason hooked a finger over the top edge of the deed and pulled it back down so he could see her face again, flushed and exquisite. "So," he said, "where do you want to go today?"

Acknowledgments

When it takes you seven years to finish a book, it's hard to be sure you're remembering all the people without whose valuable assistance you would still be staring at the end of a pen tracing a lazy helix in the air over an untouched ream of shiny new paper. Since the only people reading this page probably have a reasonable expectation of being on it, if you think you should be here and aren't, you're probably right. Sorry. And thanks!

I'd like to first thank my close friends—Keith and Jim and Mary Ellen and Russ and Doug and Dave and Joe and the whole lot of 'em: some of whom absolutely inspired characters in this book, all of whom may claim it. This book began as an exploration of friendship in that glorious post-collegiate twilight . . . that was our time, wasn't it?

I'd also like to thank my family—my ever-patient wife, Leslie, and my ever-impatient children, Chloe and Sam—who together reawaken me to the world every day. And my mom and dad, now that I know what an awesome, wonderful pain in the ass it is to raise children, and my sisters, Trish and Kath, though they know damn well they deserved every noogie.

Thanks are also due to my friends and colleagues at *Maxim* magazine and Dennis Publishing and elsewhere in "the biz"; to my agents, Dan and John, and to my excellent editor, Geoff (and I swear he didn't add the word "excellent").

ACKNOWLEDGMENTS

Finally, I'd like to thank each and every one of the demented denizens of my city, New York, where the world's best in every field have gathered for four centuries to take their shot at greatness, where the gravity of all this assembled talent bends the buildings right up to the sky, a magical island where, quite literally, anything can happen.

About the Author

Keith Blanchard is editor in chief of *Maxim* magazine. He lives in New Jersey with his wife, Leslie, and their two children.